THE IDIOTS' CLUB

ALSO BY TONY MOYLE

Standalone Novels
THE IDIOTS' CLUB

'The Circuit' Series
MEMORY CLOUDS
MEMORY HUNTERS

'Ally Oldfield' Series
THE END OF THE WORLD IS NIGH
LAST OF THE MOUNTAIN MEN

'How to Survive the Afterlife' Series
THE LIMPET SYNDROME
SOUL CATCHERS
DEAD ENDS

THE IDIOTS' CLUB

TONY MOYLE

LIMBO PUBLISHING

First Published: July 2021.

ISBN 9798529938515

Limbo Publishing, a brand of In-Sell Ltd

www.tonymoyle.com

Cover design by Xen Randall

For

The 'Beerbellies'

"Unofficially the worst five-a-side football team in history. Officially friends for life." T.M.

Four old friends.
Five dares.
Seven days.
Ten million pounds.

ONE

ERIC

Yesterday.

SEVERAL LINES OF DRIED BLOOD, which had oozed from a matted wound on his temple, chased each other down his cheek before disappearing under the collar of his ripped, once clean white shirt. His face was filthy and swollen, creating the illusion that he'd recently played a game of rugby against a team of angry rhinos, and lost heavily. None of his clothes were attached to his body in the way his expensive Saville Row tailor would have recommended. Half of one trouser leg was missing, his smart jacket was covered in lacerations, and his right shoe had been torn in two and looked more like a disposable holiday flip-flop. All things considered, he thought it was a pretty decent outcome, given the circumstances.

Stealing a lion had consequences.

Aside from the obvious physical injuries, and the even more uncomfortable thought that his appearance might damage his cherished reputation, his current demeanour was in stark contrast to his visual appearance.

A permanent wry smile carved its way through the dirt, blood and bruises. Even if he'd felt inclined to try, he couldn't have shifted it. For the first time in years - more than twenty, to be precise - he felt alive again. The events of the last week had transported him back to an era when life was emotionally uncomplicated and exponentially more enjoyable, even if most outside observers might not have described his last few days as being either. Not that he'd ever cared what other people thought of him. In his unique view, the latter was an essential prerequisite in achieving the former.

Eric Gideon had always been an outsider, and to prove his worth, he found it impossible to say no when people tested him. If there was even a shred of doubt about his self-confidence, he might have challenged why this was. Not only did he avoid exploring it, he lacked the basic self-awareness to recognise such explanations were even necessary. Why would he question it? He was completely at ease with who he was, and of what he was capable. Which, in the main, was anything people said he wasn't. When someone challenged him, even if they'd done so in jest, he agreed without flinching.

He always had.

He always would.

It was a test of his character, and a refusal to act was tantamount to failure in itself as far as he was concerned. Proving he could deal with anything life threw at him, whilst simultaneously humiliating those who had the nerve to dispute his nerve in the first place, was the foundation stone of his very existence. Without that everything else fell over, and if it did, the world would finally see a side of him long hidden from view. However outlandish or impossible the task, he'd always meet the challenge head on with a cocksure and brash grin not dissimilar to the one he wore now. Most people had boundaries. Eric couldn't even spell 'boundaries'.

Traverse the alps on a pogo stick? Absolutely.

Blag your way into a Royal wedding? No problem.

Pretend to be Japanese for a week? Easy.

Swim the English Channel? Hold my beer.

Steal a lion? Where would you like it?

The wilder the brief, the more it motivated him. The greater the chance of failure, the more it pushed him. But for him, it wasn't enough to set his own goals. To make the effort worthwhile there had to be a suitable challenger, and when you had a reputation for succeeding in the face of improbable odds, such candidates were few and far between. None of his forty-something-year-old peers, and he could count those on one hand, felt inclined to indulge him these days.

But last week, the past returned and everything changed. The game was on…again.

Grown-ups frown at other adults who choose to play silly games, not that Eric recognised himself as being one. In his opinion, a secret and disturbing transformation afflicted people as they approach the end of their twenties. They started to plan for the future, considered their health, went to the gym, opened savings accounts, worried about what other people thought, and followed rules.

In essence, they became 'sensible'.

Most disgustingly of all, they viewed 'fun' through an entirely different filter. Fun when you were twenty or younger was anything you wanted it to be and it wasn't spoilt by instructions, risk assessments, financial planning, safety nets or adult permission. The only requirements were some like-minded companions, a pinch of creativity and a furtive imagination.

Oh, and booze. You had to have booze.

Games are best played by children. Adults almost always ruin the experience. It was the game which Eric missed most when everyone else 'grew up'. He needed an external stimulus to distract him from the slow decline into old age, inevitable dementia and finally, death. An eventuality for which the majority of middle-aged people had more than adequately prepared for decades in advance of its likely occurrence before getting bored and running out of interesting things to do or say.

If you played the game as frequently as Eric did, then you had to accept there were downsides to your childlike over-exuberance – today it was mostly bite marks. You also had to accept that there would always be adults who not only disapproved but were intent on stopping you. These were often authority figures who believed that your reckless disregard for safety put others in unnecessary danger. Down the years, they'd presented themselves in many forms: teachers, neighbours, bosses, friends and family. Today, they owned handcuffs, drove noisy cars with blue blinking lights and employed detectives expertly camouflaged in everyday clothing, which annoyingly made them that much harder to spot, and avoid.

Eric stared patiently at the mirror on the far wall, his wry smile still clinging to his face like it was fixed on with super glue. He wanted whoever was watching from the other side of the glass to know that he was having a lovely time despite what they might believe. It wouldn't take long before he found out whom they'd selected to take him on. He hoped it was someone suitable, but either way, he was prepared for anything or anyone. A lifetime of bravado and a long history of run-ins with the 'Rozzers' had taught him some valuable lessons. Lacking the internal capacity to back down from a dare meant he'd wisely adapted his approach.

Catch him, they did frequently.

Arrest him, they did often.

Charge him, so far they'd never managed.

Every dare had the potential to cut across legal boundaries, which is why Eric always had a contingency plan. A deception designed to confuse the investigators and provide an alibi or alternative version of events to keep the police off his tail. To date, this had worked well, but his ability to bamboozle and mislead would never be more under pressure than it was today.

Today, he'd need more than words.

Today, he'd need to play his joker card.

The door swung open, and a smartly-dressed brunette in sizeable stiletto heels strode confidently into the interview room clutching a silver travel mug in one hand and a bulging folder in the other. Medium build, pale complexion, average height and, Eric guessed, about ten years younger than him. Her precise mannerisms and stiff posture immediately illustrated to the sharp-minded Eric what kind of woman he was dealing with. A fiercely ambitious, no-nonsense type who'd stop at nothing to get the job done. Uncompromising, righteous and prepared to use her sexual aggression against him if it was called upon to secure a confession. It wasn't just Eric's galactic self-confidence which led him to this conclusion; he was an expert at reading body language.

Eric's primary job in the world of advertising was to sell ideas to people. That was made somewhat easier to achieve if you knew what customers were thinking before they expressed it verbally. Assessing eye cues, body language, micro expressions and idiosyncratic gestures might lead an expert like Eric to deduce, and then influence, a prospective client's likely decision making. Eric had spent years assiduously studying techniques such as Neuro Linguistic Programming, the sometimes dark art of using word suggestion to programme someone's behaviour. Whether it was unleashed during a business meeting or at difficult times in his personal life like this, the effect was much the same. Eric's talent for persuading people to do what he wanted, even when they were steadfast in their desire not to, was legendary throughout the industry.

The newly arrived Detective Inspector dragged the metal chair away from her side of the table, its legs scraping noisily across the tatty grey laminate floor. She lowered herself gently into the plastic seat and shuffled it back to the table with her long heels. She placed the folder on the smooth metal surface before fiddling with it obsessively until it was exactly perpendicular to the edge. For the next few minutes, the two opponents stared each other down, each unleashing an arsenal of invisible weapons to establish an opinion on the other without uttering a single word. The pressure of their eye contact intensified, yet the smile on Eric's face never once looked prepared to emigrate.

"DI Iris Whitehall," offered the woman impolitely.

Eric nodded in acknowledgement.

Of the many adversaries Eric had faced down the years, none had truly matched him for cunning or skill, or at least that's how he wrongly remembered it. The brain has a knack of reframing the truth to protect the false narrative it is partially responsible for building. Even though he failed to recognise those who'd fought and won in the past, the chance of finding a worthy adversary in Frome Police Station, a sleepy town in deepest darkest Somerset, was somewhat improbable.

"One-way glass," Eric said, nodding his head at the wall behind her. "Isn't that a little old-fashioned?"

"Old building, new tech," she replied impassively, pointing to the camera on a bracket in the corner of the ceiling. "This is Frome, Mr Gideon, not Edwardian England. You'll be amazed how much of the modern world has managed to reach us. We have a Starbucks, mobile phones and everything."

"Fair enough, and I've enjoyed my brief experience of it, but I think I'll be going now," Eric suggested confidently.

"I hate to break it to you, but *Star Wars* came out forty years ago and Jedi mind tricks don't work on Her Majesty's Constabulary."

"Even so, I'd still like to leave."

"Leave!" she laughed dryly. "Why would we let you leave?"

"Don't you have a duty of care? I need these wounds seen to." He pointed at his head and then some unidentifiable places under the edge of the table. "Look at my hands."

Eric held his hands in front of him in an overly exuberant manner and alternated his gaze between them and her as if he was trying to make a connection.

"You'll live," she added sternly. "It's bound to happen if you decide to mess around with a dangerous animal."

"I've no idea what you're talking about," he replied plainly.

"Yes, you do."

"I really don't."

"Last night, you and a bunch of friends stole a lion from Longleat Safari Park."

"No, we didn't."

"You livestreamed it!"

This accusation wasn't entirely without merit. Eric had indeed broadcast last night's events on a number of social media channels, and, to the untrained eye, it might have appeared that he was stealing a lion, but videos can be very misleading. That alone certainly wasn't enough evidence to charge him, and she knew it. For a start, if he did steal the creature, where was it now?

"We've already interrogated your mates, you know."

"Mates?" he replied innocently.

"Yeah, the other two idiots you were with when I arrested you. Fascinating bunch."

Eric shrugged, his smile still fixed petulantly to his lips. His cocksure expression hadn't gone unnoticed. DI White-hall was accustomed to dealing with arrogant criminals who believed in their ability to escape punishment with ease. She was frequently the one to disappoint them.

"They were most helpful with my enquiries. Do you know whose name came up most during their interviews?"

Eric made no attempt to answer the question.

"Gaddafi," she said, pointing at him with a single outstretched finger. "Nickname, is it?"

"It's actually pronounced 'Gaydafi'," scoffed Eric indignantly.

"I'm guessing they call you that because you're the ringleader, right?"

"No! They call me that because years ago someone accused me of having a dictatorial - yet rather camp - walk."

"Are you fucking with me?" growled Whitehall.

"Am I?" he pondered uncertainly.

"I wouldn't. You'll regret it."

Eric shrugged, unconcerned by the threat.

"You and your friends might think all of this is a big joke, but a crime has been committed and it doesn't need Inspector Morse to work out who's responsible." She opened the black folder and placed it on her lap so the contents were out of his line of sight. "By the looks of your file, this isn't the first time you've had run-ins with the law either, is it?"

"How many convictions does it say I've received in your little book?"

"None," she confirmed.

"Charges?"

"None. Forty-two arrests, though."

"As you will certainly know, arrests count for nothing when it comes to a criminal record check."

"Correct, but I'm not conducting one. I'm using intelligence collected about you which describes forty-two separate arrests for a variety of unusual crimes, not all involving the theft of large jungle mammals, going back twenty-five years."

"I must have a guilty face," he offered in rebuttal. "When you look like me, the police tend to be a little over-zealous."

"Are you suggesting every one of these arrests was motivated by racism?"

"Evidently."

"Perhaps you've managed to get away with it every time and it has nothing to do with the colour of your skin."

"It's always about the colour of my skin."

"I'm interested in solving crimes, Mr Gideon, not racial profiling."

"And what crime do you think I've committed, exactly?"

"Several, but shall we start with the recent theft of a very big cat?"

"That wasn't me."

"Do you know what classifies a theft? Taking something that legally doesn't belong to you. This lion was yours, then, was it?"

"What lion?" he replied in pretence.

"There's something you should know about me, Mr Gideon. I always discover the truth, whatever it takes. My nickname is easier to interpret than yours."

"What do they call you?" he asked.

"Elephant."

"Because you never forget," stated Eric knowingly.

"Because elephants have the best sense of smell of any animal and I whiffed your stench a few days ago," she replied, flaring her nostrils.

Eric leant forward, eager to know what backed up this claim. A few days ago, he'd had nothing to do with lions but he did have something to do with the removal of a rather large World War Two bomb, not that he was willing to let on at the moment.

"This isn't your only crime this week, is it, Mr Gideon?"

"I've no idea what you're talking about."

"Over the last few days, an idiotic group has perpetrated a series of crimes from London to Exeter, each as bizarre and inexplicable as the last. The only common thread to these events is the people responsible. I can smell the unmistakable stench of arrogance, a smell that is almost overpowering in your company. Once I've identified a motive, and collected all the necessary evidence, I intend to charge you for all of them."

"Good luck with that."

"Don't worry, I won't need luck." She shook her head. "You see, I'm a brilliant investigator; didn't they tell you?"

"I'm sure you are, but you're wasting your time."

"Funny, that's exactly what the others said. I'll ask you the same question I posed them. What on earth possessed you to steal a lion?"

"We didn't."

From her jacket pocket, DI Whitehall removed a mobile phone which had been set up to replay the video that would prove otherwise. She held it in front of him and pressed 'play'.

Dark, grainy footage showed four men struggling to cajole a stumbling, partially-tranquilised lioness into the back of an inappropriately small black hearse. The video was filmed at night, and only the light from the hearse's weak headlamps and the illumination from the flash of a handheld camera phone lit the scene. The clearly damaged vehicle had been parked unconventionally on the side of a country road lay-by, and next to it a large irregular hole had been punctured in the hedgerow.

One of the men was mirroring the disorientated movements of the hairy mammal, wobbling and slurring his words like a drunk trying to convince his local publican to announce a lock-in and keep serving. Another member of the gang, wearing an absurdly colourful jester's hat, was attempting to replace one of the hearse's tyres, while the punctured one lay on the muddy ground covered in bite marks. The job was being made more difficult by his relentless need to toke on a rolled-up cigarette every ten seconds. A lanky, semi-respectable-looking gentlemen was wallowing on his knees a good distance away, shaking his head and muttering anxiously to himself.

"Turnip, don't just stand there, come and help!"

shouted the fourth figure, both wrestling and remonstrating with the ever more sleepy queen of the jungle who, incidentally, had never even seen a picture of a jungle let alone the real thing. Nor, as it happens, had she seen this section of road on the A362 between Frome and Warminster. After all, being bred in captivity meant you were frequently restricted to it, and rarely had the opportunity to take road trips with a bunch of middle-aged idiots.

"That last voice does sound awfully familiar," said DI Whitehall sarcastically.

"Does it?"

"I notice he's also missing the same trouser leg as you."

"They don't make clothes like they used to, do they?"

"Are you really trying to deny that it's you in the video, Mr Gideon?"

"No, of course not. That would be incredibly foolish."

"So, you did steal a lion."

"No."

"Hold on. Let me summarise this. You agree that you're in the video, it's definitely not your lion but you're not stealing it?"

"Perfectly framed."

"Mr Gideon, if you want my help, you have to help yourself. No judge in this country is going to dismiss this evidence as circumstantial."

"I don't need your help, thank you. I've never needed anyone's help ever. But I can also see you're a woman who won't stop until the truth is revealed," said Eric, dropping his defences although his smile remained constant throughout. Now he'd had a chance to analyse her, it was time to weave his magic. "I'll tell you what's been happening, if you have the time?"

"Frome Police Station is hardly the Bronx. You might be my only case this month."

"Nevertheless, it is…complicated," added Eric. "A rather long story."

"Then you'd better start from the beginning," she replied, clicking her pen open and preparing to capture the important details in her folder.

"That'll be twenty years ago, then."

TWO
THE IDIOTS' CLUB

TWENTY-TWO YEARS AGO.

THE FOUR FOUNDING members had originally called it the *Who Dares Wins Collective.*

Everyone else simply called it *The Idiots' Club.*

This was a far more appropriate name because across Exeter University, and the wider city region, their reputations preceded them. Anyone living in the area had either been on the receiving end of their activities or was forced to read about it in their local papers. For a two-year period, the club's mysterious antics were an indelible part of city life. Some residents found them entertaining. Most found them disruptive. But no one had the first idea what they were trying to achieve, including the members themselves who, despite their best efforts, couldn't avoid the name being thrust upon them. *The Idiots' Club* stuck and eventually even they resorted to using it.

One of the great benefits of attending higher education was the opportunity to advance your extracurricular passions, or to sample ones you'd never previously experienced. The options at Exeter University were almost endless. Lacrosse, journalism, belly dancing, flute playing, pigeon racing, judo, croquet, pole fitness, hide and seek, baking and philosophy were just some of the two hundred official societies a student might join. *The Idiots' Club* certainly wasn't official, because there were prerequisites a new club had to demonstrate before being approved by the Guild of Students.

Societies must have at least twenty members.

Societies must work in harmony with other clubs.

Societies must not contravene University policy.

Societies must, at all times, uphold the University's motto, *Lucem Sequimur* – 'We follow the light.'

The Idiots' Club never had more than half a dozen members and although it wasn't their singular purpose to disrupt other groups, or contravene policies, they wanted the freedom to do so if their activities called for it. And, as it was impossible to know what their next activity might be, they couldn't in good conscience agree to anything. As for 'follow the light', they'd decided the motto was ambiguous at best and as long as they did their unique hobby in the daytime, or at the very least whilst carrying a torch, they were probably in the clear.

For most clubs, being Guild affiliated did have its perks – access to financial support, use of University facilities and help with risk assessments. The last of these was something on which *The Idiots' Club* definitely didn't need guidance. If they had to rely on risk assessments, they'd never do anything. There was a more fundamental reason why they refrained from applying for official status. Most of their members saw themselves as outsiders, and the last thing they wanted was to be on the inside.

Many of Exeter's official societies boasted award-winning exploits, hundreds of active members, and famous alumni who'd gone on to achieve global acclaim in the fields of science, art, politics or literature. Yet none of these clubs had the seismic, although brief, impact that *The Idiots Club* had in its tenure of chaos and notoriety. A reputation which lingered long after the club was forced to disband.

University life in the United Kingdom in the nineteen-nineties was quite a different place than it is today, because the country was a very different place. A wave of positivity had swept the country on the back of Britpop, progressive politics, cultural diversity and a genuine sense of national pride. It was a time of prosperity, increased tolerance and, most importantly, a palpable belief that almost anything was possible. Back then, attending University had already become a common step on the educational ladder for almost fifty percent of school leavers, and achieving it represented much more than an advancement in one's future prospects.

It represented an important lesson in life. Vital development on the journey to adulthood.

For Eric Gideon, it represented excessive drinking, fornicating with the opposite sex as frequently as his limited sobriety allowed and testing himself against a much wider field of opponents. Whilst the bulk of students broadly understood what was expected of them, Eric staunchly refused to jump the hurdles that society placed in his way. The perennial underdog, he'd always had to fight just to survive. When life dealt you a poor hand, the only way to compensate for it was to learn how to bluff. If the playing field remained uneven, there was no other option than to play dirty to win.

Eric knew almost instantly that he wouldn't fit in with the other students who lived in his hall of residence, or the fellow academics who packed out lecture theatres. They looked different, spoke differently and treated him differently. Their interactions with him were always conducted covertly, as if a campaign of distrust had been uploaded simultaneously to every student and staff member to impede his access to their restricted circle. His place was always on the edge watching those who had the privilege of being protected by the system. Such had it always been. In the poverty-riddled streets of London, in the classrooms of Brixton, in his own home and now here.

But he knew everyone who was tightly packed inside the privileged inner circle would be suffering from claustrophobia. There wasn't enough room for everyone, and the boundary rope kept you firmly restrained and forever excluded. The people like him, who had either been refused access or chosen not to enter, had much more freedom on the outside. Eric was both, and to his delight, he wasn't the only one.

There were others.

People who refused to compete in a race which had different starting lines and more dangerous obstacles in some lanes than in others. These outliers weren't always easy to spot. They didn't congregate, have their own dedicated haunts, or seek an audience to broadcast their ideas. They were adept at blending in with the enemy to avoid being detected and condemned as weirdos and freaks. If you wanted to survive in this hostile environment, camouflage was your only choice.

One of them was Josh Foxole, and as soon as Eric met him, he knew instantly that he'd found a kindred spirit.

Their introduction happened quite by accident one Monday night. There was one night in the week which was deemed unacceptable to be at a night club, and that was because none of them opened: a Sunday. Every other night favoured a different venue and a specific theme. Monday's entertainment was at Rococo's, and the theme was always fancy dress. Everything from 'Nuns and Vicars' to 'Viz Characters'. Think cosplay with much less effort on display. On this particular evening, the theme was a seventies night.

Eric had tagged along with a group of students from his halls whom he didn't like very much. They'd spent hours selecting their outfits like they were auditioning for *Stars in their Eyes*. Eric was content with chucking on a pair of flairs, a kipper tie and a gaudy coloured silk shirt. He knew the score. This, like everything else in life, was a glorified popularity contest, and he wasn't remotely interested in winning. Even though most of the revellers spent hours attempting to stand out, they all inevitably ended up looking like clones of each other anyway.

Which is exactly why Josh stood out.

Amongst the long-sleeved floral dresses, fluttery bell bottoms, handlebar moustaches, tight trousers and turtle-necks, Eric noticed a bloke who was ostensibly wearing nothing more than a nappy. Eric watched with fascination as the man appeared ignorant of the odd stares and confused expressions at his strange choice. He certainly had the body to pull it off, though, and loud shouts of harassment seemed to have zero effect on his confidence. All night, Eric observed with interest this man's bold attempts to chat up the girls. Not just any girls, either. He aimed his affections at those who were quite obviously out of his league. No one else acted like this. Normal people were too concerned about what others might think, or how it might damage their reputation to put themselves out of their comfort zones. This man clearly didn't have one.

"What's with the outfit?" shouted Eric over the blaring music, as the man approached the bar to refresh his empty glass.

"It's a nappy...well, it's a towel wrapped around my waist to make it look like a nappy, if you want to be picky."

"I gathered. You do know tonight is a seventies night, don't you? Creche night is next Monday!" joked Eric.

"Yes, I know. I was planning to go to that one dressed as a Duplo rabbit."

"Now that, I've got to see," laughed Eric. "What's with the nappy, then?"

"It's what I was wearing in the seventies," the man grinned in response.

"Brilliant. That level of creativity deserves a drink. Let me get these..." he said, pausing to encourage an introduction.

"Foxie."

"Eric Gideon," he offered, shaking his hand. "Foxie?"

"Josh Foxole, but my friends call me 'Foxie'. Sadly, there aren't many of those, so everyone else has taken to calling me 'J-Hole', which is unfortunate. I'll have a WKD blue cheers."

Eric handed the barmen two one-pound coins in return for two bottles that contained an alarming neon blue liquid not to be found naturally outside of an exploding nuclear reactor.

"I couldn't help noticing that you were flirting with Vanessa Ballantine."

"Who?"

"Over there." Eric pointed out a drop-dead gorgeous blonde dancing mesmerically a few metres away to Rose Royce's *Car Wash*. "She's on my English course and I hear she's incredibly picky when it comes to men. I wouldn't waste your time, mate."

"I wasn't actually flirting with her," corrected Foxie. "I just went over to let her know she left her watch at my place last Monday night."

Eric analysed his expression. There wasn't a hint of a lie in it. Blokes were rarely honest about their sexual exploits and felt compelled to embellish even their limited success. Conversations with juvenile men, and for juvenile read any period between the ages of six and sixty, often followed a pattern much like this.

"Yeah, I snogged her," he replied, making grunting noises and shoving a clenched fist in the air. "She bloody loved it."

"Wasn't she doing a charity kiss-a-thon at the time?"

"No!"

"I saw you give her a pound."

"No…no I didn't. I enticed her with my boyish charms and sexual magnetism."

"And a pound."

It was some way from how Foxie reacted. There was something highly believable about his rather matter-of-fact response. If someone wanted to exaggerate the fact they'd had sex with Vanessa Ballantine, they'd have made more out of it. Foxie skipped over it like he was reading out the football scores.

"Prefer the supermodels, do you?!"

"Not really; they're often quite high maintenance and don't have much going on up there," he said, nodding his head. "I only do it to piss off the other blokes. Look at the sad losers."

Eric watched as a collection of timid, half-drunk, seventies rejects blundered around the poorly-lit nightclub hoping to catch the eye of their favourite student crush. This mostly involved a series of techniques doomed to fail, such as dancing too closely like a frightening sex pest, consciously avoiding any eye contact that strayed their way, grinning vacantly or muttering some distasteful chat-up line they'd read in *Nuts* magazine.

"They're all useless," claimed Eric, increasingly loudly to battle the decibels booming out of the DJ booth.

"They're scared, which is why I do so well. I don't care if the girls tell me to bugger off. Mostly they don't. Want to know why?"

"Enlighten me."

"Girls like it when a guy pays them a compliment; they find confidence sexy. Anyone can do it, if they have the guts."

Eric's internal sensors started to tingle. Was this guy going to suggest he didn't have what it took? He really hoped so. Eric liked this straight-talking outcast and he'd like him even more if he was willing to try, or do, anything in the pursuit of entertainment.

"Who're you with, Eric?" asked Foxie, glancing around at the other lost souls along the bar.

"That lot," answered Eric, pointing over to a cubicle on the far side of the dance floor.

"But you've been stood here all night?"

"I'm with them, doesn't mean I like them. They don't share my idea of fun."

"What's that, then?"

"Mixing it up a bit. Doing whatever I want whether the rules say I can or not. Making an impression."

"I like your style, my friend. I think you could have a lot of success in a place like this with an attitude like that."

"I don't have time for girlfriends."

"Nor do I," winked Josh. "I'm rather fond of sex, though, and that's always more fun with others, if you know what I mean!"

Everyone knew what he meant. Josh might be a hit with the ladies, but he was evidently the least subtle person in the whole club. The nappy didn't help, mind.

"I bet you could pull that girl…there." Josh pointed out

a beautiful, petite brunette in a revealing satin dress and white knee-length boots. She was currently teasing a small circle of bewildered human sacrifices who were playing along with her false mating ritual, convinced they all had a better-than-evens chance of pulling her. They couldn't have pulled a pair of curtains.

"Are you daring me?" qualified Eric.

"Do the words really matter?"

"Oh yeah."

"Then, okay, I dare you."

Eric's eyes lit up. The game was on, but every deed deserved another. "If I do this one, then I get to return the favour."

"Fair enough – you'll have to go a long way to embarrass me, though."

It was a claim that Josh would soon live to regret.

Unbeknownst to them at the time, *The Idiots' Club* was born, with Eric receiving a fierce slap to the jaw from the sexy brunette and everyone in Rococo's being briefly forced to witness a man strip off his adult-sized nappy before dancing to the seventies classic *It's Raining Men* completely in the buff on the central podium. The end of the evening also marked the first time in months that Josh left a nightclub with a bloke and not one of his conquests. He didn't mind in the slightest. The pair hiked several miles back to their halls, semi-inebriated and unable to stop laughing hysterically all the way home.

It was the first of many dares that academic term. "I dare you to…" became a regular riposte of their evenings from then on, although their determination to outdo one another often meant the night ended in a stalemate. As much as they enjoyed trying to humiliate each other or push themselves to the limit, a club of two members restricted their options. They needed new blood. A like-minded student who shared their sense of humour and desire to shock normal people. Someone whose sense of decency fell well below the standards expected by respectable citizens. Someone whose sense of fun and disregard for rules matched their own.

They found him.

But they weren't expecting it when it happened.

One morning, they were sitting in Josh's ground-floor dormitory bedroom listening to the new Blur album, smoking Craven A cigarettes and deciding whether they could be arsed to get some lunch when a streak of blue dashed past the window. It went by so quickly that the pair of them stared at each other to verify whether it had happened at all. Five minutes later, it went past again.

"What is that?" said Eric, spluttering from an overlong drag and standing to open the window.

"Students are mental," uttered Josh, almost accepting the oddities that occurred on campus as normal.

"This guy certainly is; come look."

Josh pulled himself out of his beanbag, can of Foster's in hand - even though it was only early Sunday - and lumbered over to the window. He rubbed his eyes to check whether they were working.

"What's he doing?"

"Laps," suggested Eric.

"Of what?"

"The halls of residence."

"But he's naked and covered from head to foot in blue paint!"

"Curious, isn't it."

"Mental! Why would he do that?"

"Charity fun run?" Eric searched for answers.

"Then he's either got himself lost or he's the only runner."

"He's coming around for another pass – let's ask him."

"Why not - we're not busy," replied Josh with the understatement of the year.

"Hey!" called Eric as the blue man ran along the wall towards their window. He was going at a staggering pace, probably as a result of limited air friction that jogging bottoms never really give you. "What are you doing?"

"Dare…" shouted the man as he went passed them without stopping.

"Promising," Josh said with a nod. "What's the dare?"

"How should I know? We'll get him on the next pass."

In the history of communication, the next hour probably broke records. The duration between answers and follow-up questions was delayed by about five minutes as Eric waited for the strange blue man to return on his next lap. The delay gave Eric and Josh plenty of time to collect their thoughts, debate the man's last answer and consider all manner of other philosophical questions mused by students, like what percentage of lectures could be missed each week without drawing attention to yourself or impeding your ability to pass an exam. They agreed it was twenty-five percent. It became clear, although it took ages, that the blue man's name was CJ, although on a later pass he confirmed this was short for Callum Jollie, and he was in the middle of running one hundred laps of the complex whilst being painted to look like a Smurf. This in itself was fairly ballsy, but when they later discovered the reward for his mania was nine pints of lager, it told them a great deal about the man's character.

Just the type of person they were looking for.

"How many laps left?" asked Eric.

"Two!"

Five minutes later.

"Come back here when you've finished; we've got an offer for you."

"Okay."

Callum finished his challenge and sauntered over to them, sweat making the blue paint run, his 'gentlemen's sausage' still swinging freely for all to see.

"Well done," offered Josh with a salute.

"Thanks."

"Was it worth it?"

"Nine pints, definitely. That's a night out, and I don't get a lot of money from my parents."

"Do you always do dares for beer?"

"Most weeks, but they're getting less frequent," puffed Callum, resting his back against the wall next to the window. Both Eric and Josh leant out, purposefully looking upwards to avoid their eyes colliding with his family jewels.

"We have a club," said Eric, "and we need members with…balls."

"But they don't always have to be on show," added Josh quickly, still looking in the opposite direction.

"What sort of club?" asked Callum.

"The Who Dares Wins Collective. We dare each other," said Eric pointing at Josh. "Want in?"

Callum thought about it for a second. He'd not joined any societies to date, and as far as he could tell, the University hadn't opened its own Alcoholics Anonymous group yet.

"Yeah, okay."

"Nice. Welcome. We meet on Fridays in the Ram."

"Fine. I'll be there. What sort of dares are we talking about?"

At that moment in time, none of them envisioned the future might involve lions.

ERIC WAS SOMEWHAT selective when recounting his memories of the Exeter old days to Detective Inspector Whitehall. Getting away with the unusual events of the last week meant he had to walk a fine line between truth and non-disclosure. She had to implicitly believe everything he told her, while at the same time being satisfied she'd received the whole story.

Which was a problem for Eric.

Because she didn't.

Detective Inspectors were equipped with built-in scepticism radar, doubt detectors and highly tuned bullshit antennae. This was never more the case than it was with Iris Whitehall, who had plenty of reasons to distrust criminals and, more importantly, men.

"Let me get this straight," sighed Iris, after enduring twenty minutes of seemingly pointless nostalgia. "You and some immature friends established a club twenty-odd years ago with the express purpose of humiliating each other and disrupting the lives of ordinary folk so you felt more manly about yourselves?"

"No, to push ourselves. To see what we were capable of."

"Because you felt ignored by the world?" she said, bemused and hoping a motive for the crimes perpetrated over the last week might become clearer.

"Stop anyone in Exeter High Street and ask them if they know who Eric Gideon is, then you'll see if I'm anonymous."

"But anyone can achieve infamy by creating chaos. The rest of the world tries to accomplish recognition by being a force for good through science, art or charity. But you just didn't have enough talent for that, did you?"

"You can't goad me," stated Eric calmly. "I'm immune to it."

"No, you're not," she replied confidently. "Actually, I believe it's your greatest weakness. As disinterested as I am in your attempts to frame yourself as the victim and distract me from my investigations, I still don't see how your past has anything to do with stealing a lion?"

"Let me repeat – for continuity – I didn't steal it," Eric repeated, again holding his hands in the air to send a metaphoric message to the surveillance camera that they were clean.

"Then why the bloody hell do you think you're here!" growled Iris, losing her patience.

"Because that has everything to do with twenty years ago."

"*The Idiots' Club*?" Iris suggested disbelievingly.

"Yes."

"A group of puerile friends daring each other to do ridiculous and dangerous things in the name of…fun."

"In the name of feeling alive."

"Perhaps you could have tried hiking?"

"Anyone can do that. It's not enough to know you're alive; that's simply surviving. Billions of people live like that from their first breath to their last, sheltered by their reluctance to take a chance. *The Idiots' Club* was about attempting the impossible, whether we succeeded in doing so or not. Haven't you ever had the compulsion to do something you weren't allowed to do? Or do something someone told you that you couldn't?"

"No," snapped Iris, not entirely honestly.

"Why not?"

"Because, unlike you, I'm an adult."

"Is that what makes us adults? Suppressing our desire

to be more than we are? Do you have children in your family?"

"A niece," grumbled Iris.

"How old?"

"She's four."

"And when you watch her play, do you judge her?"

"No, she's four; she doesn't know any better."

"But does she look happy?"

"Most of the time, unless she can't do something or someone interrupts her."

"There you go! As soon as an adult interferes, the fun is ruined. If they left her to her own instincts, unconstrained by adult rules, she'd learn the resilience needed to keep going until she succeeded. Kids have a natural sense of curiosity, but adults aren't judged in the same way."

"That's because we learn responsibility, danger and a sense of morality. My niece doesn't know those things yet, so she has to be protected."

"Let kids be kids, right?" said Eric sympathetically.

"Of course."

"But we don't, do we? We don't let them keep that childlike wonder - we force it out of them. We quash it. What was acceptable and encouraged at one age is punished and ridiculed at another. If society wants me to live like that, then you can count me out."

"Mr Gideon, if you want to act like a child no one is going to stop you, as long as you respect the rule of law."

"Laws that were created by ancient, disillusioned men, sometimes hundreds of years ago, with the express purpose of controlling freedom and restricting pleasure."

"What if we lived in a society where everyone did whatever they wanted, as you seem to - what then?" she said rhetorically. "The world would descend into anarchy and other people's actions would inevitably hurt you as a consequence. What if someone stole your lion?"

"I don't have one," he confirmed.

"You're holding on to a fantasy world," countered Iris.

"I'm promoting one that doesn't disapprove of others just because they're different, even though they don't know why. Society isn't equal but we're all told to follow the same rules, laws and disciplines."

"And you believe the perceived discrimination against you is justification enough for your actions."

"Yes."

"No! There's no defence for breaking the law."

"That's good, then…because I haven't."

"What you have done, as far as I can make out from your cryptic and rather meandering story, is reform this *Idiots' Club* of yours because you and some other loser mates are suffering a collective midlife crisis!"

"Age is simply a number. A midlife crisis is triggered in people who sleepwalk into middle age only to wake up to realise the clock is ticking. Tick tock, tick tock," added Eric in a haunting and purposeful tone. "They realise their lives are miserable and the aspirations they've been blindly working towards for decades are a façade to keep people out of trouble, pushed by the system like a drug dealer. They suddenly accept there isn't a pot at the end of the rainbow, just the unavoidable and looming end of life. By the time they discover the deceit, they're institutionalised and too knackered to do anything about it."

"And that's why you reformed the club, is it? To rediscover your youth. Most men buy a Porsche," she replied, redirecting Eric's rant back towards his obvious culpability.

"I had no choice but to reform it."

"The forced narrative of a guilty man." She smirked. "Everyone has a choice. It's called 'self-restraint'."

"I've never been very good at that."

"That's clearly true if your police record is anything to go on."

"No charges," he repeated proudly. "As it happens, self-restraint wouldn't have made much difference on this occasion. Reforming *The Idiots' Club* was forced upon me."

"Are you saying you were provoked?"

"In a way, yes."

"Explain."

"I find it almost impossible to say no when someone places an idea in my head. I have to prove I can do it."

"That doesn't sound like provocation. It sounds like an inability to manage your internal compulsion…or to use another phrase…self-restraint," she repeated.

"It's a disease," he rationalised solemnly. "I have to take the bait."

"And someone dared you to steal a lion?"

"Yes."

"Is that a confession?"

"No."

"It sounded like one."

"They challenged me to steal a lion. That doesn't mean I actually stole one, does it?"

"I refer you back to the evidence contained within the video, something you don't deny personally filming and posting on your social media accounts."

"Which still doesn't prove I stole it."

"What were you doing, then – taking it for a walk!?"

"I was…improvising."

"No, you're lying. You've been lying since the moment I walked in here. I've had enough of your games, Mr Gideon. The facts are simple. Last night, a lion was removed from its enclosure at Longleat Safari Park. A few hours later, a video was posted of you and three friends bundling the same lion into the back of a knackered old hearse. We've recovered the vehicle and arrested three of the suspects; it won't be long until we catch the fourth. The whereabouts of the lion remain a mystery, and other than a stupid lads' club that existed more than two decades ago, I can't for the life of me work out a motive that doesn't result in all of you being sectioned for your own safety. You're not denying someone dared you to steal it, yet you refuse to accept the overwhelming evidence that you succeeded."

"That's about right…apart from the bit about succeeding, obviously."

"Then where the fuck is the lion?" Iris's normal composure snapped and her fist struck the table with a bang.

"Maybe you should ask Sean Heschmeyer."

THREE
SEAN

Twenty-one years ago.

Sean Heschmeyer was the fifth and final inductee to *The Idiots Club*, but his appointment wasn't universally popular. Eric certainly wasn't in favour of it because Sean wasn't like the rest of them. The other members were united in having unorthodox backgrounds and holding odd views of the world that were uniquely different from regular people.

Josh had experienced a disjointed upbringing, most of it spent bundled from one foster family to another until the local authority ran out of willing suitors and he ended up on the streets. Micky, the fourth member of their group to join, grew up with an authoritarian father who ruled with a level of strictness most army cadets would find hard to live with. Callum definitely had something wrong with him, but no one felt qualified to pinpoint exactly what it was.

Then there was Eric, a poor black kid growing up in a world of white privilege, although he certainly wasn't unique in that regard. The youngest of four brothers and the son of first-generation Nigerian immigrants, on all levels Eric was an underdog. Poorer than even his London neighbours and mercilessly bullied at home, in school and by the general public at large who seemed to own a collective dislike for people like him. He grew up with very little, but it would not always be that way; he'd promised himself that much.

The Idiots' Club was a sanctuary for misfits, cast out by their families and communities, only to drag themselves out of the gutter to make something of their lives through an abundance of resilience and a bloody-minded refusal to accept their designated place in the world. University wasn't a certainty for them as it was for most eighteen-year-olds; it was a bloody miracle. If overcoming adversity were a degree course, all four of them would have earned first class qualifications before the end of their second term. The intense prejudice and inequality they experienced every single day were the very forces that drew them together. These were the only things that connected them, and in all other ways they were starkly different characters.

But not Sean.

He was different.

Not regular by any means, but also definitely not similar to them.

Sean was born into a self-made, reasonably affluent German family who'd afforded him an easier upbringing than the majority of students on campus. He'd had the best education, a loving supportive family and a sense of belonging, and his route up the slippery pole of success had already been degreased. All he had to do was earn a decent degree in engineering before joining the family firm where, as the only child, one day he'd inherit it. Sean was the embodiment of the system the others were keen to escape. At Exeter University, people with Sean's background were two a penny. They wore the most expensive clothes, owned cars, joined the debating society, drank fancy cocktails and pretended to be grown-ups by hosting dinner parties that served baked seabream, hasselback potatoes and crème fraiche sauce.

Eric despised them, and not purely because he didn't know what crème fraiche was.

He hated their white privilege, their heritage, their perceived superiority and, most importantly, their total lack of balls. They talked a good game, but when it came to the crunch, they were always left wanting. There was only one way to beat them. Eric would make a name for himself achieving feats they'd never even dream of. By his second year of University, Eric Gideon had certainly achieved that. There wasn't a fresher or postgraduate on campus who didn't know who he was. But it went much further, too. Every professor, policeman and administrator was aware of Eric and *The Idiots' Club*.

His club.

Incomparable, unauthorised, notorious and, until Sean's arrival, exclusive.

Callum had been the main instigator in Sean's induction. CJ had a miraculous talent for acquiring lost causes. The girls he dated were always head cases liable to break down in tears at a moment's notice or threaten him with a pair of scissors for breathing too heavily in his sleep. One old flame had even left a whole salmon hidden in the bottom of his wardrobe after Callum announced he wanted a 'cooling off' period. It was weeks before he located the source of the foul, rotting smell. The friends Callum accumulated outside of the group were generally eccentric nutjobs who had a tendency to talk about subjects only they could possibly find interesting. Callum never thought them odd because, in truth, he was stranger than all of them – the metaphorical mothership for all freaks on campus. Sean was just the type of kook that Callum collected. Not a weirdo, exactly, but certainly strange. But peculiarity often carried hidden benefits and, unknown to them at the time, Sean was also a bloody genius.

It was evident, from the club's first observations of him, that Sean was neither a popular student nor someone who found it easy to navigate social situations. Every late Friday afternoon, when *The Idiots' Club* formally gathered in The Ram - the main student bar - to plan their weekend and consider prospective dares, Sean would always be sitting alone in a booth by the window. It was the only day of the week anyone saw him there, possibly a symbolic gesture on his behalf to embrace what student life might have to offer outside of the lecture theatre. It was this unusual weekly pilgrimage that brought him to the club's attention. Sean stood out like a sore thumb because student attire, behaviour and appearance were regimentally divided into three distinct class groups.

The 'Sloane Rangers' were the upper class students. The men were normally fitted with red corduroy trousers, had perfectly ironed white shirts, wore natty shooting jackets with patches on their elbows and occasionally sported flat caps. They drank Guinness or wine, spoke fifty percent louder than anyone else in the room and had pompous, unimaginative nicknames for each other, like 'the captain', 'smudger' or 'porky'. The women who mingled around them were always pristinely presented in designer outfits which they were never seen in more than once. They were always doused in two kilos of make-up, which they tirelessly readministered at least three times a day. Their faces had a distinctively orange hue, the dazzle from which was more powerful than the sun. They drank cocktails, padded their bras to boost their confidence and cackled like witches on work experience. Most of all, they had long pointy noses which they raised a fraction so they looked down on people they thought beneath them, like Eric.

The 'spods' were on the bottom rung of the student class system. These individuals were the easiest to identify and yet the most elusive to spot in the wild. They were the students who attended University purely for educational reasons. They created the illusion they were having fun but failed to understand that 'fun' wasn't found in high-brow literature, decaffeinated herbal tea, country walks, candle making or eighteenth-century Austrian church music. They had pallid skin due to a reduced exposure to natural light, listened respectfully to what others had to say, raised their hands when they wanted to speak, created work planners that were so complicated Stephen Hawking would struggle to comprehend them, knew where the library actually was, and never ever missed a lecture. Most of all, they were almost never spotted in the student bar after five o'clock in the afternoon. They mostly visited at lunchtime, ordered shandies and ate falafel paninis. Eric knew this because he spent most of his time in the Ram rather than in lectures, based on his and Josh's twenty-five percent rule.

The final demographic were the 'sheep' who were the middle class students. Almost everyone who didn't fit one of the other two categories slotted comfortably into this one. A curious mixture of football lovers, lager swillers, Britpop boffins, scruffy urchins and shabby-clothed clones. Whatever the trend on any particular day, the 'sheep' followed unswervingly towards it, desperate not to be left out in the cold like Sean. If the word on the street confirmed everyone was now drinking Baileys and black-currant cordial, stocks in the Ram would run dry within hours. If the NME music magazine proclaimed 'Shed Seven' as the next big band, everyone would miraculously procure one of the band's t-shirts by the following morning. If David Beckham was pictured with a mohican haircut, the 'sheep' would soon follow his lead and campus would look like a nineteen-seventies punk crowd.

But Sean didn't fit any of these stereotypes.

He stood out from the crowd because he'd somehow managed to strike a weird amalgam of all three: the demeanour of a 'spod', the dress sense of a 'sheep' and the drinking preferences of a 'Sloane Ranger.' It was like a cross between Prince Charles and Paul Gascoigne with a gentle nod to Sir Patrick Moore. His unorthodox appearance was the very reason the group noticed, and eventually targeted, him.

Friday night was always dare night. *The Idiots' Club* would meet at around six o'clock for an evening of relentless drinking and mischief making. After a few pints had been swiftly consumed, they'd present the ideas they'd been working on for a week. There were no conventions or rules. They'd simply pick out one of the club and present their challenge and wait for him to decide if he wanted to take it on.

"Micky, I dare you to go over to that flock of sheep and ask the ugly bloke with the bald head if he'd like to dance the foxtrot with you. If he says no, I dare you to do it anyway while commentating in the third person."

This was a great example of the dares they exchanged in the early days, simple and mostly accepted with glee. Week by week, they became more inventive. Some were deemed to be 'team dares' that would require a significant amount of planning, like the time they managed to clear the Biology block by setting off all the fire alarms. They all laid claim to creative high points but out of the group,

Eric's dares were always the most inspired. He had a genuine talent for constructing the most impressive challenges and where others in the club might occasionally veto, he never did.

Not once.

Sean entered their lives one Friday evening because Micky had been somewhat less creative that week and simply ran out of good ideas.

"Callum, I dare you to go over to that funny geezer in the corner and have a conversation with him in a high-pitched Scottish accent for as long as you can. I'll buy you a pint for every ten minutes you manage it."

Dare accepted.

He kept it up for three hours.

There were two main reasons for this.

Firstly, if it came with the condition of free alcohol, there wasn't a single dare that Callum wouldn't do - shave his head, wear a dress, set a flare off in the Vice Chancellor's waste paper bin, canoe the Ex river blindfolded. Student life was centred on a drinking culture, and as such, Callum's behaviour didn't seem particularly unusual. Only in the post-University years did the others realise that he might have a serious problem. The second reason he managed to maintain the conversation for as long as he did was because he actually enjoyed it. He found Sean fascinating, and what's more, Sean had absolutely no suspicion that Callum's squeaky, and extremely poor, Scottish accent was anything but authentic. A dare is a lot less enjoyable for onlookers if the subject of your wind-up doesn't even know it is one.

After that night, Sean stuck to Callum like a limpet. Which meant Friday dare night was never quite the same again. It wasn't the irritation of his presence that finally convinced Eric to let Sean join. It was something much more sinister. If Sean was in, then Eric could break him. He'd invent the most despicable, dangerous dares and revel in Sean's failure to complete them. Proof that those who'd had an easier ride in life were inferior to him.

Sean, on the other hand, just wanted some friends. He did his best to complete the dares they assigned him but mostly he failed abysmally, to their endless amusement. Sean also found it incredibly difficult to offer the others suitable challenges, something that only increased Eric's disapproval of him. The others broadly accepted him into their midst and did their best to protect him from some of Eric's more callous attempts to humiliate him.

By their third and final year of University, *The Idiots' Club's* dares got out of hand. It wasn't enough to embarrass one another; Eric wanted to attempt increasingly dangerous and outlandish dares that involved large groups of people, buildings and institutions. As a result, the police were regular visitors to campus on the backs of their pranks and the Vice Chancellor, Sir Andrew Carrington, had threatened to expel them on several occasions if he caught them in the act. An opportunity that presented itself on the third of March, nineteen ninety-seven.

"He'll never make it," expressed Micky, staring up at a solitary figure grappling with the side of a red brick tower.

"Obviously," Eric answered sternly.

"He's got further than I thought he would," commented Josh, who was propping up an old, thick wooden door that allowed access to the structure.

"Glue monkey!" called out Callum with a burp, as he careered around the tower, legs working entirely independently from the rest of his body. He clutched a half-empty bottle of Hooch and tried desperately to achieve the required co-ordination to deposit the rest of it into his mouth. Most of it ended up on his shoes.

"You're about half way, Sean! Keep going," encouraged Micky.

"What is the dare, exactly?" asked Foxie, attempting to roll a cigarette with one hand.

"Remove one of the clock hands," confirmed Eric.

"Cock hands," giggled Callum, who stumbled and landed in a heap on the curb which encircled the clock tower. A lack of motivation to move suggested to the others that he'd decided to turn in for the night. He'd slept in much more ridiculous places than this down the years.

The hundred-year-old Miles Clock Tower took up position on a small roundabout on Queen's Street at the far end of town. It had always been a notable landmark for wayward drinkers on their quest to return safely to their student accommodation. Eric and Foxie lived in the row of houses behind the curry house - one of many restaurants and pubs which surrounded the monument to the late Mr Miles. The bottom six feet of the tower were made up of a central square core attached to four buttresses which featured the heads of stone horses. From there, smooth grey masonry blocks and long thin dirty windows, which in theory allowed anyone climbing the internal staircase to look out, extended for another twenty feet. Once this was scaled, the climber faced an overhang that further impeded access to a white and gold clockface and two large black metal hands.

Sean was currently clinging precariously to the upper reaches of the second section by his fingertips.

"Should we get him down?" asked Micky caringly.

"No!" insisted Eric. "He's routinely failed every dare

I've given him over the last twelve months. He's earnt this one."

"I think I can hear him weeping," added Foxie, peering into the gloomy clouds. It was the early hours of Saturday morning if the clock was still working accurately.

"No, that's just nervous excitement," fibbed Eric.

"Excitement! He's barely moved an inch in the last hour," argued Micky. "You know, you can be bloody cruel sometimes, Eric."

"Me!"

"Yes."

"What about you?"

"What about me?" replied Micky innocently.

"You dared him to dress up as a guinea pig on a visit to a pet shop."

"When?!"

"It was yesterday," confirmed Foxie breezily.

"Oh yeah," he replied forgetfully.

"But Sean accepted the dare," continued Eric.

"He often does," Micky remarked casually.

"We all have a veto."

"I think he's trying to prove himself."

"That's why we should let him continue," said Josh staunchly.

Another long, pathetic Germanic wail floated down from high above them. It was followed a few seconds later by a shiny black brogue which bounced off a buttress and landed on Callum's head. It didn't wake him. Being struck by a fast-moving removal truck wouldn't shift him once he'd passed out.

"Maybe he should try harder, then," insisted Eric. "It's not like he comes up with anything clever for us, is it? The best he's managed in twelve months is daring me to knock on my neighbour's door and run away."

"Maybe they don't do dares in Germany," mumbled Foxie, through an imperfectly-rolled cigarette that he was attempting to light with the wrong end of a match.

"He's just not up to our standard," huffed Eric. "Sean! Stop messing about and get on with it. I'm giving you another five minutes and then we're going home."

"Did anyone know this door was unlocked?" said Foxie, twisting the handle of the clock tower's door and finding it unexpectedly easy to open.

"It's amazing what you can do drunk," explained Micky, believing Josh had managed to force open the locked door. "It gives you super powers!"

"What's Callum's, then?"

"Unconsciousness."

The sound of a siren broke the loud, chattering voices of the three inebriated friends. A police car pulled up alongside the tower, fortunately not on the face where a poorly-prepared German was still hanging on for dear life.

"Boys," said a uniformed constable through the passenger window in a thick but calm Devonshire accent.

"Evening, officer," said Micky, who was the most presentable looking and had a knack of pretending to be sober even when he wasn't. It was a skill he thought he was better at than those on the receiving end.

Eric turned his back to avoid detection. He had a reputation to shelter.

"On your way home, are you, boys?" suggested the policeman.

"Stopped to check the time," lied Micky, half pointing at the clock face and then thinking better of it.

"And does he belong to you?"

Micky followed the policeman's nod to a body lying spreadeagled on the road in an Oasis t-shirt only partially visible through chunks of kebab, chilli sauce and lettuce.

"Yes. He's a bit tired, occifer."

"He's a traffic hazard. Remove him from my roads or I'll nick the lot of you for littering."

When Micky shuffled over to Callum to crane him up off the tarmac, an untimely second brogue tumbled out of the sky and bounced off the top of the police car. Before the officer got a chance to see where it had come from, the air was split by a hysterical scream. Seconds later, a falling body struck a buttress with a bone-crunching crack before landing in a heap on the roundabout right in front of the police car. Sean attempted to keep up the scream until the sight of his own bloody, shattered legs persuaded him to give up and pass out.

"Shit!" bellowed Micky.

"Run!" shouted Foxie.

"Eric Gideon! Stop!" demanded the policeman as Eric's escape route revealed his full identity.

DI IRIS WHITEHALL rustled hastily through the pages of her ring binder. She normally memorised case files, but there were so many pages in Eric's that it was impossible to retain it all. Sean Heschmeyer. She'd heard that name before. On the very last page of his file, she found it. A record of the very first time her interviewee had been arrested.

"Here it is," announced Whitehall triumphantly. "You were arrested for fleeing the scene of a crime."

"Falsely arrested," added Eric. "Again."

"It says in my notes that Sean suffered a pulverised pelvis, broken left leg, punctured lung and suspected brain damage when he fell twenty-five feet from the Miles Clock Tower. Statements taken from witnesses at the time indicate that you forced him to climb it and the authorities wanted to charge you with grievous bodily harm."

"But…"

"The charges were dropped."

"Precisely."

"Sean retracted his statement after claiming it had been an accident, and he took sole responsibility for his injuries."

"Which meant it wasn't a crime…therefore I couldn't be charged with fleeing it."

"We both know that's not true, don't we."

"You have the right to think what you want, but you weren't there."

"What happened to poor Sean after that?"

"He had reconstructive surgery on his leg, spent a month in hospital, missed his final exams and returned to Germany without a degree in engineering."

"Did you visit him?"

"In Germany?"

"No, in hospital."

"Only once."

"And what did you say to him?"

"I apologised."

"I find that very hard to believe."

"And I thanked him," said Eric, displaying the first signs of remorse in the interview to date. "It was a brave thing he did. My attitude towards him changed. I realised I'd treated him rather unfairly. I was inflicting my anger at the world on him, and afterwards, I took a long hard look at myself."

"And did he accept your apology?"

"He never said a word to me the whole time I was at his bedside. I put it down to the morphine."

"And what happened to the rest of you after the 'accident'?" she said, using ironic quotes with her fingers.

"Nothing. The Vice Chancellor tried to have us thrown out but he had no evidence to force it through. He had a vendetta against me from day one. After that, we knew we were on our last chance, so we disbanded *The Idiots' Club* there and then. We never wanted anyone to get hurt. We'd learnt our lesson the hard way. It was the last time the five of us were all together."

"Until last week."

"Yes."

"But what's Sean got to do with all this? He's not in the video footage from last night. He's not a suspect in any of these crimes."

"He has everything to do with it."

"How?"

"It was his idea. It was his invitation."

FOUR

CALLUM

Two weeks ago. Clerkenwell, London.

CALLUM JOLLIE POURED a large measure of whisky into a massive chipped tumbler from an ugly crystal decanter. It was eight thirty in the morning and most of his staff hadn't had their first coffee yet. He swiftly downed the contents and placed the glass back on its unorthodox coaster: a sea of paperwork. It was probably sprawled across an office desk, but a positive ID was impossible because none of the desk was visible. There were hundreds of opened letters, each printed in red and black ink with threatening fonts. Some had official government emblems, others featured the logos of well-known blue-chip corporations and a few had been written in angry handwriting.

All the letters demanded the same thing.

Money.

The first one arrived about a month ago. It began as a gentle trickle of individual grievances, but in the last few days the postman had been struggling to deliver the daily avalanche of court summons, final warnings and creditor demands to the second floor. The writing wasn't only on the letters; it had been on the wall for months. Callum though was an optimist. He believed in miracles long after all hope was lost. What if they landed a big order? It would be enough to keep the wolves from the door for another few weeks. As far as he knew, his team had been working tirelessly over recent days to convince customers up and down the land to commit to their next order by offering huge discounts. Savvy business people smelt desperation a mile off, and so far, there had been no takers. Maybe one of the angel investors he'd been courting in the city would provide a financial lifeline? They'd all seemed so enthusiastic about the opportunity. Corporate vultures always did when they knew they were getting a free lunch out of it. Even at this late hour, Callum believed a last-minute reprieve would save them, but in under thirty minutes the last chance saloon would finally close its doors for good.

Through the glass wall of his austere office, recently stripped of all comforts and devices necessary for running a small business, his loyal staff were forlornly packing their belongings into cheap self-built boxes. Some of the girls were sobbing, and a line of sympathetic colleagues were falling over themselves to offer moral and emotional support. It should have been Callum's shoulder they were crying on. After all, this was his business and these were his people. Every one of them he hired and selected personally; every one of them faultless in their dedication and perseverance. It wasn't their fault - how could it be? It wasn't their unwavering loyalty that failed, it was his leadership and few of them would have seen it coming. Such was the smokescreen that executives like him used to hide the truth. For some of the younger members of staff, this was probably their first experience of redundancy.

It definitely wasn't Callum's.

It happened more frequently than Easter.

In the last twenty years, Callum had launched more new businesses than the average person bought shoes, and they fell apart considerably quicker than a cheap pair of trainers bought from a dodgy market stall. In total, he'd seen more than a dozen misguided ventures peak and collapse in less time than most companies took to hire an accountant. Every time he incorporated a new business, he was convinced this was the big one, but every venture's fate was as predictable as the last. Even though the gestation period between success and ultimate failure was getting longer, it was always a matter of time before they committed financial hara-kiri. The current faltering race-horse in Callum Jollie's business stable had been active for well over three years before the gods of commerce decreed it was destined for the glue factory.

Callum was a dreamer. He always had been. All he ever wanted, for as long as he could remember, was to build a business both reputable and recognised. Most of all, he wanted to be seen by others as a business Goliath. Someone who was famous for a magic touch that turned failing businesses into money spinners. Notorious for spotting untapped trends, talent and opportunities. The recipient of awards from peers, the public and the business community. Known as much for his extravagant lifestyle as he was for his business acumen. Regularly interviewed by the big financial broadcasters seeking his unique insight into the day's economic twists and turns.

To date, the only interview he'd conducted was a few column inches on page twenty-four of the *Croydon Gazette* about the surge in people buying sheds.

It was indicative of how his dreams had so far failed to materialise. Not that he'd ever give up. Each failure brought him closer to what he knew was inevitable. Unlike other business gurus notorious for their global success, his achievement would not get a helping hand. Trump, Musk, Branson, Gates and so many others all had an advantage. They started out with something in the first place. It was mostly money, but Callum failed to understand they had something else he lacked.

Good ideas.

Callum's unshakeable belief in destiny clouded the unarguable truth: he totally lacked good business judgement. Rather than demonstrating an unnerving knack for picking out untapped innovations or seizing on products before the market woke up to their potential, he routinely demonstrated exactly the opposite. He jumped aboard a business bandwagon only after one of the wheels had fallen off. He bet the farm in the face of hurricane warnings and went big on fads which everyone else dismissed. The extensive list of his corporate blunders was almost enough to grant him the notoriety he so craved.

Straight out of University, he wasted no time in building his legend. Swept up, as many investors were, by the exciting prospects of easy money offered by the accelerating dot.com market, Callum's first company sold window cleaning services online. The demand from customers seeking to have their Microsoft programmes decluttered was extraordinary but, sadly, almost none of them wanted their actual window panes washed.

Not deterred by the first bump in the road, he invented a revolutionary lawnmower which was able to instantly compost cut grass. This tremendous environmental advancement worked well if you overlooked the inconvenience of the lawnmower catching fire every other time you used it. The businesses that followed included bereavement counselling for pet owners, affordable housing from renovated shipping containers, ergonomic beanbags, a recruitment company focused solely on placing entertainers in circuses and an import company that specialised in Syria's natural resources. In PR terms, Callum Jollie was to commerce what Michael Jackson was to child minding.

Believing he'd learnt the lessons of past mistakes, the current, and soon to be former company, was the most orthodox yet. Callum decided to enter a mature market – printing. Not just any old printing, though. His firm claimed to be able to print on anything the customer wanted. From the mundane world of paper instruction manuals to the rather more bizarre one of etching a brand name on the side of a submarine, it was all in a day's work. At least it would be if they still had any. The downside of anything described as 'mature' was the risk that it might die from old age. As investors and advertisers spent more of their budget online, the market for physical printing was shrinking as quickly as an old age pensioner's height. Recently, costs had outpaced revenues, and the investment required to maintain their promise of 'printing on anything' became uneconomical. Once you've lost your unique selling point, you quickly disappear in the crowd.

Callum was shaken from his daydreaming by a sharp tap on the glass of his office door. His personal assistant, Cindy, eyes raw from her tears, stood on the other side clutching today's mail in her hand. Callum waved her away, but she remained resolutely immovable. Finally, he motioned for her to enter.

"You might as well stick those straight in the shredder," insisted Callum, pointing at the two dozen letters in her hands.

"I can't."

"Oh, don't get all judgemental with me. It's not like I'm trying to shirk my responsibilities."

"You sold the shredder last week," Cindy snapped in reply.

"Oh…yeah. Better stack them here with the others, then."

She dropped them on the desk where they merged effortlessly into the heap. She only kept hold of one.

"Do you blame me?" said Callum pathetically, his eyes wide and watery like a scorned puppy.

"What for?"

"All this." He gestured at the employees packing their things out in the main office.

"Of course I do. It's not like I did anything wrong, is it?" she chuntered through pierced lips.

"What will you do now?"

"I'll get a good job with a proper company. One with decent benefits and managed by someone competent."

"I'm sure you'll be fine," Callum sympathised.

"Don't patronise me! I've already had five job offers."

The only offers Callum received recently were from bailiffs, and the only benefit to accepting was the avoidance of harassment by some borderline psychopaths. At least she had some career prospects. He'd pissed off every money lender in the city, official and dodgy. Even if he did want to start again, who would back him with his record? He glanced around at his crumbling empire, still officially his until nine o'clock.

"Oh good," added Callum. "Let me know if you need a reference."

"Not necessary," she said curtly.

"It was fun while it lasted though, wasn't it," he smiled.

"Fun! That's your idea of fun, is it? Lying to creditors about where my boss is? Deceiving investors? Pretending to uphold a sunny disposition for the other staff, even though I knew the truth? No, none of that was fun."

"Never boring…" Callum tried to put his usual positive spin on the situation.

"Boring is underrated."

"Variety is the spice of…"

"I kept this letter from the others," Cindy said, interrupting him and feeling no guilt about it. He hadn't paid her wages for weeks so what value was there in pandering to his ego. "It looked like private correspondence. Because I'm a dedicated, competent and professional PA, I thought I'd point it out to you before you ignored it along with all the others you've been dodging."

Callum leant across the desk and analysed the intriguing letter with suspicion. He didn't receive personal mail in the office very often, although the occurrence was fairly infrequent at home, too. His dwindling group of friends and acquaintances struggled to keep up with the constant changes to his business address, and as he owed money to most of them, he was quite happy about it. He rarely saw the few genuine friends he had left and couldn't actually remember the last time they sent him anything in the post. Callum wasn't married, lived alone and felt most comfortable around people who avoided crowds. A crowd for Callum was more than five, and as he didn't know that many people, he rarely found himself in one outside of work commitments.

In the top left-hand corner of the handwritten letter was the embossed name of *Heschmeyer Industries*. He knew they were a recently-won client, but to Callum they meant much more than that. He quickly snapped it out of Cindy's hands and nervously struggled to break-through the seemingly hermetically sealed envelope. Maybe this was it? The eleventh-hour reprieve he'd been praying for to stave off the financial zombies. He finally managed to tear through the outer wrapper with his teeth and nails, and unfolded the cream-coloured notepaper that sheltered inside.

It wasn't exactly the solution he yearned for, but it might still turn out to be one, nonetheless. He scanned the words three or four times to reinforce their meaning.

"Oh please, god, don't tell me the business is saved," pleaded Cindy.

"Not yet."

"I'm still leaving, you know."

"Probably a wise decision."

"Much wiser than the one I made three years ago."

Callum leapt out of his seat still clutching the letter. He grabbed his jacket from the corner of the room, where until recently a coat rack had stood to attention, and proceeded to head for the door.

"Where are you going?" demanded Cindy.

"Out."

"Oh no. Not this time!" She threw her more than sizeable frame in front of the exit to block his escape. "I've covered for you for the last time. You will accept accountability!"

"Couldn't I accept it tomorrow?"

"No! You have a meeting with the liquidators in less than twenty minutes. I've already rescheduled it three times this week. I won't lie for you anymore. If you want to postpone again, then you'll have to ring them yourself."

"Cindy, I'll give you one hundred pounds if you delay them one more time for me!" begged Callum.

"I know for a fact that you don't have one hundred pounds."

He cursed his luck that he'd granted Cindy access to his online bank account because he needed a recognised adult to check it for him. He was always too frightened to look.

"Then you can have whatever's left in my account!"

The last balance she'd seen showed a total liquidity of nine pounds and twelve pence.

"Sit down," she barked aggressively, shepherding him towards his chair like a bad-tempered sheepdog. "I'm not letting you out of this room until they arrive."

Callum slumped back into his uncomfortable, cheap plastic canteen chair. He used to have a big auspicious leather one but like the shredder and the coat rack, it too had been sold off. Cindy reversed through the door, closed it firmly and returned to her packing, one eye pinned on his door. This was it. There was no escape from the inevitable now. He opened the letter once more and reread the instructions. A QR code was printed at the bottom. It was a boarding pass for a flight that left this evening. He had to be on it. The business might still fail but if he followed these instructions, like a phoenix he might still rise from the ashes.

At nine o'clock precisely, the phone on Cindy's desk buzzed impatiently. It was one of the last items left on what had once been a fully-equipped workstation. Gone were the computer, keyboard, stationery, complimentary calendar from one of their suppliers and the framed photo of two rather plump children wearing ponchos and enjoying a day out at a water park. She guessed correctly who was causing it to ring, and as a consequence, even the phone might be missing by the end of the day. She immediately buzzed the caller into the building. A minute later, Callum's visitors were exiting the second-floor lift of his shared services office building.

Two soulless-looking men carrying humourless expressions extended their hands in unified greeting. They were pale, slim and exceedingly dour corporate clones. Balancing slender spectacles on their sharp-edged noses, they shared a preference for slimy side partings and were uniformly shrink-wrapped into identical, unblemished designer suits. Cindy shook their clammy hands meekly and offered a reluctant smile. These would be the final visitors she'd ever welcome to the office. Institutional grim reapers, they would depart in an hour or so with the withered soul of someone's once barely solvent hopes and dreams. That was their job, and from their expressions, they thoroughly enjoyed it.

"Please follow me," directed Cindy politely.

The two men floated along a few feet behind her like they were attached to a pulley system. They passed the empty office cubicles, dried up water coolers and barren notice boards before Cindy stopped at Callum's office door. The blinds along the glass partition had been drawn as if the PVC slats were the final wall of defence against the firm's impending liquidation. There was one way to delay men like this from fulfilling their duties, and Callum knew full well that nine pounds twelve pence wouldn't cut it.

"Mr Jollie is waiting for you." Cindy held the door open for them. She hoped it would be her last unpaid duty on her very last day.

She was very wrong.

The cold rushed out to meet the warm air of the open plan office. Both men glanced inside the empty room, then at each other and finally at Cindy.

"He's a little strange, but totally harmless," Cindy assured them, a frequent response to people's alarm at his frequently bizarre behaviour.

"Madam, he's not in here."

"What?" she gasped, peering into the room for the first time to notice that the second-floor window was open and the wind was causing the final reminder letters to jitter nervously on his desk. "Selfish bastard!"

"We don't like to be left waiting," said the elder of the two men.

"We get paid before any creditors, however long it takes," stated the second.

"I do apologise, gentlemen. I'm sure Mr Jollie has simply popped out for a moment."

"Out of the window?"

Cindy hurried over to check whether there was an injured forty-something director shattered on the pavement or hobbling away from the scene. To her disappointment there wasn't, which was annoying, as she was quite prepared to personally drag him back to the meeting by his earlobes. On the window ledge, a post-it note was doing its upmost to remain sticky in the face of sustained external harassment.

'Cindy. Just popped out to find ten million quid. Please ask them to come back next week. Sorry.'

Two weeks ago. Holborn, London.

"Take a seat please, Eric."

"I'll stand, if it's all the same with you."

"Your choice."

The smartly-dressed, striking brunette tapped the keys of her laptop to retrieve his personnel file. A universal truth of owning a computer is the collection of files. Bloody millions of them. Most are organised securely in the event they should be needed at some point in the future. Rarely is this true, but people keep them anyway just in case. Although when a particular file does become urgent, it will become so elusive that it might as well have been deleted. Files have a habit of behaving like that. They're sneaky. They're stored in folders with logical naming conventions in the belief that they'll be easier to find. In reality, it'll take several days to locate them and even then they'll only come to light by accident or after the seeker spends hours rewriting the original document or demands that every single colleague check their own terminals in case they happened to save a copy when the originator pointlessly copied them in.

There were some files on Monica Silver's laptop she'd struggle to find with the assistance of the FBI. But as HR Director at Peperit Creative, there was always one document which was easy to find: Eric Gideon's personnel file.

It was usually in her 'recents' folder.

"How many disciplinaries have I conducted with you?" asked Monica with a suppressed smile.

"That depends what time period you're referring to."

"This year."

"Three."

"And it's only mid-March," she confirmed. "You're on for a personal best."

"I like to aim high."

"We encourage our employees to have a representative with them - trade union member, colleague or lawyer - but you know that already."

"I do."

"And…"

"Why break the habit of a lifetime."

Everything HR did followed a process. Eric thought it must be exhausting to stick so regimentally to local country laws, company manuals and ACAS advice. Following arbitrary guidelines was a misnomer in an industry like his. Creativity didn't work like that. Nothing in the pantheon of human endeavour had ever been achieved by following rules. It was the disruptors and rule breakers who made names for themselves and changed the world. He doubted whether anyone would remember an HR Manager a hundred years from now for some great leap forward in human progress. Not only was it irritating to sit through, it was also clear the process didn't work very well. None of his disciplinary hearings had ever succeeded in adjusting his behaviour. But as he regularly walked the tightrope between pushing the envelope and continued employment, he had to play along with their game. Which meant he had to do what he always did in these situations – nod, confess and offer fake contrition. A skill he'd perfected over many years.

"Do you want to start?" asked Monica.

"No, I think I'll let you go, in case you don't have as much information as I do about the situation," he grinned.

"You do know how serious this is, don't you? It's normally three strikes and you're out."

Eric nodded and purposely adjusted his body language to make sure he was sending all the right signals. At the last count, he was well into double figures, and experience had taught him this was nothing more than an idle threat. They wouldn't fire him. They needed him. Peperit Creative would have been nothing without him. When Alan West, his boss and the owner of the firm, initially hired him fifteen years ago the business was a struggling minnow in a sea of hungry sharks. Now they were one of the biggest ad agencies in the city and, as Creative Director, Eric was responsible for winning and designing the campaigns for their biggest clients. Unilever, Pepsi, Apple and a dozen other big brands were in Peper-it's stable all because of him, and he knew they'd bolt out of the door if he blew the hinges off. The value of an agency like this one was measured almost entirely by its human capital and good will. There were no assets, no products, limited services and only short-term contracts. Take the creativity away and there was nothing much left to sell.

"There's an intern in intensive care," said Monica gravely. "Do you want to explain why?"

"He didn't pass."

"Pass what?"

"His initiation test."

"We've banned initiation tests," she stated assertively.

He nodded multiple times in a style which suggested his head was about to fall off.

"You can stop with the NLP, Eric. I'm a master practitioner."

She was a novice. Theoretical application only. He used it as frequently as he used his lungs.

"Why did you wrap the intern in heavy chains, padlock and hang him upside down from the fire escape?"

"It wasn't just me."

"No, but you have an aptitude for encouraging people to do what you tell them. You're a senior executive with an exceptional track record, equally feared and respected by the rest of the staff. In a fiercely competitive industry like this, people are hungry and ambitious. They will do what you tell them because they think it's good for their careers, and you know it."

"Which is exactly why we need initiations."

"They're banned. It's policy."

"Do you know how many people want to work in advertising?" he asked rhetorically. "Thousands. There isn't enough room for all of them. We can't judge them purely on the quality of their degree or their past experience. They all claim to be equally capable. The only way to know for sure who will make it, and who will not, is to test their ingenuity under pressure. Talent acquisition requires a touch of creativity."

"Then give them a psychometric test or IQ challenge; don't hang them from their ankles fifty feet off the ground!"

"Pfft! Those online tests are easily fooled, and they don't recreate the pressure of a deadline or the jeopardy of performing under stress. When people experience true fear, they either panic or meet the challenge head on."

"The young man on whom you inflicted your spurious ideology is only twenty. How would you have fared at that age?"

"Perfectly well, thank you."

"Your arrogance is breathtaking."

"It's only arrogance if you fail. It's called 'self-confidence' if you succeed, and I always do."

"Just so you know, although I'm certain you don't care for him any more than you do any of the rest of us, he's suffered a broken ankle, whiplash and a suspected hernia. All because you insist on disregarding health and safety."

"Nothing serious then, and he's learnt some valuable lessons as a result. If he'd had what it takes, he'd have found a way to escape. Now he knows he's in the wrong industry and he can move on with certainty."

"Do rules mean absolutely nothing to you?"

"No, they mean someone is trying to control me. Rules are designed by the privileged to stop people like me joining in."

"Or they're sensible steps to stop idiots like you injuring interns," replied Monica.

"You wouldn't think like that if you'd had to struggle through life."

"You don't know me," she snapped angrily. "You don't know what I've had to do to get here. You think you're the only one who's been discriminated against because of who you are. Women have had to fight for parity, too, and most of us have managed to do it without the wanton disregard for others or resorting to testosterone-fuelled pranks. Get your head out of your arse, Eric. You're not unique. You blame your background for a lack of opportunity, but maybe it isn't that. Maybe you're just a dick."

Receiving an insult like this might offend some people, but not Eric. His skin was thicker than a dehydrated hippo. He was impressed by the unexpected fire inside her, though. He always had respect for those who stood up for themselves. Before he had a chance to offer a defence for his actions, his phone rang loudly in his pocket. Without flinching, he removed it. Rather than silence it and offer Monica his sincere apologies, as was the accepted convention in situations like this, he answered it.

"Gloomy! Long time no hear."

"Excuse me, we're in a meeting," Monica said indignantly.

"It's my representative," whispered Eric, cupping his hand over the speaker. "You did encourage me to have one."

"In person, not on the phone."

Eric made a 'quiet down' sign with his palm and turned his back on his infuriated HR Director.

"No, I didn't get an invite…post…all paperless in this office, mate…I'll check my emails…who…I'm not going to see him…calm down, Callum…I'm sure it is important to you but…no, I don't owe you one…"

"PUT THE PHONE DOWN!" screamed Monica, springing from her chair and attempting to rip it out of his grasp.

"No, no…it's not a bad time…just a disciplinary…not that uncommon, no…I have them in my diary as a recurring meeting…yeah…go where?…Scotland?…why would I go there?…I'm sure it is important to you but…look, I'll go if Josh is going…how should I know if he got a letter, I'm not his keeper…I'll give him a call…look, I've got to go…she looks like she's about to go nuclear…talk later."

"Never in all my years as a professional have I met a ruder, more conceited, ill-disciplined, arrogant or entitled man than you, and I used to work in the Civil Service. I don't care how important you think you are to this firm – we have to make an example of you. I'm suspending you for two weeks until a formal disciplinary hearing can be arranged with the board of directors."

"You know I can reverse your decision in an instant with one brief phone call to Alan," he replied calmly.

"I don't think so," she said with a smirk. "I have more sway with him than you do."

"What makes you think that?"

"Because I'm having sex with him."

"Ah."

FIVE
JOSH

Two weeks ago. Royal Tunbridge Wells.

It was midafternoon when Josh Foxole received the call. Not the first one. He ignored that. Nor the second or even the third. He'd heard them surely enough but he'd been a little preoccupied. It was about the caller's sixth attempt to reach him when he eventually picked up. Josh slid his naked arm from under the duvet and searched around the floor for his discarded trousers. Eventually, he located the back pocket where his phone was demanding attention in dual attack mode, vibrating furiously and ringing like a fire alarm. He checked the number before deciding to answer. It was unrecognised, so they weren't in his contacts list. He thought this was always a blessing, because it meant it was probably a customer and not someone trying to figure out where he was.

"Josh Foxole, Moby Pet Products," he replied in his most professional sales voice.

"Do you sell ringworm tablets?" said a scraggily voice which fluctuated between Welsh and Pakistani accents.

"Yes." Josh shuffled up in bed to display his bare chest to the room. The curtains were closed, but a shard of sunlight was forcing its way through the gap. "What animal is it for?"

"Flamingo."

A body stirred in the double bed next to him, and a manicured hand with red painted nails slid across his body. He felt five digits and the warm metal of a wedding ring gently massaging his chest hair.

"Flamingos?"

"Yes."

"I don't think flamingos get ringworm," replied Josh, who had no real knowledge on the subject to fall back on. "What's wrong with them?"

"They've turned blue," replied the Welsh Pakistani.

"Eric?"

"Is it that obvious!"

"Your accent is ridiculous," Josh chuckled.

"Had you going for a minute, though."

"I was just playing along," fibbed Josh.

"Where are you?"

"Work. Ouch!" he replied as the woman next to him pinched his right nipple.

"Work?" asked Eric sceptically.

"Yeah."

"What's her name?"

"I don't know what you're on about. I missed your calls because I've been in a meeting."

"Pull the other one."

The middle-aged blonde kissed Josh's neck seductively and he reluctantly nudged her away. There were many temptations that Josh struggled to deny himself, but the opposite sex was way out in front on that list.

"What do you want, man? I'm a little tied up right now."

"I'll bet you are!"

"Not like that."

"Did you get Sean's invitation?"

"Sean who?"

"Heschmeyer!"

"Who?"

"You're kidding, right? Sean the Yawn. Simple Sean. Sean Coronary. Sean Schnitzel…"

"His second name was Heschmeyer? Never knew."

"Josh, you struggle enough with first names! I'd bet you don't even remember her name, do you?"

He glanced across as the blonde's nymphomaniac lips tried to circumnavigate his body. A list of names flashed though his brain like a carousel, but none of them seemed to identify her. "What invite?"

"Apparently, Sean's holding a big opening ceremony for one of his projects and he's invited Callum."

"But not us."

"That's why I rang you."

Josh spent the majority of his waking hours in social settings, whether work-related or not. He disliked being on his own, and hated being excluded from a function. It didn't matter what it was. He'd go to the opening of an envelope if there was a free buffet and people to talk to. Sporting event, awards ceremony, dinner party, the opera, a kid's birthday party – as long as he didn't have a better offer, he'd be there. A better offer usually meant lying in bed in the middle of a weekday afternoon with a sex-starved stranger.

"Why didn't he invite us?" asked Josh despondently.

"I suspect it's because we haven't seen him for twenty years, and the last time we did, he was laid up in hospital with life-limiting injuries."

"Then why is Callum invited?"

"Maybe because he didn't run away," suggested Eric.

"Only because he was unconscious at the time."

"It doesn't matter. That's all in the past and I only look forward these days. Callum has two spare tickets and he's begging me to go with him."

"What did you say?" replied Josh, trying not to be distracted by his companion's hand, which was trying subtly to move south.

"I'd go if you did."

"You know me, Eric - I'd willingly attend an invitation to my own execution. I'm not sure why you'd want to go, though? You hate the guy."

"Yes, I do, but apparently I owe Callum a favour and he seems really agitated about something. Friends have to be there for each other when it matters, even if we seldom are when it doesn't."

"When is it?"

"Tomorrow."

"Fine. I can clear my schedule," said Josh, offering the blonde a sly wink.

Salespeople didn't really have schedules, only what they chose to report on their CRM system for management to scrutinise. As long as it looked like they were in meetings with customers, no one really cared very much. It was certainly a lot more flexible than being a vet, Josh's original profession. If Mrs. Tarrant booked an emergency appointment for her sick cat, it wasn't easy to change plans at the last minute. Josh knew this because he frequently had, which is probably one of the reasons Mrs. Tarrant's cat could no longer be described in the present tense. It certainly wasn't the only reason he'd been fired by more veterinary practices than cats had lives. It was hard to concentrate on animal surgery when his employers insisted on hiring hot student veterinary nurses. Arsonists make very poor firemen. Selling pet products definitely wasn't a lucrative career, but it did offer freedom, and the vast opportunities for social interaction suited him perfectly.

"You'll have to clear today's schedule, too," persisted Eric.

"Why?"

"The plane tickets are for today only."

"Plane tickets? Where are we going?"

"Scotland."

"Scotland! What the fuck is he opening, Scottish-German trade talks!"

"A bridge, apparently."

"So, what is he, a minor celebrity or something?"

"No. I think he built it."

"Must have taken him ages," chortled Josh.

"Our flight is from Gatwick at eight; I'll meet you there."

"Okay…Jesus, what was that?"

Their conversation was interrupted by the riotous sound of glass smashing out in the street, which even Eric heard down the other end of the phone. It was quickly followed by a series of dull thuds from a wooden object hitting aluminium. Josh hurried to the window and peeked carefully through the gap in the curtains. A muscular man in a builder's hi-vis jacket was in the process of annihilating a small Vauxhall Nova with a cricket bat. Josh recognised the vehicle immediately. It was his. The man, on the other hand, he'd never seen before in his life.

"What's all the commotion?" asked Eric.

"He's home early!" whispered the nervous lingerie-clad

blonde who'd joined Josh at the window to see what the disturbance was.

"I might have a transport problem," remarked Josh rather more calmly than the situation demanded.

ERIC PARKED his brand-new black Nissan GT-R R35 sports car outside a small semi-detached house. He didn't need to check the address, which he'd typed into his phone, to know he was in the right place. The presence of a battered small hatchback was enough evidence to mark out this otherwise unremarkable suburban street. Royal Tunbridge Wells was a relatively affluent area, but by the looks of its housing stock and the cars parked up and down the road, he was in the rougher end of town. Not rough compared to the area in which he grew up, but run-down enough to cause anxiety about leaving an expensive sports car unattended. He gazed across the road to number seventy-three where he expected to see his friend waiting for him, eager to leave.

Josh wasn't there.

His car certainly was, though.

Well, mainly there.

Parts of it were also over there and some critical components associated with automobiles had disappeared entirely. But the broken chassis, shattered windows and missing doors were by no means the only events worthy of attention.

The first-floor bedroom window of number seventy-three was open to its widest possible position and a series of objects were being jettisoned through the semi-closed curtains, creating a rather brave and totally new front garden design. A pair of women's thigh-high boots, a laptop case, a poorly-packed set of luggage, a bedroom lamp and a man's leather jacket were some of the items that came through like a vengeful version of the *Generation Game*.

Eric chuckled to himself nostalgically. Josh hadn't changed a bit. Still up to his neck in it. If Eric was incapable of saying no to a challenge, then Josh was equally unable to resist the attention of women. Not just those who took a fancy to him, either. He had to prove that he could win the affections of anyone who caught his eye. Generally speaking, he'd been bewilderingly successful at it, too. Eric only recalled one occasion when a girl had rejected his boyish charms. It was such a momentous event that Josh stayed in his room for weeks, convinced he'd lost his mojo. Self-belief is fragile like that. It can take one small bump in the road for an engine to fail unexpectedly.

Eric often wondered how Josh had managed to continue his streak well into his forties. Eric could sell almost anything to anyone, but his high conversion rate in work didn't translate to the dating arena - not that it bothered him in the slightest. He'd had his fair share of relationships, but they never lasted longer than half a year. People bored him. They wanted to settle down, relax and spend hours watching television. He wanted to be pushed, to mix things up and live life on the edge. When he did meet someone he saw as his equal, they saw through him as easily as he did others. It also became over-competitive and often ended in confrontation and a huge, ugly breakup.

Eric believed the most alluring characteristic that made Josh attractive to women was his utter coolness under pressure. The attribute had worked a charm in the nineteen nineties and was obviously still working now. Confidence was the winning formula. That and the fact that Josh had one of the dirtiest minds of anyone Eric had ever met, and he'd know - he worked in advertising. Most people who met Josh for the first time would describe him as aloof, non-committal and even, on occasion, a little cold. It didn't surprise Eric that the female students in University found his complex bad boy image intoxicating, but it did surprise him that middle-aged women still fell for it.

No doubt Josh was having to delve deep into his customary coolness to smooth over whatever situation he'd got himself into today. By the sounds of the full-scale shouting match in progress on the first floor, he had his work cut out.

"Psst," hissed a noise from the conifer bush that separated the garden of number seventy-three and the neighbouring plot.

Josh hadn't broken out his boyish charms after all, he'd simply moved to stage two of his playbook – running away. Eric pressed the button to lower the electric window.

"Nice car," came Josh's unmistakable voice from behind the foliage. Only his floppy fringe and nose were partially visible.

"Thanks, it's new."

"What model?" the bush queried conversationally.

"GT-R."

"Wow, must have been a good sales quarter."

"Always better than the last," explained Eric, a little perplexed by his friend's decision to make casual chitchat at such a time. "Mate, what are you doing in there?"

"Waiting for you."

"I'm here."

"Yes, I know. But you need to swing the car around over to this side of the road and open the passenger door."

"Why?"

"I don't want to cause a scene."

Eric glanced up again as more items were ejected from the window, including something that was accompanied by a noise that sounded remarkably like the howl of a cat. "I think there's already a scene, mate!"

"I know, but trust me...I can make it worse, " he added calmly. "Swing it around."

The front door of the semi-detached house flew open and smashed against the pebble-dashed front wall, cracking the frosted glass. Having run out of suitable possessions to chuck though the upstairs window, the agitated bodybuilder who'd been responsible for obliterating the Vauxhall Nova spotted the Nissan GT-R driver chatting to an unseen figure in his garden. Now he was going to take his fury out on both of them.

"Quickly," encouraged Josh, still as composed as he was before the annoyed builder arrived.

Eric pressed the ignition button, stuck the car into a right-hand lock and squeezed the accelerator pedal. The sports car screeched and a semicircular trajectory took it to the other side of the street. Josh, almost fully naked, scuttled out of the hedge and dived into the passenger seat.

"What the..." stated Eric before he was interrupted.

"You can go now," indicated the new passenger, "before he puts a dent in your nice new car!"

"If he does, I'm sending you the bill."

The Nissan burst off down the suburban street somewhat faster than the round speed limit signs approved of and certainly faster than the irate thug pursuing them on foot could manage. In moments the red-faced husband was merely a speck in the rearview mirror.

"Thanks." Josh offered a thumbs-up sign.

"Is your naked butt on my heated leather seats!"

"Yes."

The only piece of Josh's clothing not strewn liberally

around the shrubs of number seventy-three, and still attached to the veterinary salesman's body, was a pair of comedy boxer shorts. Not just any boxers but ones designed exclusively for intimate private moments, and only then if you were a certain brand of sexual deviant. Eric tried desperately to avoid direct eye contact.

"Is this a normal day for you?" he asked sarcastically.

"Not really. I normally don't get caught," Josh replied, placing his wallet and phone on the sports car's dash, the only other possessions he'd managed to grab before his retreat.

"You must be getting sloppy in your old age."

"Occupational hazard."

It was unlikely that any occupation included unexpected vehicle vandalism, shimmying down drainpipes and hiding in a bush naked within its job profile.

"Who was she?"

"One of my customer's employees," Josh answered nonchalantly. "Only met her yesterday. Bloody lovely girl, though."

"What happened to Jane?"

"Who?"

"Your wife."

"Oh, Jane…ex-wife."

"I was at your wedding less than two years ago."

"She's not even my most recent wife."

"What?"

"Yeah, I got married again late last year to an oncologist."

"And you didn't invite me."

"It was a shotgun thing and I wouldn't be too upset; we got divorced last month."

"What was her name?"

"I want to say Celine…"

"You don't remember?"

"…but it might have been Zoe."

"They're not even similar names!"

"I do remember she was an oncologist, though."

"Well, that's great, Foxie, much more important than remembering her name. That's three in total, then?" Eric didn't shock easily, but his best friend's marital record was beginning to compete with Elizabeth Taylor's.

"I'm done now," he insisted. "No more wives for me."

"Just other people's."

Josh grinned childishly. "Can you swing by my place so I can grab some clothes?"

"Nope."

"What do you mean, 'Nope'?"

"Our flight leaves in less than two hours and it's at least thirty minutes to Gatwick Airport. You know what Callum is like with timing; he's not going to wait for us if he thinks he's going to miss it."

"I can't go to the airport looking like this!"

"I dare you," said Eric, shooting him a mischievous wink.

"Oh no. That's not fair. Carrington banned us, remember?"

"Pah! Carrington doesn't own you. What's the matter, lost your bottle?"

"I think the events of this afternoon prove conclusively that I haven't. Is it legal?"

"What, entering an airport wearing nothing but boxer shorts? I doubt there's a specific piece of legislation against it. I think if you had your tackle out they'd be able to get you on indecent exposure charges, but as long as you don't pull them down, I think you'll be fine. One way to find out, isn't there."

"These aren't your average pair of pants, though, are they?"

"Pants are pants. Either wearing only pants in a public place is acceptable, or it isn't."

"Sod it, we've done much worse down the years!"

"Absolutely. I'll tell you what: if you get through departure and security, I'll buy you a brand new suit before we board the plane. Can't say fairer than that?"

"Deal."

Twenty minutes of high-speed driving later, the Nissan exited the motorway and carved through the traffic on the airport's approach road.

"Why does Callum want to see Sean?" inquired Josh.

"He didn't say, but he was quite insistent that we were there with him."

"Has he even seen Sean since the last time we did?"

Eric shrugged.

"And Callum insisted that you 'owe him one', right?"

"Yes. Apparently we both do."

"I don't owe him anything," replied Josh aggressively.

"Yeah, you do. You just have a terrible memory."

"My memory is excellent."

"Apart from when you have to remember the names of people you were married to not that long ago."

"I'd have remembered something as important as a debt to a friend, though."

"It's not a debt as such; it's an unavoidable truth which deserves acknowledgement and repaying with a favour of his choosing. This appears to be it."

Josh failed to remove his clueless expression by rubbing his stubbly face with his hand. "Huh?"

"When Sean had his 'accident'," explained Eric, choosing his words carefully, "you and I bolted. We left

Callum and Micky to deal with the police, the medics and the aftermath."

"Callum was unconscious, though, so really it was only Micky."

"Don't you believe it. You know what happens to a drunk person when something serious goes down."

Scientists across the world, both mainstream and homeopathic, have been eagerly developing ways to artificially sober people up for decades. There are many schools of thought as to what works best. Suggestions range from drinking strong coffee, breathing fresh air, consuming a gallon of water, or taking pills that speed up your metabolism, to forcing yourself to vomit. Millions have been spent on this research, but none of these methods works the best. Any piss-head will tell you that the surefire way of achieving sobriety is to place the subject in a situation of immense stress and danger. Anything that involves the emergency services usually works in a heartbeat.

"What did Callum do then?"

"Sobered up, initially. Then he gave Sean first aid before the medics arrived, and a few days later, he convinced Sean to drop the charges against us," explained Eric.

"Shit, how did he manage that?"

"I don't know. He's clearly a better influencer of people than I am…what am I saying…obviously that can't be it."

"I guess we do owe him one, then. Strange that he's waited twenty years to call it in – and over this of all things," speculated Josh, who had begun to shiver as a result of the evening temperature.

"Yeah."

The sports car drove straight up to the valet parking where they were immediately met by three official-looking young men who squabbled over who was going to get to park the automotive eye candy. The losers had the consolation prize of not having to deal with a man in his boxer shorts. Josh stepped out into the English drizzle from the comfort of the heated seats and carpeted floor well. He exhaled a deep sigh. The entrance to the airport was crowded with excitable holiday makers. Airports were always busy, whatever time you arrived. As they walked towards the glass entrance, anyone in their general vicinity was caught in a juxtaposition between averting their eyes in horror and a weird curiosity to work out exactly what Josh was wearing. When it became clear what it was, they mostly squealed and returned to averting their eyes.

After years of putting himself in the line of fire with Eric's dares, Josh had learnt a valuable lesson. If you were going to do something dumb, then you had to act like everything was completely normal. If he behaved like a man wearing nothing but boxer shorts in the shape of a rhino's head, equipped with a grey rubber appendage that stuck out diagonally from the front and the words 'I've got the horn' printed on the rear, then he would be doomed. If, though, he acted like he was just another passenger heading out on a business trip to Amsterdam or a holiday in the Seychelles, it would have the effect of disarming the general public.

Most of them.

Not all of them.

Some mothers threw themselves at their children to protect them from an image which might give them permanent nightmares or create a bunch of questions that no parent wanted to answer.

Some stared agog and pointed.

One woman almost fainted, but Josh wasn't sure if it was out of fright or whether she actually recognised the briefs. She did look a little familiar.

The security guard manning the entrance to the departure foyer clearly didn't see the funny side or fall for the act that this was normal behaviour.

"Where do you think you're going, sir?"

"Edinburgh," replied Josh confidently.

"Not dressed like that, you aren't."

"Technically, I don't think he's dressed at all," Eric pointed out unhelpfully.

"I know my rights," lied Josh. "It's not illegal."

The security guard didn't know whether this was true or not. Memorising the vagaries of the British legal system wasn't normally called upon in a job that involved little more than looking angry and treating everyone with suspicion. He was being intellectually stretched and he didn't like it. In situations like this, jobsworths only had one escape route.

"It's against airport policy."

"What is?"

"That is."

"Wearing boxer shorts?"

"No, you can wear them as long as they're not on show."

"It specifically says that in the airport policy book, does it?" argued Eric.

"Not specifically, but there's a general note about dress code."

"I don't believe you," said Josh, finding himself surprisingly irritated at the thought that someone might stop him expressing his fashion choices. "Show us."

"No," the man replied gruffly. "Look, it's indecent."

"I actually agree with you," said Eric. "But that's how I found him and as much as I disapprove, we're late for our flight."

"Unless you can give me a good reason why I can't fly

wearing these, then I'm going to do it anyway," insisted Josh, puffing his chest out.

"It's at odds with my morals," countered the guard rather weakly.

"Then I'd discourage you from spending two weeks with him in Magaluf," added Eric, enjoying himself more than he had in months.

"There are young children in there," said the security guard. "It's just wro…"

"Thief! Stop him!" came a scream from inside the departure hall.

A few seconds later, a youth in a hoodie and ripped jeans sprinted past them, clutching an expensive-looking, feminine handbag. He only briefly slowed down when he caught sight of Josh's groin region. Then he ran even faster.

The guard instinctively gave chase, believing his firm's resources were better employed stopping muggers than debating morals with a grown man and his lewd under-wear choices. As Eric and Josh were about to respond to the distraction by going about their business, their way into the terminal was blocked again.

"It could only be you two," said Callum, holding out two boarding passes.

SIX

THE BRIDGE

QUEUING TO SCAN HIS BOARDING PASS WAS PRETTY embarrassing, but that was nothing compared to how Josh felt once they reached the other side. Passports might not be required for domestic flights, but every passenger was still required to go through security. Josh placed two of his three belongings - his wallet and phone - in a plastic tray and took his third possession with him. To his utter surprise, he was the only one of the three of them who set the scanners off.

He stepped out of the machine, and a dispirited female security operative waved him towards her with an expression that merged contempt, bewilderment and exasperation. The staff here had to deal with all sorts of oddballs on the average shift, but this wasn't something they were likely to experience again anytime soon. She asked if he was hiding anything down below, and Josh managed to suppress an answer guaranteed to result in a full and painful cavity search. After he denied any hidden objects, the woman grabbed a long, thin metal pointer which she used to poke tentatively at the minimal fabric. Having convinced herself potential hijackers or terrorists would probably not arrive at their target in such a fashion, she waved him through.

True to his word, Eric, struggling to stem the tears of laughter that cascaded down his face, immediately escorted Josh to the shops. Finalising a quickfire round of assertive buying decisions, Josh was kitted out in an expensive BOSS suit, Ben Sherman shirt and a pair of matching Hush Puppy shoes and instantly found it easier to blend in with the general public. They wandered the vast terminal until they found a place to sit and wait for their gate to be called.

"That's two you owe me," expressed Callum.

"Two?"

"Yeah. I had to pay a young lad and his mum to help me out. You owe me a nice watch," he said, brandishing a wrist complete with tan marks.

"What kind of watch?"

"Omega," he lied.

In truth, it was a really old Casio, but the youth seemed to think it was retro.

"Jesus, Gloomy! Why didn't you just give the kid some money?" asked Josh.

"I don't carry cash," replied Callum, hiding the fact that nine pounds twelve pence probably wouldn't have swung it, even though the Casio was probably worth a fraction less.

"It's good to see you, Callum," said Eric, squeezing him on the shoulder. "Been a while."

"Eighteen months," he answered, counting back in his mind to the last occasion. "How is Jane?"

Eric drew his finger under his chin to strategically give news of Josh's current marital status.

"Oh...and business," Callum said, changing subjects hurriedly. "Things good with you boys?"

"Better than ever," announced Eric, who wasn't entirely sure if he'd have a job by the time he got back from their unexpected trip. "You?"

"Yeah, fine. Big plans." Callum struggled to give the correct eye cues and, as normal, Eric noticed immediately that his response was some distance from the truth.

"Have you seen Micky recently?" inquired Josh.

"Not for years," responded Callum with a tone of regret in his voice. "You know how Natasha is - she has him on a pretty tight leash these days."

"These days! She's been like it since we left Uni. Never been keen on us lot."

"That's not strictly true," amended Eric. "I seem to remember she was extremely keen on one of us. Isn't that right, Rhino Boy!"

"All in the past," replied Josh, without demonstrating the slightest sign of embarrassment. "So, what's all this about, Callum? Why do we have to go to Scotland with you?"

"You're my oldest friends...and I had three tickets. Why wouldn't I invite you along?"

"It's precisely because we're your oldest friends that tells us you're hiding something," said Eric pointedly.

The crackly, barely audible, tannoy announcement drifted over their heads to partially indicate that their gate number had been called. A glance at the huge electronic boards hanging from the ceiling confirmed it.

"That's us," announced Callum eagerly.

"We'll continue this conversation on the plane."

They certainly tried, but once they were squeezed into their budget airline excuses for seats, Callum quickly dominated the subject matter - when he wasn't guzzling down overly expensive cans of lager, that was. The flight from Gatwick to Edinburgh was in the air less than an hour, but it didn't stop Callum from seeing off four or five small cans before touch down. Some things had changed in twenty years, but obviously some habits had not. Callum still fuelled himself with a steady stream of booze, and neither time nor location was ever going to stop him. Eric wouldn't have minded so much if it weren't for the fact he'd offered to buy the round.

After the plane landed safely in Edinburgh and the three of them passed through security with the minimum of fuss, Eric tried to raise the subject of Sean again. He failed. In the hotel, which was adjacent to the airport and had been paid for in full by their host, Josh attempted to reignite the topic down in the bar. Seven pints and less than two hours later, they'd failed to make any inroads. Callum offered only nostalgic stories or the occasional proclamation of how pleased he was they were all here enjoying themselves. Following this stage in proceedings, Callum entered what the boys always referred to as his 'karaoke phase'. This normally involved singing a collec-tion of famous nineties songs without the benefit of any background instruments besides the general mutterings of the disgruntled patrons. It was impossible to sing along with him, because the lyrics and melodies to different songs were constantly being changed and merged together.

Once Callum passed through this period, they knew they'd soon lose him to the 'sleepy phase' and it would be best to get him back to his bedroom before they were forced to carry him across time zones in this seemingly endless building. With Callum securely tucked up in bed, the mini fridge emptied for his own protection, the other two decided to turn in for the night. They'd try to pose their questions over breakfast tomorrow when heads were clear and the bars were shut.

At about seven thirty in the morning, they reconvened in the breakfast hall to scoff down lukewarm scrambled eggs, baked beans with an added layer of congealed skin and anaemic bacon that appeared to have been cooked over a candle. Callum, true to form, showed zero effects of the night before. When most people have a 'big night' it tends to be a rarity, and as such, the impact in the morning is both painful and predictable. When Callum had a 'big night' it frequently came hot on the heels of the last one. This repeated pattern of liquified self-harm created a state of being that was never exactly sober and not completely drunk. He also needed half the hours of sleep of most average humans, making the transformation even more remarkable.

"Great night," said Callum chirpily.

Josh shot him evil eyes and tried to bite through a sausage that had the constitution of a rubber mallet.

"Callum, what's this really about?" demanded Eric. "You've been avoiding the subject since yesterday evening."

"Why are you so suspicious?"

"Experience," stated Eric firmly.

"There's nothing unusual about this. An old friend is having a big event and he's invited me…us."

"What's the big event?" mumbled Josh as he continued to wrestle with his breakfast.

"Bridge opening," said Callum matter-of-factly.

"But none of us has seen Sean for more than two decades," explained Eric.

Callum pretended to get up to refill his juice glass, but

Eric quickly grabbed his arm and guided him back into his seat.

"Callum?" pressed Eric sternly.

"I might have seen him since then."

"Specifically?"

"Recently."

"When?"

"A few months ago."

"Why?" said Eric forcefully.

"It wasn't planned or anything; we bumped into each other at a business function, got talking about old times and exchanged phone numbers. Nothing extraordinary about that."

Eric didn't trust Callum's explanation. He was receiving too many mixed signals which suggested his friend wasn't telling the whole story.

"Does Sean know you're bringing us along?" asked Josh.

"Absolutely. He was delighted."

"Then why didn't he invite us directly?" quizzed Eric.

"He did - it's just that you two never open your post."

Josh nodded. In his experience, nothing good ever came out of an envelope.

"Look, a lot of water has flowed under the bridge since Uni, if you'll forgive the pun," laughed Callum. "This is an opportunity to heal old wounds and move on. It'll be good for all of us. No point holding grudges, is there?"

"Suppose not," replied Josh. "I'm actually intrigued to see what he's made of himself."

"Haven't you heard of social media," grumbled Eric, who was less excited about the prospect because he already knew.

Although Sean had suffered most from the accident all those years ago, the impact had been felt by all of them.

Eric's only real passion, *The Idiots' Club*, had been forced into retirement and, more importantly, the events of that fateful night had driven a wedge into their friendship which never truly recovered. Josh and Eric had remained in regular contact, but he rarely saw Callum and hadn't seen Micky in over a decade.

"Right, the ceremony is at ten so we'd better get ready."

"That's more than two hours away. It only takes me five minutes to get ready. Did you have a sex change when I wasn't looking!" joked Josh.

"No."

"Where is this bridge?" asked Eric.

"It's a couple of miles outside the city. It's called the Queensferry Crossing, a new road bridge across the Firth of Forth."

"Shall I book us a cab?" offered Josh.

"Apparently, he's sending a limo. I hear it's got a drinks fridge in it!"

"Looks like it's going to be a long day," whispered Eric out of the corner of his mouth.

Dead on nine o'clock, a brilliantly white stretch limo glided up to the main entrance of the airport hotel where the three friends were waiting patiently for it. Once inside, they settled down on the black leather seats hidden behind tinted windows. It was obvious to Eric that their mode of transport was in line with everything else about this trip. Along with the posh hotel, free plane tickets and their VIP status, Sean was clearly sending them a message. Look at me - I'm better than you.

True to form, Callum tracked down the drinks fridge like a prized bloodhound and began the challenge of single-handedly consuming all of its contents before they arrived at their destination. The journey was about twenty minutes, but that didn't come close to his personal best. Josh was the only one of the three who'd never been to Edinburgh, and he was quite despondent to hear that the route was entirely lacking in landmarks. In the distance he occasionally caught sight of Arthur's Seat, the extinct volcano looming over the south side of the city, as it peeked through the spread of human progress that consumed much of the skyline.

Their route from hotel to bridge was via the ring road that circled the city's outer rim with the clinical precision of a pathologist's scalpel. By Callum's third glass of champagne, they spotted the three towers of the bridge stretching into the cold, clear, early spring morning. Then the road split in two, the old road leading onto the original Forth Road Bridge and the new gleaming black asphalt connecting the soon-to-be-open one. The limo slowed as it reached the construction gate still in place across the dual carriageway, joining a queue of cars that waited for access.

They inched slowly towards the eight-foot metal fence where two young women dressed head to foot in *Heschmeyer Industries* branding checked visitors' tickets. Callum wound down one of the many windows and presented his three tickets. They were waved through by the sweet smiles and powerful perfumes of the two hostesses, and it was clear when they breached the checkpoint that this opening ceremony wasn't going to be a low-key affair. There were hundreds of cars waiting to access a slipway which led off the side of the new road into a makeshift car park formerly used for construction vehicles.

The limo pulled into two marked spaces and the driver explained it was a three-hundred-metre walk to the bridge. The friends alighted, Callum topping up his glass before he left. They joined the procession of dignitaries, special guests and construction workers in ill-fitting suits on their slow march down the new road towards the bridge.

"Why do I feel so out of place?" offered Josh anxiously.

"Because you spend most of your life talking to vets about how to apply ointment to a dog's testicles. You are out of place," confirmed Eric. "I've just seen the First Minister of Scotland talking to a woman with so many gold chains around her neck she's either a famous rapper or more likely the Mayor."

"Soak it in, boys," urged Callum, a little too loudly and showing the first signs of slurred speech. "This is the high life."

By the time they reached the point where the road left the land and continued over the water of the Forth River like an engineering conjuring act, the truth of who was responsible for its construction was inescapable. The name *Heschmeyer Industries* was emblazoned on everything and anything. It descended down the towers of the bridge on massive gold banners. It was mounted on the feather flags that stretched along both sides of the roadway from one end to the other. It was written on the sashes of the staff who offered guests complimentary drinks and canapés. It was featured on banners, badges, brochures, trailed out the back of noisy biplanes circling above them and was even etched on the side of the crystal glasses being handed out to thirsty dignitaries. To Eric, at least, the intention of the branding overkill was obvious. Look at me - I'm better than you.

A temporary stage, furnished with a lectern, speaker system and microphone stand, had been erected in the centre of the bridge; that, too, hadn't avoided the virulent bout of logo rash which infected the rest of the area.

"I wonder who built the bridge," said Eric sarcastically as he accepted his first glass of champagne of the day.

"It must have been Balfour Beatty," added Josh playfully.

"Do you think Sean might have an inferiority complex?"

"I think the branding looks great," remarked Callum.

"Anyone spotted him yet?" asked Eric.

"Who?" inquired Josh genuinely.

"Sean!"

"No, but I've spotted a tidy little redhead."

"Give yourself a day off, would you."

The crowd winced and grabbed their ears in unison as the nerve-wrenching sound of feedback from the huge speaker stacks reverberated around them. Up on the stage, an elderly man tapped the microphone several times with his finger before leaning in to speak. His wispy grey hair whipped around his face from the stiff breeze interrupting his pivotal role in the proceedings. He propped it back with one hand and grabbed the microphone with the other.

"Ladies and Gentlemen. Lords and Ladies. Your Royal Highness, First Minister and distinguished guests. Please welcome to the stage CEO of *Heschmeyer Industries* and the driving force behind this magnificent feat of engineering, Sean Heschmeyer."

The crowd offered a genteel round of applause and drifted slowly towards the edge of the podium. Callum, Josh and Eric lingered at the back to camouflage themselves amongst the throng. A spindly man with fragile wire-framed glasses and the hair stylings of a Benedictine monk confidently approached the lectern with a raised fist as if he'd recently clinched a heavyweight boxing title. He waited patiently for the plaudits of a thousand guests to peter out before addressing the crowd. The vibrancy of his smile and the twinkle in his eyes was in stark contrast to the one his three old friends, hidden out of sight at the back, remembered. The only evidence that this was the same Sean at all was the slightest of limps he'd displayed as he'd climbed the small staircase and navigated the stage.

"It's my utter pleasure to welcome so many of you here today for this important ceremony," he announced in his characteristic, although less pronounced than they remembered it, Germanic twang.

Something about seeing Sean for the first time in decades was making Eric agitated, but he couldn't put his finger on the reason. Perhaps it was triggering to remember what happened all those years ago? More likely it was the visceral sense of jealously rearing up inside him. Sean didn't deserve his success, or the crowd's praise. It had only been achieved because he'd had a leg up on the class ladder since before he knew how to walk. Because the dice were loaded, it was impossible for someone like Eric to find themselves in Sean's position, even though he'd achieved more in comparison if you took their starting points into account. The subliminal message which had played on a continual loop for Eric ever since they stepped out of the limo rephrased itself. Look at me - I'm not better than you, but people think I am anyway, so fuck you. His agitation grew. He encouraged competition, but this wasn't it. This was elitism.

"The first bridge to span the Firth of Forth estuary was constructed by the Romans and was no less of an engineering marvel than the colossus of concrete and steel under your feet," continued Sean. "Man's ingenuity to solve problems is unlimited even when the technology available may not always appear fit for purpose. If the archaeologists' findings are accurate, the Romans solved the puzzle of crossing this waterway by binding nine hundred boats together from this very spot at South Queensferry all the way to the opposite bank. Like all innovations, it made their lives more efficient. It saved many days of marching to get to the north side of the channel rather than going around the estuary to the west. Our bridge stands proud in upholding that fine tradition of invention and human endeavour. It may not save us as much time as the Romans, but it will take pressure off the nearby Forth Road Bridge where I understand the congestion can be horrendous. The Queensferry Crossing will ease congestion, reduce pollution and eliminate frustration."

"If I wanted a history lesson," mumbled Eric, "I'd have chosen it for my degree."

"He does kind of drone on, doesn't he," agreed Josh. "Not like the old Sean. He wouldn't say boo to a goose."

"This momentous day is a double celebration for *Heschmeyer Industries*," Sean pronounced. "Not only do we have the honour of opening this fine megastructure - we also rejoice in our company's successful floatation yesterday on the London Stock Exchange for a market capitalisation just short of one billion pounds. I know my father, and our founder, Klaus Heschmeyer, would find it hard to believe that the little firm he started in a small business park in Cologne would one day be rubbing shoulders with the most valuable blue-chip firms in Europe."

There was a lazy round of applause from the audience.

"Blimey, the little sod must have made a killing," suggested Josh.

"Based on today's stock value," answered Callum, with an accompanying hiccup between words, "he's worth two hundred million, but it's going up by about a million every day."

"He's only invited us here to rub our noses in it!" steamed Eric. "That's all this is. I can't believe you fell for it, Callum. Come on, I'm not listening to this entitled narcissist a minute longer."

He dropped his crystal champagne flute to the ground, where it ruptured into a dozen pieces, and turned to leave. Those closest to him looked around to see what the commotion was.

"Wait!" Callum grabbed him by the arm and dug his winkle picker shoes into the ground like a dog refusing to go walkies in the rain. "You owe me."

Sean continued his address.

"I have many people to thank before we formally invite Her Royal Highness Princess Anne to cut the ribbon and declare the Queensferry Crossing officially open. I apologise in advance if I miss anyone out. Firstly, I'd like to offer my eternal gratitude to all my colleagues at *Heschmeyer Industries* and to the many subcontractors who've worked on the project."

"Let go!" demanded Eric, who was physically bigger and more prone to aggression than his friend.

Sean continued to congratulate a seemingly endless list of collaborators and supporters with the aid of a piece of paper that he'd extracted from the inside pocket of his jacket. They included the Scottish Government, the Environment Agency, his personal friend the Prime Minister, the EU Commission, the Vice Chancellor of Exeter University, local residents, hauliers, concrete suppliers, his family, Sir Isaac Newton and a number of other famous physicists no one had ever heard of. By the end of his speech, if you were in the crowd and your name hadn't appeared on Sean's list, it was probably an oversight. Though most of the gathered dignitaries had been included, even they were beginning to lose interest.

"Finally," concluded Sean with an audible sigh of relief from a thousand mouths, "I'd like to thank one very special group of people without whom none of these achievements would be possible. My oldest friends."

Eric stopped in his tracks, still battling to extricate himself from Callum's attempt to keep him there. Both their suits had taken the brunt of the scuffle.

"That's us," said Josh in surprise, jumping in the air and spontaneously waving a hand at the stage. Eric instantly shot him a frown for doing so.

Sean's long, skinny finger pointed to the back of the crowd who turned collectively to see two middle-aged men wrestling each other and a third man smiling, and waving, back at the stage like a gormless idiot.

"It doesn't look as if they've changed very much," chuckled Sean. "More than twenty years ago, four people changed the course of my life. They taught me lessons that no University could ever teach and no degree syllabus will ever include. They taught me resilience. Without the motivation they impressed upon me, none of this would have been possible. They inspired me to think bigger, act better and most of all, prove to everyone what I was capable of. Well, gentlemen, this is what I am capable of."

He pointed reverentially at the bridge that bore his name.

Eric and Josh stared at each other in confusion. Was Sean being genuine, or was there double meaning to what he'd said? They couldn't be sure, but it seemed unlikely that their poor treatment of him as a student had made such a positive impact on his future. Eric's strong desire to leave the ceremony waned. There was enough intrigue surrounding what he'd heard to want to know more, and besides that, Callum was a constant presence in his ear begging him to stay.

Sean finally brought his hour-long speech to a conclusion by inviting Princess Anne to cut a ribbon, something she'd presumably done countless times before – probably this week alone. Once the formalities were complete, the crowd returned to their private conversations and irregular formations, scattered in pockets around the three-laned section of motorway. Eric grabbed another flute of fizz and walked over to the side of the bridge to check out the view and gather his thoughts.

SEVEN

TRUTH OR DARE

THE WATER OF THE ESTUARY LAPPED HARMLESSLY AGAINST the huge concrete towers buried deep in the rock and silt of the river bed. The weather was relatively calm today, at least by Scottish standards which frequently offered a pick 'n' mix of high winds and horizontal rain which struck the face like a cold power shower. The bridge was the work of exceptional craftmanship and undoubted engineering inge-nuity, but it would still cow to the elements, forcing it to close at least twice a week to protect driver safety. Although humanity's achievements were all around him, there was no manmade remedy to the might of a Gaelic storm.

Eric leaned over the newly-painted metal partition and stared into the murky river thirty or so metres below him. In his whole life, no challenge had been ducked and no challenger remained unvanquished. Yet today he felt the uncomfortable and bitter taste of defeat. Sean had gained victory, and Eric wasn't even sure how he'd managed it. The freaky, friendless, skinny oddball with no discernible talents had achieved more than he had simply because of his bloodline. And to rub salt into the wound, Sean had the temerity to apportion his success to *The Idiots' Club*. How dare he. All Eric had ever done was humiliate Sean. The last member to join their club had shown zero propensity for innovation and yet he'd miraculously grown *Heschmeyer Industries* from a plucky regional enterprise into a superstar blue-chip phenomenon. There was no way Eric was responsible for that. If he was that inspiring, he'd have done it himself.

"You've got to say," commented Josh as he approached the barrier, "it's a bloody impressive bridge. Hats off to Sean; I wouldn't know where to start."

"That's because you trained as a vet. I'm sure Sean couldn't operate on a budgie, could he?"

"I'm not sure I could, either."

"You know what I mean."

"Anyway, I'm not so sure. With his self-confidence, I wouldn't put anything past him."

Eric shot daggers from his eyes.

Far below them, an object glistened in the light before striking the waves and instantly disappearing under the surface of the Firth of Forth. They glanced to their left to find Callum wobbling slightly against the guard rail, pretending to clutch an expensive champagne flute while his brain waited to catch up on reality.

"Whoopsie!"

"Maybe you shouldn't stand too close to the edge, mate," offered Josh.

"I'm fine," he slurred. "No danger here."

"How many have you had?"

"Couple…" he maintained innocently.

Josh assumed he was counting in dozens.

"Why do you think Sean picked us out for praise?"

demanded Eric, with Sean's words still circling around in his head. "My highly tuned instincts are suffering from acute vertigo right now."

"I'm not sure. Maybe you should ask him." Josh nodded over his friend's shoulder as someone approached them.

Eric turned slowly to find Sean aiming directly for him holding two full glasses of champagne and wearing a smile that suggested he'd never been so pleased with himself.

"Smug git," huffed Eric.

"Rich smug git," corrected Josh.

"I thought you might need another." Sean indicated to Callum as he handed him the spare glass. "Don't worry about the broken ones; I can buy more. Lots more after yesterday."

"Cheers," said Callum respectfully.

The three VIP guests stood in silence for a minute, although Eric noticed that Callum found it difficult to look Sean directly in the eyes. It wasn't the alcohol, either - it was as if some painful memory might be triggered if their gazes met one another.

"I'm so happy you could make it!" Sean burst with enthusiasm, taking control of the silence. "Do you like my bridge?"

"It's amazing…"

"It's alright," said Eric loudly, to drown out Josh's sudden bout of sycophancy. "I've seen better."

"Stand down, soldier. I come in peace," quipped Sean, opening up his body language to diffuse the tension. "There's no bad blood here, Eric. It's just nice to see everyone after all these years. How long has it been, would you say?"

"March the sixteenth, nineteen ninety-seven," replied

Josh, as if the date was permanently scarred on his brain. "Hold on…that would…"

"That's right," nodded Sean. "It's twenty years ago to this very day."

"The significance of it doesn't feel coincidental," suggested Eric coldly.

"It isn't. I chose it specifically because it's a date which means so much to me. It's the day that changed my life… and the last time I saw you, Eric."

"The fall from the clock tower must have damaged your memory, then, because I saw you a few days after that."

"Did you?" replied Sean, taking a sip from his glass and finding the revelation inconsequential.

"Don't play games with me. You must recall that I saw you when you were in hospital?"

"Nope."

"I apologised sincerely for what had happened and expressed my gratitude that you'd dropped the charges against us." Eric spoke through gritted teeth, aggrieved he was being forced to revisit a moment of weakness.

"Sincere apologies don't sound your style, if I may say," rebuked Sean.

"But you must remember it!"

"I don't."

"Liar!"

"Eric, I was high on morphine and I woke up most mornings with vivid hallucinations. Everything from nurses dressed as fruit to melting walls."

"I get that sometimes," Callum expressed quietly to himself.

"Do you really expect me to remember something like that?" continued Sean. "You weren't prone to acts of contrition, after all. I probably thought I'd imagined it and simply dismissed it. Either that or I wasn't conscious at all."

"You were, and just because you don't remember it doesn't mean it didn't happen."

"Whatever you want to believe," said Sean mockingly.

Eric's day was climbing the list of his worst ever, right up there with snapping his Achilles tendon and burying his mother. The one time he'd done what others expected of him was the one time the person on the receiving end of his genuine sense of repentance had been away with the fairies.

"You're right," smiled Sean. "It doesn't change anything for me. It doesn't change how I feel about you."

"Congratulations on the stock floatation," chirped in Josh, attempting to lower the rising emotional temperature.

"Thank you, Josh."

"Must have been exciting?"

"It's the culmination of years of hard work…but the journey is often more enjoyable than the destination," he recited, showing the first signs that life might not be as serene as he'd been keen to demonstrate during his speech. "Did you qualify as a vet in the end?"

"Qualified, yeah."

"Good for you. I'm sure you have a string of vet practices up and down the country by now?"

"Oh yeah," he replied nervously. "Lots."

"Taken it public yet?" asked Sean.

"No, the public come to me," he said proudly, not entirely sure what Sean meant.

"No, I mean have you had it listed?"

"It's in the Yellow Pages, if that's what you mean?"

It absolutely wasn't, so Sean changed tack.

"Married?"

"Frequently!"

"I'm not surprised, what with your reputation. I expect you've got a babe in every town from Carlisle to Royal Tunbridge Wells, haven't you?"

"What…"

"I've not managed to find the 'one' yet, either. I've spend too much of my time travelling for work to court a wife, but one day I hope I'll be able to settle down and start a family at Netherswell Manor. Would be a wonderful place to raise children."

"I suspect being a multimillionaire might make it easier!"

"Or more difficult," Sean acknowledged. "What about you, Eric? How's life in the creative industries," he added conversationally.

"Perfect," Eric snapped defensively.

"Oh really, I heard things were challenging."

"Did you really? From whom, exactly?"

"Alan told me there had been a bit of an incident recently."

"Alan?"

"Alan West."

"You know my boss?"

"I know a lot of important people, Eric. I've made it my job to know. I've hired Alan's firm a number of times down the years. Including for this project."

"You mean *my* firm…why didn't I know about it?" he questioned under his breath.

"Because you're not the boss, Eric, as much as you pretend to act like it. I hear on the grapevine that it's a fifty-fifty call as to whether Alan's prepared to keep you on. I shouldn't worry, though - a man of your reputation and experience will be in high demand around London firms."

"Watch out, boys," said Eric, turning to the others. "Maybe he's been spying on all of us."

"Maybe I have," Sean replied jovially. "I'm already abreast of Callum's circumstances, having bumped into him recently. As for Josh here, well I'm sure if I asked any of the women on my guest list, one of them could fill me in on his latest exploits."

"I'd like to make it absolutely clear that I have never slept with Princess Anne," Josh clarified less than convincingly. "She's not really my type."

"I'm sure it's a relief to the whole Royal Family."

"What's all this really about, Sean?" demanded Eric. "Why are we here?"

Sean paused as concerted thoughts which had been gathering pace for years settled into order. There was so much he wanted to say, but there was only time now for the most important reflections.

"Because I wanted to thank you," he suggested once more.

"For what?"

"Making me who I am."

"We were horrible to you," responded Josh honestly. "Particularly me and Eric. We spent hours devising the most ridiculous dares knowing you'd never be able, or willing, to do them. We were surprised and emboldened when you gave most of them a go. We made ourselves feel better about who we were by making a fool out of you. We bullied you relentlessly. We didn't know it at the time, but I know it now."

"But at least you did something," countered Sean.

"Sorry?"

"Everyone else ignored me. I know which one I prefer."

"You mean you liked being bullied?" said Josh.

"No, of course not, but at least it was some stimulation."

"That's weird."

"I always found you rather fascinating," announced Callum, who had already downed the contents of Sean's kind gift and was trying to catch the eye of the bar staff.

"I know. You were usually there for me when I needed you, Callum."

"But the rest of us weren't," argued Josh. "Aren't you angry?"

"No."

"Sean, we forced you to walk around campus covered in jam on one of the hottest days of the year. We challenged you to bungee jump from Devonshire House even though we knew you hated heights. We took a photo of you in ladies' underwear while you were sleeping, printed a thousand copies and stuck it on every dormitory wall..."

"Did you!?" said Sean in shock.

"That wasn't one of Sean's dares, Josh..." put in Eric, "it was actually one of yours."

"Oh...yeah...I forgot that was me. Actually got me a few dates," he said, winking.

"You're welcome."

"Even when we weren't asking you to do dares, we still found ways to belittle you," continued Josh. "And to top it all off, you ended up in hospital because of us. You still walk with a limp to this day."

"Not because of you."

"Because of *The Idiots' Club*."

"Which I was a member of. I agreed to do all those dares, didn't I? Nobody forced me."

They nodded reluctantly, knowing how good they were at manipulating people to do what they knew they shouldn't.

"Do you know what I thought about most when I was

lying in that hospital bed for all those weeks?" Sean offered.

"Nurses?"

"No, I was still thinking about how I could impress you. How I could use my failures to motivate me to greatness. I've channelled those thoughts ever since."

"Why?" exclaimed Josh.

"Because all I ever wanted was to be like him," he said, pointing at Eric.

"Me?"

"Yes."

Callum wandered away from the group to replenish his glass. He already knew what was going to happen next.

"There's no one like me," argued Eric defiantly. "You need to have the right background to even have a chance to match me. It's not something you can learn. It's something you are, and you'll never have it."

"If life has taught me anything, it's that you can achieve whatever you put your mind to," stated Sean.

"Bollocks. You don't have enough creativity to come even close to me. You never did. All your dares were predictable and dull. You couldn't do it then and you certainly can't do it now!"

"Do you dare me?" said Sean, watching Eric walk straight into his trap.

"Dare you to do what?" Eric struggled to follow.

"Do you dare me to set you the most creative challenges you've ever faced, to prove that I have what it takes?

"Have what it takes to do what?" Eric replied with a sarcastic laugh.

"To beat you."

"I think I've humiliated you enough," suggested Eric bitterly.

"And I you." Sean's face became sterner as he pointed

at the success all around them. "These people aren't here because of you. They came to see me. It's my name on the banners and up the side of the bridge. Where in the world would I find *Gideon* plastered on every wall?"

"Anyone with your background could achieve it."

"But not all of them have."

"If you take me on, your privilege can't protect you."

Almost imperceptibly, the two men inched towards each other until their noses were nearly touching and they saw the whites of each other's eyes. Eric looked for clues, signs that Sean's words were hiding his real feelings about him. There was no obvious pupil dilation. His gestures weren't giving any cause to suspect he was lying. The sound of his breathing and the gentle regular expansion of his chest didn't reveal any misrepresentation, either. He really did think he could win, but there was something else there in his expression. A signal that Sean wasn't aware he was sending out. Not doubt as such, that seemed steadfast; this was something deeper and stronger. Sinister, even - but Eric wasn't sure what it was.

"You really believe you can do it, don't you?"

"Yes."

"You'll lose."

"There's only one way to find out," Sean replied plainly.

"I think we're a little too old for all that childish nonsense now," advised Josh, who had no desire to make his life any more complicated than it already was.

"Too old for what?" asked Callum, who'd returned with a tray of glasses, all of which he'd decided were his.

"Dares."

"What dares?"

"We haven't got to that part yet."

"What are you proposing?" Eric queried, feeling the

first waves of dopamine invade his blood stream and power his competitiveness.

"Five dares in seven days," said Sean, more quickly than any of them had expected.

"I can't skip work for that long," laughed Josh uncomfortably. "I'd miss out on too many sales."

"Sexual conquests don't count towards your bonus, I suspect," submitted Callum.

"Depends what you mean by a bonus!"

"You don't have to do it," explained Eric. "Sean is challenging me."

"No," he corrected, "I'm challenging all of you."

"Then I'm not interested." Josh waved him away. "It's been great to see you, and I appreciate your hospitality, but I'm not getting dragged down by all that shit again."

"Hold on, Josh - don't be so hasty," said Callum, swaying a little. It had nothing to do with the bridge, which moved less than the Scottish mountains on the horizon. "Perhaps if there was a big enough incentive."

"I don't need money!"

"Yes, you do," argued Eric. "You're skint. I've seen what remains of your car, and I know for a fact that Maria took you to the cleaners after your first divorce and you've had two more wives since then."

"I don't want money," Josh corrected himself. "It doesn't solve a thing."

"I'll give you ten million if you complete five dares of my choosing," announced Sean.

"Umm...how many days did you say we had?" asked Josh, in a tone which had softened dramatically.

"Seven."

"You're really prepared to burn ten million pounds just to see if you have what it takes to beat me," established Eric suspiciously.

"I won't have to, because I fully intend on winning - but if I don't, the money won't make much of a dent in my fortune. I imagine it might make a big difference for you three, though. Why don't you take a moment to yourselves to think about it?"

EIGHT
TEN MILLION REASONS

YESTERDAY. FROME POLICE STATION.

ON THE WALL, the clock's small hand nestled on the number three to signal that the police interview had entered its fourth hour. As was to be expected from an interviewee, and just as he'd hoped, Eric had done the majority of the talking. The longer he managed to string it out without giving much away, the less time she'd have to charge him. While he waffled hyperbolically, Iris Whitehall struggled to separate fact from fiction. After three solid hours, she was certain the former had only taken up about three minutes. It was a strategy which often worked. Let them talk, and eventually they would give something away they'd not intended to reveal. But not Eric. It was plain to her that he was a master in the arts of deception and diversion.

"I'm going to stop you there, Mr Gideon," interrupted Iris, finally deciding enough was enough. "Are you seriously suggesting that one of the wealthiest men in the world dared you to commit all of these crimes?"

"Exactly right."

"Poppycock."

Eric's facial features scrunched themselves into a ball at the strange local lingo.

"It means you're deluded," she explained. "It's plausible, although no less mental, that your silly club engaged in a host of criminality in the name of completing some dares, but it's another dimension altogether to imply that someone made you do it. What possible motive would Sean Heschmeyer have?"

"Revenge."

"Rubbish!"

"What did the other two tell you?"

She avoided the question, because she knew full well their accusations matched his. It was obviously the best pre-rehearsed story they could concoct in the melee of their surprise arrests.

"Sean's accident was two decades ago and normal people don't hold grudges for that long – particularly when they've told you they don't have one!"

"It doesn't matter how many…miles…people travel; they always come back to where they started," said Eric, purposefully accentuating the word 'miles' and pausing unnaturally before continuing. "People don't always mean what they say."

"Tell me about it," she sighed.

"Anyone can be mysterious."

"I think we'll stick to the cold hard facts rather than some esoteric philosophy. So you claim it was Sean's idea - actually Sean's provocation," she said, referring to her notes, "that forced you to reform *The Idiots' Club* and as such put in motion the events that led to the theft of a lion."

"Not theft, but other than that, yes."

"Where's the provocation? As far as I can see from your mannerisms over the last few hours, Sean Heschmeyer read you like a book. He knew you wouldn't be able to say no to any challenge because you have an ego the size of an orbiting moon. He didn't need to provoke you, and I don't see a single iota of evidence for it, anyway."

"There are ten million pieces of evidence."

Iris Whitehall scratched her head. She'd been a detective for eight years, and spent five as a regular police constable before that. She wasn't a green recruit, easy fodder for the more intellectually competent criminal, which most of them certainly weren't. Usually, her interviewees crumbled faster than a shortbread biscuit in a mug of warm tea - such was the strength of her interrogation skills. Criminals weren't generally the sharpest tacks in the toolbox, and if they were, they'd probably be making good livings as accountants or computer programmers. Her training and experience would always outweigh their preposterous attempts to outwit her. She'd play with them for a while, using her advantage as a female in a position of authority, before setting them up with a series of well-crafted word patterns - traps they'd quickly fall into.

Eric was different, though. He wasn't your average scumbag or opportunistic petty thief. According to his case file, Eric was about as familiar with the criminal underworld as a rabbit was with a crossword puzzle. To her, this made him equally as intriguing as he was irritating. There was very little job satisfaction in charging petty offenders for crimes her four-year-old niece could solve. It was rare she was forced to unleash the full scale of her armoury, but on the rare occasions when she did, it made the job genuinely fulfilling. Today was one of those days. A day when someone like Eric Gideon was going to test her to the very limit.

Test, yes. Beat her, no.

She'd never allow it.

"Ten million what?"

"Pounds."

"That's how much he paid you to do it?"

"No. That's what it would cost us if we didn't take up his challenge."

"Blackmail!"

"In a way."

"That's the most ridiculous thing I've ever heard," she replied, bursting into a fit of giggles.

"What – you mean more ridiculous than a man in a jester's hat attempting to steal a lion in the back of a clapped-out hearse?"

"Successfully stealing," she corrected him.

"Good try."

"Why would someone who's worth two hundred million pounds need ten million more from three men with the combined assets of a group of squatters?"

"You're the detective…you figure it out," smiled Eric.

"Okay, I'll humour you for a moment and tolerate your bizarre conspiracy theories. Even if he did have probable cause, based on some grudge festering away inside him since the nineties, and I seriously doubt it - why would you allow him to blackmail you?"

"Come on, detective, you can figure that one out," Eric goaded, placing his hands behind his head and leaning back on his chair to watch her work.

"He doesn't care about the money," she surmised. "So I'm guessing if you didn't take his offer, he had some compromising information about you that might make life difficult. He knew your pressure points."

"Very good, detective. But which buttons would he press?"

"From what I know about the three of you from my interviews, he wouldn't have to do anything," replied Iris sarcastically. "Callum Jollie's company is teetering on the precipice of bankruptcy – and not for the first time, according to my records. Josh Foxole has destroyed more marriages than he's had hot dinners, and only some of them were his own. And you - well, you've been suspended from the job you love and have no obvious support network to fall back on. What more damage could Sean do that you haven't inflicted on yourselves? You've already lost everything you had."

"Not everything," insisted Eric, rather impressed by her summary. "Sean might not have declared the wars we've been personally waging on ourselves, but he can force us to surrender. But that's not enough for him. He wants to take away the one thing that only we can break."

"What?"

"As I said – you're the detective."

"Reputation?"

"Already permanently damaged."

"Power?"

"The three of us have less of that than the battery in that clock," he said, pointing at the wall.

She found herself drawn to the simple plastic time-piece. As the seconds marched unstoppably forward, it hastened her pulse. She was stumped. But why was she so curious? Had the efforts of the last few days clouded her normally granite logic? Was she falling for his tricks? She snapped out of it.

"Do you have any proof of any of this? A signed document, eyewitness accounts, confessions…"

"No. Generally speaking, if someone blackmails you, they don't place an ad in *The Times*."

"How convenient. I'll have to retreat to my original, and more probable, conclusion: the three of you are lying to me."

"I guess only time will tell, won't it."

Time was something she was running short of. She couldn't keep him here indefinitely. She needed enough evidence to charge him or reluctantly release him. Even if she did charge him, he'd probably secure bail, and that wouldn't answer the key question of where the bloody lion was. It was better to get the full picture now.

"Let's go back to the facts. There's video evidence of you and your friends engaged in a series of illegal activities. You say Sean Heschmeyer challenged you to complete five challenges in seven days…"

"Blackmailed us," corrected Eric, hoping if he repeated it enough times, she might believe him.

He was wrong.

"So far, I can implicate you in three crimes, all of which carry heavy custodial sentences. Yet you say there were five dares. The only way to corroborate your story is if you tell me what these dares were!" she said with a knowing grin.

Two weeks ago. Queensferry Crossing.

Sean left them alone to discuss his offer. He'd agreed to grant them an hour before he would return to hear their answer. There were two clear camps forming, but because of the unequal numbers, the power dynamic was always going to be one-sided.

"You know this is ridiculous, don't you!" laughed Josh.

"Why is it?" argued Callum, who had noticeably sobered up on hearing the financial aspect of Sean's deal.

"Because we're meant to be adults! We're meant to be mature."

"The evidence is overwhelmingly against us," countered Eric.

"What's that supposed to mean!"

"It means we haven't exactly nailed being grown-ups, have we? Multiple bankruptcies, failed marriages and employment disciplinaries including hanging an intern over a fire escape by his ankles…"

"How'd that go?" inquired Josh.

"Not well."

"There you go! We're not supposed to do this shit anymore."

"But," said Eric, "maybe the reason we keep screwing up is precisely because we're trying to be grown-ups."

"No, you're going to have to explain that to me."

"When was the last time you were really happy?" Eric asked Josh pointedly.

"Probably after my first marriage, to Kate."

"Your first wife was called Maria."

"Maria," he murmured nostalgically.

"Was that the insanely jealous, controlling one?" tested Callum. "Or was that the one who destroyed all your best clothes with a pair of scissors?"

"Both her."

"And how long did that period of bliss last?" solicited Eric.

"Couple of months."

"And how long has it been since you were happy with life for an extended period of time?" probed Eric further.

"Probably at the time of *The Idiots' Club* and Uni," confirmed Josh.

"There you go, then. We've been flailing around for two decades pretending to know what we're doing, yet none of our lives has improved since we left."

"Micky and Sean have done alright for themselves, though, haven't they. Maybe it's just us three who have problems."

On the face of it, it would be hard to disagree, but Eric had a gift for disagreeing with anyone about almost anything. Sean had obviously achieved great success and, although none of them had seen him in years, all the signs suggested that Micky had conformed to society's expectation and was thriving as a result.

"But are they happy?" argued Eric.

"He looks fucking delirious to me," said Josh, pointing at Sean as he schmoozed with the First Minister of Scotland in the distance.

"He isn't," insisted Eric fiercely. "If he was, he wouldn't be challenging us?"

"Everyone needs a hobby!"

"No. This is personal for him. I can sense it. It's been brewing inside him for years. He's been waiting for the right moment to strike. He might claim he's over what happened to him, but I don't believe it. The coincidence of the date isn't just about him. It's about all of us. It's about closure."

"Well, whatever *it* is can stay well and truly open, because I'm having nothing to do with it," grumbled Josh.

"I think you're missing something, mate," observed Callum. "Ten million pounds. That's more than three million each. Think about that for a minute."

"What would I do with it? I've had money, Callum, and it made me miserable. I'm not equipped to use it sensibly. Remember, we all grew up without a penny, and when I finally had more than I needed, all I did was waste it. I'd rather be happy and poor."

"But you've just said you haven't been happy since University, which means you're unhappy and poor right now," confirmed Callum. "I'd much rather be rich and unhappy."

"What do you need the money for, anyway?" countered Josh. "You have a good business. I've heard your ads on the radio."

"Of course," replied Callum sheepishly, "but businesses need investment to grow, and if they don't, they get swallowed up by the bigger fish."

Callum had always been a rather secretive man. He kept his affairs and emotions close to his chest and only ever put a positive spin on things. He hated to admit defeat, and until the death knell rang, he wasn't confessing it to his oldest friends. He hoped if all went well, he wouldn't have to. Sean's challenge was his exit strategy – the only remaining option to keep him and his business afloat. It was the miracle he'd prayed for, even if it wasn't exactly what he expected. But he couldn't do it on his own. Sean had stipulated they all had to agree or the deal was off. He had to convince the others to get on board.

"Do you know how many businesses I've started," croaked Callum.

"God, no," said Josh. "I stopped counting after the self-drying swimwear company."

"That one will come good…"

"How many?" interrupted Eric.

"No idea. I can't remember either. What I do know is this one has been the best of all of them. I can't let it get eaten up by a bigger competitor. I've marked every failure down as a learning experience and redoubled my efforts, but determination can only last for so long. Like a slowly emptying tank of petrol, the more you battle to reach the next services, the more likely they are to be closed. I can't do it anymore. I can't start all over again. I have to invest."

"Get a loan then," offered Josh.

"There isn't a bank or money lender in London who hasn't lost money on me. The investment has to come from a different source, and Sean's offer is the perfect scenario."

"I feel for you, Callum, I really do," said Josh sympathetically, "but I'm not humiliating myself for money."

"You used to do it for free!" Eric correctly pointed out.

"Then don't do it for the money," begged Callum. "Do it for me."

Josh contemplated the reasons for his objection. Most of them weren't really his at all. They spoke in his head with the voices of other people in his life. Ex-wives, work colleagues, a litany of foster parents, opinionated locals from the pub and even politicians from the telly. They didn't tell him what he wanted to do; they reinforced what he shouldn't do, because it wasn't how civilised people behaved. Having never truly experienced what it was like to be a civilised person, he wasn't really sure why he was faltering. It wasn't as if he had many commitments in the coming week. He had no dependents, no real loyalty to his employer and a diary overflowing with internet first dates and the exhausting maintenance of numerous affairs.

"What's your view?" Josh asked Eric.

"You already know my answer."

"Yes. It's always 'yes' with you."

Eric nodded. "I'm not interested in the money either, but I can't turn it down. Sean's accident wasn't just a defining moment for him; it changed everything for me, too. It made me question, even doubt myself. It alienated me from my friends and left me searching for an alternative sense of freedom and rebellion that I've never managed to replicate. I'm not done with *The Idiots' Club* - I think I always knew that. I should have been the one who decided when it was time to stop. I won't be told what to do by people who strut around like they own me and the rest of the world. Of course I'm in. I very much doubt Sean will come up with anything we can't do with our eyes closed."

"Maybe this is one of those times when you should say no, mate," suggested Josh. "Perhaps this is a test, a lesson to prove to yourself that turning down a dare doesn't make you a loser?"

"I can say no anytime I like," replied Eric angrily.

"When have you ever?"

Eric struggled to think of a suitable example to make his point, and when his delay proved Josh right, he quickly changed tack. "We don't have a choice this time."

"Of course we do."

"You don't see what I see. He's already set the trap."

"What trap?"

"Didn't you pick up on the clues?"

"Clues?" scoffed Josh, who channelled all of his available energy into decoding signals only when they came from the opposite sex.

"He knows how to hurt us. This isn't a coincidence. He knows about my work troubles; he know about Callum's business plans. He's in a position of power, and people like that always have the means to crush the little man. I'm sure he has a detailed list of all your affairs and no doubt all the mobile numbers of their husbands. How long have you been seeing the woman from Tunbridge Wells?"

"Since yesterday morning."

"And you're normally careful, right? You don't take silly risks that might get you caught?"

"As much as I can be arsed to, yeah," he said unconvincingly.

"And her husband's surprise return home yesterday – I'm guessing that's never happened before?"

"Never."

"And you think it's an accident he turned up unexpectedly, knew precisely which car was yours and just happened to be equipped with a cricket bat, do you?"

Josh suddenly absorbed the clues. "Bastard!"

"He already knows our pressure points. I don't buy that this is a fluke or he's forgiven us for what happened. He's been planning on us being here at this moment for months, maybe years."

"Then why isn't Micky here?" said Callum, seemingly defending the spontaneous nature of Sean's actions. "He's an essential member of the club, too."

"Maybe Sean couldn't find a suitable button to press, or maybe he's decided Micky has already learnt his lesson," replied Eric, recognising the hole in his argument and secretly finding it intriguing.

"Look, let's cut to the chase and stop overthinking it. Two of us are in agreement," stated Callum. "It's up to you, Foxie."

Josh hadn't heard his nickname in years. There was a time when he barely responded to his Christian name, he heard it so infrequently. It immediately sent him back in time. Suddenly, the two characters flanking him changed. The age and weight of the world dissipated from their faces; their bodies became noticeably more toned and less flabby. Their thinning hair expanded over bald patches to show styles that were longer, fashionable and noticeably more unkempt. Their faces glowed with unbridled optimism, and the atmosphere was mugged by the uncontrollable sound of laughter. He opened his eyes, and the glimpse into the past was replaced by two middle-aged losers.

"Maybe. Let's see what he can come up with," offered Josh.

"You're either in or we're all out. I'm not giving Sean the satisfaction of forcing us into failure minutes after suggesting we were willing."

"Please, Josh," continued Callum with a pathetic whine. "You owe me, don't forget."

"I have forgotten."

"Then let me remind you. I convinced Sean to drop the police charges when the authorities were desperate to pin something on us. Don't forget by nineteen ninety-seven everyone in Exeter had had enough of our disorganised mayhem. The police chief had our mugshots pinned to the station wall – that's how popular we were. Carrington had a personal grudge against us, and after what we did, he had the perfect motive to expel the lot of us. Everyone hated us for disrupting their town. Personally, looking back, I'm not really surprised. We did take things a bit too far, but you do when you're young."

"Right, and we're not young anymore," expressed Josh, who was morally seesawing from one point of view to the other.

"Which means we will be more sensitive about our impact on others this time."

"I very much doubt that," added Eric.

"Without my interference, Sean would have fallen for the police's manipulation, and all of us would have been banged up for GBH. Trumped-up charges to restore order to the city."

"And massively lower the University's cleaning bill!"

"Most likely," said Callum. "I did all of that for you, and you owe me."

"I thought we'd repaid our debts by coming to Scotland with you!" said Josh.

"I thought so at the time, but now this will repay me in full."

Josh's reluctance collapsed. "Oh, sod it. I'm in."

"Good lad," commented Eric with a smile.

Exactly an hour later, Sean returned. He'd already correctly predicted their response. When you spent your working life contemplating potentially ruinous strategic business decisions, then you were foolish if you didn't explore every risk, alternative and outcome. Whether he was engaged in a hostile business takeover or negotiating terms with his investors, it paid to have the inside line on what made people tick. He knew what floated their boats, and he also knew what would sink them.

Sean's reaction to their acceptance of his challenge lacked any obvious emotion, another indicator which Eric noted with interest. There was no surprise, excitement or delight, only cold acknowledgement of the facts.

"Give us your best, then?" goaded Eric, once Sean had shaken them by the hand in a gentlemen's agreement.

"You don't expect me to come up with five dares off the top of my head, do you?" he replied cunningly.

Eric was certain he'd already decided what they were but humoured him; it gave Eric more time to prepare his own retaliation if it were needed.

"When, then?" asked Callum eagerly.

"Your hotel. Noon tomorrow. I'll book a room," responded Sean. "In the meantime, why don't you mingle. There's plenty more champagne, Callum, and you've caught one of my team's eye, Josh."

"Oh yeah? Which one?"

Sean pointed out one of the hostesses: auburn hair, slender figure and probably only marginally over the universal equation for dating a younger woman – half your age plus seven.

"I do love a good mingle."

"We're good, thanks." Eric pinned the other two down with a paternal stare. "We'll take the limo back to the hotel now."

"Of course. I'll arrange it immediately," said Sean, scuttling off to find one of his minions.

"Spoil sport," said the other two in unison.

NINE
CONTRACTUAL OBLIGATIONS

A WEEK LAST SUNDAY. EDINBURGH.

ERIC INSISTED on an early night so they would have their wits about them for the meeting the next morning, but none of them slept easily. Callum had become accustomed to passing out rather than allowing fatigue to take its natural course, and he didn't sleep a wink. Josh struggled to shift thoughts of what might have been with the young redhead and the overwhelming sense of dread which surged up from his stomach. Eric also had a restless night due to nerves, but his weren't borne out of fear. His were nerves of excitement.

He imagined it was a similar feeling that boxers experienced the night before a big fight. Eric was the undisputed and undefeated heavyweight champion, with an overwhelming confidence in his ability to knock out his opponent. But when you fought, there would always be the cold and inconvenient reality that achieving victory would result in a certain amount of cuts and bruises. The power of the punches would depend on the size and skill of the boxer in the opposite corner of the ring. On this occasion, the contender had an utterly dismal record, but somehow he'd been granted another shot at the big time. By the looks of it, Sean had trained hard and prepared well for the bout, so Eric would need to avoid complacency.

Maybe Sean had learned some dangerous new moves that he wasn't expecting? Maybe Eric wasn't quite as agile as he once was? A distant but still lingering doubt he couldn't shift from the back of his mind. A thought which only made the challenge more exciting. He wanted Sean's best shot. He wanted a proper fight. Where was the fun in knocking Sean out in the first round? If this was going to put *The Idiots' Club* to bed, then they had to go out in a blaze of glory, rather than a damp squib.

The alarm from Eric's phone screamed at him from the bedside table. He wasn't sure how much sleep he'd managed, or whether he'd achieved any at all, but he knew he wasn't getting any more. It was seven, and they'd agreed to meet in the breakfast hall at eight for a strategy meeting. He scooped himself out of his king-sized bed, lovingly crafted to offer occupants much more comfort than it had delivered him last night. The shower fulfilled its purpose much more satisfactorily, and once he was dry and back in the only suit he'd brought with him, he made himself a coffee and drew back the curtains.

It was a typically bleak Scottish morning. Marble-sized raindrops noisily peppered the windows like God was attempting to blow them out with a bazooka. The wind howled in from the sea, and it wasn't just the gnarled trees in the garden that felt its anger. This might be a five-star hotel, but the windows weren't impervious to the draft which seeped in through unseen gaps to tickle the net curtains. Planes from the nearby airport took off at regular intervals, visibly struggling to achieve the lift and thrust required to keep their passengers from turning green. Eric shuddered at the thought of being inside the claustrophobic metal tube and thanked the stars that his flight home was scheduled for tomorrow. There was something altogether foreboding in the air today, like a great force was trying to stop the world spinning. It felt biblical.

"Bring it on," Eric mouthed to the shadows.

In the breakfast hall, the others had rejected the idea of repeating yesterday's experience of the full English buffet and were tucking into porridge and fruit salad, respectively. They, too, were presenting the effects of too little sleep and a supernatural sense of doom in the air.

"Morning," greeted Eric encouragingly.

Callum and Josh offered him subtle lifts of heads from bowls and pairs of disconsolate eyes in return.

"Jesus, Callum, you look awful."

"Thanks," he reacted bitterly. "This is what I look like when I don't drink the night before."

"You look worse than when you do. I'm no doctor, but if I was, I think I'd be prescribing Stella Artois!"

"Eric, it's not a joking matter," Josh stated delicately. "It's obvious Callum has a problem."

"No, I don't!"

"You clearly do, mate."

"My relationship with alcohol is no worse than being addicted to brake fluid. I can stop anytime I like," he said with a lighthearted but false laugh.

Neither of them joined in.

"Josh is right," replied Eric. "It's not funny. You really should see someone about it."

"I don't have a problem!"

"When was the last time you had a night without a drink?" asked Josh.

"I do it all the time."

"When?"

"Specifically?"

"Yes," the others responded in harmony.

"I don't know…sometime in April."

"It's currently March…"

"Is it? I thought it was November."

"Well, it's an easy mistake to make when you can't see your calendar because you're always so pissed," ribbed Josh.

Eric shot him an evil look.

"Callum, none of us can predict what awaits us over the next week, but what I do know for certain is I need you thinking clearly and functioning normally. I need you to take it easy…know what I mean?"

"He means keep it down to eight or nine pints a day," added Josh, estimating - based on the weekend they spent with him - that this was probably a fifty percent reduction.

"I think if we're being judgemental about addictions, Josh is the last person who should be handing out advice."

"Meaning?"

"We all have our demons, Josh. Yours have been obvious for a while."

"I haven't gambled in months!"

"Okay," amended Callum, "two demons."

"If you're suggesting I'm a sex addict…"

"We are," they replied in unison.

"…Then you're absolutely right. But my fix is free and good for my health, unlike yours."

"How is it good for you?"

"Cardio. It gets a good sweat on."

"I must be doing it wrong, then," complained Callum. "It never lasts long enough to get my heart rate up."

"That's because your dick's drunk," said Eric.

"Nice. I'll make a mental note that it's Pick on Callum Day. I guess I'm next in line now that Sean's not around, right?"

"We're just worried about you," said Josh seriously.

"I'm fine. I know what I'm doing."

"If you say so, but I'm keeping my eye on you. Remember, take it easy," repeated Eric, like an overbearing parent. "I'm going to grab a croissant, and then we can decide how we're going to play this today."

Eric returned a few minutes later with a soggy excuse for France's premier breakfast delicacy, a few indescribable pastry extras and a large steaming mug of black coffee.

"What did you mean 'play this today'?'" asked Callum. "I thought today was about receiving Sean's challenges. Not much to 'play', is there?"

"Of course there is."

The others stared blankly, and Eric glared back with pity for them.

"How many dares have I refused to accept?" he asked, stuffing half a croissant in his mouth.

"None that I can recall," answered Callum.

"And how many did I fail to complete?"

"What about the time you were supposed to replace all the light bulbs in the English block with red ones?" recalled Josh.

"That was actually one of mine," said Callum.

"Oh, yeah. It was a pretty good effort; you managed half of the rooms before they rumbled you. What about the time you were supposed to switch the Vice Chancellor's wallet for a fish sandwich?"

"I completed that one," replied Eric confidently.

"I recall there was a disagreement about the final outcome," Josh submitted.

"You challenged it on a technicality because I used a

fish paste sandwich. I told you to shut up – fish paste is still fish."

"What about when…"

"None!" Eric stopped him in his tracks because he already knew the answer. "I've never failed a task. There's a reason for that which none of you have ever picked up on."

"What?"

"I always work out a contingency plan. If the first method fails, I quickly try another. More importantly, if I think there's even the slightest chance that I might slip up, I devise a way of making the dare backfire on the person who gave it to me. Today will be no different."

"But how can we have a contingency arrangement if we don't know what he's going to dare us to do?" asked Josh.

"We can't - not yet."

"What's the point of a 'strategy meeting' then?"

"To make sure you boys keep your eyes open. I want you to observe everything: who's in the room, what Sean says, what he does. Anything that we might be able to use if everything goes tits up."

Callum nodded.

Josh pulled a face that confirmed he didn't see the point.

Josh approached the majority of life with a naïve sense of spontaneity. Planning wasn't a strength of his, mostly because he felt spending hours researching how he should do something took much longer than making it up on the spur of the moment. The outcome would generally rely on chance or his uncanny ability to get himself out of trouble but, like most skills, the more he did it, the less often he found himself in the shit, or at least the more tolerable the smell of turds became.

"Where are we meeting him, anyway?" asked Josh before the eagle-eyed Eric interrogated his disagreeable facial expression.

"Boardroom in the business centre," said Callum casually, as he polished off the last stodgy spoonful of porridge.

"How do you know that?" inquired Eric suspiciously.

"It's on the notice board in the foyer."

"What did it say?"

"The Old Boys Idiots' Club Annual General Meeting."

"You've got to give it to Sean," said Josh. "He's nothing but thorough!"

THEY MINGLED around the business centre for a good half hour before they were due to meet Sean. Around them, smart-suited delegates from a variety of well-known companies, who were also listed on the foyer's notice boards, huddled in plenary groups to debate tasks set by trainers hidden behind one of the many leather-padded doors which circled the large communal space. Dotted here and there were angry-sounding coffee machines, disarmingly comfy sofas and motivational artwork in gleaming glass frames. Eric listened as a cluster of apparent strangers wrestled for intellectual control over a group task which appeared to have nothing to do with 'business' whatsoever.

A young, suave-looking ginger-haired chap with a name badge hastily emblazoned with 'GAVIN' in large capital letters was getting overly aggressive with people he'd only met for the first time an hour ago. His forceful convictions - about the most effective method of transporting a chicken, a bag of grain and a fox across a river - were mostly aimed at an older, world-weary woman whose badge suggested her name was just as tired of this bullshit as she was. It might have read 'Sharon' if she'd been bothered to press a little harder on the label when her reticence impeded her from doing so.

The other members of the group simply gazed ambivalently into the ether, occasionally nodding or shaking their heads, depending on their changing allegiance between the two alpha delegates. They didn't really care what the correct answer to the task was, because none of them thought it remotely likely, given they were a gathering of professional buyers, that they'd come across this problem in their general day-to-day workload. Unless, of course, they happened to work for companies who regularly procured an equal volume of grain as they did chickens and the only form of transport available in the international supply chain was a small dinghy. The logos printed on their lanyards proved this wasn't the case. They all worked for well-known pharmaceutical companies who were notoriously affluent and somewhat more sophisticated with their production and logistics operations.

The task, of course, was not supposed to be taken literally. It was designed to simulate how a team of individuals might work together to overcome a problem. Right now, the team thought the most pressing problem was Gavin.

Eric had been to many of these educational events down the years. He always learnt something, but not always from the course itself. The real lessons emanated from the observation of the other characters who attended. He didn't need to listen to the conversation of the group a few metres away to understand who they really were and who they were trying to be. He drew those conclusions from signs they unconsciously projected into the atmosphere of the overly manicured business centre.

Eric had already sussed Gavin out long before he'd

opened his mouth. The answer was painted all over his name badge. The wearer would have no idea that graphology was a magnifying glass into their personality. Large letters meant he was outgoing and desperate for attention. Narrow spaces between them portrayed his need to intrude on others. The use of a slash rather than a dot over the letter 'i' indicated to Eric that Gavin was prone to excessively criticise those he saw as inferior to him. All of this data was analysed almost instantaneously and borne out a few moments later when Gavin interrupted the other woman with his overly opinionated views.

This was just one of the aspects Eric noticed about people almost implicitly. Streams of intelligence were being collected faster than a high-powered computer, merging together to create an immediate profile of the person, subject or task. He was equipped with talents which kept him one step in front of any adversary. Whatever Sean was prepared to unleash on them today, it wouldn't outsmart him.

There was only one problem with seeing what others could not. It was almost impossible to turn it off. Relaxation was something Eric struggled to achieve because he was always on duty. Not so for his companions. He glanced across at his two friends sitting adjacent to him along the wall on metal and leather-clad bar stools. Josh was asleep, head pressed backwards against the wall, mouth gaping wide, loudly sucking all available atmospheric oxygen into him. His body was slumped diagonally over the chair, calling the principles of science into question. No one could ever accuse Josh of struggling to relax. He did chilling as effortlessly as a drug user did tripping.

In contrast, Callum was anything but comfortable. His leg wobbled unconsciously against the metal frame of the stool like he was furiously trying to pump up a faulty blow-up doll. His hands shook like a category five hurricane, and a flood of sweat flowed out of his thinning hair and over his brow. Eric knew what the beer shakes looked like, but his friend's physical reactions were not entirely related to a lack of alcohol consumption over the past twelve hours. There was something else in the mix which Eric wasn't entirely sure about yet. He'd find out in time. Watch, decipher and understand - that was his mantra. The truth would escape, however diligently the defences had been constructed to constrain it.

Just before ten, the door to the boardroom swung open, and the elderly man who'd introduced Sean to the gathered assembly at yesterday's ceremony shuffled out to greet them. Eric administered a couple of sharp jabs with his elbow into Josh's ribs and eventually he unravelled like a knackered jack-in-the-box. He jabbered some nonsensical remarks about sandwiches and a girl called Tess before realising his current whereabouts and doing his best to explain his way out of it.

"Gentlemen. My name is Clarence Douville, and I'm Mr Heschmeyer's legal counsel," the man announced dryly, shaking each of them weakly by the hand. "My client would like to thank you for your punctuality. If you'd like to follow me, Mr Heschmeyer is ready to see you now."

Inside the well-furnished boardroom, Sean stood at the far end of a long polished table, hands clasping the back of a hefty black leather chair. On the left side of the room, brightly coloured box pleat tartan curtains stood guard over floor-to-ceiling windows spanning the entire wall. On the right side, a series of framed photographs featuring some notable *Heschmeyer Industries* projects had been specifically hung for the purposes of today's meeting. No doubt what usually occupied the walls were brightly coloured prints of cityscapes from around the world, like the rest of the identikit hotel.

Six chairs had been positioned around the far end of the boardroom table, leaving the other half barren. Nestled amongst the crystal tumblers, full to the brim carafes of water, hotel embossed notepads and strategically placed bowls of shiny black and white mints were six thick, bound documents with laminated covers.

"Welcome," said Sean cheerily. "Come in. Would anyone like coffee?"

Callum nodded his head eagerly, and Sean signalled for Clarence to do the honours. Eric's highly-tuned senses were immediately drawn to the hefty documents laid out precisely in front of each seat. There were six in total, but only five of them.

"I can't tell you how excited I am," announced Sean gleefully. "I feel like a young man taking his first tentative steps into a brave new world, very similar to how I felt that first day I stepped off the flight from Germany. I've missed those butterflies. We should have done this years ago."

"Get much sleep last night?" asked Eric cryptically.

"Yes, plenty. Why?"

"I imagine you must have been up late into the night designing challenges commensurate to our reputations. I mean, think how embarrassing it'll be for you if we complete them without even trying very hard. I'm sure the press would love to know how the great Sean Heschmeyer lost ten million pounds to a destitute drunk, an insatiable womaniser and a renowned advertising executive."

"Hey!" Josh chimed in. "A suspended advertising executive, don't forget."

Eric shushed him with his hand.

"That would make a good story - if it ever turns out to be true."

"It will," replied Eric confidently.

"Of course, the press might end up writing a very different account of the events. We'll have to wait and see, won't we. I have relationships with all the big media moguls, and I'm sure one of them will be interested in the story. What about you, Eric? Do you have any of them in your little black book?"

Eric remained passive, neither confirming nor denying he had such a network. Everyone knew full well that he didn't.

"Actually, these were printed off last night." Sean indicated the binders on the table. "It didn't take me long at all, in fact. I've had a very long time to think about it, you see."

"Let's hope they test us more than your previous attempts in the nineties."

"I'm confident they will."

"Only your very best effort will do," claimed Eric boldly. "And even then, I don't like your odds."

"We'll soon find out. Don't let your overconfidence affect the outcome."

"Fat chance," whispered Josh.

"Gentlemen, please take a seat," offered Clarence, waiting for them to comply before taking his own place at the table.

"Why do we need him here?" asked Callum, nodding at the legal eagle.

"Do you have a qualification in British law?" asked Sean.

"No."

"What about the rest of you?"

The others shook their heads.

"And are you expecting your designated solicitor to arrive anytime soon?"

Again, the shaking heads confirmed they weren't.

"Friends, the document in front of you is a legally binding international contract. It sets out the terms and conditions of our agreement, and as I might be liable to part with ten million pounds of my own hard-earned wealth, I'd like nothing about our deal to be misleading, misrepresented or ambiguous. That is why Clarence is present. I assure you he is more than qualified to oversee proceedings, but if you'd like to find your own qualified representative somewhere about the building, please be my guest."

Eric had already witnessed the standard of attendees congregating around the business centre. He was certain the loud-mouthed Gavin from purchasing might profess to be an expert legal negotiator, but then again, he'd probably just as easily argue he'd personally seen a Yeti and had the inside track on the whereabouts of the Illuminati. They didn't need that sort of assistance, and there was no reason to doubt Mr Douville's credentials. After all, Eric in partic-ular had signed a thousand business contracts with clients down the years, and he'd never insisted on checking the authenticity of their legal representatives before putting pen to paper.

"I'm sure Clarence is both suitably qualified and impartial," agreed Eric. "Shall we get on with it?"

"Certainly."

"Gentlemen, if you'd care to turn to page one, I will take you through the significant clauses in the contract. Then you can take as much time as you'd like to read through the details," stated Clarence dryly.

"The only clause that matters to me is what he wants us to do," said Eric, keen to get to the juicy parts of Sean's amateurish attempts at creativity.

"All in good time, Mr Gideon. As you will see from the

table of contents, the document outlines the offer, acceptance, conditions, terms of payment, terms of nonconformity, cancellation policy - which comes with associated penalties - and a detailed glossary with terms of reference."

Legal documents were not notorious for their page-turning quality and were more often associated with their eye-closing quality. It took an iron will or damaged mind to truly endure the challenge of reading such things. Often, this was exactly the intention of the lawyer who'd drawn them up. Like almost everyone faced with such a chore, all three of them would eventually flick through the dryness of the opening sections and make a beeline for the section in the file entitled 'Acceptance' which outlined what they were being asked to do.

"Do you have one in English?" asked Josh, quite seriously.

"It's all written in English, Mr Foxole."

"Not any English I use on a regular basis. It's like reading a code that stupid people don't understand."

Clarence wasn't a stupid person, and like all really clever people, he didn't have the slightest empathy for the hard of thinking.

"I mean," Josh said, "what the fuck is this?" He stabbed the contract with his finger.

"Which section are you referring to, exactly?"

"Page one, paragraph two. The parties hereto hereby form a Partnership under the name 'Old Boys Idiots' Club' (hereafter referred to as 'The Partnership') to conduct the later description of 'Activities' and all other lawful deeds as further business of 'The Partnership' as may be necessary, incidental, or convenient to carry out 'The Partnership's' activities as provided herein," read Josh, in utter bewilderment.

"On which specific part of that do you need clarification?" asked Clarence.

Josh starred at him blankly. "The words, mostly."

"It's quite straightforward," sighed Clarence. "It simply states that the five of you are entering into an agreement to work together to complete a series of activities over a period of time, with some conditions applied to how those activities should be completed."

"Why didn't you just write that, then?"

"That's not how things are done in the legal world. Can I help you with anything else?"

"Yeah, where's this party going to take place, and is it formal or casual dress?" asked Josh.

"You are the party, Mr Foxole!"

"Ah, I see my reputation proceeds me. Too right I am," he winked at Callum.

"All of us who sign it are the 'parties'," confirmed Eric.

"Oh. What's with all the hereby, hereto and herein jargon, though?"

"They have to justify their huge fees somehow," explained Callum.

"Can I continue," asked Clarence, remaining externally calm even though he was starting to get internally agitated.

"What about this part?" interrupted Josh, desperately out of his depth. "It says, 'Consequently the "Parties" agree that in case of a breach or threatening a breach of this "Agreement", the disclosing "Party" shall, in addition to any other remedies available to it at law or in equity, be entitled to the issuance of injunctive relief to enforce the provision hereof.' What does that mean, exactly?"

"To be plain and direct, Mr Foxole, it means should you breach - or even suggest in jest about breaching - any aspect of this agreement, Mr Heschmeyer can sue you remorselessly until there's nothing left of you."

"Right, but there's a hundred pages of this stuff. I wouldn't be surprised if taking a shit and sneezing at the wrong time aren't clauses in the agreement that might suggest a breach!"

"I assure you they aren't. Shall I continue?"

Josh waved him on, certain if he questioned every paragraph he didn't understand, the elderly Mr Douville might not outlive his own explanations.

While the sleep-inducing voice of Clarence Douville besieged their ears with words only found in the vocabulary of Oxford dons and seventeenth-century novelists, the group tried to follow the contents laid out in front of them. Every time Josh or Callum reached the end of the description of one of Sean's dares, known formally as 'The Activities', their expressions soured, their faces grew paler and they glanced at each other with increasing levels of distress. By the time Callum reached the fourth dare, he felt physically sick. His hand darted forward, fumbling for a carafe and glass to steady his nerves.

Eric had to hand it to their challenger; it was a lot more inventive than he'd thought Sean was capable of, and certainly more of a test than he'd faced for some considerable time. Not that he believed for a second it wasn't eminently achievable. In the unlikely event that it wasn't, all he needed was a fallback, something he was keeping his eye out for in both the weighty document and the mannerisms of the people around the room.

"You've got to be kidding!" exclaimed Josh as he reached the end of the 'Activities' section exasperated by its translation.

"My client never kids," replied Clarence indignantly.

Sean remained almost motionless throughout, further blocking Eric's attempts to read him.

"It's not moral," stated Callum nervously.

"When were *The Idiots' Club* ever moral?" inquired Sean.

"That may be," replied Josh, "but these dares aren't simply risky - they're likely to get us banged up in jail!"

"Not if you're as good as you say you are," Sean reminded them. "It wouldn't be a challenge if it was easy, would it now?"

"Well, you've made certain of that with your added clauses, haven't you," sighed Callum.

One section of the document had been titled 'Additional Clauses', and if the details of the dares had raised their eyebrows, these additions ripped them clean off their faces. In particular, the instruction that all dares had to be livestreamed at the time of completion, showing all of them actively participating and without disguise.

"Why do we need to film them?"

"Simple. I don't trust you," offered Sean. "This way, I will be able to follow your progress in real time, as will whoever else decides to tune in to your channel."

"I'm guessing you'll be promoting it, though," said Eric bluntly.

"That depends on how entertaining I find it," smiled Sean.

"How many Instagram followers do you have?"

"About a million."

"You're sick!" snarled Josh. "I don't know what you're up to, Sean, but I'm having nothing to do with it."

"But yesterday…" whined Callum before he was cut off mid-sentence.

Eric placed the top back on his pen and slid the signed contract into the centre of the table. "I'm in."

"Good," said Sean, "but as you know, the contract stipulates that all of you have to sign or the agreement is rendered null and void."

"I'm not signing it," declared Josh defiantly. "I may have agreed to it yesterday…"

"You shook hands on it," insisted Callum, who knew the symbolism of such an act amongst their group.

"I don't care. I'm forty-one and, amazingly, I've never been arrested, hospitalised, committed to a mental institution or been secluded from normal society for my own protection, all of which are very much in doubt if we do what he's suggesting."

"You've also avoided commitment, responsibility, career progression and just about every other norm of adulthood," goaded Eric. "If you don't do it, you'll continue pinballing through life with no purpose or plan. But this, this will make you a legend."

"It'll make me a bell-end."

"What do women love most about you, Josh?" asked Sean, breaking into their conversation and appearing to be on Eric's side for the first time in years.

"Rugged good looks."

"You think? Do you own a mirror? I mean, for someone of your age, I suppose you're punching above your weight, but you're definitely on the wrong side of the hill accelerating towards the finish line like an out-of-control bobsleigh. What will you do then? How will you feel when they stop admiring you?"

"I'll have to adapt."

"You already have. Your looks were never what attracted people to you. It was always your attitude. A bravery, a recklessness…an element of danger, even. If you do these things, imagine what it'll do for your street cred. And then," prodded Sean in a threatening manner, "imagine what it'll do to it if people knew you didn't even try because you were too frightened."

Josh's resistance started to ebb away as he visualised both the worst and best case scenarios.

"Slide me that contract," Callum indicated to Eric. "I'll sign."

Eric passed his signed copy over, and Callum added his signature to the bottom next to his friend's scrawled name. Clarence stood up gingerly to retrieve it, carrying it to the head of the table where he and Sean signed their own names in black ink.

"Your friends are in, Josh," announced Sean. "Are you going to let them down?"

Josh turned his head to eyeball the men sitting on either side of him. Their expressions were polar opposites, but they both wanted the same thing. "Pass it over," he wheezed reluctantly.

Josh penned his name and then slumped back into his chair like a bicycle tyre receiving a catastrophic puncture.

"Just one name left to add," offered Sean mysteriously. "And that might be more challenging than the dares themselves."

One document remained dormant on the table, untouched and as pristine as the moment it came out of the printer. Three sets of eyes rested on it. Eric knew whom it was for and he didn't need section eleven, paragraph four, clause two of the document to confirm it.

"Whose is that copy?" asked Josh after a long period of silence.

"The last member of *The Idiots Club*," said Sean. "It has to be all of you or none of you."

TEN

MICKY

Yesterday. Frome Police Station.

Iris Whitehall returned to the interview room with two plastic cups of steaming tea, her nicotine levels suitably replenished for another hour. The repulsive smell of stale smoke clung stubbornly to her clothes and poisoned the atmosphere in the room. It didn't bother her because smokers were the only people immune to it. If, like Eric, you'd kicked the habit years ago, the stench was ten times stronger than it was for regular people. He physically recoiled and tried to cease breathing but it was no good; there was no escape from it. If he needed another deterrent against the inclination to spark up again, this was it.

Iris placed a cup in front of him.

"Is it decaf?"

"It's hot and it's tea. Think yourself lucky."

"I'll be certain to leave a positive review in the visitors' book."

She opened her notepad to pick up where they'd left

off. "You said there was no proof to your claim of black-mail, but you also said you signed a contract."

"And?"

"If your story is accurate, that would be evidence, and I'm surprised you weren't keener to point it out."

"Slipped my mind," he lied.

"How does this contract show that you're being black-mailed? It might simply be an agreement to do mad stuff and unintentionally raise my anger threshold."

"The contract specifically states that should we fail to complete the tasks in the time allowed, then we owe Sean ten million pounds. Actually, it states it in words which are a lot less easy to understand and include phrases like 'sub-ject to', 'not withstanding' and 'without let or hindrance'."

"How can you be sure that's what it means if the words were ambiguous? You know how corrupt lawyers can be."

"We asked for an explanation."

"*The British Legal System for Idiots?*" replied Iris, suggesting a new addition to the famous series of books.

"If you like."

"And do you have a copy of the contract?"

"Yes."

"Where is it?"

"I'm not sure, exactly," admitted Eric honestly.

"What a surprise! Because if I'd signed a contract that might ruin me, I'd definitely treat it like junk mail." Iris took a sip from her tea but instantly regretted not waiting for it to cool down. "How many people signed this docu-ment, exactly?"

"Six."

"You, Mr Jollie, Mr Foxole – all currently on the premises – Mr Heschmeyer and his lawyer. I know about them, but who was the other signatory?"

"Turnip."

"What's his real name?" she said, rolling her eyes in disbelief.

"Micky Parsons."

"How did he get the nickname 'Turnip'?"

"Parsons sounds a lot like 'parsnip' and parsnips remind people of turnips."

"No, they don't! Not even a toddler would confuse those vegetables."

"I didn't give him the name," Eric replied plainly. "I grant you it's not that imaginative, but he already had it when we first met him."

"At least we know who he is now."

"What do you mean?" asked Eric, showing a glimpse of concern for the first time in the interview.

"Four of you stole the lion; only three of you are here."

"That doesn't mean the other person in the footage is him, does it?"

"Who else would it be? The Marquis of Kent?! The Lord Chancellor of the Admiralty?! Tarzan?!"

"I'm certain all of them would have been more helpful than Turnip."

"Stop wasting my time, Mr Gideon. A lion and a suspect are missing. Doesn't take a genius to work out that if I find one, I'll find the other. Tell me: where is Micky Parsons?"

A week last Sunday. Herefordshire.

Eric pressed on the worn, old-fashioned doorbell and kept his finger there for longer than was normally necessary. The bell was attached to a tatty, ancient front door which might have suffered storm damage every day since it was first fitted. The racing green paint flaked off the wood like a skin disease, and surrounding the door was a worn and fragile manor house, which loitered unwelcomely at the end of a long winding driveway. The state of the property might falsely trick people into believing that the owners were down on their luck, or that the house had been vacated some months before. But this was some distance from the truth, and Eric knew it.

In England, there was a certain breed of rich person who lived like this.

Old money.

It's counter-intuitive to think that affluence might be purposefully camouflaged behind a veneer of destitution, but having oodles of money didn't necessarily mean the occupants lived the high life. Quite the contrary. Spending money on the upkeep of a house of this size and age was likely to result in the owner not being rich for much longer. Not all rich people are tight. Eric had more wealth than he needed and was somewhat reckless with it, but he was nouveau riche – easy come, easy go. Old money, on the other hand, had a heritage and a responsibility. If nine generations of your family had managed to avoid blowing the inheritance, then the pressure was definitely on the next in line. A pressure which will create an uncomfortable anxiety.

A fear that one day the money might dry up.

We all fear something, but most phobias are preposterous because we've never actually experienced the notion - and in most cases, we're not likely to. There are people who fear being struck by a meteorite, the zombie apocalypse, killer clowns, excessive dryness or other peoples' knees. All of these terror-inducing non-events have complicated Latin names which make for dastardly tricky pub quiz questions. Take 'arachibutyrophobia' for example, which is the fear of peanut butter sticking to the top of one's mouth. This is a surprisingly common phobia and, unlike werewolves, something that's much more likely to happen in an average day. Other fears affect a much narrower group of sufferers, like 'anatidaephobia' which is the fear of being watched by a duck, and then there are those that have deeply ironic names like 'hippopotomonstrosesquippedaliophobia' which is the fear of long words! Of course, most phobias are irrational, but it's not always the case.

People who've never experienced excess wealth would find it difficult to truly understand what it's like. Once you've achieved financial dominance, the concept of losing it all and returning to a life amongst the riffraff might turn your stomach. This is even more prevalent if you've never truly experienced what it's like to have nothing. Eric knew what it was like, so the thought of going back didn't scare him. Wealth which was largely passed down the generations meant the recipient had never worked for it, either. The longer the family tree of wealth, the meaner the next recipient was likely to be.

This visceral anxiety will result in a tendency to keep their wallets firmly shut. They're likely to be the last to buy a round of drinks, if they do at all, will frequently be seen wearing clothes they first purchased forty years ago, will haggle over the price of every basic commodity, ration their heating consumption and reuse wrapping paper from presents other people bought them. Old money types are almost always tighter than two coats of paint.

Wealth, of course, is a relative term. The people who lived in this manor house weren't multi-millionaires like Sean, but in comparison to two of the people standing on the doorstep, they were positively loaded. On a standard deviation of British income, Eric would certainly be in the top few percent, but cash left his wallet faster than air left his lungs. He'd grown up on a sinkhole council estate in the heart of London where most of the residents aspired to achieving bank statements that had positive numbers on them by the middle of every month. He'd received no guidance to help him use his money wisely, because there was no precedent to follow. No one in his family or community knew what excess meant. 'Spend now, worry later' was their guiding principle. The family who lived in this house were more 'worry now, spend later'.

Through the thick oak door, a muffled chime did its best to notify the homeowner of the club's unscheduled arrival. With a house this big and a bell this quiet, the chances of it working rested solely on someone walking past at the specific moment someone rang. Eric gave the bell some moral support by banging a clenched fist against the wood three times. He stood back from the uneven stone step and waited for the outcome. Behind him, Josh and Callum waited in the drizzle a few feet away.

"You're sure this is the right place?" asked Josh from under the hood of his nineteen-nineties duffle coat.

"You've been here a dozen times!" said Callum.

"Have I?"

"Yes. Micky's family have owned this house for three generations, and we used to come here in the holidays between terms."

"Oh yeah…Micky's dad owned a Great Dane called Zeus," said Josh cautiously.

"That was my dad," replied Callum, in a voice he normally reserved for telling very sick people they were dying.

"Jesus, Foxie, what's wrong with your memory. Have

you checked you're not suffering from early onset Alzheimer's?" mocked Eric.

"Don't be daft. It's advantageous for a man in my position to have a selective memory."

"Explain," inquired Callum.

"Well, I have a lot of...how can I say this tactfully... female friends. Dozens, in fact, and I often meet them on the same day. It pays not to confuse one from another. It's kind of awkward if you say the wrong name when you're in the middle of...you know."

"I'm guessing you only refer to them as 'babe' or 'darling' and try not to engage in deep and meaningful conversations, " Eric speculated.

"Dead right! It also helps if they know about my terrible memory. It's endearing."

"If you say so," scoffed Eric.

"But it's not entirely false if you don't remember this house," countered Callum.

"I don't have space for remembering mundane things."

"Like the names of the women he married," joked Eric.

"I doubt anything significant ever happened here that's worth remembering," added Josh.

"Micky's dad chased you across the grounds with a shotgun after you exposed yourself to his wife!"

Josh glanced around at the boggy fields to the left of the driveway and the adjacent copse of trees. A tension of adrenaline rose in his bloodstream as the angry voice of Micky's dad echoed through history. "That'll be why I don't remember it."

They waited in the rain, hoping someone would finally come to the door and let them in. After their return flight from Edinburgh this lunchtime, they'd taken the opportunity for brief trips back to their respective London homes to freshen up and grab a change of clothes. This was particularly welcomed by Josh, who'd been wearing rhino boxers under his suit for the last three days. Normally, a man dealt with this crisis by turning them back to front or inside out, thereby extending their pre-wash lifespan three-fold, but this wasn't a feasible strategy if a large reinforced horn was extending out the front. Unless you were prepared to stick it up your arse, and Josh wasn't.

After a quick turnaround, they were on the move again, but choice of transport was limited. Micky's house was in the countryside, twenty miles from the nearest public transport links and twice that distance from an airport. Driving to Herefordshire from the southeast of England was their only feasible option given their new time constraints, even though the terms of Sean's contract gave them a limited period of grace before the dares had to begin. That's if they ever did.

Everything would hinge on what happened today.

Their choice of car was also limited. Josh's Vauxhall Nova had largely been towed away to a scrap metal merchant, although some of it was still scattered around the vicinity of where he'd last parked it. Callum confessed to not owning a car because he lived in the city of London and there was little call for it. He omitted the fact that it would have definitely been repossessed by now if he had one. That only left Eric's pride and joy.

The Nissan GT-R R35 had many selling points, and most of them proved to be accurate. Although one feature, in particular, proved to be a stretch of the truth. The car was marketed as a four-seater vehicle and no one could argue against it, in the same way that no one could argue most printers could be used as fax machines. Neither of which made these functions fit for purpose or entirely necessary. It was feasible to sit in the back two seats of the

GT-R if, and only if, you met certain conditions. You had to be no taller than a dwarf, no wider than a high jumper, have fewer limbs than a slug, have an immunity to claustrophobia and be impervious to deep vein thrombosis. On the upside, the car's top speed was over a hundred and fifty miles an hour, so at least you wouldn't be vacuum-packed in the back for as long as you might be in a Vauxhall Nova.

Josh and Callum flipped a coin for the privilege.

Josh lost.

As he stood in the rain, Eric noted that his posture was more stooped than it was before their hundred-plus mile journey, and for a normally tall man, his current extension was on a par with Callum's, who was well known for being the short arse of the group.

While Eric contemplated another set of heavy knocks to the door, it finally opened, and a conservatively-dressed woman stood in the entrance. As soon as there was enough of an angle for the woman to catch sight of who was on her doorstep, she hastily reversed direction. There was just enough time for Eric to leap forward and shove his boot in the gap.

"Hello, Natasha."

"Piss off!"

"That's not a very nice way to greet an old friend."

"No, but it's a perfectly acceptable way of addressing you!"

"Is Micky in?" Eric asked serenely, as if the previous insult missed the target.

"No!" She caught a glimpse of Josh behind Eric's head, and he shot her a cheesy smile and a raised thumb. It didn't lighten her mood one bit. "Get your foot out my door or I'll snap it off!"

"That's his car under there, isn't it?" suggested Eric, pointing at a car-shaped lump under a grey tarpaulin, both of which sheltered under a moss-covered carport next to the house.

"No, he's at work."

"On a Sunday?"

"Business trip."

"Do pharmacists go on business trips?"

"Absolutely. I'll tell him you called. Good-bye," she barked, trying to persuade the door to ignore the heavy size-ten foot that blocked its route.

"Natasha, it's lovely to see you," said Callum supportively and in a softer tone than Eric was capable of. "We were passing by and wanted to say hello, that's all."

As Callum had been blocked by Eric's broad frame, Natasha noticed him for the first time, and Eric felt the strength of her resistance against his boot lessen. "Do yourself a favour, Callum - stay away from these two idiots. Micky worked that out more than a decade ago, and life has been brighter and smoother ever since."

"Boring though, right?" claimed Eric.

"Calmer," she snapped in response. "I'm going to ask you one last time."

"We just want to see Micky. One hour, tops."

"Why?"

"What's suspicious about wanting to catch up with an old friend?"

"Everything! The three of you showing up together for the first time in over a decade, for a start. I know for a fact Josh and Callum haven't spoken to each other in years after they fell out over an unpaid debt."

"What unpaid debt?" whispered Josh.

"I've no idea what she's talking about," replied Callum, thankful that Josh's memory loss included the investment he'd made in one of Callum's failed ventures.

"Every time you turn up, chaos is always close on your

heels. Micky's left that life behind him. He's left you behind him. We don't want anyone disturbing the perfect world we've worked so hard to build."

Privileged people often made such claims. Inheriting wealth or success wasn't easy to stomach when your entitled peer group knew the truth. Keeping up with the neighbours meant wearing a mask. Eric didn't begrudge Micky his fortune, but he did take umbrage at Natasha's attempts to rewrite history. Most of what they called their 'perfect world' they'd not worked for. The house, the fifty acres of farmland nearby, a collection of classic cars and the status that came with it. In normal circumstances, Eric generally despised those who'd benefited from an unfair system which made it easier for the rich to get richer to the detriment of people like him. But every story was different, and Micky had more than paid for it.

Growing up in the presence of Major Reginald Parsons, and being an only child, was price enough for poor old Micky. The Major was a fourth-generation military bigwig, and each predecessor had cleared the way for their successor to step up to higher office. The Parsons had served with distinction in every major British war since the Crimean War. The Major once told them proudly that his great grandfather, James Parsons, had been one of the few officers to survive the 'Charge of the Light Brigade', and there was no suggestion whatsoever that he'd been involved in planning the catastrophe. None of these past glories made Micky's life easy.

Living up to the standards of ancestors was hard enough, but when you had a brutal father and no interest in joining the family business whatsoever, it made life complicated. Tough love can go one of two ways. It can be a powerful control mechanism to keep you in line, or occasionally, it creates rebellion. When Micky refused to conform, he had to suffer the slings and arrows of a domestic war as a result. Physical beatings, psychological torture, neglect and coercive control were the Major's weapons of choice.

Micky's comfortable lifestyle had been paid for in blood and trauma, but it wasn't true for Natasha. She'd paid no such sacrifice. Natasha Wilmot-Jones, as she was known back in the day, studied at Exeter University at the same time they had. She was part of the Sloane Ranger brigade, although she lacked the social standing and background of many in that group. It was only chance that her orbit collided with Micky's and, unsurprisingly, the actions of *The Idiots' Club* were entirely responsible.

"Is it perfect?" asked Eric, casting doubt on her claim.

"Yes!"

"Because if it was…" Eric paused to consider how best to weave his talent for creating doubt in her mind. "If it was, you'd be at ease with your husband meeting up with old friends. You'd trust him enough to know what was in his family's best interests, wouldn't you? If you didn't trust him, it would suggest an anxiety and diffidence to your notion of perfection, wouldn't it?"

"You can't manipulate me, Eric. I'm immune, remember!"

"Yes, but he isn't," replied Eric, pointing through the gap in the door to the figure listening carefully at the other end of the corridor. "How's your business trip, Turnip?"

"Don't call him that!" snapped Natasha.

"Try yoga," recommended Eric sarcastically. "I'm told it's relaxing."

"Hello, Eric," answered Micky, as he approached the door in old-man slippers, ill-fitting corduroy trousers and a frayed beige smoking jacket. "To what do we owe the pleasure?"

"The Queensferry Crossing."

It was a strange reference, given the two had been estranged for more than a decade, but Micky understood it immediately and there was only one reason for that. All adults over forty fell victim to the same addiction – the compulsion to watch news reports at least nineteen times a day. For some adults, giving up crack cocaine would be easier. Even though the Parsons consumed wall-to-wall news bulletins, Micky was certain his wife wouldn't understand the significance of Eric's reference. He'd clearly done so on purpose to avoid using a name she would have recognised: Sean Heschmeyer.

"What's he on about?" snarled Natasha, convinced she was being kept out of a loop.

"Investment opportunity," offered Eric, not dishonestly.

"Josh, Callum," said Micky as he took control of the door from his wife and allowed full visual access to the corridor's faded paisley wallpaper. "Been a while."

"Not through want of trying," replied Callum, who had single-handedly attempted to keep the group together over the years.

"Micky doesn't need any crackpot investment advice from people like you," brooded Natasha. "If he wants to lose money, I'll send him to a casino."

"Why don't you come in?" invited Micky before he was quickly challenged.

"Over my dead body! If they even take a step into this house, I'll make your life a misery," she threatened.

Micky's demeanour shrivelled in front of their very eyes. Eric had seen it happen to him many times before, but it wasn't always influenced by the same person.

"But you didn't say anything about him coming out here, though, did you?" winked Eric.

ELEVEN
THE GEORGE & DRAGON

THE BRITISH PUB IS AN INSTITUTION NOT REPLICATED authentically anywhere else in the world. France might lay claim to the village bar, Germany has its bierkellers, Australians call theirs 'hotels' and Vienna has coffee houses, but none rival the history and pedigree of the humble British pub. Even in former Commonwealth colonies, where the rise of 'fake pubs' has hit epidemic proportions, no establishment truly mirrors the ambient feel of the original, however much mass-produced mock memorabilia is thrown at them.

If you want a proper pulled pint - as opposed to the miserly measures served in the United States, lukewarm beer - an experience that forces most European tourists to send it back in disgust, the company of men of a certain vintage and aroma, bar billiards - a game even veterans don't fully understand, sarcastic bar staff, ancient horse brasses, semi-submerged beer gardens and pickled bar snacks first placed in vinegar sometime around the last war, then there's only one place to go.

Actually, not one.

There are ten thousand examples up and down the length and breadth of the country.

Traditional British pubs can be found in locations no business planner worth their salt would ever endorse. As well as the more commercially viable places - like built-up areas where lots of people live – they are also found on the sides of mountains, in the middles of fields, underground, on largely uninhabited islands, on isolated beaches and often in small clusters in rural villages with permanent populations measured by a single person's fingers and toes. But however remote their location, it's reassuring to know that they all feature an abrasive drunk Scotsman, irrespective of how far the pub is from his original birthplace.

Genuine pubs, as opposed to those which have succumbed to being secretly converted into bland soulless gastropubs, will have iconic names: The Rose & Crown, The Anchor, The Red Lion, The Plough and The Railwayman. In total, one hundred and twenty-four of them are called The George & Dragon and at least four of those were a reasonable driving distance from Micky's house.

One, though, was within walking distance.

After Micky had been subjected to a bout of verbal domestic abuse which registered a nine on the Richter scale, he plucked up the courage to step outside. He'd at least contemplate what Eric wanted to say, even if he had to deal with the messy marital clean-up operation later that evening, hopefully when Natasha's mood had softened somewhat. He knew, as well as any husband did, it wouldn't. Wives had a genetic talent which made them incapable of forgetting even the slightest irrelevant detail of an argument several decades after it first occurred.

Which was a shame, really, because last orders at The George & Dragon was at eleven.

Micky swapped his comfy slippers for a pair of mud-caked welly boots and slunk off down the driveway, shoulders hunched to the soundtrack of aggressive high-pitched threats. Every step along the pot-holed lane dampened the volume of her hysteria and decreased his obvious cowardice.

"I don't know how you put up with it," said Josh, giving Micky a friendly pat on the back. "I've divorced wives for much less."

"You divorced one of them because you forgot her name," Eric reminded him judgementally.

"True, but I think not remembering it was a good sign it wasn't going to last."

"Natasha isn't normally this combustible; she just has an intense dislike for you three. Normally, she's a pussy cat."

"I imagine that's how zookeepers describe their Bengal tigers," suggested Callum.

"You can't really blame her. Trouble stalks you lot like a plague of locusts. Plus there's...you know...the history."

All four of them nodded.

"That's not the only reason for her behaviour, though," expressed Eric boldly. "I don't think you realise what's happened to you. She's poison."

"What right do you have to judge me?" snapped Micky, stopping dead in his tracks near the gate to the main road. "Look what you've done with your lives - it's hardly a case study on how to master adulthood, is it!"

"How would you know?" Eric replied angrily. "You were the one who withdrew from us, weren't you. We didn't alienate you from the group. You and your harpy wife were responsible for that."

"I made a choice," barked Micky in his most forceful tone, which was comparable to most people's normal one.

"The chaos of your friendship or the calmness of my family."

"You call that calm! I only remember one person shouting, don't you, boys?" asked Eric.

The others nodded, Josh more forcibly than Callum.

"You wouldn't understand," explained Micky. "Committing to someone requires compromise. You just can't have it your own way and do whatever you want. You have to make sacrifices for the other person."

"What sacrifices is she making?" asked Josh.

"None of your business."

"You did make a choice," said Eric, "but it wasn't about us."

"What do you mean by that?" demanded Micky, folding his arms.

"You chose to replace your authoritarian father with a bossy and controlling wife. You fought against it once, but now you need it. You have a compulsion to serve so that you feel needed. It's the reinforcement of a life script that makes you feel inferior to others. Your dad really screwed you up, Micky, and for a short period of your life, we protected you from it. We helped release you from it, but now it's seeped back in like a shadow."

"Bullshit! I don't have a need to do what I'm told," he said firmly. His face had turned to thunder, and he considered turning on his heels to return to the comfort of the house.

"You do," confirmed Josh.

"I don't!"

"Look, stop being a twat and come with us," insisted Eric.

"Oh, okay," Micky replied subserviently.

"See what I mean!" said Eric. "The old Micky would have told me to piss off. You don't have to do what others tell you. We've come here looking for your help, but ulti-mately, you have to decide if you want to. We won't make you."

Micky's defences crumbled.

"Come on; let's get a pint," begged Callum.

"Okay."

They ambled down the country lane in silence, shad-owed on both sides by five-foot-high, ancient twisted hedgerows that bustled with hyperactive sparrows. After five minutes, the sight of grey smoke billowing from a chimney greeted them warmly in the distance. The homely smell of burning cherry wood and the imagined scent of brewed hops quickened their steps. The weathered sign of The George & Dragon stood guard over an almost empty car park and squeaked eerily as it swung in the breeze. The lights of the seventeenth-century building called them in, and they ducked to avoid cracking their heads on the low lintel of the bowed doorframe.

Inside, a scattering of lost souls, mostly accompanied by well-mannered Labradors, nursed frothy tankards of amber beer, read newspapers, or stared vacantly out of the windows. Most were hiding from something: wives, D.I.Y. projects, the weather or life in general. This wasn't the kind of pub that appealed to sports fans – there was a strict no television policy in pubs like this - and they weren't here for the culinary delights, either, most of which came directly from a microwave or were served between two enormous slabs of bread. No one went to church to be entertained or well fed. Parishioners went out of duty and faith, and pubs were no different.

A few of the patrons nodded in acknowledgement of Micky's arrival, which immediately reduced their dislike of the people he was with. Even then, though, Eric knew he made them uncomfortable. A non-local stepping on their hallowed floorboards in the company of someone they knew was one thing. A black man in an almost exclusively white rural district was quite another. Eric knew the truth about modern racism. Most white people had been shamed into examining their cultural and personal bigotry over the last few decades, but it hadn't vanished. Just because people refrained from verbalising their views for fear of being labelled a racist didn't stop the thought swimming around in their heads. In many ways, it made life more difficult for people like him. When people said what they believed, at least, he knew where he stood. Now he assumed everyone was thinking it. The disgruntled looks, inaudible mutterings and agitated shuffling of chairs told him everything he needed to know. He'd not studied psychology, human behaviour and communication theory for work purposes alone.

"Right, I'll get them in," said Callum, keen to replenish the depleted levels of alcohol in his bloodstream.

"I thought you were skint?" inquired Josh suspiciously, having noted that Callum had paid for nothing during their entire trip to Scotland and back.

"My new credit card," he said, flashing the gold plastic to the others proudly while carefully covering the details on the front with his thumb. "It came in the post while we were away."

"You'd better get yours ready," Josh whispered to Eric, "in case it bounces!"

Callum approached the bar, his hands shaking with nervous excitement at the thought of his fingers finally being set free to wrap themselves around a cold glass. A jolly-looking publican wobbled over to take his order. The end of the barman's beard swayed just above his pot belly, making him a prime candidate for a ZZ Top tribute band.

"Four pints of lager," said Callum eagerly.

"Not for me, Callum," interrupted Micky. "I don't drink anymore."

"…that was only my order," explained Callum.

"Fuck it," said Josh to the barman. "I'll have what he's having."

"Mineral water for me," Micky requested with a frown.

"How long have you been dry?" asked Eric in an interrogational tone.

"Eight years last Christmas."

"Feel any better for it?"

"Not particularly. It wasn't entirely my decision."

Eric didn't need to ask more. It was obvious who wore the trousers in Micky's household. He wondered, with a sense of dark curiosity, what it would be like to live like that, cut off from the things which once offered so much joy. It was evident Micky's avenues of pleasure had been permanently converted into cul-de-sacs. A life of servitude and prohibition was no life at all, and it was up to Eric to show him the light, as he had done once before.

"Eric?" Callum mimed out the internationally recognised sign language for 'do you want a pint.'

"Just one for me; I'm driving."

Ten drinks were arranged on two buckled brewery branded metal trays, along with the omnipresent beer spillage that sloshed around the bases of the glasses. Josh and Eric carried them tentatively over to one of the quiet booths between a roaring open fire on one side and lead-lined windowpanes on the other. As soon as the trays landed safely with minimal further liquid overflow, Callum shakily lurched for a glass before emptying its contents down his gullet at record speed.

"Steady on, Callum," said Micky. "There's no rush."

"He has a problem," observed Josh.

"No, I don't."

"You really do," confirmed Eric. "Do you want to talk about it?

"Talking wastes drinking time."

"We're all friends here, mate - you can tell us," offered Micky warmly.

"Are we, though?" interjected Eric.

"What do you mean?"

"Well, this is the first time we've been together in more than ten years. You'd hardly describe that as a close friendship group, would you?"

"I don't judge friendship on the frequency of contact; I measure it on the depth of the bonds formed. Real friends are those you can meet after ten years and it doesn't feel awkward," explained Micky.

For a good few minutes, no one spoke.

Micky played restlessly with his glass and avoided their gazes. He searched desperately for something interesting to say which wouldn't make it sound like he'd just met them. He hummed nervously between gulps of mineral water and slowly felt himself sinking further into his seat in the hope the shabby, faded material might consume him.

"You mean like this," said Eric, ending the silence.

"How's work?" Micky uttered, hastily breaking the ice with the type of question only boring people asked.

"We're not here for chitchat, Micky. We need your help. If you have any attachment to the past, to our past, then we might not have come in vain."

"Of course I do. The old times were amazing, completely life changing. It was probably the happiest time I can remember, and the three of you will always be more important to me than I can ever express. But they were the old times. I've moved on. We all have to in order to grow."

"But if one of us was in mortal peril, you'd help out,

right?" submitted Eric, laying a trap he might need to activate later.

"Definitely, no question," he replied honestly, but not
expecting it to be called upon anytime soon.

"That's why we're here."

"Who's in mortal peril?" gasped Micky, casting his gaze
around the group.

"All of us," announced Josh dramatically.

"You're all dying!"

"Well, not as such," added Callum, already nearing the
end of his second pint.

"But that's what 'mortal peril' means."

"Death doesn't always refer to the loss of life…"

"As a pharmacist, I'd take umbrage with that," challenged Micky.

"With words like 'umbrage', you could have been a
lawyer," groaned Josh, who disliked words with more than
two syllables.

"Death can also refer to someone's reputation, business
or career," continued Eric accurately.

Micky had always been susceptible to manipulation,
particularly by members of *The Idiots' Club*. It was hard to
avoid such effects when you'd grown up with the painful
consequences of disagreeing with someone more powerful
than you. He'd been caught off guard by their surprise visit
but the voice of his wife, still ringing in his ears, was
making him recognise it now.

"What's this really about, boys?'

"The Queensferry Crossing," repeated Eric.

"*Heschmeyer Industries*. Sean's company."

"We saw him."

"Sean! How is he?" asked Micky buoyantly.

"Rich," replied Callum enviously.

"Let's just say he's done a lot of thinking," remarked Eric.

"Where did you see him?"

Eric described the events leading up to and including their unexpected invitation to Sean's opening ceremony. He stopped right before the point at which Sean made his proposition.

"I wonder why he didn't invite me?" Micky said regretfully.

"Because you wouldn't have come," stated Eric.

"Probably not," he concurred, taking a sip of mineral water. "What did he say?"

"He made us an offer."

"An offer? What sort of offer?"

Eric took a few seconds to ensure the words conveyed the message exactly the way he wanted. "He dared us to complete five challenges in seven days."

Micky responded by spluttering his mineral water down his chin via a dry, uncomfortable laugh. "Why would he do that?"

"Because he's bored," explained Eric, before the other two took the opportunity to disagree. Eric was convinced there was a greater motive to it, but this wasn't the time to explore it.

"What did you say in response...hold on...I already know what *you'd* say."

"Yes," Eric confirmed.

"And the rest of you?"

They nodded.

"Why?"

"He's offered us a share of ten million quid."

Micky gawped at them disbelievingly.

"It's not about the money, though," disputed Eric.

"It is for me," countered Callum, digging into his fourth lager.

"It's the last chance for *The Idiots' Club* to go out in infamy. To rediscover the excitement of living on the edge and feeling the adrenaline rush through our bodies. Not because we've been instructed to, but because we want to."

"But you have been instructed to…by Sean," pointed out Micky.

"No, we haven't. He's dared us…it's different."

"It sounds mental, if you ask me."

"I was with you to begin with," Josh told him, "but how often do you get the chance to do something unique and exciting like this."

"We did it twenty years ago - wasn't that enough?"

"Not for me," Eric refuted. "I need to prove I can still meet the challenge, that *The Idiots' Club* still have what it takes."

Micky's face went pale from a sudden and terrifying realisation. They hadn't travelled all this way only to tell him about their ridiculous plan. They said they needed his help. They said it was about an investment opportunity in *Heschmeyer Industries*. Eric had purposefully framed it as a reformation of *The Idiots' Club*. A club in which he played a fundamental part.

"No!"

"Hear us out…"

"I'm not having anything to do with it. I'm forty-two, I'm married and I have three kids. I run a successful chain of pharmacies. I'm on the school's board of governors, for Pete's sake. I have standing. I have principles! If you want to act like fools, running around the country completing daft dares set by a multimillionaire for his own amusement, and most likely for his own agenda, then beat yourself up.

I'll read about it in the newspapers but I'll have nothing to do with it! Nothing!"

"Two and a half million pounds," tempted Callum.

"I don't want the money."

"What about the chance to test yourself," suggested Eric.

"I have no interest in boosting my ego, thank you very much."

"Girls will fancy you again," said Josh desperately.

Micky stared at him blankly.

A thin layer of frost settled on the atmosphere in the lounge bar which the raging fire did nothing to melt.

"I wish you the very best of luck," announced Micky, draining his glass and preparing to leave.

"Sean says it has to be the four of us or there's no deal," implored Eric. "We need you, Micky."

"Why is it so important to you?"

"Callum needs the investment and Josh is frightened of losing his sexual magnetism."

"Not them - you, Eric. Why do you want to do it?"

"Because I can't not do it."

"Yes, you can. Maybe it's time for you to learn how to say no. Maybe that is your test, Eric. Maybe you can't move on to the next phase of your life until you do. You don't always have to fight. You have a great car, you're talented, have opportunities and maybe one day a family. What more do you need?"

"I don't have what Sean has," he said angrily. "I never will if I play by the rules. Unlike you and him, I didn't get a leg up, so I have to fight."

"I'm not following you into battle this time. It's been good to see you, genuinely it has, and I hope our next gathering will be under different circum-stances. I'm sorry I haven't tried as hard as I should to keep in contact with you. I'll try to do better in the future."

Micky buttoned up his smoking jacket and headed off into the drizzle for the short walk home. The others gazed into half-empty glasses like jilted lovers.

"That's it, then," conceded Josh.

"I'm getting another round," announced Callum. It was obviously going to be a big round, because he grabbed both trays before marching back to the bar.

"We're not beaten yet," said Eric under his breath.

"Sean was right. He knew getting Micky onboard was going to be our toughest challenge. There's no way we can convince him to change his mind."

"How many dares have I failed?" Eric repeated his earlier boast.

"This isn't a dare, though, is it?"

"Everyone has a pressure point. Sean has proven that by the research he did on us. Sean wants Micky to compete. He needs him to, and he's not going to leave that up to chance. We just have to work out what Sean already knows – Micky's pressure point."

"But if it's not money, ego, power, girls, nostalgia or reputation, what is it?"

Eric processed everything he'd witnessed since Micky first came to the door earlier this evening. What was he missing? Micky had confessed to having everything he wanted in life, but that wasn't the only motivation people reacted to. It wasn't always about what someone might gain; it was sometimes about what someone might lose.

A shaky, clinking symphony, like a musician playing a drum kit packed with light bulbs, signalled Callum's return from the bar. The trays were packed with shot glasses, filled from bottles the barman had evacuated from the cellar before a concerted dusting off to verify their contents.

Most of them contained sticky brown liquids, but whether this was the distilleries' desired intention would remain unclear until the drinks were consumed.

"What's Micky most scared of?" asked Eric.

"Natasha," answered Callum confidently, dishing out the first round of shots.

"I'm driving," Eric said, waving Callum's eighty proof pick-me-up away.

"You and me then, Josh!"

"Oh, what the hell. Bottoms up!"

The viscous liquid scorched a path down their throats, and like a Wi-Fi hotspot losing reception, it took their vocal cords several minutes to come back online.

"Cointreau?" wheezed Josh, tears visibly watering his cheeks.

"What scares him more than Natasha?" Eric asked searchingly.

They shrugged.

"Natasha when we're around her. Nothing triggers her temper more than us. More than you, in fact." He pointed at Josh.

TWELVE
NATASHA

THERE WERE SEVERAL LEGITIMATE REASONS WHY NATASHA Wilmot-Jones-Parsons despised all but one of *The Idiots' Club's* former members, and she was far from the only person who felt that way. Almost every student who'd attended Exeter in the period between ninety-five and ninety-eight had reasons to hate them. To this day, the club was still banned from entering most local pubs, barred from certain shops, had been red flagged as malcontents by the local Council and disavowed by the Exeter Alumni Association.

But people's dislike for them didn't end there.

Even twenty years on, Eric and his crew were still about as popular as a fart in an elevator. Dozens of Josh's sexual conquests had launched social media accounts dedicated to warning unsuspecting potential victims of his philandering behaviour. Every investor, both institutional and private, had learnt to shun any venture backed by, or associated with, Callum Jollie, and a number were still pursuing him through the courts for damages. Although the creative industries had a begrudging respect for Eric, he wasn't winning any popularity contests. Advertising was famous for attracting people with more faces than twenty-sided dice, though, so he got away with it. They pretended to like him because they wanted to climb the greasy pole of progress, and if you were committed to that, you'd kiss anyone's arse.

In a world where the vast majority stuck to the rules imposed upon them by work regimes, relationships, business practises or politics, anyone circumventing the norms was treated like a leper with halitosis. Either those refusing to comply were doing rather well as a consequence and the 'sheep' ridiculed them because they were too frightened to follow, or the rule breakers had spectacularly failed and had become justifiable targets. Whereas Sean and Micky were firmly back in the mainstream, Eric and the boys were still proud outsiders.

Natasha didn't like outsiders. She also had no time for the poor, minorities, immigrants, retirees, people from Yorkshire, children – even her own, Norwegians, football fans, single mothers, delivery drivers, bookmakers, and anyone called Ken. The cross-section of people she disliked didn't leave much room for those she did, but even after all of these prejudices, there was still a very specific reason why she hated *The Idiots' Club* most of all.

His name was Josh.

Her ex.

Members of *The Idiots' Club* sat outside the three branches of the student kingdom - Sloane Rangers, sheep or spods - and as a consequence, attracting girlfriends meant incursions into enemy territory. For someone with Josh's desire to win any girl who took his fancy, these forays were frequent, weekly in fact, and his covert courting helped him build up a formidable understanding of the sub cultures, habits and behaviours of all three. Being accepted into a community you had no right to infiltrate was impossible unless you had exceptional powers of deception, and Josh was a master.

He knew exactly how to imitate their traits to wheedle his way in and gain their trust, although it became exponentially more difficult with every passing term. After each successful conquest, Josh moved on to his next fancy, often in a completely different section of students altogether, which meant revealing the disguise he'd adopted the previous week. Fortunately for Josh, there was a fresh intake of students at the start of each new academic year who were not familiar with his tactics, and off he went again.

Josh was never interested in committed relationships, like some students were. For him, the excitement of the chase and the increasing difficulty of the challenge, and the extent to which his reputation preceded him, trumped the boring familiarity of the same partner and being nagged relentlessly to do things he didn't want to do, like watching chick flicks and...talking. Josh got easily bored and not just with the opposite sex. He fell asleep during lectures, quickly lost interest in hobbies, got demotivated in jobs by a lack of variety and even occasionally became fatigued by the longer of *The Idiots' Club's* dares.

Friday night at University combined two of his favourite passions. Dares and women. On one occasion, both were called Natasha - a dare that had sizeable and lasting implications for all of them.

Ironically, it was Micky who suggested, for the club's entertainment, that Josh chat up the Sloane Ranger who stood at the bar waiting to be served. It wasn't imaginative or particularly challenging, but it was always illuminating to watch Josh work. Like a talented neurosurgeon or a great sculptor at the peak of their fame, Josh's incomparable tactics were mesmerising. However far out of Josh's league they pushed him, somehow he always found an approach which worked.

Except for one momentous occasion, that was.

The night he strolled nonchalantly over to Natasha, the chase was over almost before it began. Unbeknown to them, she'd had her eye on him for months, and she wasn't looking for a casual fling. Which was a problem, because most of Josh's relationships had the shelf life of a Danish pastry. The inevitable end of his infatuation would come a few days later, accompanied by one of his trademark routines. If you had every trick in the book to seduce people, you also had to develop a range of methods for letting them down gently.

It's not you, it's me.

I think we need a break.

I'm not sure we want the same things.

I need to concentrate on my studies.

Catholic? My Protestant family will never allow it.

I know, I thought it was unusual for foster parents to plan an arranged marriage, too.

The clinic called; it's not good news!

You mean you're not bisexual? That's awkward.

Josh never felt guilty about these lies. He genuinely believed he was protecting women from the truth, and they often accepted the alternative without disagreement. Not so with Natasha, though. She wasn't going to allow him to get away with that behaviour lightly. A Sloane Ranger wasn't accustomed to rejection or being told they couldn't have what they wanted. They'd grown up in families who spoilt them. They had watertight egos which had been pelted with platitudes and unreasonable expectations of what they'd accomplish from day zero. They had no idea how cruel the world was when the security blanket of a blinkered, overindulgent family was peeled away. Most of them would suffer the fall at some point, but that didn't mean they'd accept it. Natasha first experienced it at Josh's hand and she'd never let him forget it.

A few months later, after Josh had passed through a number of unsuspecting victims, Natasha made her move on Micky. She didn't think he was that attractive or find him remotely interesting, but of Josh's known associates, he was certainly the best candidate for her revenge. Micky's family at least had standing, class and wealth, even if he looked like a life-sized two-dimensional stick man with comedy glasses. If she couldn't have Josh, then she'd destroy what he cherished – friendship. It was a game she'd played for years to get her own way, but when it came to Josh, there was only one problem.

It didn't work very well.

Rather than drive him into a jealous rage, Josh actually encouraged the relationship. To him, it was the perfect outcome. Micky had struggled to find a girlfriend so he was happy, and Natasha had moved on. Win-win. Natasha realised she'd have to play the long game. Really long. Over the next decade, she slowly poisoned Micky against them, but disappointingly, Josh didn't recognise what she was doing. He was still none the wiser twenty years later, which only heightened her hatred of him. Eric, as usual, had noticed. He'd worked it out years ago, and in their current predicament, it was the perfect ammunition to influence Micky, but he'd need to act fast.

Sean had granted them a short preparation period before the dares were officially due to start. This, Sean claimed, was to allow *The Idiots' Club* enough time to work out how the challenges might be completed, although Eric suspected there was an alternative reason. Sean knew only too well that it would take them time and skill to wear

Micky down. They only had five days, including yesterday, and the longer it took them to get Micky's signature on the contract, the less time they'd have for reconnaissance and, crucially, for Eric to devise his Plan B.

The secret to overcoming Micky's refusal was to make his life uncomfortable, or to annoy Natasha, which amounted to the same thing. The morning after their trip to the pub, the three friends put their plan into operation. They each had individual briefs, designed to cover all bases and maximise their efforts to be a pain in her arse.

When Natasha left the house to muck out her horses in the early hours of Monday, Josh was waiting on the doorstep. He attempted to engage her in casual conversation, but she blanked him. When she arrived at the stables ten minutes later, he'd managed miraculously to beat her there. Then when she was exercising one of the ponies, he was there again, leaning on the fence, sipping tea from a travel mug and waving menacingly at her. An hour later, when she returned to the house, he'd stolen a march on her once more. This time, he'd erected a small blue tent on the lawn near the front door. Later in the day, he rang the doorbell and asked if she could spare some milk. She was horrified to find he was brewing a kettle on a small camping hob. She stomped back inside, threatening to call the police if he didn't get off her property. Every time she looked out of the kitchen window there he was, rocking back and forth on a camping stool, smoking a roll-up and waving. Every time their eyes met, her blood pressure soared.

She wasn't the only member of the Parsons family who was dealing with unwanted attention.

When Micky arrived in town to open his local pharmacy shop for the day's trade, Eric had formed a queue of one outside the shuttered door. Micky offered him a pleasant yet disaffected 'Good Morning' before unlocking it and dashing inside. Once the sign was flipped to 'Open', Eric marched in and pretended to browse the shelves, fascinated with everything from shampoo to verruca cream. After an hour, his lingering presence in the background was damaging Micky's concentration. He'd already dropped a container full of tablets over the floor and received several complaints from customers who'd been given the wrong prescriptions. At lunchtime, when Eric wasn't looking, he slipped out of the back door, only to find Callum waiting outside the bakery with a haggard grin.

Eric was still milling around the pharmacy like a nervous first-time shoplifter when Micky returned from a rather disappointing sandwich.

"Can I help you, sir," he inquired coldly.

"You can sign this," said Eric, removing a single piece of paper from his pocket and brandishing it in the air. Next to their names were five scrawled signatures and a gap by Micky's own.

"No!"

"Then…I'm just browsing," mumbled Eric, returning to his pedantic assessment of the shop's very limited range of sun creams.

When the time came to close the shop for the evening, Eric was still there, contemplating whether to finally buy something. While he'd been stalking the shelves of cosmetics, condoms and cataract cures for ten hours, Callum had been milling about outside the school gates to greet Natasha when she picked up the kids. She hurried away, and Callum was forced to follow her home by bus. Back at the house, Natasha noticed that Josh had relocated his tent to the other side of the driveway after being politely instructed to do so by a recent police visit. He'd filled the remaining time sending ninety-six text messages to Micky

– only a fraction of the ones the pharmacist received from three separate numbers today.

When an infuriated and exhausted Micky eventually returned home, he found all three camping out on the edge of his land, and he knew things were only going to get worse for him when he got in the house. Josh left his mobile phone near the door so they could get a full and detailed broadcast of the argument that raged for many hours.

The following morning, a bleary-eyed Micky arrived for work, where Eric was waiting patiently out the front looking remarkably fresh and ready to go again.

"Morning, Turnip."

Micky grunted.

"We had a splendid evening last night. Campfire, sausages on bits of whittled stick, glass of Pinot and marvellous company. How about you?" said Eric mischievously.

"Leave me alone!" implored Micky.

"If you sign this, I will...eventually," he said, holding the single page up once more.

"No!"

"Natasha in a good mood last night, was she?"

Micky frowned.

"She must have enjoyed having a bit of company yesterday. I'd imagine it must be lonely for her during the day when you're at work and the kids are at school?"

"Eric, you have to stop this. It's harassment."

"Is it?"

"Yes! She's going to make my life unbearable if you don't stop."

"I know," he grinned. "And that was only what we're capable of in a day. You know us; we always commit. We have staying power. None of us is being missed and none of us has anything better to do. How long do you think we can keep it up? How long do you think you can?"

"Eventually you'll leave, but Natasha will always be there. I fear her more than I fear you. If she found out I was involved in Sean's deal, she'd make the rest of my life a misery, not just a couple of days."

"We can make sure she doesn't find out."

"She'll find out. Women always find out."

"Well, it's your choice, Micky, but just so you know, I'm going to come here every single morning until you sign it. I'm going to loiter in your shop scaring off your customers and making your work intolerable every single day. Josh will follow Natasha like a hawk, and Callum's going to get drunk and bad-mouth you around the village until he destroys your reputation in the community."

"Jesus, Eric! That's a cheap shot."

"Oh no, you don't understand. I didn't instruct Callum to do that…I imagine that's what'll happen naturally."

"We're meant to be friends," whined Micky pitifully.

"Yes, and friends help each other out."

"And they don't launch campaigns of terror against each other!"

"Desperate times call for desperate measures. We need you," replied Eric, "and clearly, you have a very short memory."

"What do you mean by that?"

"July, nineteen ninety-nine, do you remember?" Eric said with a look of judgement.

Micky nodded subserviently.

"When your mum passed away - removing the last line of defence between you and your hostile father - who came to offer you support first?"

"You did."

"And in nineteen ninety-seven, who received a vicious

beating when they intervened in a bunch of townies lynching you on your way home from the nightclub?"

"Josh did."

"And in two thousand and six, who was it that lent you money to set up your first pharmacy shop?"

"The HSBC Bank," Micky responded.

"Oh…I thought it was Callum?"

Micky shook his head. "He's always skint."

"But he was there when your sister needed somewhere to hide when her mental boyfriend got aggressive with her, wasn't he?"

"It was a choice between Callum or Josh."

"It doesn't alter my point. We've always been there for you when you've needed us," argued Eric. "What have you done for us in return? You withdrew because Natasha holds a grudge."

Micky's defence began to crumble. His conscience, so long smothered by fear and a sense of duty to his wife, was sending him warning messages and idle threats.

"Now we need you," added Eric. "Are you going to help, or do I have to prepare for a protracted sit in?"

"What does Sean want us to do, exactly?"

"Nothing too taxing - remember, he was never any good at thinking up dares," Eric lied convincingly, knowing full well from the contract that he'd got a lot better at it.

"Fine. I'll sign, but only if we can come up with a convincing way of appeasing Natasha."

"I promise once we're done, it's the end of *The Idiots' Club* for good, and we won't bother you unless you formally invite us."

"I don't think that's likely, do you?" he replied, taking the sheet of paper and pen from Eric and signing it on the window of the shop. "How are we going to stop her finding out?"

"Don't worry, I'll come up with something brilliant!" he said with a wink.

"That's what I'm worried about," sighed Micky.

As THEY CAMPED on the roadside near Micky's house for a second evening, they floated some options to appease Natasha. They knew she wouldn't fall for anything mainstream, particularly now she smelt a rat. Sudden business trips, training events, sick relatives and jury duty were ruled out because they were easily rumbled and didn't allow the twenty-four-seven access to Micky that they needed. Josh suggested staging a kidnapping, which had legs for about half a pint – not a long period of time, based on Callum's pace of consumption.

Another favourite idea was to fake an accident designed to leave Micky in hospital, unable to receive visitors. This was tricky to pull off because if the injury was real, Micky wouldn't be much use to them, and faking it meant involving a huge number of collaborators. Callum advocated paying one of the lonely beer drinkers he'd met at The George & Dragon to pretend to be Micky. His ridiculous plot involved wrapping the decoy head to foot in bandages as a result of 'Micky's' exposure to harmful chemicals during a leak at the pharmacy. Then all they had to do, Callum explained, was bribe the local hospital to accept the wounds were real and agree to quarantine him for his own safety. Other than the obvious issues of getting everyone to agree, and keep it a secret, the main sticking point was how they explained his lack of wounds the following week when they finished completing the tasks and 'Micky' got discharged.

Eventually, the most suitable answer came from an

unexpected source.

Josh.

He recommended they tell her some of the truth in return for the only thing she really wanted – to see the back of them. It was a genius idea, and Eric was a little annoyed he'd not thought of it himself. There were risks, though. They couldn't take it back once they'd told her what they were doing, and that might prove fatal. It had to be organised and phrased right. Unless she had some control over the situation, Natasha would never agree to it.

That evening, after several phone calls and the clandestine use of Micky's printer, the group signed their second major contract of the week. This one gave Natasha guarantees that if she allowed Micky to come on 'holiday' with them for a weeklong reunion, they'd agree never to contact him, his family or her ever again. They also agreed never to enter Herefordshire in future, to avoid the unlikely event of bumping into her. Micky was pessimistic about the chance of it working, but reluctantly he agreed to follow the plan, as it beat pretending to be in a burns unit for the next seven days. As darkness descended over their camp, Natasha walked down the driveway clutching a piece of paper.

"Is this what it's going to take to get rid of you?" she announced grumpily as the men crouched over a camping stove waiting for the kettle to boil.

"Yes," said Eric, making the sign of the cross on his chest.

"And if I don't sign?"

"Then you'll have to put up with us at the end of your driveway like a bunch of middle class gypsies…forever."

"I'll call the police again," she threatened.

"They've already been. Nice guys. Apparently, there's nothing illegal about what we're doing now and they also mentioned that if we saw you, we should advise you to stop calling or they'll arrest you for wasting police time. Message sent. Sausage?" He waved a stick at her with what smelt like burnt roadkill on the end.

"No!"

"Suit yourself."

"How can I be sure you won't go back on the deal?" she probed aggressively.

"If you look at the contract, you'll see we've included a special clause in the unlikely event that would ever occur."

Eric had never hired a personal lawyer before, Josh only knew divorce specialists and Callum hadn't paid his corporate legal fees for some considerable time. Fortunately though, they all knew one who might help. Up against considerable time pressure, they'd reached out to Clarence Douville, who was only too happy to draft the contract and agree to act as an intermediary should there be any future disputes. He'd been a little too helpful in truth, which only cemented Eric's opinion that the situation was not as it appeared.

"What clause?"

"Section nine," stated Eric.

Natasha ruffled furiously through the pages like an aggrieved sibling challenging an inheritance.

"We, the undersigned," she read out loud, "agree that if any conditions in paragraph six fail to be met, the claimant will have access to all documents held by Mr Clarence Douville. What documents, specifically?"

"If you can provide evidence that any of us has broken our commitments to stay away from you, your family and the county of Herefordshire after a period of ten days from now, Mr Douville will grant you access to information the three of us would prefer stayed private. Every misdemeanour, moral misjudgement and undiscovered illegal act we've been responsible for over the last decade would be yours to use at your leisure. Our current reputations and future prospects would rest in your hands."

Natasha smiled demonically. "Part of me hopes you breach the contract."

It was a high price to pay to secure Micky's involvement. Natasha wouldn't hesitate to use the information, and now Sean's lawyer held their darkest secrets in perpetuity. The list of indiscretions was explosive, and in the wrong hands, it would be enough to bury them several times over. Callum's industrial-scale tax evasion, Josh's collection of sex tapes which were so risqué they'd not even make it into Amsterdam's Sex Museum, and Eric's multiple lapses with his employer's expense accounts, client confidentiality and black market wheeling and dealing.

"Do we have an understanding?" asked Eric calmly.

"Ten days?"

"Yes, and not an hour more."

"That's next Friday evening at eight thirty-four," she indicated precisely.

"I'll even round it down to eight-thirty for you," replied Eric smugly.

Micky was between a rock and a hard place. If he helped them complete whatever tasks Sean had set, Natasha won. If they failed, she hit the jackpot. He'd never wipe the smile off her face. Her control over him would be absolute. What's more, now he had to engage in a load of juvenile stupidity with a bunch of unpredictable human time-bombs likely to leave him in even more trouble. All because he felt obliged to help them even though they'd given him few reasons as to why.

Natasha added her name to the bottom of the contract, planted a cold uninterested kiss on her husband's cheek and almost skipped back to the manor house.

"Pay up!" demanded Callum jubilantly.

Josh removed ten pounds from his wallet and passed it across the circle.

"What's that for?" asked Micky.

"I didn't think she'd go for it," replied Josh.

"It was your idea!" gasped Eric.

"I know, but I'm not as confident about my ideas as you are."

"I didn't think she'd go for it, either," uttered Micky, looking glum. "I've had enough for one day; what time do you want to meet in the morning?"

"Morning? We can't wait that long. We have to start planning immediately," insisted Eric. "Sean has given us until Wednesday midnight before the dares begin. That's tomorrow. We need every spare second if we're going to pull this off."

"If it's any consolation," Josh offered sympathetically with a nod to the house, "I don't think you're getting any tonight."

"A normal evening, then," sighed Micky.

"Really? You surprise me, mate. When Natasha and I were dating, she couldn't get enough of it! Like an animal, she was."

Micky's self-confidence hit the ground floor. It rarely got much higher than level two these days.

"That's not helpful," Eric maintained sternly.

"I still don't know what Sean wants us to do?" mumbled Micky, as if the events of the last twenty-four hours had occurred only in his nightmares. "I've signed the damn thing without even looking at it."

"Pub?" suggested Callum, glancing around at the others.

"Pub," agreed Eric.

THIRTEEN

THE FIVE DARES

The atmosphere in The George & Dragon was not dissimilar to their last visit on Sunday evening. The regular patrons were slightly more jaded, the smoke from the open fire was a little thicker, the background soundtrack – courtesy of a lone guitarist exclusively playing Bob Dylan covers extremely poorly – was a little noiser, and as before, the landlord cut the appearance of someone with the sole purpose of haranguing anyone responsible for keeping him in business.

Two heavily laden trays were escorted over to their now regular spot next to the fire. The draughty lead-lined panes struggled to adequately protect them from the weather outside, where night had drawn in and only the rutted car park was visible under the dimly illuminated pub sign. It wasn't much lighter inside. Apart from the fire, only the dull glow from grime-coated bulbs on dodgy wall fixtures struggled to cut its way through the heavy shadows of the lounge bar. Eric wiped the table clean of spillage with a beer towel, laid Sean's contract in front of him and turned his phone's torch on to help them read.

His eyes settled on three faces he'd known for more than half his life, worn down and weathered from the passing years but as familiar to him as a cherished pair of slippers, and a wave of nostalgia washed over him. His expression softened, and the group tuned in to the trans-formation in his demeanour. Gone was the bitterness which burnt ferociously in his eyes. Gone was the emotional barricade which kept others from getting too close. Cracks had appeared in his rigid iron-like will and, most unusually, a warm smile hijacked his normally dead-pan, often unwelcoming, expression.

"You okay?" inquired Josh in concern.

"Perfect. I've just experienced something."

"Is it a stroke? We had a TED talk at work about it once. Your face has gone kind of…droopy," observed Callum, who almost instinctively mimicked the effect.

"Nostalgia," corrected Eric. "Don't you see?"

The others shrugged, failing to understand the significance.

"The four of us, in a pub, about to discuss what dares we're going to do," explained Eric. "For a split second, I went back in time. I didn't see your world-weary faces; I saw youthful excited smiles, long unkempt hair and hope."

"That's odd, because I see four middle-aged losers, in a shit, barely solvent pub, about to embark on a campaign of lunacy almost certain to eviscerate any threads of hope we've blindly held onto in our naive quest to achieve even a modicum of normalcy," declared Micky grumpily.

The moment of nostalgia popped, and reality forced its way back into focus.

"I'll bet you're a great laugh at reunions!" said Josh.

"Let's cut the soppy flashbacks and read it, shall we?" demanded Micky, pointing at the contract, still the only one who didn't know what it contained.

"I will read out the dares in the order I think we should tackle them," expressed Eric assertively. "Easiest and least likely to propel us into internet celebrities first, most difficult at the end."

"Why would any of them make us internet celebrities?" asked Micky nervously.

"Because we might go viral," professed Josh optimistically.

"How?"

"We have to livestream our dares," clarified Callum between gulps of lager.

"WHAT!"

"It's in the contract," confirmed Eric. "Maybe you should have read it before you signed!"

"Maybe I would have if I'd not been subjected to psychological warfare and stalking."

"Too late now, I'm afraid," Eric responded curtly.

"You've always been a deceitful, manipulative asshole!" growled Micky. "You knew I wouldn't have signed if I knew the truth."

"Yes, because you've become a wimp who's frightened of everything."

"Up yours," he mumbled.

"Calm down, boys," insisted Josh, attempting to take the heat out of the situation.

"Oh, you want me to be like you, Josh! Is that it? Your approach is so horizontal you make the Equator jealous. Not all of us want to bumble through life avoiding accountability. You take what you want and leave before the cleanup operation begins. Don't tell me to calm down!"

Josh shrugged, immune to all degrees of insult. "Remember, Micky, I've had sex with your wife...lots of sex."

Micky jabbed him in the nose with an instinctive

clenched fist, knocking him backwards off his stool. Josh bounced up like a Subbuteo player, primed to retaliate, but his offensive parry was suffocated by Callum's hasty intervention. When Callum was in his, rarely experienced, idle pre-binge drinking mode, he behaved like a passive coward. But after he passed the six pint threshold, fear and consequence were locked away in a restricted part of his brain alongside shame, logic, brevity and moral decency. He manoeuvred his body in between them.

"I might be lost, Micky," said Josh coolly, "but at least I'm not trapped."

"Sit down and have a drink," advised Callum, who was still holding an aggressive pose even if his words were incongruously mild. "We can't do this, boys - not today."

"It's you I'm actually most angry with," announced Micky. "You've always been the sensible one, the most trustworthy. Why didn't you warn me?"

"I couldn't. I knew you'd say no."

"Too right I would."

"Look, I need Sean's money to grow my business. When you've had a past business failure…"

"Eleven," interrupted Eric.

"…the options are limited," he continued.

"But there's bound to be a better way than this," countered Micky.

"No. I've tried everything."

"I'm sorry, Callum," said Micky honestly, "but Sean's money isn't going to solve your problems. Sometimes you have to rely on your own resilience rather than some get-rich-quick scheme."

"That's not the point," growled Eric. "If the normal banking system won't let Callum in, then we have to circumvent the rules. That's how we survive."

"But it did let him in - eleven times - it's just he didn't

repay his loans! It's not discrimination; it's simple economics. Maybe it's time to accept the system is there for a reason and you will have to live within it."

"I'm going to," said Callum before Eric reengaged with the argument.

"What?"

"It's no good, Eric. I've tried my best, but it's time to admit defeat. I'm not cut out to be an entrepreneur. Once we've completed Sean's dares and secured the money, I'm going straight. No more risk taking, no more 'next big thing' and no more delusions of grandeur."

"What about the booze? Are you going to give that up, too?" inquired Josh.

"Even regular people drink moderately."

"Yes, they do…and you're neither."

"Don't judge him," countered Micky.

"I'll do what I like, thanks."

The booth at the back of the bar by the fire descended into a tennis match of forceful disagreements and incriminations even overpowering the inaccurate mumblings of the Bob Dylan impersonator. The landlord glared threateningly at them and, worried about being ejected, Callum took matters into his own hands.

"Stop! This is stupid."

Shaken by the unexpected force of their telling off, they ceased fire.

"Whatever grudges we hold against each other, we have to put them behind us. Right now, I need my friends to help me out, and by the looks of it, none of them appear to like each other very much. Let's focus on what we're up against. Five dares in seven days, one day remaining to plan and ten million quid if we succeed. I want that money, but there's something more important to me. I want the chance for the four of us to rebuild bridges.

To bring the curtain down on *The Idiots' Club* the way it deserved, not the way it ended. One last opportunity to join forces and remember what we used to be...friends," said Callum grandly, gripping the side of the table for both balance and dramatic effect.

Life had altered immeasurably since the last Friday dare night some twenty years ago, but as their eyes met, a flickering connection, once stronger than reinforced concrete, drew them together. Back then, all they had was each other. *The Idiots' Club* against the world, their shared experience of life's hardship the glue which kept them together. Their commitment to protect each other from danger, a reassuring safety net from the cruel blows life had in store for them. From a young age, they'd faced plenty of hardship, but those challenges never seemed so difficult when they worked together.

"Callum's right," agreed Micky. "We've been worn down by the world we once tried to hide from. I'm sorry I haven't been a great friend over these past ten years."

"None of us have," added Eric.

"Whatever it is that you need, Callum, I'm behind you one hundred percent."

Eric reached across the table to exchange a firm hand-shake and a subtle knowing nod with Micky.

Josh did likewise but couldn't help adding, "You'll probably regret that statement when you hear about dare two!"

"At the moment, I don't know what any of them are," responded Micky, giving Eric an encouraging nod to read through the contract.

"Dare number one," announced Eric. "Sean wants us to evacuate Exeter University campus in the middle of a weekday afternoon."

"Easy," scoffed Josh. "*The Idiots' Club* did that plenty of times back in the day."

"It won't be as easy now."

"Why not?"

"There are twice the number of students, more buildings and tighter security. You can't just wander around campus the way you did in the old days."

"Bloody terrorists have ruined everything," joked Callum as he failed dismally to build a tower of beer mats.

"And we have to livestream it? How does that work?" said Micky.

"We all have to be identifiable during the dare at some point."

"But not throughout."

"No. Sean said as long as he can see that we've all been involved in the dare, then that's enough for him," confirmed Eric.

"And what does Sean consider evacuated?" probed Micky who always possessed a deeply analytical mind. "Surely he won't know if one person stayed inside, would he?"

"Once the emergency services arrive and the Vice Chancellor triggers the evacuation plan, then it's likely to be their policy that everyone has to leave. But it won't be simple. Each University building has a separate alarm system, so even if we set one off it would only result in emptying that building, not all of them."

"How do we manage to do all of them, then?"

"Don't worry; I have a plan."

Eric always said he had a plan. Most of the time he did and it was considered, effective and ingenious. Occasionally it was slap dash, last minute and dodgy. Once in a while it didn't exist at all - like this one - but Eric's confident statements would always confuse them as to which of the three it was, to the point where it was best not to challenge him and go with the flow.

"Dare two is where it gets really interesting."

"Go on," Micky noted nervously, reminded of Josh's earlier reference to it.

"One of us has to propose to Jessica Connelly…and she has to accept."

An uncomfortable silence enveloped the booth as the three of the occupants who already knew this information waited anxiously to see how the newly informed one might react.

"Sean's a prick," moaned Micky.

"Oh yeah."

"Got to admit, though, he's better at this than he used to be," said Callum, adding his positive spin.

"Propose what?" questioned Micky.

"Marriage," confirmed Eric.

"Are you sure?"

"Yes."

"What makes you sure?"

"It says so in the contract," replied Eric, pointing it out in black and white.

"Bollocks."

"Does anyone even know where Jessica is?" quizzed Josh after a period of silence.

"She's an actress working in the West End, London, but I think her whereabouts are probably the least of our worries, don't you?" said Eric.

Jessica Connelly earnt a First-Class Honours degree in drama from Exeter University. Such distinctions were rare, but she earnt an even more rare one. Jessica was the only girl from any year group, hall of residence, faculty - student

or lecturer – or resident of the entire county of Devon who
successfully spurned Josh Foxole's advances. Not just once
either. He tried multiple times, believing, quite falsely, that
she misunderstood his intentions on the first few occasions.
He pursued her for months, shocked that his charms
appeared to be failing him. Every time he tried, a total of
twenty-three if the records kept by Eric were reliable, she
turned him down. The more he asked, the more he wanted
her, blind to all others. Josh spent many dry months after
his last attempt, disabled by self-doubt until she finally
relented and told him the truth.

She fancied Micky.

Which was a problem, because Micky had recently
formed a relationship with Natasha and the Sloane Ranger
wasn't letting go anytime soon.

"She'll never go for it," declared Josh confidently.
"She's definitely a lesbian."

"Just because someone doesn't fancy you, it doesn't
make them homosexual," Eric pointed out.

"There's no other explanation. Do you know how
many heterosexual women have turned me down?"

"One," confirmed Eric. "Jessica."

"Go on, guess."

"Is it…Jessica Connelly."

"Heterosexual women!"

"JESSICA CONNELLY," they stated harmoniously.

"Lesbian! I know for a fact she is, because she was in a
relationship with Sally Harmer," he argued, more flustered
than they were ever used to seeing him. "God's truth!"

"Sally Harmer, the Snake Charmer!"

"No…the third-year geography student," disputed
Josh.

"Yes, exactly. She shagged more men than Christine
Keeler."

"You're thinking of someone else."

"No, I'm not. Google her," pressed Eric. "I think Sally Harmer married Paul Cousins from your business studies course, didn't she, Callum?"

Callum was preoccupied with a bout of hiccups and the challenge of holding his breath between gulps of beer in order to shift them.

"The point is, whether she's gay or straight doesn't make a blind bit of difference - somebody needs to propose to her," said Eric, eyeballing Micky and dispensing one of his persuasive nods.

"No! I'm not doing it."

"You said you were behind us one hundred percent," Josh reminded him.

"I was rounding up from ninety-nine."

"It has to be you," Eric asserted. "She's not going to say yes to any of us."

"I'm willing to have another crack at it," maintained Josh confidently.

"I think the rejection might tip you over the edge, mate. It has to be Micky."

"Number one," Micky counted on his fingers, "I'm already married. Number two, if Natasha found out she'd flay me alive and then I wouldn't be. Number three, it's a despicable thing to inflict on someone."

"I'm buoyed by your answer," replied Eric.

"Are you? Why?"

"Because you didn't say it couldn't be done, only that there were reasons it shouldn't be done."

"Four, it can't be done."

"Too late. Anyway, I already have a plan. It's not illegal to ask someone to marry you if you're already married; you just can't go through with the wedding. We'll make sure Natasha doesn't find out, and I'm sure we can make it up to Jessica in some way after Sean has handed over the money. She's a minor actress in the theatre. You know what that means, don't you?"

"She works…hic…nights?"

"She's skint."

"You can't buy everyone," said Micky.

"Dare number three," continued Eric, ignoring Micky's growing moral resistance and quickly changing the subject. "Abduct Logan Cobley."

"God, I hate that guy," uttered Josh furiously. "Fucking snitch."

Everyone nodded. It was the first sign of unity since they'd arrived on Micky's doorstep two days ago.

"Me, too," agreed Eric. "Logan was the single most annoying man to ever study at any University…ever. Bloody do-gooder."

Logan Cobley was a one-time roommate of Sean Heschmeyer. One of the most identifiable 'spods' on campus, he took it on himself to stop *The Idiots' Club* at all costs and at every opportunity. His desire to protect the University's reputation was on a par with Sir Andrew Carrington's, and Logan was frequently seen leaving the Vice Chancellor's office after disclosing intelligence he'd collected on the club's next dare. When confronted by the group about his reasons for curtailing their fun, his only defence was, 'It's the right thing to do.'

It was the main, but not the only, reason the group hated him.

Logan's attitude was the antithesis of their own. The kryptonite to their determination not to be restricted, silenced or controlled. The battle raged for most of their time in Exeter, but by their third year, Logan had success-fully disrupted the group's activities so often they had to devise a decoy plot to keep him off their scent. Typically, Logan's determination to impede them only spurred Eric to devise even more elaborate and risky challenges for them.

"Why have you put that in third?" asked Micky. "It shouldn't be too hard. Logan was a puny man; he won't put up much of a fight."

"It's third because the last time I checked, abduction is still a crime and as we'll be livestreaming it, I imagine by this point the authorities might put in an appearance - making the final two tasks even harder."

"Why don't you put it in last, then?"

"Because dare four is even more illegal."

"How can something be more illegal?" said Micky, puzzled. "Either it's against the law or it isn't."

"Did I say more illegal? I meant to say more difficult."

"What's dare four, then?"

"Another abduction."

"Then why is it more difficult?"

"It involves a lion."

"Wh…at?" gasped Micky, struggling to get the word out of his mouth.

"Sean wants us to steal a lion."

After pulling a number of faces which Micky's brain couldn't fully decipher because they suggested a range of emotions from hysteria to genuine confusion, he finally spoke the only appropriate word he could find. "Why?"

"The dude's rich," explained Josh. "Rich people buy everything they want legitimately, and after that, they want what money can't buy."

"M'ybe…itz a pet?" slurred Callum, who'd quietly disengaged from the group to finish off a round of small shot glasses filled with brown liquid, the medical effects of which the publican of The George & Dragon insisted he took no responsibility for.

"Who'd want a pet lion?!" blurted Micky.

"Hermann Goring," answered Eric.

"Hermann Goring had a lion?"

"Seven, but not at the same time."

"No, because that would be stupid," mocked Micky.

"Goring must have had balls of steel," added Josh inconsequentially. "Not satisfied with dodging the nightly threat from allied air raids, Goring thought, 'How can I up the danger level? I know - let's put a lion in the house!' Hardcore."

"I think you're forgetting the man was a mass murdering Nazi," said Micky sternly.

"Obviously not. I'm just saying it's bold, that's all."

"I don' sees…what…hic…'meyer has in common with Goring?" ruminated Callum, mostly aiming his comments at the beer-drenched table.

"Both German?" Josh speculated.

"It doesn't really matter why Sean wants us to steal a lion. The fact remains it's our fourth dare," summarised Eric.

"But you've got a plan for that, too, no doubt?"

"Obviously. It's the single hardest thing we've ever had to take on, so it's going to take one hell of a plan. I have six ideas currently."

Eric knew this to be an overstatement designed purely to put the others at ease. The actual number of options he was working on was smaller by the count of six. It didn't faze him; if David Copperfield could make an elephant disappear, he was confident he could have the same effect on a lion.

"What's the final task?" asked Micky, expecting Eric to

describe something impossible like playing soccer on the moon or infiltrating the Pentagon.

"Dare five is the easiest."

"Why leave it until the end, then?"

"Because it's also the most significant and personal. Sean wants one of us to climb the Miles Clock Tower in Exeter and remove one of its hands."

The symbolism wasn't lost on anyone. Even Callum, who was nodding backwards and forwards on his stool desperately trying to ward off unconsciousness, knew what it meant. The clock tower dare had been the last any of them had attempted before *The Idiots' Club* was forced to fold. It had resulted in Sean's injuries, Eric's arrest and the erosion of their friendship. Everything changed that night, and not only for Sean, who clearly was making a point by including it.

"Why don't we get that one done immediately?" asked Josh. "Give us a boost before the trickier ones."

"No. It has to be last," insisted Eric forcefully. "It ends at the Miles Clock Tower as it did before, but this time in success."

Callum fell backwards and landed in a heap on the twisted, ancient floorboards. He narrowly avoided cracking his head on the wooden booth behind him. The only notable reaction to this by the others was to check their watches to confirm the time before nodding their affirmation and breaking into a collective smile. Right on schedule. Much had changed down the years, but it was reassuring to find not everything had.

"Evacuate a major University, propose to a lesbian, kidnap a spod, steal a lion and climb a tower," summarised Josh. "Should be an interesting week."

"A toast!" Eric stood up from the table and raised his glass.

Micky picked up one of Callum's unfinished drinks.

"I thought you were off it," pointed out Josh.

"Not this week," Micky replied solemnly. "I'm going to need it."

"To *The Idiots' Club*," announced Eric.

Drinks were necked and glasses struck the table.

FOURTEEN
THE PRICE OF SUCCESS

On account of his self-inflicted blackout, Callum missed the rest of the evening and their agreed strategy for the next twenty-four hours. Each of them would focus on one specific dare before reporting back to the others at Eric's apartment in Battersea the following night. The only dare which needed no further reconnaissance was the final one. They all knew where the clock tower was, how to climb it properly and the ideal time of night to scale it. The risks would be the same as they were twenty years ago - the police, security cameras and nosy neighbours - but this time they'd approach it without the added pressure of being pissed. The only outstanding question about the fifth dare was who would do the honours, and as there was a reasonable chance they might not get that far, they put the decision off until a later date.

The other four tasks were allocated based on each man's personal knowledge of the target. Josh would travel by train to Exeter from Herefordshire to run reconnaissance on dare one. Eric already had a well-formed plan about how to achieve a full evacuation of campus, so Josh was given a list of information to check how feasible it might be. Micky was going to run point on dare two. He'd need to find out as much data about Jessica Connelly as he could. Place of work, home address, friends, potential relationships, pressure points, hobbies and, most crucially from their perspective, whether she was already married or not – to a man or a woman, Josh pointed out less than helpfully.

Callum, who had no say in the division of responsibilities because he was cluttering up the walkway to The George & Dragon's toilets for much of it, was designated dare three. None of them had seen or heard anything about Logan Cobley for almost twenty years. None of them moved in the same circles as he did, and they weren't connected through any of the social media streams. Primarily this was because they hated him, but also, and crucially, he didn't appear to be on any. Tracking him down might be more of a challenge than Micky stalking Jessica. The first thing Callum had to establish was whether Logan was still alive. A negative answer would require a lot more shovelling and a lot less chloroform to achieve a successful abduction.

Finally, Eric would tackle the not inconsiderable task of how to best relocate a lion without anyone noticing. A day was an insufficient amount of time to solve such a quandary when the list of unknowns was long enough to fill a phonebook.

How many lions were there in the United Kingdom?

Which were closest?

How were they housed?

What was the security like?

What would it take to knock one out?

How long would it take before the animal was docile enough to carry?

How much might one weigh?

How would they move it around?

What transport would they need?

Where would they put a lion once they'd caught it?

And so the list went on.

By the end of the following day, Eric had answered none of these questions. Not one. Not because the information was that hard to find. It wouldn't have taken him five minutes to discover that lions were, on average, about two hundred kilos in weight and the best tranquiliser to use was a combination of medetomidine and zolazepam-tiletamine. Eric hadn't even pretended to look. In fact, he'd reserved none of the allotted time to focus on the subject of lions at all. Instead, he'd spent the day focusing on a rather different mammal entirely. Stealing a lion was one thing, but convincing the authorities they hadn't, when the evidence would be overwhelmingly against them, was another level of cunning altogether. The contingency plan was more important than the dare and would invariably require the involvement of a third party. Someone who'd jump at the chance to get one over on Eric and the boys, and he thought he knew just the person for the job.

At around eight o'clock on the Wednesday evening, the team arrived in dribs and drabs at Eric's flat. Only Josh had been before and he would almost certainly be the last to get there, having been forced to spend much of the last twenty-four hours imprisoned on British Rail trains. Micky was the first, boringly punctual as always. There were upsides and downsides of being born into a military family, but being late couldn't be categorised as either.

Micky stretched out his arm to knock on flat sixty-three's door only to find it flew open before his knuckles made contact.

"Turnip!" said Eric warmly. "Come on in."

"How did you…"

"Over the years," Eric preempted his guest's question, "I've timed exactly how long it takes for someone to reach my flat on the sixth floor the moment I buzz them in from the foyer. I like to test myself, see if I can open the door before they knock. Bang on again."

"Have you heard about something called 'hobbies'," offered Micky sarcastically.

"Huh?" said Eric, helping Micky escape his jacket and hanging it on the posh coat stand next to the door.

"If you're bored - why don't you try squash or golf?"

"Too many rules," huffed Eric.

"Fine, but I think you need something more to fill your spare time than estimating how long someone's journey will take in your lift."

"I do. That's why you're here, isn't it."

Micky strolled down the corridor and into a lounge which was blessed with spectacular views over the city. In the distance to his right were the iconic landmarks of the London Eye and Big Ben, and to his left, much closer to the flat, Battersea Power Station. It was shrouded by idle cranes that waited patiently for the contractors to return and continue work on its massive redevelopment. The murky brown waters of the Thames struggled slowly towards the sea as if several centuries of pollution weighed them down. The opulence of the apartment's interior took Micky's breath away. He knew Eric had a successful career in advertising, but this place was straight out of one of those celebrity magazines his wife was obsessed with.

A huge TV which wouldn't have been out of place at an open air concert had hijacked one side of the room. In the centre, a long elegant table was penned in by ten cream leather chairs, and everywhere he looked a vast collection of expensive art - sculptures, oil paintings and glistening trinkets - grabbed his attention. The styling demanded one overwhelming descriptor from anyone who might utter it.

Bling.

"Shit," wheezed Micky.

"Is that a review?"

"No. But...how did you...I mean...it's...what can I say..."

"Fabulous, isn't it?"

Micky nodded. "Do you flat share with a rapper?"

"No, it's just me."

"What did it cost you?" asked Micky insensitively.

"Couple of million, but that was a few years ago now. Drink?"

Micky nodded vacantly as if his head wasn't properly attached to his shoulders anymore. Eric approached a leather-panelled cabinet and swung the double doors open to reveal a drinks bar stocked with an array of expensive single malts, ancient bottles of brandy and rare liquors.

"Scotch?"

Micky's head wobbled again in agreement.

"This is a very rare nineteen eighty-four Rosebank single malt." Eric passed Micky a crystal tumbler with a double shot of amber liquid swirling around the bottom. "They decommissioned the distillery in the early nineties, so there's only a limited supply of it left. What do you think?"

Micky put the glass to his lips and took an impossibly small sip, as if this shot was the very last one left. "Superb. Really smooth, and I'm not usually a connoisseur of the stuff."

"That's about fifty quid's worth, so I suggest you don't get used to it. When Callum gets here, not a word of this," smiled Eric, waving his hand at the collection of bottles. "He can have a weak lager from the fridge."

"Sure. Probably best if…blimey…is that…" Micky advanced excitedly towards the wall and a framed picture of colourful dots painted in a square pattern. "…is it a Hirst!"

"Yeah. One of only a hundred. Cost me a pretty penny at auction, I can tell you. When Josh saw it he said it was 'barely better than what his nephew could produce' - which is true, but that kind of misses the point," explained Eric.

"And what is the point?"

"Josh's nephew isn't Damien Hirst. Cheers." Eric chinked his friend's glass before taking a sizeable gulp of whisky.

"Eric, if you have all of this," Micky waved his hand vaguely around the pristine apartment, "why don't you enjoy it?"

"I do," he replied unconvincingly.

"People who enjoy life don't tend to place incendiary devices underneath themselves. You don't need Sean's dares. You don't even need to work if you have all of these assets. Why do you want to put yourself through it?"

"Do you like the painting?" inquired Eric, pointing back to the Hirst and appearing to quickly change the subject.

"Yes."

"And would you like it any more if I told you I paid twenty thousand pounds for it?"

"Christ, Eric! Of course I don't like it more, I just wouldn't pay that much for a print."

"Why not?"

"Because it's a small painting of some colourful dots, and for twenty grand, there are other things I'd rather spend my money on. Like a car."

"And what if I told you that it isn't even a genuine

Hirst but a forgery by an eighteen-year-old art student from Dartford? What would your reaction be then if I told you I'd spent twenty grand on it?"

"I'd say you were totally out of your mind," replied Micky, leaning in closer to examine the signature in the bottom right-hand corner. "Very convincing fake, though."

"It's not a fake. Not even I'm that crazy. My point is that the value of an item changes dependent on our view of factors outside the object itself. The art becomes almost irrelevant. If Damien Hirst vomited on a canvas, put a wooden frame around it and called it 'Inner Self', someone would pay through the nose to own it. If Callum did that, they'd probably have him sectioned."

"I still don't see what that's got to do with you?"

"The reputation of the creator is more important than the quality of the object itself," said Eric.

"Only if you're an easily impressed fool. I don't change my view on an item's beauty or quality based on how rare it is or how famous its creator was," scoffed Micky blindly.

"Of course you do."

"I don't!"

"You're being naïve, Micky. It's only human nature."

"Prove it!"

"Okay, I will. The whisky you're drinking isn't a rare single malt worth fifty pounds a shot. It's a cheap over-the-counter blend from the supermarket around the corner. The really shit stuff which tramps drink from brown paper bags while they sit idle on park benches, scaring the general public."

"I don't believe you."

Eric retrieved the bottle from the bar. It had a vaguely Polish-sounding name and smelt like singed fabric. Micky sniffed the glass and the bottle to compare.

"I tampered with your sense of taste and smell simply

by telling you a convincing story about the whisky you were supposed to try. In the context of the apartment, its contents and my lavish lifestyle, it was almost impossible that you'd say you didn't like it."

"What's the real Rosebank like?" asked Micky curiously.

"Delightful."

Micky was disappointed to see that Eric wasn't going to pour him a glass to find out for himself.

"In answer to your original question – why, if I have all this, do I need Sean's dares? Because I have enough stuff to last me several lifetimes, but what I want most doesn't come with a price tag. I want to be held with the same esteem as the notorious Mr Hirst here."

"Perhaps you should join an art class?" proposed Micky.

"No need. What we are about to do this week will be my masterpiece."

The intercom buzzed before Micky was able to explore the conversation further. Eric pressed the telephone receiver and unlocked the ground-floor entrance to allow Callum access to the building.

He raised his shiny Rolex watch. "You took one minute and seventeen seconds. I factored in how you march rather than walk. I imagine, given the time of the evening, that Callum is on at least his sixth drink, so he's at more of a swaying stage rather than a staggering pace. I'm going to estimate one minute and forty-three seconds. Shall we make it interesting?"

"A bet?"

"Fifty quid."

"Yeah, why not. If I win, I'll swap the fifty for a shot of that whisky. It has to be precise, though; there's no leeway on this."

"I started my stopwatch the moment I buzzed him in," replied Eric, displaying his wristwatch. "I won't take even a second either side."

The two men sauntered down the hallway to wait patiently at the door. Eric held out his arm so both of them were able to follow the watch ticking by one second at a time. One minute passed and there was still no knock. One minute and thirty seconds went by and there was no sound of movement on the other side of the door. Micky's pulse was picking up pace, and without expecting it, he let out an excitable giggle. Eric grinned. It wasn't about the money; it was purely about the game. A little moment of shared nonsense to break the monotony and ease the stress of modern life, just like they'd done so regularly in the past. On exactly one minute and forty-three seconds, Eric firmly grabbed the handle and threw open the door.

He'd been supremely confident about the readjustments he'd made to the timings and was certain the outcome would be identical to when Micky arrived earlier that evening. The timings had been perfectly recalibrated, but time was only one of the variables he should have taken into account. 'Perfectly calibrated' was never an appropriate description when it came to Callum. Outside flat sixty-one, across the corridor from them, Callum was propped against the wall and banging furiously on the door.

"The Dobichevs are in the Bahamas this week," sighed Eric. "You're welcome to come in here, though."

"Boys!" hollered Callum to celebrate his achievement.

Micky held out his hand, and Eric removed a crisp note from his wallet. He immediately passed it back and whispered, "One shot of the rare stuff, please, barman!"

Callum's trench coat was hung next to Micky's and a can of weak lager removed from the fridge. Eric poured the contents into a glass for his new visitor. Once Callum's admiration for the apartment had been subdued with the necessary answers, the three men pulled up a leather dining chair and reviewed their research. There was no time to wait for Josh's arrival which, if his text message was accurate, wouldn't be for at least another hour. They'd fill him in on the other dares when they got the opportunity.

"I suggest we start with you, Callum," announced Eric.

"I thought my dare was going to be number three?"

"It is, but Josh isn't here yet, and while you're still able to pronounce consonants, we should take advantage of it."

"Don't mock me," blasted Callum indignantly. "I've built and run a dozen businesses over the last two decades, you know."

"And like your sobriety, they all begin with promise and enthusiasm, and end broke, tired, damaged, disorientated and with kebab sauce down their shirts."

"If you were self-employed, you'd know what it was like," scoffed Callum. "Drinking is the only way to get through the day."

"Did you find Logan?" demanded Eric, changing the subject before he was drawn into a wasteful debate with a drunk unable to face up to his own addiction.

"Yes." Callum removed his phone and scrolled through his recent photos. He selected one and placed it in the middle of the table. "That's him."

"Bollocks it is!" insisted Eric.

"Logan was a nine-stone weakling," added Micky in agreement. "He was thinner than a rake and geeky looking."

"People change," replied Callum.

"But he's massive. I mean, look at him - he's too big for the photograph."

"Sorry, I zoomed in."

"Oh yeah, that's much better! So you took the photo from about twenty metres away and yet I can still see his massive biceps. How do you know this is Logan Cobley?"

"It's not."

"Huh…even for you it's early."

"This man's name is Peter Francis..."

"Well that's not him, then, is it, you idiot," huffed Eric before Callum could finish.

"Which is what he calls himself now…" continued Callum, "…for security reasons."

"He has an alias, why?" enquired Micky.

"To protect himself and his family, I'd imagine."

"From what?"

Callum necked the remaining dregs of lager and nodded to Eric for another. Eric shook his head. "Mr Francis here, formerly known as Logan Cobley, works for a company called Stonehouse, who specialise in foreign security projects. He and his colleagues are hired as private operatives in war zones to protect foreign dignitaries, guard property and sweep for enemy hostiles or explosive devices."

"Shit."

"Shit indeed," interjected Callum. "I'll tell you more for another can of lager!"

Eric went to the fridge to fill up Callum's glass so he didn't notice the contents of the can were actually alcohol free.

"How did you find him?" asked Micky.

"When I couldn't find any record of Logan online, either dead or alive, I contacted a friend of mine who works for the Ministry of Defence. Safe to say we've both broken quite a few laws in the process."

"Sean must have known," growled Eric. "He's

connected to hundreds of politicians and civil servants. What else do you know about Logan's new life?"

"He's in the country at the moment, but he's due to fly out to Yemen at the end of the month to protect British interests. When he's at home, he lives here in London."

"And is he," Eric paused, "equipped?"

"The man has been shot twice, lost several body parts - including a foot - in an IED explosion, rescued several hostages from ISIS captors, has access to an arsenal of weaponry the mafia would be proud of and is likely to have the most technologically advanced security system that money can buy. And that's only the half of it. He also has friends."

"Friends? What are we talking here, mates from the pub?"

"A brotherhood who will stop at nothing to keep him safe. The other employees of Stonehouse."

"Anything else," muttered Eric.

"Yes. He's a black belt in several martial arts."

"We're screwed," confirmed Micky. "Abducting any old Joe would be hard enough, but Sean wants us to kidnap Rambo!"

"Nothing is impossible," said Eric confidently. "Any pressure points?"

"Weaknesses!" Callum snorted. "Didn't you hear what I said? The guy's a black ops mercenary."

"Everyone has a pressure point; we just need to find Logan's."

"I didn't find any."

"Wife? Family?"

"If there are any, their identities are protected."

"Ambitions?"

"I'd imagine it's not getting killed in Yemen."

"What about this 'brotherhood' you mentioned?" asked Micky.

"According to my MoD contact, they call themselves 'The Five Horsemen'. It used to be six but one of them was blown up in Afghanistan, the same incident that claimed Logan's foot. They always work together. They've sworn an oath of allegiance to watch over one another. They're almost one symbiotic organism - take one of them on and you take all of them on."

"Five Rambos," huffed Micky. "Lovely! Can I go back to being a pharmacist now?"

"No," snapped Eric. "We knew Sean wasn't going to make this easy. He has a point to prove, and so do we. This is a defining moment. It's like that Hirst over there. Which of us is going to rise to the top? How many other unknown artists as talented as Hirst are there in the world? Thousands. Hundreds of thousands. It's Sean or us, and it has to be us."

"For fuck's sake, Eric, can't you just admit we're out of our depth on this one?" argued Micky.

"No."

"How do you expect four middle-aged, unfit chumps like us to overcome a bunch of hired mercenaries? They're used to war zones; we'd be out of place in a Shoe Zone!"

Eric's face burst with laughter.

"It's not funny," insisted Micky, beating his fist on the wooden dining table.

"Yes, it is. I've waited so long for someone to make a game of it, and now, from the unlikeliest of sources, Sean has offered us one. But that's not even the funniest thing."

"Then what is?" asked Callum.

"Brotherhood. That's the pressure point."

"How? It would be just as difficult to abduct one of the others."

"We don't need to. You don't see it, do you?"

The others shook their heads simultaneously.

"Why do you think Logan ended up in this job and all of its dangers?"

"Money?" said Callum. "The pay must be amazing."

"I'll bet the death in service policy is pretty good, too," offered Micky.

"Neither."

"He's mentally disjointed?" guessed Callum.

"Wrong again. He wants to belong to something. To be part of a group. Why do you think he worked so hard to disrupt all of *The Idiots' Club's* dares back at Uni? He was jealous of Sean. Sean didn't really belong in our club, and Logan was jealous."

"How does that help us? 'Hello, Logan, if you let us abduct you then you can join our immature old boys' club?' Something like that?" mocked Micky.

"Not quite. We're not going to kidnap him or any of his gang. We're going to pretend to."

Callum and Micky glanced at each other cynically. They'd learnt to act on faith when it came to their friend's bravado. However much they doubted his schemes, they always ended up with a big dollop of humble pie on their plates for suggesting Eric was wrong or deluded. Now was not the time to test whether he'd lost his touch. After all, they all had something to lose if things turned ugly. They needed to show faith until a time came when it was obviously futile to do so.

"Let's move on," announced Eric forcefully. "What did you find out about Jessica?"

"Are we also going to 'pretend' to get her to agree to marry me, too?"

"Oh, no, not at all. This one will have to be genuine."

"Did I offend you at some point without knowing it?" asked Micky honestly.

"Probably, but I don't hold grudges against friends. Jessica?" he prompted.

"She also lives here in the city. She's an actress working in theatre, currently performing in *Cats* at the London Palladium."

"Big part?" enquired Callum.

"She plays a cat," replied Micky.

"All the actors play cats, Micky. The clue's in the title."

"Oh…I'm not really into the theatre."

"But you've heard of Andrew Lloyd Webber?"

"He runs all those tennis clubs, doesn't he?"

"No, you're thinking of David Lloyd," sighed Eric. "Lloyd Webber is responsible for some of the biggest West End musicals in modern history. *Phantom of the Opera*, *Jesus Christ Superstar* and…*Cats*."

"A musical about cats! People will watch anything these days," said Micky, tickled by the thought.

"Which character does she play?" asked Callum.

Micky checked his phone for the notes he'd made about Jessica to jog his memory. "Cassandra."

"Small part," commented Callum, who appeared to have a worrying level of knowledge on the subject. "Continue."

"She's not married, and as far as I can tell, there's no significant other half."

"I have to ask before Josh gets here: is she a…"

"No. Not as far as I can tell. I spoke with a few of the backing singers after a rehearsal to get the lowdown on her. I said I was posing as a talent scout," he divulged, clearly proud of his ruse if his wink was anything to go on.

"MI6 must be beating a path to your door," offered Eric sarcastically. "What else did they tell you?"

"Not much. She's been struggling to get substantial roles since an incident a few years ago in a production of *The Lion King*."

"Incident?" the others posed in unison.

"Apparently, she fell asleep in the middle of the second act."

"That doesn't seem a serious enough crime to bar her from bigger roles. Why was it such a big deal?"

"She was on stage at the time."

"Oh."

"Apparently, she was performing the role of back left leg of an elephant and while she snored loudly at the rear end, the other three actors had to drag her around the stage. By all accounts, it made it look like the beast had been shot, and the kids in the audience were all in tears. It's not really her fault; I found out from the internet that she suffers from narcolepsy."

"Poor lass," said Callum. "Must be tough."

"Apparently, as long as she avoids working afternoon matinees, she's able to manage the condition with medication."

"Can we use anything else about her?" asked Eric.

"She loves rugby."

"Does she like to watch or play?"

"No idea, but if I had to guess, I'd say watch. She wouldn't be much help if she fell asleep in a scrum."

"I'll bet she's never been to Twickenham," remarked Eric. "Not on an actress' salary."

"I'm not following you," said Callum, rubbing his chin.

"Okay, this is what we're going to do. Micky, I'm going to buy you a ticket to see *Cats* - apart from anything else, you could do with the cultural education. When you're there, you'll need to find a way to bump into Jessica. Invite her for dinner, just as old friends. We can't go in too hard or we'll scare her off."

"You mean I shouldn't ask her if she'll marry me straight away, then!" Micky stated, tongue in cheek.

"That's more second-date territory. Over dinner, I want you to invite her to a rugby match. Tell her you have two tickets for this weekend's International."

"But I don't have any tickets."

"Leave that to me. I have clients who are falling over themselves to invite me to these things. When the two of you are there, that's when you'll propose. It can't fail."

"It definitely can."

"Trust me."

"What, again?"

"Are you sure this is lager," commented Callum, staring into the dregs of his glass. "I don't think there's any lager in it."

Eric's phone vibrated in his pocket. "Josh, where are you?"

"Outside the door."

"Why didn't you press the intercom?"

"Because I'm already inside the building. I'm outside *your* door. I didn't want you to have the pleasure of winning fifty quid off Micky for guessing how long it took me to get here."

"Spoil sport."

As soon as Eric opened it, Josh burst through and lobbed his jacket at, but not on, the coat rack, a perfect analogy to how he treated his apartment compared to how Eric looked after his. If Eric's was opulent, pristine and furnished with beautiful art, Josh's by contrast was tatty, unkempt and furnished with eBay castoffs. The difference wasn't only down to their divergent characters; it had a lot to do with the fact Josh had been married, and divorced, three times. Keeping hold of your possessions, cash and dignity became a challenge after that.

Josh bustled into the kitchen like he owned the place, grabbed a beer from the fridge, and plonked himself down on the settee by the side of the dining table. He rested his dirty trainers on the glass coffee table. "What did I miss?"

"It's better you don't know," said Callum.

Josh gazed at Callum for a moment, a little shocked. "Umm…it's not like you to be talking straight at nine thirty in the evening. How many have you had?"

"Eight or nine. I think I might have become immune to alcohol."

Josh glanced down at the label on his beer bottle to find it had zero alcohol by volume. Eric shook his head violently to ensure Josh didn't give the game away.

"Got it. Good thinking."

"How was your trip?" asked Micky.

"Not good."

FIFTEEN

BRAINSTORMING

SECOND ONLY TO SCALING A MODERATELY-SIZED LATE nineteenth-century clock tower in the centre of a moderately-sized Devonshire city, the next easiest of their dares appeared to be the evacuation of Exeter University. But after a circuitous journey from Herefordshire to London via the target, Josh's tired and glum expression didn't look encouraging. Eric granted him the opportunity to catch up on non-alcoholic lager and smoke a few cigarettes out on the balcony before it was time to find out exactly how bad it was.

"Did you follow my instructions?" asked Eric.

"To the letter."

"What's the problem, then?"

"Your plan won't work."

"Why not?" he asked, disgruntled.

"Things are a little different on campus than you and I remember them."

"Do you know, I haven't been back since graduation day," expressed Micky nostalgically.

"You wouldn't recognise the place, Turnip."

"What's changed?"

"Almost everything."

"Example?" asked Callum, who had been back since graduation but not for about ten years. He'd applied to the alumni foundation for a business grant. He was still waiting on an answer.

"For a start, no one goes to the Ram anymore."

"What do you mean, no one?" said Eric.

"No one. I went at lunchtime, and other than a geeky spod working on a laptop and drinking...water," he said with a shiver, "it was empty!"

"Where were all the students, then? It's not the holidays, is it?"

"No. They were in the library."

"How do you know? You never even went there," Micky reminded him. "Come to think of it, I don't believe any of us did."

"I went once," replied Josh.

"When?"

"I had sex with Susie Cavendish in the psychology aisle. Just to be clear, I went in specifically to have sex with Susie. I wasn't already there and happened to get lucky. I think it was a dare?"

"Yeah, one of mine," said Eric.

"Nice! One of my favourites."

"You're welcome."

"I tell you something, though - you couldn't miss the library now. They've built this bloody big atrium over the top called the 'Forum'. It's where the shops used to be. They have these humongous staircases that descend about two floors under ground level. It's like somebody landed a bloody spaceship on campus. There's the library, barely recognisable to the one we don't remember, a load of lecture theatres, cafes, seating areas and no bar! Not a single one. The Ram is where it always was, but now it's hidden away like no one wants the students to find it."

"I don't think they do want to find it, Josh," explained Micky. "Students are a resourceful bunch, always have been, and if they wanted to go badly enough, a twenty-foot-high barbed wire fence wouldn't keep them out."

"What are you saying?"

"Students have changed. My nephew is studying at Oxford, and according to his mother, all they ever do is study."

Josh gasped in horror. "Study! Where are all the sheep?"

"They've followed the spods."

Josh grabbed at his chest as if he was experiencing a heart attack.

"Think about it. Twenty years ago, we didn't have to pay a penny. Now these poor kids are going to finish their education with forty thousand pounds of debt hanging over their heads. If they don't get a decent job, they're going to be paying for it until they retire."

"What about the less well-off students?"

"Them, too."

"Jesus, why didn't someone protest about it?"

"They did. Everybody under twenty voted for the Lib Dems, but they sold them out for power and gave up their 'no tuition fees' policy."

"Assholes."

"Don't worry - they barely exist anymore."

"I still can't believe it. Students aren't supposed to be in libraries. They're supposed to be stumbling around wearing traffic cones on their heads, experimenting with cannabis and learning how to chat people up. That's the point, isn't it?!"

"Not anymore."

"I thought *The Idiots' Club* might have left a legacy," Josh professed angrily. "A path for future generations to follow."

"Sadly not."

"I think my belief system just imploded."

"You'll have to get over it," replied Eric, pressing on eagerly. "What about the fire alarm system I asked you to find out about?"

"State of the art. Every building has its own, each monitored from a dedicated control post in the Forum. It was updated at the same time as the building work. Oh, and here's a funny thing. Have a guess who the contractor was that built it?"

"*Heschmeyer Industries*," stated Eric knowingly.

Josh nodded.

In a rage, Eric spontaneously threw his crystal tumbler against the wall, where it shattered into a hundred pieces. "Fucker! Devious, conniving, snivelling little German prick!"

Micky leapt out of his chair to restrain his friend from inflicting any further damage on his luxury apartment. "Eric, calm down."

"Looks like Sean has been planning this for a while," suggested Josh.

"Oh, you think! I'm going to eviscerate him. We're going to complete his dares and then we're going to burn down his empire and piss on the ashes."

"That's a bit extreme, isn't it?" said Callum nervously. "It's just a game…that's what you used to say."

"A game with no rules," added Micky.

Eric took a moment to compose himself. He wasn't just angry with Sean, he was irritated with himself for not seeing what was happening sooner. "Is there any way of setting off the alarms?"

"Yes, but we'd have to find a way of doing it simultaneously in fifty separate locations. The moment they investigate the source of one and find out it's a hoax, they'll reset the alarms and the evacuation will be called off."

"How long before that happens?"

"With the number of fire marshals and surveillance cameras they have in place, I reckon it'll be less than a minute. The evacuation would be over before the students smelt the fresh air."

"Callum, remind me what the contract terms are for this dare?"

Callum retrieved his trench coat and removed the contract from his pocket. "We have to prove that all students have been moved from Streatham Campus. It doesn't say for how long, but I'm guessing Sean will want to see there's no one on site."

"I imagine, unless a higher authority like the emergency services demand it, a mass evacuation would only be possible if it was sanctioned by the Vice Chancellor," maintained Micky.

"Who's that these days, Josh?" inquired Callum.

"Same one as when we were there."

"You're joking!" cried Micky. "He must be bloody ancient."

"Not really. Maybe we thought he was old at the time because we were young."

"Sir Andrew bloody Carrington," hissed Eric angrily. "That prick was the bane of my life. He's the biggest racist I've ever had the misfortunate to encounter."

"I don't think he's necessarily just a racist. He didn't like students in general, which is odd for someone who exclusively works with them," Micky commented.

"If Carrington's in charge, there's no way he'd sanction an evacuation even if every single undergraduate was being simultaneously threatened by armed assailants. The man's a total arse-wipe," confirmed Josh. "We'll need a plan that circumvents his authority."

Everyone nodded, apart from Eric, who had other ideas.

"There is an upside to this," Josh determined. "If we succeed, we might beat Sean and Carrington in one fell swoop. Imagine that. Carrington's had it coming for decades."

"Every one of us wants that outcome, but we still don't have a plan," Callum pointed out correctly.

"We need to brainstorm," announced Eric, moving towards a broom cupboard and excavating a flipchart. He struggled to set it up in front of the panoramic window, and when it was eventually stable, he encouraged the others to join him in the lounge area.

"Why do I have this strange compulsion to draw a comedy penis!" chuckled Josh.

"Because you have the mental age of seven," Micky reminded him.

"This is what we do at the agency when we have a new creative project," revealed Eric, waving the flipchart pen around flamboyantly like a carnival baton. "Everyone throws out ideas, and we play off each other until our collective talents find the best solution. It's important to understand that there are no outlandish or stupid ideas - you have to speak your mind and put it out there, however ridiculous it might sound."

"Maybe you should give Callum the good stuff, then," suggested Micky. "He always comes up with the best nonsense when he's plastered."

Eric grabbed a less expensive bottle of whisky from the cabinet and three more glasses, a new one for himself and one each for the latecomers.

"Okay. How do we do this 'brainstorming', exactly?" inquired Josh excitedly. As a veterinary rep, the limit of his brainstorming was reserved to which route to follow each morning on his rounds to see customers.

"First, we focus on the problem."

Eric wrote 'Evacuate Campus' at the top of the page with a big red marker pen.

"I'm brilliant at brainstorming," declared Callum self-confidently, already helping himself to a second measure of whisky. "All of my business ideas were formed that way."

"I'd love to see which ideas you rejected," sniggered Josh.

"The secret to brainstorming is to let go of any inhibitions," explained Eric. "Don't restrain an idea because you believe it's unworkable or implausible. There has to be trust within the room or we'll hold things back. Listen intently to what others suggest and refrain from excessive judgement just because you don't agree or understand their idea. We will debate ideas using logic, not opinions. We will select winners based on evidence, not conjecture. Is everyone clear?"

Callum nodded eagerly. Micky shrugged, not in the slightest bit interested.

"So…we can say any mad shit that we like?" queried Josh tentatively.

"Anything at all," agreed Eric, who'd spent much of his adult life engaged in such meetings.

"Brilliant! I feel so liberated all of a sudden."

"So, let's get the ball rolling. How would the four of us successfully evacuate thousands of students from over fifty buildings?"

There was a moment of suspense as everyone waited to see who'd be first to contribute to the plenary session.

"Botulism," Callum blurted out.

"Expand," urged Eric.

"It's a toxin produced by bacteria travelling through the water system, air or on food. If there was a confirmed case on campus, that would be enough to empty the place."

"Okay. I'm not sure how to spell 'botulism'," confessed Eric, "but I'll just write 'tiny bugs' as I'm guessing it doesn't specifically have to be that one."

"I guess not."

"Excellent. We're off to a flyer. Next."

"Terrorist threat," offered Micky, who was feeling a little more comfortable with the process after Callum's opening gambit.

"Topical, but we'd need to explore it further," responded Eric, writing it in shoddy handwriting under the first entry. "There would have to be a realistic motive as to why Al Qaeda wanted to disrupt a rural British university."

Josh stewed in his seat, desperate to get in on the act but unable to shift one immovable thought from his mind that crowded out all other brainwaves.

"I'll add one to the list," said Eric. "World War Two bomb. They're still finding those all over the place."

"Good thinking," exclaimed Callum. "What about a chemical spill of some sort?"

"Or a natural disaster," submitted Micky.

"I'll add them on too although, sadly, we don't get many earthquakes or tsunamis in the UK."

Josh fidgeted in his seat, aware he was still the only person yet to add anything. Everyone else's suggestions had been greeted with enthusiasm and yet doubt still hijacked his mouth's ability to express itself. Surely his idea wasn't any worse than some of theirs. The others turned their attention on him and his mouth was compelled to let loose.

"A comet impact."

The room was enveloped by an awkward silence.

"Write it up," demanded Josh.

"What else do we have?" asked Eric, redirecting their thoughts.

"Why haven't you put mine on the list?"

"Because it's stupid," answered Micky, butting in uninvited.

"Apparently, there are no stupid ideas," bristled Josh, badly mocking Eric's accent.

"There aren't."

"Apart from that one," confirmed Micky.

"What's wrong with it!"

"Factually speaking, you mean?" replied Micky, summarising the procedures. "Well, firstly, we can't fake a comet strike because I'm fairly certain NASA would have identified any cosmic threats some years before. Secondly, even if we could encourage a massive lump of space rock to take a sudden detour towards the planet - where do you recommend we evacuate the students to? Mars? You're advocating an extinction level event, not a short-term relo-cation of some gullible teenagers so we can win a pointless dare. Thirdly, you only said it because your limited intelli-gence struggled to find anything more appropriate to say and you don't have a verbal filter."

"Fuck you, Turnip."

"Truth hurts, Foxie!"

"Do you want me to beat you to a pulp again, like I did outside the *Turk's Head* that night, remember?" growled Josh, rolling up his shirt sleeves and lunging at Micky. "Let's go!"

Eric cut him off in the middle of the lunge and placed him in a bear hug. "Not today. You can settle old scores on your own time. Right now, we're all friends, and our focus is on dare one. Understood?"

"He started it!" hollered Josh.

"You suggested a comet strike!"

"Both of you stop," commanded Eric, raising his voice. "Josh, you're entitled and encouraged to offer any suggestions you want, but we're not going to falsify a large meteor striking the planet in the next day and a half. Micky, you need to lay off him. We're a team, and if we fail to act like one not only will we lose, but all of us will find our lives fundamentally less enjoyable at the hands of Sean Heschmeyer."

Both offered mumbled apologies, and Eric went back to considering the alternatives already listed on the flipchart. He ran his pen through a number of them while offering an explanation as to why they lacked feasibility based on their current resources and time constraints. By the end of his redactions, only two options remained for consideration. An unexploded WWII bomb or a chemical spillage. In either case, the threat had to be genuine for the emergency services to be called out and campus to be emptied. On balance, they all agreed that unleashing dangerous chemicals on the town might have long-lasting health implications for the students, and, more importantly, the four of them. An unexploded bomb, however, only posed a threat if it ceased to be one.

"There's only one tiny hole in the plan as I see it," announced Callum.

"What?"

"We don't have an unexploded World War Two bomb."

"Obviously, that's why we need to 'borrow one'." Eric indicated, using quotations with his fingers.

"Well, as fortune would have it," mocked Micky, "a

friend of mine has a spare thousand-kilogram German ordinance just lying about in his garden. He tried eBay but no takers."

"Do you think he'd lend it to us?" asked Callum eagerly.

"I was kidding, obviously. What do we do now?"

"If you say brainstorming, I'm going to be the one who explodes." Josh wagged his finger at Eric threateningly.

"I'm guessing we only have two choices. Either we steal one from a museum or we scour the internet to see if any have recently been dug up."

"Islington!" exclaimed Callum with a burst of energy.

"What about it?"

"It was in the news this morning! Builders discovered one."

"But it'll be armed, won't it?" quizzed Micky nervously.

"It's been in the ground for more than seventy-five years. I think if it was going to blow up, it probably would have done so by now. Think of all the disruption it's been subjected to since it landed. Construction projects, tube trains rattling underneath it, new road systems. The firing mechanism probably disintegrated years ago. It'll be useless."

"That's a bloody big presumption."

"For once, I agree with Micky. What if it goes off when we're trying to remove it?" said Josh.

"I've seen the movies. We'll put an ear to it and if it's not ticking, I think we're safe."

"Great," he replied sarcastically.

"We'd better get a move on, then. I hear they're planning a controlled detonation in the morning," added Callum. "We should go now!"

"Hold on a minute. We need to think about this,"

stated Micky. "We haven't even talked about your plan for the lion yet."

"Don't panic; I have that under control," lied Eric. "And right now, I think we have enough to be getting on with."

"But we can't simply saunter into Islington, lift up a bomb and carry it away!" beseeched Micky.

"Why not?"

"Because they're heavy…and what's that other thing… we don't know what we're doing!"

"When has that ever stopped us? We just need to pick up some supplies."

"What supplies? A massive bomb removal machine!"

"Josh, do you by any chance own a fireman's outfit?"

"Of course."

Micky stared at him quizzically.

"It's for…entertainment purposes," he replied with a wink. "The ladies love a costume."

"Good, we're going to need it," said Eric. "We're also going to need a small van and possibly a crane. Anyone got any contacts?"

"I can ask Dubious Barry," replied Callum.

"You know someone called 'Dubious Barry'?" said Micky.

"Yeah. He's done some work for me down the years. He's in the delivery business."

"But isn't he…well…dubious?" pointed out Josh.

"Occasionally, he's been known to mislead people when it comes to what he's promised, but he won't do it with me. We have an understanding."

"I'm not sure anyone popularly known as 'dubious' is someone we should put our trust in."

"We don't have much choice," Eric responded. "Unless you have any contacts who might have what we need?"

They shook their heads.

"Can you reach him now, Callum?"

"Barry's a wheeler dealer - he'll sell you anything whatever time it is."

"Great, get on it."

"I'm totally against this," avowed Micky. "It's bloody suicide."

"It does seem a little hasty," agreed Josh.

"There's a only a small window when we can steal it, and I have a great feeling about this," Eric reassured them, nodding his head repeatedly.

"Let's vote on it."

"Callum, I think I'm going to need you to say the words, please, before these two losers back out."

"Don't you dare!" Josh and Micky shouted in unison.

SIXTEEN

BOMBS AWAY!

"I DARE YOU" WASN'T A PHRASE BANDIED AROUND WILLY-nilly if you were a member of *The Idiots' Club*. It wasn't used in jest or in anger. Once uttered, at least in Eric's presence, there was no going back. Like the duels of old, when the gauntlet was thrown down, it became a test of honour and bravery. Eric knew daring himself to do it was preposterous, because it removed one of the essential characteristics of the dare. The challenge itself was only half of it; it also mattered who was standing on the other side.

A suitable rival.

It didn't necessarily have to be an enemy, either. It might as easily be a person you respected or loved, but the greater your sense of feeling towards them, the more significant the dare.

Today, it was Callum.

Whenever Eric asked him to "say the words", he was always willing to oblige, and once the phrase left Callum's mouth and entered Eric's ears, the rest of *The Idiots' Club* were powerless to stop him. Either they helped, which was the usual convention, or they stood back and watched the carnage.

All for one or not at all.

"I dare you to steal a World War Two bomb."

There would only ever be one reply.

"Yes."

That was it. They were going to steal a bomb.

There were some items in the world which were almost impossible to steal. The Crown Jewels, official government secrets, the Mona Lisa, the Magna Carta - all good examples of objects beyond the capabilities of even the very best of thieves. Not that the scale of the task had put people off down the years. There had been numerous attempts, some even temporarily successful, but ultimately each one futile. Acquiring notable artefacts like these was both impractical and inconceivable because the value to their owners, and the nations that treasured them, was beyond measure. As a consequence, they were afforded a level of surveillance and security that couldn't be fooled or disarmed by four plucky middle-aged men with plenty of creativity but almost no genuine talents. Even if you factored in that three of them were still moderately sober, it was still way beyond them. It wouldn't have stopped Eric trying if someone had 'said the words', mind you.

At the other end of the spectrum, some things were incredibly easy to steal, because they lacked intrinsic value. As such, their owners afforded them almost no protection against theft, because a person might fail to notice if they went missing. Who's going to call the police if someone pinches some of your loose change, or a few penny sweets from a pick & mix jar, or junk mail from a letterbox? Technically, such acts are still crimes, but compared to stealing Tutankhamun's Death Mask, being caught isn't likely to result in the same length of sentence.

Massive unexploded WWII ordinance didn't really fit into either category.

Compared to, say, a Faberge egg, they aren't particularly valuable, which makes spending buckets of money to mitigate against anyone stealing one hard to justify, and it's unlikely to be insured against such an eventuality. The potential threat to life of an unexpected detonation also means recruiting security guards is a real challenge. Plus, what was the point? Who in their right mind would want to steal a bomb? The only purpose of having any form of security would be to keep people safe and away from the area.

However, unlike a simple flower pot being pinched from someone's garden, people will definitely notice if a large German shell goes missing - not that this isn't necessarily a bad thing. It would be fair to assume that the few hundred residents of the Borough of Islington who had the misfortune of living in the vicinity of this one wouldn't mind in the slightest if someone removed it. After all, that's exactly what the bomb disposal team were planning to do the next morning. What did it matter to them if the team assigned to take it away weren't the highly trained professionals and relocation of the device was left in the hands of four inappropriately-dressed idiots? All they really cared about was spending one less night sleeping on the floor of a local leisure centre. That and not returning to discover all their windows were missing because the team responsible cocked something up.

∼

Yesterday. Frome Police Station.

. . .

"You know we'll catch him, don't you?" said Iris confidently.

"Who?"

"Micky Parsons."

"Why? What's he done?"

Iris rolled her eyes. She was getting a little tired of Eric's games and, after multiple attempts, she'd failed to trip him up.

"I understand his wife is very anxious to see him."

"I'd bet she is."

"And I'm sure she'd be most grateful if you were able to offer information that led to his safe return."

"I seriously doubt that. Natasha's not my biggest fan."

"I've yet to meet anyone who is."

"My tailor."

"I'd say you won't be needing him for a good few years."

Eric purposefully glanced up at the clock, something he'd done repeatedly throughout the interview, much to Iris's irritation. It was, she presumed, a subliminal reminder from him that her time was running out.

"Why don't you just tell me where Micky is and stop this charade?"

"I might be able to help you, but there would have to be certain conditions," contended Eric, the smile still tattooed to his lips.

"I'm listening."

"You'd have to let me leave."

"Ha! No chance. Your powers of persuasion don't appear to be working very well."

"Surely if my information led to you finding both Micky and the missing lion, that would end any interest the police had in me, wouldn't it?"

"Nope."

When playing poker, it's always useful to have a trump card, and it wasn't only Eric who was planning to use one. Iris had been sitting on hers since the very start of the interview, biding her time before throwing it down. The lion theft wasn't the only crime she wanted to solve. Over the last few days, there had been other unexplained events that appeared to lead to his door. She opened her folder, took out a black and white photograph and slid it face up across the table to him.

"Do you know who this is?"

Eric met a lot of people in the course of his job and had an uncanny talent for remembering faces. None looked like this man, though. In fact, Eric thought there would be few people in the world who'd tolerate looking like the subject did without resorting to an extensive course of reconstructive surgery. A huge square face featured several deep scars, a nose that changed directions at least three times before it reached the tip and more eyebrow hair than skin. After a long period of contemplation, Eric gently shook his head.

"Barry Benson."

Eric shrugged.

"He's frequently known to his network by his alias. Dubious Barry."

Eric's body went into high alert and he momentarily closed his eyes to compose himself. If he left his body to its spontaneous reaction, he'd send out a mass of signals which might accurately be read as genuine surprise. So this was Dubious Barry. He'd never met or seen him before, but he certainly knew who he was. More importantly, DI Whitehall knew, too.

"Strange nickname," said Eric, opening his eyes and retaining his composure.

"I thought so, too, but then I learnt a bit more about

him and learnt that his moniker is more than warranted. You see, Mr Benson, here, is currently in custody in a London interview room being hosted by some colleagues of mine. Want to know what he's doing right now?"

"Not particularly."

"He's looking at a photo of you."

"I hope it's a better one than this."

"No doubt he's not hiding his emotions nearly as well as you are. I imagine he's trying to work out what you and he have in common."

"Well, it's not the same barber - that's for sure."

"Would you like to share what it is, or shall I?"

Eric waved her on, hoping she was going on a hunch rather than fact.

"Last week, a World War Two bomb was discovered on a building site in Islington. It's not uncommon, of course; they turn up all the time, particularly in the capital, which was peppered during the Blitz. What's much less common, however, is discovering it one day and miraculously finding it gone the next."

"Erosion," offered Eric, trying unsuccessfully to reposition his strategy, given the seismic power shift he'd experienced over the last five minutes.

"It's been in the ground for more than seventy years, Mr Gideon. I think if it were going to erode, it probably would have already done so."

"Bloody kids," Eric suggested weakly. "I'm sure it'll turn up if you do a campaign of stop and search."

"I also doubt we'll find it in someone's pocket."

"No, but one of them will confess to where it is."

"No point. We already know."

Eric's mouth dried up and his smile faltered.

"You see, the same bomb reappeared the following day two hundred miles away in a very similar construction site near some University buildings. Now, I know you like a good puzzle, Mr Gideon. Would you like to hazard a plausible theory as to how it might have got there?"

Iris grinned. She was finally enjoying herself, and for the first time in their battle, she had the upper hand. She'd let him squirm on the end of her line a little longer until he was intellectually shagged out, and then she'd reel him in.

"I've no idea, but whoever managed it would have brainstormed it for hours, I'd imagine."

"Given the mental fortitude of Mr Benson, I very much doubt his brain would provide more than a gentle breeze. In fact, based on his gormless reaction to our questions I believe he hasn't got the first idea why he's even been arrested. But you do, don't you, Eric?"

It was the first time she'd used his first name and he knew the significance. It was a trick Eric often used himself. Using it was an act of friendship which made the interrogator appear sympathetic rather than hostile. The effects were easy to avoid as long as you saw it coming. Eric had anticipated that the vehicle they'd hired from Dubious Barry might eventually come up in conversation. But he hadn't expected it to be connected to the bomb, or that Iris would know about both.

"No idea."

"Come on, now, you can do better than that. Dubious Barry is in custody because a vehicle registered in his name was used to remove the bomb. Amazingly, it also happens to be the same vehicle that four idiots used yesterday to transport a lion to an unknown location. A vehicle that, as yet, we've failed to recover."

"That doesn't implicate me in what happened in Islington, though, does it?"

"Why do you say that?"

"Because I bought the hearse from a garage in Salisbury yesterday morning."

"Did you, indeed," scoffed Iris. "Can I see the receipt?"

"I think the lion ate it," said Eric, pointing out that most of his clothes were no longer capable of storing anything, let alone a wallet.

"Where were you at around two in the morning last Thursday?" she demanded.

"Asleep."

"Can anyone verify that?"

"Yes, I was with Callum Jollie and Josh Foxole."

"That's interesting, because we know exactly where Josh Foxole was at two o'clock that day."

"My spare room."

"Not exactly," replied DI Whitehall, gleefully reaching for her phone. "Let me show you."

ISLINGTON. Last Thursday. Two o'clock in the morning.

ONLY THE DIM lights from nearby streetlamps cut through the early morning gloom. Directly behind them was an eight-foot-high wire fence recently vandalised by a pair of bolt cutters. In front of them was a huge crater which contained all manner of construction machines and equipment. To protect against someone falling in, the six-metre-deep hole was secured by a series of concrete barriers encircling the rim. On this particular section of the three-foot-high partition, two men, each with a rope lashed around his waist, peered into the abyss while a third man attempted haphazardly to retrieve useful information from his mobile phone.

"Have you found anything out yet!" Eric whispered aggressively, as he strained under the weight from the other end of the rope.

"What colour did he say it was?" asked Callum, who swayed like bamboo in a gale, frequently losing control of his phone and having to rescue it from the mud.

"Rust coloured," wheezed Micky, "but I think after seven decades, they're probably all that colour! Does it matter?"

"Apparently, the Germans dropped a load of different types, colours and sizes. Oh, that one's pretty," mumbled Callum.

"Focus," strained Eric.

"The small ones were about fifty kilos, but one was eighteen hundred, which they called 'Satan'."

"I'd bet it's that one," huffed Micky.

"Josh," Eric called down in a whisper which he hoped was somewhere between audible and inconspicuous. "How big would you say it was?"

"Big enough," came the echoed response.

"How else are we meant to distinguish it?" quizzed Eric.

"It says on the internet that some were designed to blow up immediately and other had timers that were programmed to explode between two and eighty hours after impact. Fascinating."

"It's definitely been down there longer than that, so it must be alright," announced Eric confidently. "Unless it landed on something soft!"

"Jesus, this is dodgy. Why are we doing this?" begged Micky.

"It's exciting."

"It's liable to get us all killed!"

"Does it say anything about how to pick one up?" Eric asked Callum.

"That depends on what condition it's in," offered Callum, holding the phone so close to his face it was almost up his nose. "Apparently, you can move some easily, while others might blow up if you breathe on them."

"I want to go home," moaned Micky desperately.

"But how can we tell which one we've got here?" demanded Eric.

"I'm not sure. Tell him to give it a kick!" laughed Callum, who was having a lovely time, mostly as a result of being well past the nine pint mark, which officially made him immune to danger.

Eric whispered some concise instructions down into the crater where a frightened, meek voice echoed back up to him.

"Josh says it's about a metre long, rusty, in one piece and has a '17' marked on one end. He also says he's wet himself, but that's probably less relevant."

"Ah, hold on…I saw something about numbers," said Callum. "A seventeen means it's got a timer."

"So as long as we don't disrupt it, we should be okay, right?"

"Totally."

"And if we do," said Micky solemnly, "we'll die sometime between two and eighty hours."

"I like those odds," proclaimed Eric. "Right, get it on."

Josh tied slipknots on each rope and gingerly slid them over the ends of the bomb. Once he'd finished, he legged it and waved up at them from a safer distance.

"Are we really doing this?" wept Micky. "I've got kids!"

"Stop whining and pull…but go slowly."

They tugged simultaneously on the ropes, and a dull

thud reverberated up the crater as the bomb clattered against the side. The more they pulled, the more they winced, and the closer the bomb advanced on them. Finally, after ten minutes of intense pressure, it came into view below them. Micky closed his eyes as he waited for the inevitable explosion that would wipe out his miserable existence. When he opened them again, Callum was casually tapping on the rusty metal with his clenched fist while giggling like a school-girl. "They don't build them like this anymore!"

"Stop that, you blithering idiot."

"Lighten up, Turnip. We've just dragged it up the side of a wall; I don't think my fist is going to set it off."

"Don't tempt fate," warned Micky. "Come on, let's get it out of here before someone catches us or we go up in smoke."

"Fine," agreed Eric. "You grab one end and I'll grab the other. Should be light enough to carry."

They'd already reversed their getaway car through the wire fence and as close to the crater as was feasible. The back doors were open, ready for its new cargo.

"Now I know why they call him 'Dubious Barry'," whispered Micky as they carefully slid the bomb into the back. "What did you ask him for, exactly?"

"A van," slurred Callum. "Something incon…spilious."

"Inconspicuous," corrected Eric. "I'd say it was neither."

"It's a bloody hearse!" exclaimed Micky.

"It's like a van," argued Callum.

"At least if the bomb goes off in transit, we're going to save everyone a lot of time."

"Come on, let's rescue Foxie and get out of here," advised Eric.

Removing Josh from the hole was considerably easier than lifting the bomb. For one, they didn't suffer heart attacks every time he bounced off the sides of the wall - which he did frequently. Once he was back on their level, a heated argument broke out as to who was going to sit where. The hearse was based on a nineteen eighties Ford Granada which only had two front seats. Two of them would have to crouch or lie in the back next to the bomb. Eric was deemed to be under the alcohol limit and the best driver. Josh argued fairly that as he'd been forced to retrieve the bomb, it was only right he sat up front. Callum accepted their assessment that he'd probably pass out sometime soon, which only left Micky infuriated by the decision-making process.

They did their best to prop the bomb up with some decorators' sheets to protect it from any bumps in the road, and once they were all in position, Eric gingerly drove away from the building site and out onto the main road.

Yesterday. Frome Police Station.

"That's what you're relying on for evidence these days, is it?" said Eric disdainfully. "Some long-range CCTV footage of man in a crater wearing a fireman's uniform. Have you considered that it might be an actual member of the fire service?"

"We've already checked. They have GPS trackers these days, and there was no one on site at that time."

"That still doesn't prove it was us, though, does it?" argued Eric.

"No, but this does."

Iris threw a tatty wallet on the table. Most men's wallets were indistinguishable from each other, at least from the outside. They were usually leather, pocket-sized and plain. It was unlikely anyone would confuse theirs for this one. It was made from a strange blue fabric and had the word 'FOXIE' embroidered in red thread on the front. Even Eric found it difficult to offer an alternative explanation for this one.

"It's a very common nickname."

"The army disposal team were a little surprised to find a bomb had been substituted for this."

"I've got to say, it really doesn't look good for Josh."

"Or you."

"How so?"

"You gave me Josh Foxole's name as your alibi," she said, confidently reeling him in for the catch.

"Yeah, I did, didn't I. Not looking great, is it?"

"No, but I'm struggling to understand why you're still smiling like the cat who got the cream."

"Honestly," he replied, "I'm enjoying myself."

"Sorry?" she muttered a little confused.

"It's not every day you meet a worthy opponent." He pretended to doff his cap in appreciation. "And you certainly are one. Could I ask you a question, Inspector?"

"I suppose..."

"In the video footage you showed me from last night, it's impossible to see the hearse's registration plates - so how did you trace the vehicle back to Barry?"

"I was already looking for it."

"How so?"

"Because I was in Exeter when they found the bomb."

THE JOURNEY from London to Exeter took the average car approximately three hours. 'Average' was not the first word that came to mind with their vehicle. They certainly didn't pass any other thirty-year-old hearses containing four grown men and an even older unexploded war relic in the boot. The combined weight of people and goods extended the journey by a couple of hours even before considering the cautious way Eric drove, not something he was accustomed to doing in his Nissan. Every time they hit an uneven patch of road, their hearts leapt into their mouths. Micky, who was closest to the device and remained awake throughout, would place an ear next to the rusty shell to reassure them that he couldn't hear any ticking. But after he was convinced he heard something as they passed Brent Knoll on the M5 motorway, they hurriedly bailed out in the nearby service station and legged it to a safe distance. After a considerable delay which didn't include the nearby motorway being splattered by chunks of Ford Granada, they plucked up the courage to drive on.

Just before eight o'clock in the morning, they chugged into Exeter and immediately went in search of a suitable location to deposit their load, preferably before every building site was packed with hairy-arsed builders. On the edge of Streatham campus on the east side of the University, they found the early excavation of a new hall of residence. Concerned at the potentially fatal consequences of someone discovering it accidentally, they dropped the bomb with a heavy thud on a big pile of sand in clear site, right in the middle of plot.

"What now?" panted Micky, physically and emotionally exhausted.

"We start filming," responded Eric, whipping out his phone and turning on the camera. "I've set up a YouTube Channel called the 'WDWC Live'.

"What does that stand for?"

"Who Dares Wins Collective," smirked Eric.

"Why don't you use our proper name," suggested Josh.

"Maybe at the end of the week, but from the moment I press 'record' on this device, we're no longer incognito."

"I suspect that might have ended last night in Islington," deduced Micky.

"Possibly."

"God, I wish I had your confidence," replied Micky. "Help me out here, because there's something I'm not clear about."

"Go on."

"How are we supposed to evacuate campus? Do we inform the authorities about the bomb and then mingle about campus pretending that it's us rather than the police who are clearing people out?"

"Not exactly. Here's the plan. Josh, I want you to go to the Forum in your fireman's uniform. Unless you hear otherwise from me, I want you to raise the alarm at precisely ten o'clock."

"How do I do that?"

"Use your initiative, but you shouldn't raise any suspicions if you're dressed like that. Callum, I want you to go with him and film Josh on your phone. Make sure Sean sees you on the video, too, and film Micky and me when we arrive. I'll set up your phone so it's streaming directly to the YouTube channel."

"What about me?" asked Micky.

"I want you to call the police and inform them that you've discovered the bomb, but not until nine thirty - that's very important. If you get a call from me before that, don't call them, and we'll move the bomb back into the van. Most building sites open at around nine, so it's possible someone might discover it beforehand, but let's hope not. It's just gone quarter past eight, so you have barely under an hour to get into position."

"Hold on," probed Micky suspiciously. "What about you? What's your job?"

"I have an appointment."

"To see…?"

"Sir Andrew Carrington."

SEVENTEEN
THE VICE CHANCELLOR

LAST THURSDAY, EXETER.

IN A QUINTESSENTIALLY ENGLISH WAY, the meaning of some words is not always obvious, or consistent. For example, the inhabitants of a small antiquated island just off the coast of France use the word 'public' when referring to 'private' schools. Public schools in England are anything but. Fortunately, this linguistic misnomer does not extend to other amenities that include the same word. Imagine if you followed a sign for 'Public Toilet' only to discover that eligibility for having a wee was strictly limited to those prepared to pay nine thousand pounds for the privilege and only if they proved their aristocratic bloodline. In case you're planning a visit, rest assured public toilets do mean what you think they do.

There are plenty of examples in the British vocabulary of words that misrepresent their meanings. To understand why these oddities of language continue to survive many centuries after the rest of the modern world has mostly moved on, it's necessary to delve deeper into the fabric of English culture and, in particular, the population's intractable grip on that most cherished of national identities.

Tradition.

Almost everything the English do can be explained or excused by labelling it an act of tradition.

For example, the ridiculous pursuit of running after a lump of cheese purposefully rolled down a Gloucestershire hillside - even though it frequently results in broken limbs for those stupid enough to participate – is perfectly accept-able, because it's a tradition.

Eating a Sunday roast dinner in the middle of July when the outside temperature is pushing a hundred degrees Fahrenheit is a reasonable behaviour because it's a tradition.

Even though most Brits complain bitterly about the inequality in society, give them a Royal Wedding and it turns out equality is much less important than putting up bunting. Poverty and pageantry - both traditions, apparently.

Christmas hats, roast turkey, crackers and all manner of paraphernalia that have diddly squat to do with the birth of Jesus Christ, all tradition.

Wearing the right type of tie in a specific building on a specific day. Tradition.

Disliking Europeans, foreigners and ethnic minorities - that's also a tradition, but it does depend on where you live.

And woe betide any politician bold enough to suggest that these customs are outdated and should be consigned to history. The English can stomach being stripped of all manner of privileges – freedom of speech, data privacy, money, dignity and essential public services – but tell them they can't wear bells on their trousers and prance around a pole on May Day and don't be surprised if it triggers widespread social unrest. The fact that the official number of people regularly participating in Morris Dancing wouldn't fill a moderately-sized bingo hall won't matter in the slightest. Bingo also happens to be a tradition, but only if you're over the age of eighty.

Traditions continue to be repeated because an entrenched, sentimental public are encouraged to act in such a way by the very descendants of those people directly responsible for constructing them in the first place.

The upper class.

People love tradition, but paradoxically, they don't have a lot of time for toffs.

It escapes most peoples' attention that the traditions they cling to are almost exclusively established by elitist elements within society. It seems, whether you like it or not, you can't have one without the other.

Sir Andrew Carrington was a firm believer in both.

He knew he was superior to others because of his distinguished roots: where he was born, which schools he attended and because he understood the rules of polo. He was also wise enough to realise that the nation's obsession with tradition was an essential tool for protecting the inequality which kept people like him in positions of influence.

Carrington's playground of power was Exeter University and he was its Vice Chancellor. The title further illustrating the idiosyncrasy of the English language. The most important member of staff at any University was not, as a logical mind might assume, the Chancellor. That role was purely a symbolic position often bestowed upon distinguished luminaries who'd visited the institutions they represented so infrequently they probably couldn't point them out on a map.

It was the Vice Chancellor who held all the power, and Carrington took every opportunity to wield it. He believed in a set of rather old-fashioned values like subservience, speaking only when spoken to, and respect for authority. These traditions weren't behaviours often associated with students. Students were more likely to challenge rules than follow them and believed it was their absolute right to stand up, speak out and shine a light on any aspects of modern life which fell short of their ideological utopia.

Carrington also had an overriding objective that all students should behave like 'spods', although even some of those pushed the boundaries of what he thought acceptable. No one who took their education seriously needed jigsaw puzzles or buckets of elderflower cordial! Frivolous distractions didn't deliver first class degrees; they were achieved through hard work, sacrifice and talent. Universities weren't places of experimentation; they were places of dedication. They existed to prepare young people to be the new cogs in the economic machinery, engineered some centuries ago to keep the fiscal pump flowing and line the pockets of wealthy engine drivers. Educational attainment promised to smash the glass ceiling for those who demonstrated the right attitude and ability.

But not everyone fell for the false advertising.

Carrington's carefully honed external profile was built on his unwavering drive to produce future captains of industry, Nobel prize-winning scientists, public servants and award-winning creatives. But his persona was a façade. The real reason for his strict approach on campus was founded on his own ego and an insatiable desire to win.

The one and only characteristic he shared with a certain Eric Gideon.

The modern world is obsessed with league tables. Almost every aspect of our lives has to be graded, compared and measured. Employee performance, schools, favourite sports teams, local plumbers, books, the most efficient airlines and which countries have the most democratic system can all be found on a league table somewhere. But the so-called 'evidence' of what is best and worst can't shift how someone feels about it. A football club might be bottom of their league but that won't stop its fans from insisting that their team is the best, and certainly much better than yours. This reaction will be even stronger if the team's past victories outweigh its recent performance.

It didn't matter where Exeter sat on the 'Best Universities' league table, because in most people's eyes it would never compete with Oxford or Cambridge, even if it sat at the very top. Like Eric, Carrington sought respect from others. He might control educational performance, revenues, investment, capacity and talent acquisition, but perception wasn't so easily manipulated. Even thirty years after his first appointment, he was still striving for his University to be mentioned alongside Yale, Harvard and Ipswich. Okay, maybe not Ipswich.

Anything, or anyone, who jeopardised his crusade was an enemy to progress, perfection and power.

A description Eric Gideon took as a compliment.

Sir Andrew Carrington leant back on his heavy leather chair and surveyed his huge office. Almost every inch of the barely visible magnolia-painted walls was obscured by a shiny picture frame. A great deal of them displayed photos of Carrington, smiling and shaking hands with some visiting VIP, or opening one of the many new buildings constructed during his tenure. Some showed him clutching bulky glass trophies laser etched with the name of some notable prize. A few were reserved for certificates of achievement, mostly his rather than those of the institution he represented.

The clock on his wall confirmed that it was just before nine o'clock on Thursday morning, and the gentle spring sunshine was reflecting off his photographic achievements like a glitterball. In precisely three minutes, the day would officially commence with a cup of tea and the first of today's meetings with senior managers to approve their strategic agenda. A knock on the door gave notice that the first of these key milestones had arrived. Every morning, the finest china teapot was delivered to his desk by his long-time personal assistant, Elsie. It was always Earl Grey and it was always served at exactly seventy-three degrees and occupied by a freshly-sliced Sicilian lemon.

"Gud mornin' ter ya, Sir."

An arthritis-riddled old woman, well beyond normal retirement age, struggled with the daily challenge of opening the door and carrying the tray at the same time. The cup and saucer chinked precariously against the teapot as her hands vibrated like a category five hurricane. Carrington waited patiently with no compulsion to assist. She might have worked for him for more than twenty years but she was still staff. Why should he help? She worked for him, not the other way around. The moment she was unable to fulfil her duties was a matter for him, not her, and when that moment came he'd fire her on the spot.

She mustered the strength to push the door out of the way long enough to lurch into the room, still juggling the tray precariously with her spindly, frail hands. She shuffled forward with the speed of plate tectonic shift, finally reaching the desk and arranging the teapot, sugar, cup and saucer in exactly the right formation.

Everything had to be precisely the way he liked it.

"Oy wus ya weekend?" she croaked inquisitively.

"Perfectly acceptable," he replied, not once looking up from a thick document to which he was making additions in red pen.

"Nice weather for dis time av year."

"Spring," he murmured, struggling to offer a reply, because he wasn't interested in taking the discussion any further.

"Me sista' come dun from Ilfracombe, an' apparently de weather dare wus inclement compared ter 'ere, at laest from er point av view…anyway, we foun' a gran wee tay room near Dawlish, da you know it…scones dare loike I've never tasted an' we saw the most bonny row av azaleas, al' pinks an' blues. Deidre, dats me sista…"

"That will be all, thank you, Elsie."

"Roi yer are, sir. Yer do av a visitor, though," she added tentatively.

Carrington looked up for the first time, disappointment etched across his face. He didn't dislike visitors - it was normally a welcomed opportunity to bask in their syco-phantic praise - but he did get agitated about receiving unscheduled guests. Carrington's diary was always mapped out like a highly considered military exercise. Everything had to be in its place. Meetings ran to schedule and not one minute longer. Every working day started and ended at the same time with no exceptions.

"I'm busy," he snarled.

"Yer man wus very insistent on seein' yer, sir," rasped Elsie in reply.

Making alterations to his schedule without his express permission had, down the years, resulted in ire and fury being showered down on her, so whoever wanted to see him must have made a compelling case for her to even suggest it.

"Who is it?"

"Student," she replied airily. "Yer pride yerself on alwus bein' available ter dem."

He frequently claimed to being both approachable and interested in student welfare, but the reality was somewhat different. Bosses liked to express that 'their door was always open' to employees but failed to pinpoint the exact location of the door in case any of them felt inclined to walk through it. Carrington absolutely despised talking to students in all settings. They were bubbly, overly excitable, opinionated and lacking in basic personal hygiene.

"What does he want?"

"To see yer," Elsie reaffirmed.

"Yes, I gathered that, but why?" he replied gruffly.

"It's aboyt mental 'ealth."

He thought on balance there was more evidence for the existence of the Yeti than there was for depression. Carrington strongly believed that mental health was an excuse bandied about by feckless layabouts more interested in playing the victim than overcoming minor obstacles in their lives. The Victorians didn't complain about burnout. Alexander the Great didn't stop when he got to Mesopotamia because he was feeling a bit down. Sir Isaac Newton didn't need a few hours of mindfulness because he was getting overly anxious about the flight of apples.

"Tell him to go find the pastoral team, or better still, he can waste his time trawling through the plethora of resources on our intranet if he's worried about stress." He waved her away and returned to his document.

"He didn't say he wus concerned aboyt 'is mental 'ealth, sir. He's worried aboyt yers."

"Mine! Only weak-minded fools whine about being depressed. My mental fortitude is, as it always has been, indisputable. Who is this student?"

"Eric Gideon, sir."

A vein on Carrington's temple quivered and a cold shiver reverberated down his spine. It was the first time he'd heard the name for over twenty years but even now it still had the capacity to trigger trauma. If Gideon was here, then chaos wasn't far behind. Peace and harmony had stood guard over Exeter University since Eric and his friends had graduated, and Carrington would make damn sure it remained that way. There was only one way to control it.

Face it.

"Send him in," said Carrington bitterly.

Elsie shuffled out of the office and a few moments later an imposing, middle-aged man replaced her. Without invitation he bore down on the leather seat on the opposite side of the desk and flopped himself down in it, swinging both legs up onto Carrington's desk.

"Hello, Andy. Did you miss me?"

"Mr Gideon. To what do I owe this unexpected and unpleasant courtesy call."

"During your graduation address, I distinctly remember you saying, 'Come back and see us.' Ta dah!"

"I was being figurative."

"That's the problem with language, though, isn't it. Love what you've done to the place. There have been so many changes around here, I struggled to find my way to your office, which is ironic given how many times you invited me here. I seem to remember you even had a photograph of me and the boys behind your desk." Eric pointed to the largest of the frames hanging on the wall right behind Carrington's head. "I must say, I dislike what you've replaced it with."

The photo was taken at the opening of the Forum and featured two smiling characters shaking hands enthusiastically. The older figure was unmistakably Sir Andrew, a man who'd made an indelible mark on Eric's formative years. The other was a man he'd not seen until very recently, Sean Heschmeyer.

"What do you want?"

"I imagine awarding the Forum contract to *Heschmeyer Industries* was an easy decision. A successful past student from the right side of the tracks. Someone you'd feel comfortable with in a photograph. Someone suitable to hang on your burgeoning hall of fame. No doubt it was personally lucrative, too, I imagine?"

"I never take a penny from our suppliers," he said staunchly. "Sean Heschmeyer is an Exeter University success story. A man of honour with firm principles and his firm's proposal was overwhelmingly the best fit across every measure."

"Was it," Eric replied suspiciously. "I wonder whether you'd have come to the same decision if I'd been CEO."

"My opinion of you has nothing to do with race or background. You, Gideon, are a lesser human not because of who you are but because of how you are. Not expelling you is still the biggest regret of my illustrious career."

"Expressed that to Sean, did you?"

"Why would we waste any time talking about you! You're an irritating footnote in both our histories. Irrelevant, inconsequential, forgettable. Your mark will fade the very moment your body expires," he said maliciously. "Yet our work here will live on in what we've built, and future generations will celebrate our achievements."

"What did he offer you?" questioned Eric, allowing Carrington's jibes to wash over him.

"Who, Sean?" he responded, bewildered. "What are you insinuating?"

"Both of you have unfinished business, uncomfortable scars which cannot be removed. You've had to bear the indignity of losing publicly to someone you see as a lesser foe. That can't sit well with men like you? Imagine a black kid from an impoverished, broken home making you look foolish, day in day out, for months on end. How many times did you tell me, in this very room, how my life would turn out? That I'd never make anything of myself. Well I have, and yet I still don't see my face on your wall."

"That's because of how you've achieved it."

"Come to think of it, no black faces at all," he said spinning his chair around to take in all four walls.

"You didn't come here to insult me, Mr Gideon. Spit it out or be on your way; I have a University to run."

"You're absolutely right, and today it's going to be a bigger challenge than you imagine unless we can come to some arrangement."

"What have you done?"

"It's not what I've done, it's what I am capable of doing. You see, your friend here," he said, gesturing at the picture of Sean, "has forced me to reform *The Idiots' Club*. I initially misunderstood his motives, but now I see them clearly. It's not just closure for him, it's closure for everyone he perceives we have wronged."

"I consigned *The Idiots' Club* to history. Disbanded, and disgraced. Just a juvenile group of vandals and anarchists."

"And yet here we are. Back again. But you can put a stop to it if you choose to."

"There is nothing you can do to disrupt the smooth running of this University."

Eric glanced up at the clock on the wall as the minute hand crept towards the half-hour mark. "In a few minutes' time, I'm going to evacuate campus. It'll be messy and embarrassing. People will question your governance, and even possibly your position. I'm offering you a chance to avoid that."

"Are you," he said calmly.

"Yes. I'm asking you nicely to call for an orderly evacuation."

"You want me to evacuate eleven thousand students for the sake of a dare." The notion was so preposterous Carrington struggled to complete the sentence without laughing.

"Yes. I thought it was only fair to give you the chance to protect your reputation, given how equitably you treated me down the years."

"Get out of my office!" he hollered, launching to his feet and pointing the way out.

"I'll take that as a no, then."

"Leave!"

"Of course…but, before I go to cause great mayhem to your beloved peace and harmony, tell me one thing… why did you really treat me the way you did?"

"If I tell you, will you leave?" snapped Carrington.

"Absolutely, if I believe you're telling me the truth."

"I treated you as such because you represent everything that is wrong with this country. You don't belong here. As Enoch Powell once warned, 'In fifteen or twenty years' time, the black man will have the whip hand over the white man.' Well, not here, you won't. I will not be terrorised in my own country by an immigrant with no right to grace these corridors with people like me from families who built this great nation. I don't care how successful you are, Mr Gideon, because in my eyes, a black man should never be allowed to compete with someone like me!"

His response was even more explosive than Eric had hoped. So much so he was almost shocked by the vindictive rhetoric. He knew Carrington was a racist, but he'd never believed for one minute the man would lower his guard and confess to it.

"Those whom the gods wish to destroy, they first make mad," replied Eric sternly, quoting from another section of Powell's speech. "Enjoy your day."

Eric swung his legs off the desk and headed for the exit. The moment the door settled against the frame, Carrington's hand leapt for his phone. He was being threatened and it would not stand. The police would have to act to protect the safety of his students. In circumstances such as this, most people dialled three simple digits before navigating a series of faceless operators who passed them to the most appropriate service before someone interrogated them about the reason they'd called.

Carrington was not most people.

"Commissioner," he said assertively as soon as the call was answered. "We have a problem on campus."

"You're not kidding," came the stressed out response.

"*The Idiots' Club?*"

"Who?"

"You remember, Eric Gideon?"

There was a long pause as the name settled and the memories reignited. "Oh him."

"He was just in my office. He's threatened to evacuate the University unless I announced it first. The gall of the man."

"But…that's exactly what you need to do," came the anxious reply. "Urgently."

"Ridiculous, Terry. Get a grip, man. Whatever they're up to it'll be a hoax, that's all."

"But it's not a…"

"I simply won't tolerate them disrupting the students' education and I certainly won't be bullied. I want you to assign one of your best inspectors to investigate Gideon, immediately. I want to know what he's up to. I want him arrested and charged with harassment and anything else you can pin on him, do you hear me!"

"This really isn't the time, Andrew…we're dealing with…"

"How long do you have left until you're up for re-election, Terry?" Carrington asked ominously.

"The election is in two months, as you well know."

"Did you know that students vote more frequently than any other demographic outside of old age pensioners?"

"Yes, but…"

"Be a shame if twenty percent of the electorate were encouraged to vote for someone else, wouldn't it?"

"Andrew, you don't understand the severity of what's…"

"I want Gideon stopped. I want him inconvenienced. I want him harangued at every turn. If he tries to buy a coffee I want someone watching him. I want a detective all over him like a rash. DO YOU UNDERSTAND!" Carrington shouted down the phone, face red and body convulsing violently.

"Fine! I'll post DI Whitehall to the case as soon as I can spare her, but you've got to listen to me, Andrew…there's a…"

Carrington hung up the phone and the Commissioner was left talking into the ether. He jumped out of his chair and threw on his jacket. Until the detective got here, it was down to him to stop them.

EIGHTEEN
OUTGROWN. GOGGLE. HAZELNUTS

AT PRECISELY NINE THIRTY, MICKY MADE THE CALL TO THE emergency services as planned. Unlike Carrington, he didn't have the luxury of a direct line number to someone senior, so he went through the normal hoops. The operator asked him which emergency service he wanted and straight away it made him stop and think. Police, fire service or ambulance? That decision was likely to depend on the condition of the bomb at the time they arrived. At present, it was sitting on a pile of sand not doing very much, so he decided the police were probably needed first. After a short exchange with the operator to ascertain the purpose of his call, they asked him to give a more accurate location for his bomb sighting than 'on some sand in a building site'.

"Are you nearby, sir?"

"Near enough, thanks."

"And do you have access to a phone?"

"What do you think this is!"

"I mean can you access the internet."

"Why?"

"There's a website called what3words. It will give us a precise location point. Can you find it?"

"Are you asking me to get closer to the bomb?" asked Micky, who didn't divulge that he'd spent most of the morning big spooning it in the back of a clapped out hearse.

"No, sir, you should be able to locate it from a distance."

"Hold on," he said, pulling the phone from his ear and switching access to an internet browser. He found the website easily enough but struggled to identify the exact square the bomb was on, as there weren't any recognisable features on the map to go by. It might have been diamond.bagpipes.engravings or strain.comical.character. It was no good; he'd have to get closer to the bomb and use the proximity settings. He strolled casually through the still empty building site.

"Okay. I've got it. It's outgrown.goggle.hazelnuts."

"Thank you. We have it on our system. Please move to a place of safety. We're sending a team now to cordon off the area."

It was the first time Micky had been close to the device without the background noise of chattering voices or the roar of the hearse's exhausted engine. The tranquillity of morning, unsullied by local roads or residential comings and goings some distance away, sharpened his hearing and revealed sounds that might otherwise have gone unheard. One sound in particular.

"They should be with you within ten minutes…"

"Shush," insisted Micky straining his ears to pick up a specific and faint noise somewhere below him. He stooped down towards the bomb.

Yep, it was definitely ticking.

"Shit…are you still there…I've changed my mind! I

need fire service and quite possibly ambulance too…
hello…HELLO…

THE ONLY INSTRUCTION he'd been given was to use his 'initiative' and that was exactly the way Josh liked life to be.
Improvisation took a lot less effort than thinking, and
making stuff up as you went along meant you never got
anything wrong. It takes a brave man to complain about
the outcome if they haven't set any expectations in the first
place. The history of improvisation is littered with false
starts and glorious failures that no one will ever remember,
but Josh thought it unlikely his attempts at 'thinking on his
feet' would be quite so easy to forget on this occasion.

Below him, hundreds of students mingled around the
vast open areas of the Forum as they switched lecture
theatres, stopped to chat with friends or grabbed an early
morning skinny latte macchiato. They generally looked
happy and focused, but that was all about to change. On
the balcony to his right, Callum was primed and ready to
record Josh's big moment on his mobile phone.

Josh pushed up the visor on his fake fire helmet and
lifted a loudhailer, which he'd stealthily pinched from the
building site before they'd left, up to his lips. Micky was
currently wishing he hadn't, because he could have used
one right about now. Outside the Forum, the bells of clock
tower on the campus grounds clanked noisily to indicate
the passing of the hour.

Ten o'clock.

His cue.

"Ladies and Gentlemen! Please remain calm. Leave
your belongings where they are and head towards the
nearest fire exit."

The majority of the occupants of the Forum ignored him. Most of them had AirPods stuffed in their ears and were listening to some ghastly grime music or intellectually stimulating podcast. A few of them noticed him gesturing exuberantly from the top of the stairs, but until the fire alarms went off, there didn't appear to be any need to rush. After all, they were students and coffee was expensive.

"For your own safety, please move to the nearest exit," he repeated a little louder but receiving the same level of ambivalence. "STAY CALM!"

"They look positively comatose," added Callum, who'd moved over to get a closeup.

"Kids these days," huffed Josh. "No respect for authority!"

"That's rich coming from you, don't you think?"

"I see your point."

"Maybe it's not turned on," said Callum, trying to take it from him.

Josh jerked it away like a toddler defending his favourite toy. "It's on!"

"Perhaps you just don't look…firemany…enough."

"Firemany?"

"It's a word," insisted Callum.

"Well, I've got the outfit, haven't I? What more do they want from me? Do I have to be literally on fire to get their attention?"

"Try again…but a bit louder and more gruff."

"Gruff?"

"Firemen are always gruff."

"I'm not sure what programmes you've been watching."

Callum encouraged him to go again to avoid answering the question.

"DANGER! EVACUATE IMMEDIATELY."

If anything, there was even less response as most of the students had decided this was only a drill and no one was going to move in case they lost their seats.

"THERE'S A BOMB. EVACUATE BUT ALSO… STAY CALM…LEAVE VIA YOUR NEAREST…oh shit," Josh's voice tailed off to a whisper as he spotted the disgruntled figure of the Vice Chancellor marching across the atrium floor flanked by a gaggle of security guards. He had his finger outstretched towards them and he didn't look very happy.

"Stop that man!" he instructed angrily.

A novice might have panicked, given themselves up or run away. An expert like Josh knew that the key to pretending to be someone you weren't was to resolutely defend your false identify at all costs. The more convincing the act, the more doubt was sown. He dropped his visor again to cover his features and Callum shuffled off into the background to act like a mature student, a disguise he pulled off less well than Josh's fireman.

Carrington bounded up the staircase with the energy of a much younger man, but his face was redder than an asthmatic octogenarian.

"Sir, you need to evacuate the building!" said Josh indignantly when the Vice Chancellor reached his elevated position.

"I'll do no such thing."

"Please move to your nearest exit. This one behind me will do fine. A fire marshal will point you towards a…"

"Who are you?" demanded Carrington.

"Sir, I must insist for your own safety," repeated Josh, flashing a fake ID which looked remarkably genuine. "There is a developing situation at the Bellfield construction site nearby that requires…"

"Nonsense. This is all Eric Gideon's doing."

"Who?" feigned Josh.

"*The Idiots Club!*"

"Currently, there's only one person acting like an idiot, sir," he replied, extending a judgemental finger in Carrington's direction. "Who do you think you are, anyway?"

"Who am I! How dare you?"

"It's a fairly standard question, sir. I'm not asking for inside leg measurements."

"Take his megaphone," instructed Carrington to the nearest security guard, who looked unwilling to pick a side. As far as the guard was concerned, he looked authentically firemany.

"I'm only going to say this one more time, sir. Please move to the nearest exit and make your way to the evacuation point."

"The only person who can authorise an evacuation from this site is the Vice Chancellor," said Carrington boldly. "And that, my lad, is me."

"You sure, sir?"

"Of course I'm sure!"

"What about them?" said Josh, pointing to the furthest side of the Forum where a surge of police officers in body armour were streaming through the entrance.

"Brought some friends, did you!" concluded the Vice Chancellor. "Gideon stepped it up a notch, has he? Well, I'm not falling for it."

"What are you talking about?"

"It's just a dare! A juvenile prank."

"I assure you it's not a drill," countered Josh. "People's lives are at risk. You need to raise the alarm."

"I'll do no such thing."

While the two security guards struggled to balance their employer's instructions and what appeared to be an increasingly tense situation, Andrew Carrington stormed back down the stairs to confront the 'fake' police crew. A brief and heated exchange with a senior police officer ensued until Carrington thought it wise to rip the police badge off his jacket and petulantly knocked his hat off his head. A one-sided melee broke out before Carrington was swiftly placed in handcuffs.

"I think you've got a choice here," Josh whispered to the two security men. "Save your boss or save yourselves."

In unison they scarpered out through the nearest exit.

"Oh, please tell me you're getting this on film," begged Josh as Callum rejoined him on the steps.

"Oh yeah."

More than thirty police officers were now joined in the Forum by a flock of legitimately employed firemen, and within a few minutes, the buildings' alarms were ringing out far and wide. There remained, however, a deep sense of reticence to act accordingly. Students casually packed laptop bags and art folders as slowly as possible, convinced it was a drill. It took ages to get a seat in the Forum and they weren't giving them up in a hurry.

Eric paced nonchalantly across the smooth floor from the far side of the building, stopping only briefly in Carrington's eyeline as they led him away for assaulting an officer.

"Arrest him!" shouted Carrington angrily when he saw who it was. "He's responsible for this. Arrest Eric Gideon!"

"I did ask you very nicely," whispered Eric as he sauntered past. "And I even told you what would happen."

"Let me go! I'm friends with the commissioner!"

Eric reached the top of the stairs and surveyed the chaos they'd created.

"Is this what you had in mind?" asked Callum.

"No, I didn't think it would be this easy," said Eric as

he stared into the camera. "Is this good enough for you, Sean?"

"I doubt it," suggested Josh. "We haven't got Micky on the video yet."

"He'll be here soon."

"PLEASE MOVE TO YOUR NEAREST EXIT."

"Josh, you don't have to do that anymore. The professionals are here now."

"Sorry, it's the outfit. Power rush."

"I'm amazed how casual they are," said Callum as he filmed the snail-paced student exodus below them.

"Well, they think it's a false alarm, don't they."

"It's still impressive…they're all so calm."

"All apart from him," said Josh, pointing into the crowd.

Down in the centre of the slow retreat someone was acting hysterically. A thin middle-aged man with glasses was pushing people aggressively towards the exits while screaming furiously at them. When he finally spotted the three of them alone on the balcony, he raised his voice even louder to compete with the deafening sound of the alarms.

"Is that Micky?"

"I think so," replied Eric squinting.

"What's he saying?

"It's sticking?" wondered Callum.

"What is?"

The others shrugged.

"IT'S TICKING!" shouted Micky at the top of his lungs.

∿

YESTERDAY. Frome Police Station.

. . .

"LET'S PLAY A LITTLE GAME," proposed Iris, in a manner which suggested Eric didn't have much choice in the matter.

"What sort of game?"

"It's a guessing game."

"I thought you'd be more interested in facts."

"I have enough of those for now."

"Okay. Lead on."

"How much do you think the insurance companies have estimated is the cost of the damage caused by the explosion?"

Eric shrugged casually.

"I can't accept shrugs as guesses, I'm afraid. I need a number."

"Twelve," he huffed.

"Twelve what?"

Eric didn't have the first idea, but that wasn't the point of her game. It was her intention to foster a sense of guilt inside him for the damage done as a result of his involvement, and it didn't matter if it was a broken car window or a flattened city. He didn't feel remotely guilty about what had happened. As he and the boys bolted for their lives down the hill of Streatham campus and out onto the main road, he'd witnessed the blast for himself. It was loud enough to cause his eardrums to ring for the next few hours, so he was convinced structures nearer to it hadn't escaped unscathed. As they retreated from the scene in the hearse, they'd tuned into radio news reports, relieved to hear that everyone had been evacuated safely. Yes, it was true to say that no one would have been in harm's way if they'd left the bomb where they'd found it, but he felt they deserved more credit for their part in initially notifying the police.

"Thousand," murmured Eric.

"Ten…million. Half a dozen houses were destroyed or condemned, most of the glass in the Forum was smashed, not to mention the cleanup operation and lost learning time."

"Maybe they should send Sean the bill."

"He's already donated five million to the repairs."

"Of course he has," sulked Eric.

"This is the cost of your brand of 'fun', Eric."

"Are you, again, baselessly suggesting I had something to do with it?"

"I arrived at the scene around lunchtime. Must have been a couple of hours after the explosion, but I wasn't there because of the bomb. You see, I'd been summoned by my superior officer, at the request of Sir Andrew Carring-ton. You're not going to deny knowing who he is, are you?"

"No…he's a prick."

"He's not keen on you, either. He called my commis-sioner an hour before the evacuation because he said you'd threatened him. Is that right?"

"Absolutely not," answered Eric. "If anything, he threatened me."

"It's always someone else, isn't it, Eric?"

"It's true," he replied calmly.

"And how did he do that, exactly?"

"He quoted Enoch Powell at me."

"Oh, that well-known hate crime," she mocked. "You admit to seeing him, correct?"

Eric nodded proudly.

"After your visit, he demanded that the police investi-gate you on suspicion of harassment. I went to see him later that day and I'd describe his mood as incandescent. What do you think might have caused that?"

"One of his pictures drooped a fraction."

"Not quite. Apart from his anger that some of my colleagues had handcuffed and arrested him for interfering with a police operation, most of his discontent was aimed at you and a group I'd never heard of before called *The Idiots' Club*."

"So you already knew about us," Eric replied, realising how well she'd pretended not to know.

"Only the name. I didn't know anything else about you at the time. It was the last time I heard the name mentioned until you confirmed it earlier today. I was much more interested in something called 'WDWC Live'."

Eric stared unresponsively, unwilling to let on that he already knew she'd watched his channel.

"In the old days, investigations like this took weeks and wore out several pairs of shoes. We used to traipse about knocking on doors in search of eyewitnesses, or we had to scour through undergrowth for single strands of hair or trawl through hours of grainy black and white security films. Not these days. All you need these days is one of these," she announced, holding up her phone. "There's always someone who decides the most sensible thing to do in a crisis is to whip a phone out and film it."

"Find anything good?"

"Oh yes. I've been watching your channel ever since. You see, to me it sounded suspiciously like Carrington had a vendetta against you and he was using his influence on the commissioner for his own personal gain. But the more I explored, the more I realised something else was happening. I just didn't know what or why."

"I'll hand it to you, Iris," he said again, showing his

hands when he used the word. "You're a bloody good detective."

"Tell me something I don't know."

"Okay, I will. I'm beaten," replied Eric honestly. "Now charge me and I can try to arrange bail."

"If I wanted to do that, I had enough evidence to do it hours ago. Catching you is not the only thing I care about. There's something strange going on here and I'm going to work out what it is. So far in the past week, I've witnessed four of your dares, but I haven't worked out what the fifth one was going to be."

"That is a shame."

"Tell me."

"No. I don't think I will. You'll have to work it out for yourself."

NINETEEN
AUBERGINE DIP

Last Thursday.

There wasn't much conversation as they drove back from
Exeter. It was hard to communicate when two of them had
to lie horizontally in the back of a hearse nursing perfo-
rated eardrums. The radio blared in the background,
struggling to cut through the relentless humming inside
their heads. Unsurprisingly, Callum slept through it like a
baby. Even the apocalypse wouldn't wake him up.

The mood in the car should have been celebratory, but
they struggled to raise even the narrowest of smiles. The
first dare was done and within the first day of their deadline, but it hadn't gone smoothly. Although, according to
radio reports, and quite against the odds, no one had been
seriously hurt as a result of the unexpected detonation that
redecorated a one-mile-square area of the city. Someone's
dog was missing and an old woman couldn't stop sneezing,
but apart from that and the humongous cleanup operation,
they'd got off lightly. Even more miraculously, given their

proximity to the blast, they were almost in one piece and were still talking to each other.

When it came to team dares, history showed theirs rarely ran smoothly. Teamwork requires compromise and collaboration, two attributes with which they all struggled. If four strong characters are told to work together, all of whom have a rigid sense of self-reliance and resilience imprinted on them from difficult upbringings, then disagreements are bound to happen. Most of the club's individual dares suited their personalities perfectly. But when the dare required a team effort, rarely did they share a unified approach.

Historically, this resulted in vitriolic arguments, physical bust ups and world class name calling. But if they descended into that this week, they'd surely fail. Hopefully they'd matured sufficiently enough over the last two decades to avoid it. Eric glanced over at Josh as he pulled faces and made rude hand gestures at fellow drivers through his passenger window. Hopefully some of them might have, at least.

As the miles on the signs for London ticked down into single figures, and the spring daylight edged out of view, Eric's thoughts returned to what came next. The first dare had left a trail. The footage was online and, according to Micky, who'd checked the feed on his phone, it was already getting attention. Certainly, Sean had seen. His text message a few hours later confirmed that he was satisfied with their efforts. Given the size of his personal network and burning desire to beat them, there was a good chance Sean would be promoting their YouTube channel far and wide. They had to assume that the general public would be watching and waiting for their next post. Which meant their faces were no longer private and secrecy was a luxury they no longer owned.

It wasn't the only change in circumstances they'd have to consider in the run-up to dare two.

Carrington was not someone who surrendered without a fight. Both their actions and his own would have inflicted serious reputational damage on the Vice Chancellor. Eric had always envisioned the introduction of a third party to act as a suitable decoy and Carrington had fallen right in his lap. But such a move would raise the heat on them still further. Carrington knew people. Serious people. Powerful allies within his community and a loyal army of alumni stationed across the world to act as his eyes and ears. How would Carrington mobilise these weapons in order to seek retribution for the structural and reputational damage inflicted on the University? It was possible he might send an email to tens of thousands of former students asking them to keep a lookout for the group.

The alumni who'd studied at Exeter at the same time as Eric would certainly remember who they were, even if they didn't instantly recognise their faces after all these years. Unless you counted online dating sites, which made Josh one of the most recognisable men in the Northern Hemisphere, none of the idiots were active on social media, which increased their chances of anonymity. But there were some ex-students who would easily pick them out in a identity parade, and one of them was the subject of their next dare.

Jessica Connelly.

If she received news of what they'd done, it might make their challenge more difficult.

"Wake the others," Eric instructed Josh.

It was seven o'clock in the evening and the traffic along the South Circular was predictably onerous, at least for most of the drivers forced to remain fallow in their cars. One benefit of being in a hearse was that other drivers did their best to shuffle out of the way to allow their vehicle a smoother passage. It wasn't just drivers who noticed them, either. In built-up areas, pedestrians frequently showed their respects by removing their hats, or standing head bowed on the side of the pavement. When the shabby, spluttering black Granada got closer, they stopped when they saw it was empty.

But it wasn't.

A pair of arms reached for the hearse's ceiling as Micky, the tallest member of *The Idiots' Club*, stretched his muscles to shake off cramp. This did nothing for the weak heart of the frail old lady at a zebra crossing. She fainted at the sight of several arms grappling up the side of the hearse's windows. A little further on a group of youths, who'd mostly been staring into their phones rather than talk to each other, became wildly hysterical when they heard terrifying moans seeping through the glass and a head poking into view.

"Are we nearly there yet," Micky yawned, prodding Callum in the groin who was lying top to tail next to him.

"Almost."

"Thank Christ for that. I haven't been this uncomfortable since the last time I went caving and at least then my ears still worked."

"How is everyone's hearing?" shouted Eric, demonstrating his own continuing struggles.

"Fine," replied Josh, who was the only one wearing some form of protection when the bomb went off.

"I feel like I'm suffering the world's worst hangover, and I barely touched a drop yesterday," mumbled Callum.

"You didn't have any," insisted Micky.

"Then you weren't paying attention," coughed Callum, who could find and consume alcohol via osmosis if that was his only option.

"We need to get organised for dare two," Eric announced loudly. "There's only a narrow window for this one."

"How so?"

"Because I've booked tickets for Micky to watch *Cats* tonight and it starts in a couple of hours."

"Two hours! What will I wear?"

"Chill out, Cinderella. We'll find you something," answered Josh with a hint of annoyance in his voice, still convinced out of all of them he had the best chance of wooing Jessica.

"Do I really have to sit through a musical? It's bad enough you're forcing me to go through with the dare, but that makes it ten times worse."

"It'll be good for you. Plus, you'll have something to talk to Jessica about over dinner."

"What, cats?"

"No. Musicals."

"I know more about cats," he groaned. "So while I'm doing dare two - all on my own - I suppose you'll be lounging around relaxing."

"No, we'll be covering our tracks from today and figuring out how to abduct Logan Cobley. Want to swap?"

"Not really," he said meekly.

Theatre followed by dinner with an old friend was a better deal than second-guessing a man who'd annoyed most of Afghanistan.

"We'll hide the hearse in the underground car park at my apartment," Eric affirmed. "Callum, give Dubious Barry a call and see if he's experiencing any undue attention."

"On it."

"I've also got a couple of calls to make before Micky's date tonight."

"It's not a date," huffed Micky.

"That's because you're not a lesbian!" stated Josh.

Micky had initially argued against Josh's repeated and baseless allegations about Jessica's sexuality, but right now he secretly hoped they were true.

MICKY WAITED near the rear entrance of Drury Lane Theatre unknowingly humming to himself. He wasn't going to let the others know, but tonight's performance had been a revelation. Musicals had always been Natasha's thing, and as a result, he'd been staunchly against them. Which he now acknowledged was a little short-sighted. He concluded that the only reason for his vehement dislike for musical theatre was a desire to annoy his other half. And this unavoidable truth got him thinking. Why would he do that?

The answer was quick and obvious.

Because she did it to him.

In fact the more he thought about it, the more he realised how much she hated everything he was passionate about. Cricket, skiing, Moroccan food, classic cars, comedy clubs, prog rock and soft porn magazines. It was obvious why she disliked one of them. After all, most people hated prog rock. Yet, like his own antipathy for musicals, she didn't show the slightest willingness to give them a go, even if it was only for his benefit. She never had, because their relationship had always been confrontational. In his opinion, she used passive aggression, and occasionally active aggression, to make him feel guilty about doing the things he loved and within their dynamic, he only had two ways to respond.

Put up or fight back.

Divorce wasn't even an option.

He felt a strong obligation to their marital vows. It had nothing to do with religion, though; he thought that was a stupid concept. What really compelled him to stay with her was a duty to family history. If his mother could endure fifty years of his father's abuse and fury, then living with Natasha was a doddle. It was the equivalent of exchanging a rabid, dangerous pit-bull for a docile golden retriever. Nobody in the illustrious Parsons family tree had ever been through a divorce and, as an only child, he felt the full weight of that personal history on his skinny shoulders. Perhaps when his mother passed away he'd feel differently about it. Given her determination to live forever, it was unlikely to change anytime soon. Then there was the impact on the kids to consider.

But it wasn't just family pride that stopped him from leaving her.

It was mostly because she petrified him.

Natasha had a vicious streak, and there was no knowing what she'd do if he asked for a divorce. People with her background weren't used to being second best and didn't let bygones be bygones. He only had to look at her reaction to Josh for proof of that. While Josh only dated her for a couple of weeks, Micky had been married to her for almost two decades. He shuddered as he visualised police forces up and down the country finding bits of his mutilated body inside parcels posted to everyone in his address book.

In recent years, married life had been more like minor warfare than matrimonial bliss. Like the conflict in the Middle East, they'd reached a status quo. Neither of them was prepared to accept their faults, nor were they willing to see the other's point of view. Being unhappy was one thing, but going out of your way to make someone else miserable was quite another. Micky considered himself to be on the right side of the argument but as he stood whistling *Rum Tum Tugger* in an alleyway behind a theatre waiting for a 'date', reality dawned on him.

Micky had approached tonight's performance of *Cats* with rock-bottom expectations, and after spending five minutes inside the theatre, he thought it was unlikely they'd be met. The foyer was packed to the rafters with punters, most of whom felt compelled to cackle loudly and refuse point-blank to give up any of the space they'd commandeered. There was little doubt from the expensive jewellery, overpowering perfumes, natty waistcoats and fake furs what type of crowd they were. This was the ultimate hangout for grown-up Sloane Rangers. No wonder Natasha loved it. These were her people, not his.

The experience didn't improve inside the auditorium. The seat he'd been allocated was just big enough for a Lego man. Directly in his eyeline, a giant pillar obscured his view and was so fragile he was scared to touch it in case the circle above collapsed in on itself. The stage was located some miles below him, presumably only inches above the London tube station he'd used to get here. To compensate for the poor visual experience, the theatre provided a small pair of red binoculars which could be hired for the same price as full laser eye surgery.

But when the curtains parted and the first musical notes were played, discomfort and low expectations evaporated instantaneously.

Carried away by the captivating music, magnificent set and engrossing narrative, he soon forgot why he was meant to be there. Thoughts of Jessica were consigned to the back of his mind and all that remained at the front were dancing cats. When he did remember his sole purpose for being there, he struggled to identify Jessica from the other cast members, and not simply because he'd not seen her for twenty years. The incredible costumes and realistic makeup would have made it difficult to spot members of his own family if they were in the cast. The main characters were easy enough to pinpoint because they were frequently mentioned in the story and had eponymous songs about them. As for the rest of the actors, establishing what gender the cats were, let alone who was underneath, was almost impossible.

In the end, he gave up and settled down to watch the show, which he enjoyed considerably more than the people sitting closest to him. According to the sour-faced old crone in the row directly behind his head, some behaviours are not tolerated at the theatre.

Clapping was fine.

Singing along was borderline acceptable.

Standing throughout the performance, shouting "he's behind you", foot stamping, attempting to stimulate a Mexican wave and returning for the second half with a family-sized bucket of Kentucky Fried Chicken, apparently weren't.

When the curtains finally closed, to a rousing yet polite round of applause, Micky returned to the business at hand, full of wonder and a newfound appreciation for the oboe.

A few actors sneaked out of the stage door, pursued by young fans attempting to grab an autograph of anyone they might recognise from TV. Almost all actors appeared on *Holby City* at one point in their career so they'd probably get lucky. Micky was hoping for something a little more significant than a scribble on a notepad; he needed a date. Recognising Jessica dressed in full catsuit had been impossible, but he was hoping to do better when he saw her in civilian clothes. A few middle-aged women came through and for a brief second his mind tried to deceive him. All he had to go on was Jessica's black and white head shots, which he'd found on her agent's website, and his own memory.

Both sources were somewhat misleading.

They still pictured her with long flowing blonde hair, saucer-sized eyes and a smile able to melt even the coldest of hearts, but it wasn't just her appearance that was flooding back to him. The kindness in her face perfectly matched the way he remembered her character. Unless you included Josh, who entirely deserved it, she was extremely caring and had a talent for putting people at ease with her engaging, inquisitive and bubbly manner. She was calm, relaxed and smart and he struggled to understand why, only now, he realised how incredibly sexy she was. The thought retreated rapidly in case Natasha had secretly wired a surveillance system directly into his conscience.

Micky suddenly felt very anxious and out of place. Acting suspiciously around the back entrance of a theatre was liable to get you arrested or punched, particularly now so many of the actors had already left. Had he missed her? Perhaps she'd fallen asleep in her dressing room, or decided to go out the main entrance. Just as he was about to give up and head back to Eric's with his tail between his legs, the door flew again and clattered against the wall with a bang. If he'd doubted his ability to recognise her before, he really shouldn't have worried.

"Michael?" said the woman the moment she set eyes on him.

Few people called him Michael anymore. Only his mother, and whenever he heard her use it, he assumed he was in trouble. Apart from that, it was only ever used in formal settings, like at the bank or when signing legal documents. He never introduced himself that way. He always used 'Micky', and the only other one he answered to was 'Turnip'.

"Jessica?" he said, mustering his most plausible surprised voice. It wasn't very good, but then again she was the actor, not him.

"Wow! I can't believe it. It's so good to see you," she gushed, moving out from under the illuminated stage door and into the street to embrace him. "You look great! How have you been?"

"Well, life's…" He stopped to consider the most suitable adjective to sum up his week so far. Bewildering, chaotic, desperate, surreal, bonkers, depressing were all suitable but he picked the one word everyone fell back on when needing to describe all of them simultaneously. "…interesting."

"Sounds…interesting," she laughed. "What are you doing here?"

Micky waved his official *Cats* programme, which he imagined cost more than the price of the ticket. "I was flicking through at half time and to my utter surprise I saw your name. I thought I'd hang around and see if it was you or someone else."

"And here we are. Me and you! What a lovely surprise," she said, stroking his arm over-familiarly. "You don't go to the theatre very much, do you?"

"What makes you say that?"

"It's generally known as the intermission rather than half time!" she chuckled.

"It must be a regional difference," he argued quite ridiculously. "I see loads of shows in Bristol - as many as I can get to."

The lie tripped off his tongue before his brain was even aware it had formed. He didn't fully understand why he felt the need to deceive her, other than a desire to endear himself to her. Unknown to him, he really didn't need to.

"Who're you with?"

"Just me."

"Where's Mrs Michael Parsons?"

Micky stalled. Did she know the truth or was she making a reasonable assumption?

"There's only a former Mrs Parsons these days," he lied, before quickly moving away from the subject. "A friend of mine couldn't make it tonight and offered me his ticket. I have to say, you were magnificent."

"Thank you. I'm not in it very much but it's a massive honour to be part of the cast. What did you think of Miranda Lewis - isn't she phenomenal?"

Micky nodded energetically, belying the reality that he had no clue which one of the hairy specks some distance from him had been played by an actress he'd never heard of until now.

"What about Piers Stronsky as Old Deuteronomy, he's breathtakingly good, isn't he. He recently joined us from *West Side Story*; have you seen that one?"

"Not yet," Micky replied glumly. "I've only just managed to see *East Side Story*."

"Ha!" she giggled, giving him a friendly punch on the arm to reward the joke.

"Ouch."

"How did tonight's performance compare with plays you've seen, Michael?" she asked, eager to get some positive feedback.

"Best by far."

"Really? What have you seen recently?"

Nothing. There was no way to crawl out of the huge hole he'd dug for himself still clutching the truth. He glanced down the alleyway to the brightly-coloured signs hijacking Victorian architecture to hypnotise corruptible onlookers.

"I've seen Phantom."

"So you're a big Lloyd Webber fan, then?"

"Yeah. I've seen all of his classics…Phantom, Cats…Dogs…Joseph and the Dream Catcher…Ryvita…"

She burst into laughter again and gave him an enormous hug. "You always were a terrible actor, but you're as funny as you ever were."

"At least that's something. Hey, what are you doing now?"

"I was going to head home."

"Have dinner with me?"

"What, now?"

"Yeah."

"It's ten thirty."

"Supper then."

"I really should get back."

"Someone waiting for you?" he said inquiringly.

"Only pot plants and housemates."

"You've no excuse then."

"I get really tired, Michael. Late nights aren't good for me."

"I promise to have you in bed by midnight," he answered.

"Will you now!" she winked.

"Um…I didn't mean it like that," he said, blushing.

"Shame."

Micky panicked. The last time a member of the opposite sex used innuendo on him was sometime in the last millennium and it wasn't even his wife. "Just dinner. That's all. It would be great to catch up."

"It really would. Okay, but only if we go halves," she insisted. "And I get to pick where we eat."

"Done," he agreed, offering his arm. "Lead the way."

London was rarely quiet. There were always people on the streets, day and night. The West End at this time of the evening was positively bustling as the crowds simultaneously filtered out of the vast number of theatres. Jessica, the city equivalent of a mountain goat, weaved her way through them effortlessly. Micky less so. Whichever way he moved, someone was in his path. Without Jessica grasping his arm, he'd have lost her to the melee in seconds. Her movements were instinctive and her knowledge of the area matched only by a black cab driver. She escorted him through the narrow side roads, down the suitably named Exeter Street, along the busy, bus-filled Strand before finally turning up Bedford Street.

"Here it is," she said as they approached a small independent Greek restaurant. "One of my favourite places in the city."

Micky had never been to Greece, and as far as he could remember he'd never eaten authentic Greek food before, either. Natasha was a fussy eater and avoided experimenting in case it wasn't to her liking. When they did go out, which was incredibly rare these days, they always went to the same place – The Crescent Rooms, a pompous, stuffy, expensive and rather uninspiring bistro. Mostly Natasha liked it because she knew he didn't.

"Greek. I'm game."

"Inside or out."

"They have a heater so maybe out."

"My thoughts exactly," she beamed.

Outside dining consisted of three sets of two-seater tables hunched up against the window and only marginally on the pavement rather than the road. A European plaza it was not. Fortunately, very few cars used Bedford Street other than the occasional London Taxi. Within seconds of their bums hitting their fold-up seats, their waiter, Niko-laos, was attending to their needs. His name might have been traditionally Greek but it was obvious he'd probably been there less frequently than Micky. His accent sounded distinctively like he was from Bolton.

Jessica ordered them a mezze and a carafe of red wine, and soon they were conversing freely like old friends who met up every week. They skipped through the more mundane subjects - work, kids, friends, hobbies and family - until it was impossible to avoid the topic of their shared past.

"So, what happened to Natasha?" asked Jessica, picking at the remaining olives in a glazed terracotta dish. "I'm somewhat surprised she removed her claws from you."

"We just grew apart," Micky replied, not entirely dishonestly.

"I'm not convinced you had anything in common to begin with."

The more he thought about it, the more he struggled to offer a suitable answer. What did they have in common back then? Outside of their similar upbringings, they'd liked different music, enjoyed different hobbies and had vastly divergent values. She hadn't even been his type phys-ically. He preferred blonde, petite and smiley girls - like Jessica. But Natasha's sexually aggressive pursuit of him made it almost impossible to resist. The real, yet hidden, response to Jessica's statement was simple. Josh was the only thing they'd had in common.

"We both liked rugby and wine," answered Micky finally, as if that was a stable enough foundation to prop up a two-decade-long relationship. "I think she still likes wine."

"It's not much, though, is it. I mean, I love rugby but

we're not married, are we," she responded, playing with her shiny blonde hair and piercing him with her blue eyes.

He laughed uncomfortably.

"And you have three kids?"

"Yes. But they've coped really well with the divorce. Everything has been very amicable."

He considered what might happen in reality if he actually did have the balls to leave her. His balls would probably be the first casualties. 'Amicable' was not the first word that sprang to mind. 'Irascible' might be closer to the mark. He'd probably be living in a caravan with a scabby rescue dog, zero income and no access to his children. He'd drink cans of Special Brew for breakfast, walk around in a string vest and growl at unsuspecting locals.

"Still, it must have been tough," she offered with a sympathetic stroke of his hand.

"I imagine it would...for someone who lacked resilience," he quicky added, drifting back from his nightmarish visions of an alternate reality. "What about you? I'm surprised you didn't settle down."

"Oh, I've had my fair share of psychos, players, emotional retards and catfish," she said with a smile. "And that's just the actors! Unlucky in love I guess. I met 'the one' some years ago but life didn't pan out the way I hoped."

"You never know, it's never too late," he said encouragingly, but lacking suitable consideration for what she really meant.

"Let's hope so."

Her irises expanded and the intensity of her eyes displayed more information than the contents of a Tolkien trilogy. It became obvious to him who she thought 'the one' was. If the boys had been livestreaming the date, Micky was pretty confident she'd say yes to a marriage proposal right here and now. A few days ago, the thought of this dare made him incredibly uncomfortable. Now it felt wrong on so many levels. Such an act of deception wasn't only offensive - it was liable to break this girl's heart all over again. The other dares Sean devised seemed almost impossible, yet this one now appeared ridiculously easy, if he choose to go through with it. Did Sean know how she felt about him? Was there an angle he was missing? Whether there was or not, he knew he couldn't go through with it.

"Do you still see Josh?" asked Jessica, removing the metaphorical dustsheet from the elephant in the corner of the room, or more appropriately the corner of the pavement.

"Occasionally."

"How's he doing?"

"It's hard to say. I mean, from one perspective it appears he's enjoying life, but deep down I'm not convinced he is. He hasn't changed much since University."

"Still chasing women then?"

"Yeah, I think the internet age has helped him immeasurably. Do you know you're still the only one who ever rejected him?"

"Shouldn't I get a blue plaque on my house for that!"

"I think you should!"

"I didn't mean to hurt him."

"Don't feel guilty. It was an excellent lesson for him. He needs to learn another one soon to bring him back down to earth. After your rejection, his confidence collapsed for months, but he's papered over it by convincing himself that you're a lesbian."

"Ha! Well, he would. One day, Josh will have to face up to his demons and realise that the life partner most suited to him is quite different from his view of perfection."

"I don't think he'll ever give up the chase. That's why he got so depressed when you spurned him. You took away the only thing that powers him. Belief."

"Well, for one I didn't fancy him, and I also had a massive crush on you," she admitted. "It's just a shame Natasha got to you first."

An awkward silence kidnapped the atmosphere. The flickering candle in the wicker-wrapped bottle cast pepper pot shadows across the tablecloth. The heater above their heads and the wine in their bellies kept the temperature warm inside and outside of them. Micky offered her a stuffed vine leaf from one of the pots closest to him and noticed something odd about her face.

"You okay?"

"Yeah, why?"

"Your eyes are flinching."

"Oh, are they? I don't notice it these days. Sometimes when I get tired I experience these involuntary facial movements. It's usually a sign I need to go to bed. My condition is actually one of the reasons I'm still single."

"Condition?" feigned Micky, who already knew but had to play along.

"I have a form of narcolepsy, but it's mostly under control these days."

"Can I get you anything for it?"

"Maybe the bill," she yawned.

"Back in a tick."

Micky dashed inside to use the facilities and track down Nikolaos. When he returned a few minutes later, the scene outside had shifted from romantic to catastrophic. Jessica's head was face down in a full bowl of Baba Ghanoush which, sadly for her, neither of them had found particularly appetising. Her body was slumped precariously against the side of the table, arms hanging limply by her sides, and only one buttock kept her from falling out of her chair. A glass lay on its side and red wine gushed across the table, staining the white tablecloth and washing her immaculate golden locks. The scene had all the hallmarks of an assassination by a lone sniper on a rooftop high above them. Only one element about it made this snap theory unlikely.

She was snoring loudly.

The current world record for the loudest snore is one hundred and eleven decibels. To put that into context, imagine the noise of a working chainsaw three feet away. Anyone attempting to beat this record would need perfect conditions. Sound waves travel best through the air where resistance is low. They travel less well through aubergine dip. That said, she was having a bloody good go at it.

Being unfamiliar with narcoleptics, Micky didn't know how best to deal with the situation. Did you try to wake them? Could you wake them? If you did, how would they react? He gave her a gentle nudge, but there was zero response. He tried a firmer prod but still nothing. He raised his voice to rouse her and that had no impact, either. He sat down to contemplate his next move. He couldn't leave her here like this. The situation was already starting to get awkward. People were staring and pointing as they left nearby pubs on their way down the road to the nearest tube station.

As requested, Nikolaos brought out the bill. He stopped in his tracks when he witnessed Micky's collapsed date.

"Do you accept credit cards?" Micky inquired casually.

"Did she eat any?" said the waiter, pointing at the

aubergine dip, which she was mostly using as makeup foundation.

"I don't think so, although by the looks of it she might have swallowed some on impact. Do you think she'll choke?" added Micky, suddenly concerned.

"STAVROS!" Nikolaos shouted hysterically, as if one of the tables had unexpectedly exploded. "We've got another one!"

"Another one?" said Micky in shock. "How many have you had before?"

"Quite a few," he replied alarmingly.

Micky had no idea that narcolepsy was so popular.

A huge hulk of a man, wrapped in a greasy apron and sporting more facial hair than a hipster convention, rushed outside looking panicked. He muttered something in Greek which sounded like profanity even if it wasn't. He and Nikolaos exchanged mutterings under their breath, nervously scanning the street for witnesses. Then Stavros broke out into something that sounded like English, just much more aggressive.

"Ambulance come. You take money," he said, slipping a huge roll of bank notes from under his apron and counting out some twenties.

"I really don't think an ambulance is necessary, she's only..."

"Pump stomach!" barked Stavros, demonstrating the procedure through the medium of mime with impressive accuracy. "Always same...never speak it...best Greek in town...Repeat!"

"What?"

"Say it! Best Greek. Repeat!"

"Best...Greek...in town," mumbled Micky timidly. "But what about her..."

"She live...if doctors fast."

To Micky's relief, they were. Two minutes later, an ambulance pulled up alongside the curb, its flashing blue lights reflecting off the glass of nearby shop fronts. Two crew members sauntered out like they'd stopped to order dinner.

"Stavros," said one of them in familiar greeting.

"Mr Brian," Stavros replied subserviently, with a little bow.

"Was it the Baba Ghanoush again?"

Stavros nodded shamefully.

"That's the fifth time this week."

"Never speak it…best Greek in town. Repeat!" replied Stavros, dipping into his apron and removing an ever decreasing roll of bank notes.

"No, you don't understand," said Micky, finally catching up on to the confusion. "She's not eaten…"

"Never speak it…best Baba Ghanoush…Repeat!"

"Are you her husband, sir?" asked Brian the ambulance man.

"No, just an old friend."

"Name?"

"Michael Parsons," he replied for the first time in decades.

"Not yours, sir."

"Oh, Jessica Connelly."

"Jessica, we're going to take you to hospital," shouted Brian.

"I'm not sure she can hear you."

"Sir, would you like to accompany her?"

"Yes," replied Micky, realising that this might be the best way of getting her back home without having to fire-man's lift her limp body across London. Everything would be fine as long as he explained to the crew about her real condition before they stuck a tube down her throat and evacuated the remnants of dinner.

They checked Jessica's vital signs before gently lifting her onto a stretcher. Once she'd been lifted into the back of the emergency vehicle, Micky picked up her handbag and hastily snuck an envelope inside. Stavros planted a handful of crisp notes into his grasp before making some rather ambiguous threats about what he and a man called 'Alianos' would do to his face if the Food Standards Agency paid the restaurant an unplanned visit.

Micky jumped into the back of the ambulance and it screeched off into the night.

It wasn't the worst first date in history. Yes, his companion had ended the evening unconscious and covered in Greek food, but it also included an incredibly fast ride home, two hundred quid profit, a free meal, new experiences and, until the end at least, extremely pleasant company. Most importantly of all, he'd secured a second date, even if strictly speaking, she didn't know about it yet.

TWENTY

AN INDECENT PROPOSAL

Last Saturday morning. Battersea.

LAUGHTER IS A VERY personal emotion because we all find different things funny. It's impossible to work out a formula when there are so many complicated factors to consider. Age, culture, country, mood and personality, to name a few. This is true of everyone except toddlers, who find everything hysterical. Grass, a dog's tail, their fingers, your fingers, fishfingers, someone falling over, their own reflection, anything that has shape, brightly-coloured objects, eyebrows, food, and someone laughing. When everything is new, everything is funny, but as we get older, life becomes more predictable and we laugh less frequently as a result.

We wait in hope for the humour holy grail. It's that rare moment in life when our reaction is so strong it leaves us physically debilitated. Tears will flow uncontrollably down our cheeks, our face muscles will ache, simple acts - like speech or coordinated movement – will no longer be possible, and the merest mention or thought of what we found funny will instantly set us off again in fits of giggles. It's impossible to know what the trigger will be because such levels of eye-watering comedy occur when we're least expecting them.

For Josh Foxole, it was Micky's date.

Comparisons between Josh and a toddler couldn't be overlooked.

After Micky recounted his evening, it took Josh at least twenty minutes to fully compose himself, and that was only after he was forced to excuse himself. He'd retreated out onto Eric's balcony where his laughter still broke through the double glazing and worried the neighbours. He finally re-joined them, trembling like jelly and ready to blow again at a moment's notice.

"Did you tell the ambulance crew about her condition?" asked Eric.

"She was snoring so loudly I didn't have to. They ran a couple of checks, cleaned her up and then dropped us back at her place."

"What happened then?"

"Her flatmate let us in and we helped her to bed."

"And…blah ha…did you…haaa…" giggled Josh, "give her…paaah…another aubergine!"

"I do know what that means, you know."

"Did you invite her to the game?" demanded Eric, who found Micky's date a lot less funny than the others.

"Kind of?"

"What does that mean?"

"I left the ticket and a note in her handbag."

"So you didn't ask her?"

"What use would that have been! She was asleep. I could have asked her a hundred times but I still wouldn't have got a response."

"You should have asked her earlier," snapped Eric.

"When?! Hello Jessica, lovely to see you for the first time in twenty years, do you want to come to a rugby match with me tomorrow! It's like foreplay; you have to work up to it."

"It depends how much time you have," replied Josh, still struggling for breath. "Sometimes...the most foreplay I get...is closing the car door!"

"What if she doesn't show up?" challenged Eric. "I've gone to a lot of trouble to set this dare up."

"She'll show. I checked the theatre performance times and the game doesn't clash. But even if she does come, I can't go through with it," announced Micky defiantly.

"You have to," begged Callum. "You've signed the contract."

"I don't care. We've pissed a lot of people off down the years but most of them have, in some ways, brought it on themselves. I can't do it to her. She's totally innocent."

"Don't go growing a conscience on me," grumbled Eric.

"She's not like us, Eric. She's lovely, kind and sweet."

"Sounds like someone has a crush."

"Yes, that's the problem," sighed Micky. "I'm genuinely convinced that even after one date, if I asked her to marry me tomorrow she'd say yes and it wouldn't matter what you'd set up to try and manipulate it."

"Brilliant!" Callum merrily raised his half full glass. "Dare two is in the bag."

"I'm not going through with it," repeated Micky.

"Then we'll have to go with Plan B," said Eric.

"There's a Plan B?"

"There always is. Josh, you'll have to do it."

"With pleasure! I'd love to have another crack at her now I know she's definitely not still a lesbian...like she was the first time I tried," he clarified.

"That's not the reason you failed. She just doesn't fancy you."

"Bollocks. She's playing hard to get."

"For twenty years!"

"Obviously."

"You're actually unhinged," replied Micky in disbelief.

"I understand you want to protect her. I think it's to your credit but it won't stop us," said Eric. "How do you think she'll feel if Josh comes on strong again, particularly if you do nothing to block him?"

"Do the dares really mean this much to you?" asked Micky aggressively. "More than my feelings and our friendship?"

Eric considered this for a moment. Victory was paramount, but it was always sweeter when they achieved it together. Failure was unacceptable, and if he gave up, it was liable to damage his friendship with Callum or Josh. They had to do it together or not at all.

"No," Eric responded, to their surprise. "I care about your feelings and hers."

"That's a first, " Micky huffed.

"How do you know she feels that way about you?" asked Eric.

"She has 'Michael' tattooed on her ankle; I saw it when she was being treated in the ambulance."

"Who's that?" asked Josh.

"Me, you idiot!"

"She's an actress - it's probably an homage to Caine or Gambon," speculated Callum.

"How would Gambon know it was about him?"

"Because that's his name," suggested Josh.

"And it's also…mine."

They stared blankly at him.

"Why didn't she get 'Turnip'?"

"Because only you three call me that and who wants the name of a vegetable on their ankle!"

"A grocer."

"Shut up. Don't you see? She's clearly in love with me. I think she has been for years if her relationship history is anything to go on."

"And how do you feel about her?" asked Eric.

"It's irrelevant," he replied, unwilling to reveal some of the feelings he experienced last night. "I'm married."

"But you're not happy."

"Says who?"

"Anyone who owns eyes or ears," added Josh.

"And do you want Jessica to be happy?" continued Eric.

"Yes, of course."

"And that's never going to be with you, right?" prompted Eric in full-scale sales mode.

"It can't."

"Be fun watching Natasha hunt you down with a crossbow, though," Josh remarked.

"If you told Jessica you're not interested in her, what would happen then?"

"Not a lot. She's kept her feelings for me hidden ever since she knew I was with Natasha."

"But she'll never move on, will she?"

"I guess not."

"Then I see it like this. If you want Jessica to be happy and move on, you need to demonstrate that you're not the man she thinks you are. You've got to make her hate you. It'll create short-term pain, of course, but in the long run you'll be doing her a favour. She'll forget you and move on," argued Eric.

"He's right, you know," confirmed Josh. "I've had to do it thousands of times."

"It will be a cold day in Hell when I take relationship advice from you, Foxie."

"It's the only way to set her free," advised Eric sympathetically.

Micky didn't entirely disagree with their logic even if he knew they had ulterior motives. Maybe it was the best way of helping her to move on. It was certainly better than subjecting her to Josh's unwanted attention. Then again, maybe a part of him wanted to do it anyway. He needed someone in his life to serve. Natasha was cruel and mean but maybe at the time that's what he had needed. He feared the loneliness of her leaving him – something she threatened on a monthly basis - but what if he had an alternative? What if he'd made the wrong decision all those years ago and now he had a chance to put it right. What if Natasha found out and condemned him to a lifetime of torture. He visibly shivered at the thought of it.

"So what's it going to be?" asked Eric. "Josh's unique brand of sexual depravity or you letting her down gently."

"Okay. Let's hear your plan for tomorrow and then I'll decide."

"Excellent. You're going to love it."

"I doubt that."

EIGHTY-FIVE THOUSAND EXCITABLE RUGBY FANS, draped in white or red outfits, besieged the sprawling car parks and bars that surrounded Twickenham Stadium. It was a dry but cold spring afternoon, and fans of England and Wales were engaged in lighthearted banter and competitive beer drinking. When the score was level, like it was an hour before kickoff, both sets of supporters shared an equal confidence about the outcome. In three hours' time, the atmosphere would remain amicable even if one side's chants would overshadow the other. The losers would lick their wounds, cry into their shirts and drown their sorrows.

When it came to the elite sport of beer consumption, international rugby fans faced an annual battle to be crowned champions. They'd eventually lose a competitive final to darts fans, as they did every year, but they'd still crawl in a brave second. The average rugby fan consumed the equivalent of ten pints per game. Taking into consideration that one in five supporters was a designated driver, this either put the drinking average up considerably or explained why road traffic accidents increased five-fold on match days.

International rugby matches created the sort of environment not suitable for unstoppable binge drinkers or recovering alcoholics. Callum happened to be both, and Twickenham was his idea of paradise. From the start to the end of the day, there were pubs and bars everywhere. Around the train station, served on makeshift trestle tables in homeowners' front gardens on the walk to the stadium and in the car parks around the ground. Then there were the bars in the concourses under fans' seats and the mobile sellers with their chunky square backpacks.

Callum was determined to sample all of them.

With an hour to go before kickoff, he'd already exceeded the recommended weekly alcohol allowance – for all four of them. Now all they had to do was hope the final member of their group would arrive.

Jessica had already accepted Micky's invitation and offered her gratitude via a flirty text message first thing that morning. By all accounts, her recollections about the previous night were limited, which was good because nothing which happened after the Baba Ghanoush was worth recounting unless you were Josh's funny bone. After a few messages back and forth, the lovebirds had agreed to meet inside the West Gate around half an hour before kickoff. The others, who had tickets in the row in front of the couple, would film the moment for prosperity – and however many people were watching online.

"Do you have the ring I gave you?" Eric said between sips of Guinness.

"Yes," Micky responded meekly.

"Now remember, we've made arrangements at half time which will make it almost impossible for her to say no."

"I'm much more concerned about her saying yes."

"Don't worry about that - we'll explain everything to her at the end of the week when the tasks are complete and we're all considerably richer. We'll find a way to compensate her."

Micky's face soured, unconvinced by his confidence.

"Right, it's time you met your date; you don't want to keep her waiting."

Josh, Eric and Callum watched as he dawdled off into the crowd.

"See them off, boys, and let's get into position. Probably best if you keep that cap over your eyes, Josh. We don't want to scare her off."

Eric drained his plastic vessel and placed it back on the bar.

"No! You take it…hic…wiv you," stuttered Callum, fumbling to pick it up again. "Look…it's reusable."

Jessica didn't appear to be any worse for wear after yesterday's excitement. Being unconscious throughout might have helped, and between them, Micky probably suffered the most.

"I was a little surprised when I found your note," she said softly. "I thought after the last night I'd never hear from you."

"Don't be daft. You can't help it."

"No, but most dates don't want to know me after they've witnessed it. You're a braver man than most, Michael Parsons."

"Then they're all shallow fools."

She blushed.

"How often does it happen?"

"Most days," she replied casually, "but not usually in Greek restaurants, thankfully. It's more common when I'm tired, stressed or have had too much to drink."

"How much is too much?"

"Two or three normally."

"How many have you had today?" he said, having recently bought her a large beaker of white wine.

"Three," she said, noticing the change in his expression. "I always drink more when I'm stressed."

"But you said stress was also a factor!"

"Looks like I've hit the narcolepsy full house today," she chuckled.

"Brilliant," Micky wheezed, removing his ticket from his wallet and glancing up at the concrete behemoth of Twickenham Stadium. Their seats were in the Upper West Stand which he estimated involved at least twelve flights of stairs. Scaling it on his own would be knackering enough but carrying someone on his back might take days.

"What say we go find our seats."

"Yeah, sure."

When the match kicked off, Micky got a glimpse into why Jessica got tired so easily. Throughout the first half, she leapt to her feet every time a player passed the ball. She encouraged nearby fans to sing along with her songs, clapped like an auditioning circus seal and roared like a tiger every time either team scored a point. It was obvious Jessica had the same amount of energy as everyone else, only she exhausted hers in short, sharp bursts. Micky loved his rugby, but he didn't love it as much as she did. He fully expected her to keel over at any moment. To his surprise, when her exuberance was suppressed by the half time whistle, she sat down again, still full of life.

"Great game," she exclaimed, sliding her hands over his arm and giving him a grateful cuddle.

"It can't be great," he replied despondently. "Wales are winning."

"I never mind who wins as long as there's lots to cheer."

Micky imagined she'd find reasons to get excited by a head injury assessment or the touchline getting a new coat of paint.

"My round," she added, shaking her plastic pint mug.

"You can't go now," begged Micky.

"Why not, it's half time…or shall we call it intermission," she giggled.

"We might miss something."

"What?"

He had no answer because he'd exceeded his capacity for bullshit. In the end, he just offered her a pair of cow eyes and a big hug. It did the trick although not going to the bar had consequences. Micky fiddled with the little felt-covered box in his pocket and waited nervously for the moment. He had to hand it to Eric, it was a beautiful ring which would appreciably reinforce the sincerity of the gesture…even if it wasn't. In the row in front, a few seats to their right, three men hid under their hats to avoid being recognised. Micky glanced over nervously. Callum demonstrated all the hallmarks of being hammered, Josh looked aloof and uninterested, and all Eric did was nod reassuringly while holding up his phone to indicate he was ready.

The big screens at both ends of the stadium stopped playing first half highlights. Now the cameraman searched around for the two seats he'd been told to find, a serious feat when there were eighty-five thousand of them. West Stand, Upper 3, Row Q, seats 109 and 108. The camera zoomed in from thousands of tiny unrecognised faces until it focused on Micky's. There he was, as plain as day on the big screen. His nervous system exploded. This was it.

To explain to everyone else in the stadium why a skinny, bespectacled, middle-aged man was being afforded so much unwarranted big screen coverage, the stadium's announcer crackled over the sound system.

"Ladies and Gentlemen, we have a very special couple here in the stadium with us today, Micky Parsons and Jessica Connelly, and I think one of them has a question they'd like to ask!"

A collective cheer rang out around the stadium. As convention demanded, Micky placed one knee down on the beer-flooded concrete, removed the ring from his pocket and gazed up into Jessica's eyes.

They were both closed.

Her chin was resting on her chest and anyone within the vicinity of rows Q, R, and P heard her answer before he'd even asked the question.

"Zzzz…hekhrk…oink…fzffre."

Micky panicked.

Half of the stadium waited with mild interest - mostly because they'd already refilled their beers and had nothing else to do because the second half hadn't started yet. Fortunately for Micky, ITV were broadcasting expert analysis from Martin Johnson and some bloke from Wales whose name no one could remember, rather than what was happening in the stadium. It didn't matter, because Eric was streaming it live on his phone and they were certain Sean would be watching. But watching what?

The dare was clear.

They all had to be in the footage. Tick.

Someone had to propose. Tick.

Jessica had to accept. Snore.

The stadium cameraman wasn't going to linger on them forever, so they were going have to improvise. Eric instructed Josh to crawl over the seats and get up behind her. He scrambled over red plastic, barged past old men in Parker coats and kicked over enough beer to send a tsunami to wipe out the lower tier. Remarkably, he got into position in less than ten seconds.

"What do I do?" Josh whispered through Jessica's flowing blonde hair.

"Put your hand on the back of her head and give it a nod!"

"Right."

"Not that much! She's not a rag doll!"

Micky slid the diamond-studded gold ring onto her wedding digit as Josh wobbled her head back and forward with the dexterity of a prison guard. Micky put his thumb in the air to pronounce the outcome to ten thousand barely interested onlookers.

'SHE SAID YES!!!' flashed up on the big screens moments later and the crowd gave a rather reluctant round of applause, mostly because it had distracted too much time from drinking beer.

Josh scuttled back to Eric to ensure that his presence wasn't missing from the video for longer than might be viewed as suspicious.

Finally, after nearly twenty years of waiting, Jessica was engaged to the man of her dreams and she hadn't witnessed any of it. Micky flopped down in his seat and wept. In hindsight, he wished he'd acted differently but his emotions got the better of him. If only he'd spent the time removing the ring before she unexpectedly woke up moments later as the raucous, drunken crowd excitedly welcomed the players back onto the pitch for the second half.

Eric felt his pocket vibrate and removed his phone. It was Sean. The call was over in a matter of seconds.

"What's the verdict?" asked Josh.

"Success. Two down, three to go."

"Now it's going to get really tricky."

"Logan Cobley."

"Peter Francis, you mean," corrected Josh.

"I don't really care what his name is as long as we abduct him."

"I have great respect for you, Eric, you know that, but even you can't pull this one off."

"Want to bet?"

"Nope."

"There's always a way; we just need to find it. Come on, let's scoop Callum off the floor and head back to mine."

"Up you get, mate," said Josh, grabbing Callum by the arm.

Eric drained the last remnants of beer from his plastic mug to celebrate a job well done, but as he watched the frothy dregs flow towards him something seized his attention. An embossed logo at the bottom in the plastic. He'd seen it before somewhere, although it took him a while to make the connection. Then it came to him. It had been inconspicuously placed in the corner of flags, banners, brochures and even champagne glasses. In fact, even though he'd only noticed it fleetingly, it had been on all of the promotional material at the Queensferry Crossing opening ceremony.

CJ Media.

TWENTY-ONE
THE WALLS COME TUMBLING DOWN

Last Saturday Evening.

WHILE THE HORDES enjoyed a tense second half, Eric, Josh and Callum left the game early to beat the crowds. They made it back to the train station in record time even with Callum held up between them. A few stops later along the line, they were safely back in Battersea, where there was zero evidence any international event was happening in the city. A quick Uber ride and they were home to the apartment before the final whistle had been blown. Hopefully, Micky would return before Jessica invited him home to consummate their relationship. How he'd manage to do that was anyone's guess, but Eric had more concerning thoughts on his mind right then.

"Get some coffee brewing," Eric instructed Josh after he'd returned from a double cigarette break to top up nicotine levels which had dropped to critical after being prohibited from smoking in or around the stadium.

"Something wrong, mate?"

"We need to sober him up," he pointed to Callum, "before he gets too comfy on my settee."

"You've got no chance. He's quaffed enough booze to bring down George Best."

"If he doesn't sober up, I'm going to hang him from the balcony by his testicles," threatened Eric.

"Bit extreme. What's got your goat?"

"Have you ever heard of CJ Media?" inquired Eric.

"No."

"I checked it out on my phone while we were on the train and you were scrolling through Tinder."

"Then I had a lot more fun than you!"

"CJ Media's Managing Director is one Callum Jollie."

"Well that's not unusual, he's been responsible for fifty percent of UK business incorporations in the last decade."

"True, but this one is still active, although according to their Companies House filings and the news reports, not for long."

"What do they do?" asked Josh.

"They claim they can print on anything. Stuff like this."

He threw the empty plastic cup across the open plan kitchen. Josh caught it but wasn't exactly sure what he was meant to be looking at. He'd seen hundreds of these today but paid more attention to the contents than the actual cup. There were half a dozen different designs, but each one was fundamentally the same solid plastic with a picture printed around the circumference.

"I thought Callum's business specialised in biogas fired pizza ovens?"

"That one went bust a few years ago. This one is next for the corporate graveyard."

"But there were thousands of these cups at the ground; he must be making good money out of it."

"If they weren't reusable, he might. One order and then you're done. It's only one of the contracts he's won, but I'm more interested in another."

"Which one?"

"The one he signed with *Heschmeyer Industries*."

"You're fucking kidding me," exclaimed Josh, his jaw crashing onto his chest.

"Nope. Remember the opening ceremony at the bridge and all those banners, flags and rigmarole? They all had 'CJ Media' printed on them. He's been working with Sean up until very recently."

"Then why didn't he tell us?"

"Because he's a lying shit."

"And you say they're about to go bust."

"Yes."

"Hard to grow a business that doesn't exist, isn't it?"

"That's what I thought," agreed Eric.

The intercom buzzed and Eric strolled over to let Micky in, dispensing with the need to time his arrival.

"Jesus, you look awful," said Eric as he opened the door.

Micky dashed in as if someone was following him down the hall. "You don't look so good yourself."

"It's all got a little complicated, but I'll explain in a minute. What have you done with Jessica?"

"I took her home. Fortunately, she managed to stay conscious for the second half and the journey back."

"Did she notice the ring?" inquired Eric.

"What do you think? It's hard to miss a bloody big diamond on your wedding finger when it wasn't there that morning!"

"What did she say?"

"I think she was a little confused as to how it got there, but played along when she realised what it meant. I tried to slip it off before she noticed but it's not an easy thing to do if the wearer is jumping up and down like a kangaroo. When I left, she was already picking out wedding dresses and calling her parents. I'm so dead."

"I can't believe she said yes," moaned Josh. "To you of all people."

"Josh, she didn't say anything, you idiot. You were there, remember?"

"Still, the idea that she fancies a stick insect like you when she could have had a hunk like me is utterly baffling."

"Don't test me today, Foxie. I don't see what you've done to help our cause so far."

"Truth hurts."

"You want to hear the truth?" he said, raising his voice. "If we're doing character assassinations, maybe if you showed women even an ounce of respect they might not shun you."

"Shun me! That's a laugh. Women can't resist me."

"Apart from the ones who want more than a quick shag."

"I'm actually good with that," he snarled. "It's more than you've managed in the last decade…and you're married."

"You don't see it, do you."

"See what?"

"You can't stop running, can you?"

"I don't know what you're on about?"

"Yes, you do. You just don't want to admit it. Everyone you've loved rejected you. Your birth parents, all those foster carers, Jessica - that's why you treat women the same way. You reject them before they can do the same to you. You substitute sex for love, and you'll never find true happiness until you stop running."

The truth did hurt.

Josh lost it.

He launched himself across the lounge, rugby tackling Micky into the settee. It toppled over backwards under their weight and a scuffle broke out on the other side.

Most forty-year-old men refrain from physical confrontations because they're mature enough to know that such action is the wrong way to deal with disagreements. They're also wise enough to know that they might come off worse than their opponent and any injuries might raise eyebrows at work the next day. Also, they don't actually know how it works. They understand the principles of fighting because they've seen others do it. It looked easy. It looked brutal, masculine and vicious. It looked nothing like this.

They grappled each other like they were cuddling.

Josh knocked Micky's glasses off.

Micky grabbed a foot and managed to remove a sock.

Josh attempted a headlock, missed and aggressively fondled a cushion.

Micky bit him on the arm.

Josh resorted to tickling.

Micky licked his face.

Josh reacted by making a noise only toddlers know how to make and planting one of his palms across Micky's mouth.

Micky tried to knee him in a place of worship.

Josh ripped a button off Micky's shirt and attempted a nipple tweak but only succeeded in removing a clump of chest hair.

After an entertaining couple of minutes, Eric had seen enough. He grabbed them both by the necks and within seconds they were pleading for mercy. Eric did know how to fight. Survival in the dog-eat-dog neighbourhood he grew up in made it a necessity. In the early days, he'd mostly been on the end of painful beatings, but when you had three older brothers and lived on a rough council estate it was part of your development. He was a fast learner, too. By the age of fifteen, he looked more like twenty. A regimen of weightlifting and boxing marked him out as someone not to mess with, particularly when the locals knew he'd always stand and fight.

"This stops now!"

"He started it," whined Micky, searching around for his jettisoned glasses and readjusting his ruffled clothes.

"We have to stick together," insisted Eric. "I can't afford to lose one of you as well."

"Why? Who have we lost?" asked Micky.

Eric pointed to the leather armchair. Callum was asleep in a wrecked heap, oblivious to what was going on around him.

"He's just drunk."

"He's betrayed us."

Micky looked flummoxed. "How?"

"Wake him up," demanded Eric.

Josh shook Callum by his shoulders until his head wobbled his brain into regaining consciousness.

"Is it opening time already," he mumbled incoherently.

When Josh stuck a large mug of steaming coffee under his nose like powerful smelling salts, Callum's eyes readjusted to the blaring lights of the apartment and an earlier than usual hangover. Three of his closest friends loomed over him and two of them looked thoroughly pissed off.

"Why did you do it?" demanded Eric, brandishing the plastic cup from the rugby match at him.

"I probably just forgot to take it back to the bar," he offered, a little perplexed as to why they were so angry about recycling all of a sudden.

"CJ Media. Your company made them."

"I know," he replied breezily.

"And you can print on anything," said Josh. "Even bridges."

"Bridges, roads, boats, people…"

"Not just any bridge, though. You worked on Sean Heschmeyer's bridge, didn't you?"

"Maybe," said Callum, rubbing his head and acting innocently. "I don't get involved in every contract…"

"Don't lie to me," Eric blurted angrily, grabbing Callum by the neck with a huge leathery hand. "You've done enough of that already."

Callum spluttered for air and Eric released his grasp.

"You told us your business was doing well," added Josh. "You said you wanted the money from Sean to grow it."

"But that's not true, is it?" continued Eric. "CJ Media is going bankrupt and you've been running around town looking for investors for the last few months. You found some didn't you?"

"What's he talking about, Callum?" asked Micky.

"I'm in trouble," sobbed Callum, breaking down on the floor with his head in his hands.

"More than you know if you don't tell us the truth."

They watched as he writhed in self-pity on the floor before Callum finally composed himself. He lifted himself up, turning towards the panoramic windows with his back to them. A tear rolled down his cheek and he quickly wiped it away. He'd been caught out; now he had to face the consequences.

"Can I have a glass of…water, please?"

The friends looked shocked. They knew things must be bad, but not this bad. Callum wasn't known for drinking anything pure. Asking for a glass of water was like a dog asking for a kite.

"I really thought this business was the one," said Callum, accepting the glass from Eric and taking a swig. His face screwed up in disgust as it went down his gullet. "Finally a solid business idea that would elevate me up the pecking order. I put everything into it but nothing worked. People want digital products these days. The green lobby has poisoned everyone against paper and plastic. When sales dried up, I went in search of new investment to shore up our finances. When that failed, I engaged in some dodgy dealings to keep the vultures from the door."

"Like what?"

"Illegal accountancy practises that falsified the balance sheet, corporate tax evasion and the misappropriation of funds for my own private needs. As soon as the liquidators get their hands on the books, I'm toast. I've been avoiding them for weeks. Even had to escape down a drainpipe the last time they were at the office. But they won't give up. If I don't correct the accounts and refund the money by the end of the tax year, they won't just disqualify me from being a director, they'll prosecute me for financial manipulation. I got desperate."

"Sean offered you a way out, didn't he?"

"Yes."

"But it wasn't what we're doing, is it?"

"No."

Two months ago.

Callum had never dined at Claridge's. Even before the money dried up, it was way out of his price range. Current budgets stretched to a McDonald's drive-through about once a fortnight. While he waited for his client to arrive, he took a sneak peek at the wine list and almost suffered a stroke. Some of the bottles would wipe out a few weeks of the national debt. Thankfully, he wasn't paying the bill today. Normal convention was for the supplier to foot the bill when entertaining a client, but today was different. He wasn't just meeting a client. He was meeting a client, a potential investor and an old friend, all rolled into one.

Their business lunch had been the result of a series of flukes. During a networking event about a month ago, he'd overheard a conversation that piqued his interest. An events company had been let down by a supplier and they urgently needed a last-minute replacement. Ever the opportunist, he'd wheedled his way into the debate and offered CJ Media's services. After a brief and successful negotiation, they agreed to supply everything the agency needed. It was only later that he discovered who the end user was: *Heschmeyer Industries*. Not long after that, Sean's people reached out directly to his people to engage them on other projects, thereby cutting out the expensive middle man. Then, finally, Sean made contact to invite Callum for lunch.

If he showed up, they might actually eat some.

The table reservation had been booked for twelve and, according to Callum's watch, it was closer to one and there was still no sign of him. The waiter had offered Callum something to drink while he waited, but after perusing the wine list he casually declined. Eventually, he accepted a glass of tap water, although it was very much against his principles. If Sean didn't show up soon, he'd probably struggle to pay for it. The waiters stared judgmentally at their lone diner, sipping and grimacing over a glass of water. They usually expected a sizeable service tip at the end of the customer's meal, and at this rate, neither customer nor waiter was getting either. Callum decided he'd leave at one o'clock if he was still sitting alone. To his considerable relief, his companion arrived in the nick of time.

Sean made no attempt to offer an apology. People waited for him, not the other way around.

"Callum, lovely to see you," he said, offering a hand-shake before hastily sitting down opposite and flicking through the menu. "Did you order yet?"

"No, I thought it best to wait."

"Very good. You should absolutely try the fava bean hummus with yellow pickled beets; it's divine."

Callum wasn't certain he knew what a fava bean was but ordered it anyway.

"I must say, I'm super impressed by what you're planning for my bridge opening. It's remarkable what your team can do."

"Thanks."

"I should invite you to see it."

"See what?"

"The bridge. The opening ceremony is the third Saturday in March."

"I'll check my diary," he replied, certain there was nothing important in it for months apart from a dental appointment.

Sean raised a single finger in the air and almost immediately the maître d' was hovering next to their table.

"Ah Pascal, I think we'll have a bottle of Chateau Lafite…unless of course you're having fish?" Sean looked to Callum for confirmation.

"No."

"Perfect. I'm sure you'll agree the Lafite is the perfect lunchtime accompaniment."

Callum nodded, even though lunch in recent weeks was accompanied by a cheap can of Red Stripe lager.

"I was quite surprised you had enough time to meet an old friend," exclaimed Callum as Pascal rushed off to retrieve their wine from a well-protected vault.

"I don't," replied Sean coldly. "But this is not purely a social engagement."

"It's not?"

"No. You see, Callum, in a few weeks from now the company I've built from almost nothing will be floated on the London Stock Exchange. It's the realisation of a goal I've had since March the sixteenth, nineteen ninety-seven."

Callum knew the date well. It was a defining moment in both of their lives. "Congratulations. It looks like you've achieved it."

"Not quite. It wasn't the only target I set for myself."

"Isn't being a multimillionaire enough?"

"No. The money means nothing to me. Anyone can make money if they put their mind to it. Anyone other than you, of course." His grin lacked humour or empathy. "But some things are worth even more to me."

"Such as?"

"Respect. You can't buy that. Not always. Of course, in a place like this, respect is about money. Pascal will stick his pointy nose as far up my arse as it will go if it means I tip him more than he makes in a week. Those who have nothing respect those who have everything. People like me, who have more than they need, respect those in a similar position. The level of respect only changes because of how someone achieved their position. Inherited wealth will always carry greater authority with the upper class, but it's easy enough to infiltrate their habitats if you mimic their traditions and customs. But there's a group of people for whom respect cannot be gained by the accumulation of wealth, status, people or power."

"Are you talking about people like me?"

Sean burst into a dry, croaky laugh. "No, don't be silly. You *can* be bought, Callum. It's doesn't take a genius to work out what you want. You crave what I have but fail to appreciate the fundamental principles of achieving it. And you'll do anything to discover the secrets."

"No, I won't," replied Callum unconvincingly.

"Why, then, did you accept my lunch invitation in a heartbeat? Why, without debate, did you accept my recommendation from the menu? It's because I intimidate you. No doubt you'll munch away at the fava bean hummus, insisting it's the best thing you've ever tasted, even though it's basically a cheap ingredient pulsed into a paste, served in a miniscule portion and accompanied by some equally boring pickles for an inflated price only justifiable because of where you ate it."

"I'm not that shallow."

"Yes, you are. The people I'm referring to are those who can see through the charade. The ones whose respect cannot be bought, only earnt."

There was only one person Callum knew who fit that description, "Eric."

"Precisely."

"Perhaps you should have invited him for lunch?"

"As I say, he can't be bought," repeated Sean.

"I have his number if you want it. The last time I saw him, he was working here in the city."

"He still does. I'm more than aware of Eric's current circumstances, thank you."

"Then, why did you invite me?"

"Eric won't accept my invitation, but he will accept yours."

"But, I don't have anything to invite him to."

"Not yet."

Pascal presented the dusty bottle of red wine to the pair as if he was about to offer a human sacrifice to the gods. Essentially, all Pascal's job amounted to was the collection, opening and pouring of wine for his customers, but in a renowned Michelin-starred restaurant like Claridge's, the process had to be delivered a little more elaborately. The wine bottle was offered up to Sean like the birth of an heir. The cork was ejected with the flair of a matador evading a bull. After a dance more elaborate than an attention seeking peacock, a mouthful of wine was finally poured into the glass and they were invited to smell it. What was in the glass was obviously wine, but that wasn't the end of the performance. Sean insisted that Callum should be responsible for tasting it.

He knew there were strict conventions for tasting wine in a fancy restaurant and that those customs were markedly different to how he acted at home. Often, he'd down a bottle before realising what colour it was. He stuck his nose in the glass. It smelt remarkably like wine. He rinsed the liquid around the crystal glass and held it up to the light. It looked remarkably like wine. He slurped the wine through his teeth and washed it around his palette so all of his taste buds were treated equally. Yep, it tasted remarkably like wine, too. The fact that you could buy several crates of ordinary wine for the same price as this mouthful didn't change any of it. He wasn't really that fussy. Ultimately, he only cared that it got him pissed.

"I understand you've been seeking financial backing for CJ Media," stated Sean, as he tucked into his starter like he'd not eaten in weeks.

"Yes."

"How's that going?" asked Sean, who'd made it his job to already know the answer.

"Nothing concrete as yet, but I have three or four interested parties."

"No, you don't," Sean replied with certainty. "You have three or four investors who prefer to say nothing than say no. I know this because I know who they are. How long do you have before the liquidators show up?"

"Oh, ages."

Sean pierced him with a stare.

"Two weeks," he blurted out, "if we don't secure any further orders."

"And what then?"

"Close up, move on," said Callum. He always mustered a positive demeanour in the face of trauma. He'd had plenty of practise.

"But you can't, can you? I hear from my sources that when the liquidators analyse your books, they'll find more than merely poor working capital and bad debts."

"I'm not sure I know what you mean?"

"How can I put this in the English vernacular – you've been cooking the books."

"Everyone uses creative accounting. I'm sure your finance team does it, too."

"I'd be disappointed if they didn't, but there's a big difference between bending the rules and snapping them in half. From what I've been told, you've had your hand in the cookie jar."

"Who told you that?" asked Callum. He'd always felt his employees' loyalty was beyond reproach and it was unlikely they'd blab.

"You're not denying it then?"

"It's simply a short-term liquidity issue and the repayment of a few director's loans, that's all. Everything will be in balance by the end of the financial year."

"And if it's not?"

Callum slurped his wine and avoided the question. His options were limited. If, in the likely event, no one was willing to extend him millions of pounds of credit then he'd need to find a new job, name and cover story. Faking his own death in a deep ocean canoeing accident seemed like a decent option, too.

"I have a proposition for you," Sean announced after Pascal had scuttled over to top up their glasses. "I will invest."

"Really? That's excellent. How much equity do you want? How much cash are you willing to put in?"

"Ten million, but I'm not interested in equity. CJ Media doesn't have a long-term future. It's a dinosaur lumbering around the digital landscape. The market is shrinking by double digits every year and customers like *Heschmeyer Industries* have to consider our social and ecological responsibilities. Our activities can't be seen to advance climate change."

"Hold on a minute, my company's actions can't possibly compare with the impact of yours. You build coal-fired power stations, skyscrapers and motorways."

"And we plant trees to balance out our environmental impact."

CJ Media hadn't planted anything. They'd changed a few light bulbs in the office for LED ones but it didn't seem a big enough gesture to issue a press release.

"I'd advise you to use my investment to sort out your financial affairs before selling off any valuable assets."

"I'll consider it. If you aren't after equity, what do you want?"

"*The Idiots' Club.*"

"*The Idiots' Club?*" he replied quizzically.

"Yes. I want to challenge them. I want to earn their respect, and the only way I can do that is by beating them. I want you to convince them to take me on."

"I can understand why you'd want to challenge Eric, but why drag the rest of us into it?"

"Because they owe me a debt."

"Even me?"

"Yes, in a way."

"Why?"

"You were the only one who cared for me after the fall, and for that, I'm grateful. It's why I'm offering you the deal rather than the others. Even so, your actions that night changed things. It was you who convinced me to drop the charges against them and it stopped the others learning valuable lessons. They got away scot-free and, in my opinion, have continued to ride roughshod over the rules ever since. I joined the club because I wanted to feel included, to be part of something, to prove myself. In return, they bullied me. If I take them on and win, then I will earn their respect and they will learn how it felt to be me."

"Let me get this straight: you're offering me ten million pounds to get *The Idiots' Club* to agree to do a dare?"

"Five dares. Seven days. All four of you."

"You'll never get them to agree."

"That's not my job. If you want the money, it's your job."

"None of us have seen Micky in years, and Josh is way too busy for such distractions."

"Then you'll have to find a way to convince them."

"Ten million," he repeated to himself. It was enough to buy half a case of Château Lafite or what was left of Threshers the Wine Merchant.

"Ten million to share if you win but that should be

more than enough to cover your debts and get yourself out of trouble. Of course, if they fail, I might be able to offer you something better."

"Better?"

"Twenty million, if you make sure they don't succeed."

"You want me to betray my oldest friends for money?"

"No. I'm offering you your only chance of avoiding criminal prosecution and jail."

"But I wouldn't need to betray them or end up in jail, if we succeed, would I?"

"That's true, but I'd be very disappointed if that happened. Don't forget this is not about you; it's about me. There is a debt to be paid and I will find a way of extracting it from all of you," he replied coldly.

There was something about Sean's expression that told Callum these challenges would be designed to make them fail. He wanted respect and revenge. Only their failure would give him what he was looking for. What choice did Callum have, he thought? They could at least try, and if it appeared impossible, then he'd not be out of pocket.

"Think it through," said Sean, rapidly lurching out of his seat. "I have to go."

"What about the bill…"

"Don't worry, I'll put it on my account. Look out for my invitation. After that, the rest is up to you."

"Treacherous worm!" shouted Josh. He lunged at Callum but the others held him back. "I should throw you off the balcony."

"It's entrapment," chuntered Micky. "You set us up to save your own skin. All that bollocks about friendship and us 'owing you one' - it was all a trick."

"Sean was going to find another way even if I didn't take the bait," pleaded Callum. "We know he's been spying on us. He knows about our lives, jobs, problems, partners – every skeleton in every cupboard. He had enough ammunition to bury us with or without my help."

"If you were in trouble, Callum, why didn't you come to us first?" questioned Eric.

"And what would you three have done, exactly? Hmm. Micky probably wouldn't have taken my calls. Josh doesn't have the means or the inclination to help me out of the shit and you, well you, Eric - you'd have used it against me."

"How would I?"

"You'd never let me forget that you came to my rescue. You'd tell everyone so they knew who was superior. It's always about winning for you, even between friends. Why do you think we haven't seen each other much recently?"

Eric was speechless. Was that how they really saw him? A cocky narcissist only ever interested in what was in it for him?

"It's hard to be friends with someone who never fails at anything," added Callum.

"Do the rest of you feel like that?" asked Eric tentatively.

"It's certainly a factor," said Micky.

"I think you're a bloody riot," contradicted Josh, who was so laid-back Eric's behaviour never felt threatening.

"Wow, and you think you know people. Well, I'm sorry you feel that way. I'd like to think I'd always come to your aid unconditionally if you needed my help. I guess we all have different perceptions of ourselves."

"Don't take it to heart, Eric. We know you mean well, it just always becomes a fight with you. The outcome can sometimes create a blast that covers everyone else."

"It doesn't take away what this snivelling little shit has done," interrupted Josh. "Don't let him distract from that."

Callum sank to his knees, hands together, seeking clemency.

"It's going to take more than prayer," stated Micky. "Why does Sean think I owe him a debt?"

"Because we all do," answered Eric quite unexpectedly. "We brought this on ourselves. We treated Sean the same way the world treated us – as outsiders. We didn't give him a level playing field to test himself. Now he has taken the opportunity to turn the tables on us."

"Are you condoning it?"

"No, I'm just saying I understand it."

"So what do we do now?" said Josh.

"We have to beat him."

"I say we stop," Micky declared.

Josh nodded in agreement.

"Absolutely not. Our only way out of this is to complete his dares and turn things back on Sean."

"But we can't trust him anymore." Josh pointed at Callum who was still sobbing on the carpet, head buried near his feet.

"He needs to prove whose side he's really on."

"I will," he blubbered.

"What were you planning to do in the event we were going to succeed?" asked Eric.

Callum's head came out of its hiding place. "I was going to disappear on the last day - if we got as far as the tower."

"God, you're a prick, Callum!" barked Josh. "Can I hit him now?"

"No. Given your fighting prowess, there's every chance you'll miss!"

"I can't believe I was ever friends with a weasel like

you, after everything we've been through," continued Josh. "We were always against the system, and you've sold us out to it."

"We all have pressure points," said Eric. "Perhaps it wouldn't be such a bad thing if Callum did disappear on the last day."

"What, and hand Sean victory?"

"And pocket twenty million," summarised Callum nervously. "I'll share it with you boys, obviously."

"What is it that Sean sees as a win?" Eric posed rhetorically. "Seeing us fail isn't the only thing he wants. It's obvious by the nature of the dares that he wants something else. He's trying to destroy our friendship. That's it! Don't you see. The dares are designed specifically to press our buttons. He knew I'd confront Carrington on the first dare, and he knew it would annoy the rest of you."

"Which it did," confirmed Micky.

"The second dare was about jealousy and tearing you two apart. It almost worked, too. You've already resorted to what some might describe as a fight. It's obvious why he's picked the fifth dare."

They all nodded.

"There's a pattern."

"I don't see how stealing a lion is a pattern."

"I do. It's specifically aimed at me."

"Why?"

"Because I once boasted to Sean that even if he dared me to steal a lion I could do it."

"Idiot! Why didn't you say a donkey? Or something that moves slower and bites less," groaned Josh.

"I'm not a fortune teller, am I?"

"Okay, so Sean's trying to break us up, but what are we going to do about it?" asked Josh.

"The next dare."

"But we don't have a plan," answered Micky. "And abducting Logan is impossible, if you ask me."

"I think you might be right," replied Eric.

"Are you feeling alright? That's the second time in the last hour you've agreed with Micky," said Josh.

"Never better. Thinking clearly now. We're not going to abduct Logan."

"But it's in the contract."

"We're only going to pretend to abduct him," Eric restated.

"How do we pull that off?"

"We're not. Callum is."

"Me?"

"It's the perfect opportunity for you to show us whose side you're really on."

"I'm all for it in principle," confirmed Josh, "but I'm not entirely sure how you expect him to do it."

"Change of plan. We're going to persuade Logan to abduct Callum."

"What!" gasped Callum nervously.

"Don't worry - I imagine you'll be perfectly safe."

"Imagine…"

"But why?" shrugged Josh. "I don't see how that helps us."

"You will. I have a plan forming, but we're going to need some supplies. Come on, we have lots of work to do and less than four days left."

TWENTY-TWO

CRIME

Last Sunday.

An elderly man in a thick, dark overcoat waited patiently behind the rails of the sawdust-covered arena for the rider to finish. It had been raining consistently in Herefordshire since the previous morning, and the ground under his inappropriate footwear was saturated. He lowered his enormous umbrella to further cocoon himself from the worst of it. The horses sploshed through the puddles, faces dipped to demonstrate their displeasure at having to exercise in conditions like this. Natasha had noticed the stranger half an hour ago when she'd returned to the stables to give the next stubborn horse its exercise. It was obvious from his business attire he wasn't there for his love of all things equestrian. As the only other human in the yard, it was clear he wanted to speak to her, and neither rain nor her desire to ignore him was going to put him off.

When there were no more legitimate jobs to do and all

the horses were safely back in the dry, she walked towards her Land Rover without acknowledging his presence. In the hand not squeezing an umbrella tightly was an official-looking briefcase.

"Mrs Wilmot-Jones-Parsons?" he asked, cutting off her route to the driver's seat.

"Yes," she replied sullenly, as if someone had ruined her day simply by being in the same orbit.

"My name is Clarence Douville," he said, holding out his business card, which she blanked. "I represent *Heschmeyer Industries…*"

"Bloody salespeople. Didn't you see the sign on the gate? Hmm. 'Private Property', or do people like you struggle with words of more than one syllable? Whatever it is, I'm not buying, good day."

"I can assure you, madam, I'm not a salesperson," Clarence replied, a little horrified that a man of his learned profession might be confused with such lesser men. "I have been sent by my employer, Sean Heschmeyer."

Nostalgia battled for space amongst Natasha's prejudice. She didn't like strangers who invited themselves onto her property without asking. Unless you were a known member of her upper class clique, you were unfairly wasting oxygen. "I don't care if you were sent by the Sultan of Brunei! I'm too busy to deal with foreigners today."

Did Scottish people really count as foreigners down here, he thought? The answer was yes. Even people from the next county of Gloucestershire were unwelcome.

"It concerns your husband, madam," he said gravely, hoping to finally get her attention.

She stopped before her welly boots made it into the foot well of the four by four. She'd barely thought about Micky for days. Whatever he was doing, it certainly wouldn't be something of which she approved. As long as he returned by the time agreed and she could go back to treating him like a servant, she didn't care much. Unless, of course, he'd done something terribly selfish like get himself killed. Surely he wouldn't dare. There was no safe place to hide from her, not even death.

"He'd better not have injured himself," she stated unsympathetically. "He's going to paint the spare room when he gets back, and I don't care how many limbs he's missing."

"He's in perfect health, madam, but my employer is worried about him nonetheless."

"Sean Heschmeyer?"

"Yes."

"Freaky looking foreigner from University?" she asked.

"Um," said Clarence unsure how best to describe him without sounding disloyal. "German."

"Why would Sean be worried about Micky?" she snapped.

"Because Mr Heschmeyer has entered into a contract with your husband and his friends."

"A contract? To do what?"

"A series of tasks to which my employer felt they were best suited."

"What sort of tasks?"

"I'm not at liberty to disclose the agreement with you."

"I'm his wife!" she fumed, never happy when she didn't get her own way. "What's his is mine. I demand you tell me."

"Madam, I'm a lawyer and I'm not willing to be struck off just because you have a hissy fit at me. I'm simply here because in the course of completing my employer's tasks it appears Mr Parsons has committed a crime."

"What?!"

"A crime," he repeated unemotionally. "Mr Heschmeyer feels it's his responsibility to inform you, so that you may decide how best to support him."

"I'd suggest you call the police," she replied.

"I'm certain they're already aware."

"Good. That's the only support he's getting from me."

One of Clarence's eyebrows lifted in response to her coldness. Lawyers were not known for their sensitivity, but even he wouldn't hang a spouse out to dry so quickly and on such limited information.

"Why are you still here?" she complained.

"Some of his crimes are against you."

"Me! He wouldn't dare!"

"It might be best if I show you."

Clarence reached into his case and removed an expensive, brand new computer tablet. He checked the direction of the sun and placed it in the shadows on the bonnet of the Land Rover.

"You'll never get a signal out here. There's none for miles."

"I don't need one. I've already downloaded what I need to show you from the internet."

"He's broken the law and it's on the internet?" she gawped in horror.

"Yes. YouTube, amongst others."

Natasha winced. Although she'd heard about YouTube, being a person born in the seventies meant she refused to accept it as a genuine alternative to television. Her kids were quite the reverse. They didn't really understand how traditional television worked. The idea of waiting for a programme to start at a specific time and place was unfathomable to them. Either way, if Micky had broken the law and the evidence was available to the general public it didn't just affect him, it affected her too, probably more so.

She had a pristine reputation to keep up and if the neighbour's kids saw her husband up to no good on YouTube, they might tell the rest of the village's kids.

"I want you to delete it at once," she demanded.

"Sorry?"

"Delete it. I don't want anyone to see what he's done."

"Madam, I don't think you understand how the internet works. If I delete it from my machine, it doesn't delete it from the rest of whole world. It will exist on the world wide web forever. The only person who can delete it permanently is the original producer."

"Fine, then I'll demand they delete it."

"By all means ask them."

"Whom do I speak to?"

"Your husband."

Natasha's confusion breached new levels. "My husband broke the law and filmed himself doing it?"

"Yes."

"What rubbish!"

"If you'll let me show it to you, then you can see for yourself."

Clarence pressed play on the three-minute video file. The shaky scene panned around a large stadium of boozed-up Wales and England supporters in rugby jerseys waving oddly-shaped inflatables. There were massive leeks, daffodils, dragons and the occasional flustered sheep. The picture moved across from the wider crowd and focused in on the row where the cameraman was seated. First Josh and then Eric appeared in shot, casually smiling and waving. Then the camera shook as it was switched to another pair of hands and a pissed-up Callum wobbled around, a beer in each hand.

"I don't even see Micky!" she exclaimed.

"Wait a second," said Clarence. "Look, there he is."

"Who's the girl sitting next to him? She looks rather familiar."

"Jessica Connelly."

"Who?"

"She was at University with you."

Sloane Rangers were an insular bunch who only recognised their own; anyone else didn't often appear on their radar.

"Is she asleep?"

"No, she's resting her eyes."

"Why is Micky getting down on one knee?"

"You'll see."

Micky slipped a ring on Jessica's finger while, slightly out of frame, Josh made her head nod back and forward like an out of time metronome. The camera then focused on the stadium's big screen where the words 'SHE SAID YES!!!' flashed in red against a white background.

"WHAT!?"

"She said yes," repeated Clarence, in case she hadn't quite understood.

"I can see that! But he's already bloody married. The cheating toerag. Wait until I get my hands on him. I'm going to bury him alive."

"My client would very much like to assist you," offered Clarence, "if you'd like his help."

"Why would I want Sean's help?" she seethed. "I'm perfectly capable of castrating my own husband, thank you."

"Very well. What are you going to do?" Clarence asked curiously.

"I'm going to hunt the pair of them down and then I'm going to humiliate them for making me look stupid. This must have been going on for months. I'll teach him a lesson for sneaking around behind my back. Oh, I'll bet that's what he's been doing at these classic car rallies. Let's see how he manages to get there after I destroy his treasured Austin Healey!"

Clarence didn't care much for people. What they did to each other was none of his business. But the Healey represented British automotive history, and it was hardly to blame for its master's indiscretion. Clarence knew full well that Micky's relationship with Jessica was considerably shorter than the months she'd suggested and had nothing whatsoever to do with classic car events.

"Oh no, not the car!"

"He doesn't deserve nice things," snapped Natasha.

"If you spare the car, I'll tell you where he's going to be," bargained Clarence.

"Where?"

"Exeter. Three days from now."

Yesterday. Frome Police Station.

"I'm really quite tired," confessed Eric. "Can you hurry up and charge me so I can get a decent night's sleep?"

"Don't think for a second I don't know what you're doing. I'm not going to stop the interview until I've worked everything out," replied Iris, biting her nails, a sign that Eric rightly took for frustration.

"I'm not doing anything. I'm just bowing to your superiority."

"From what I've learned about you, Eric, that would be the first time in your life. Let's go over everything again," she insisted.

"Really? What time is it?"

"There's a clock on the wall; look for yourself."

It was late in the evening. "I do prefer an analogue clock, don't you?"

She shrugged.

"I think it's the sound of the hands ticking around the face. It's nostalgic."

She continued to ignore his constant infatuation with clocks and drew him back to her agenda. "*The Idiots' Club* has completed four dares in six days - that much we know - and you say Sean Heschmeyer provoked you…"

"Blackmailed us," corrected Eric.

"…Which you can't prove. The first dare involved the theft of a seventy-year-old German ordinance from a building site in Islington and the evacuation of Exeter University campus. We have Josh's wallet, sightings of the vehicle, Carrington's witness statement and video footage placing you at the scene."

"You do, and it's impossible for me to deny any of it. Hence my eagerness for you to charge me."

She continued to ignore him. "The second dare appears to be less of a crime and more of a twisted prank against an innocent woman."

"I'm convinced that particular dare will work out for the best," stated Eric confidently.

"It's only interesting to see if a pattern emerges that might help me work out the fifth dare."

"Please let me know if you find it."

"The second dare was also useful because it provided me with a clue to the third dare."

"What clue?" said Eric, a little surprised by the revelation.

"At the very end of your livestream, Callum makes a mumbled reference to someone called Logan Cobley."

"Does he?" Eric replied.

"Yes. You have to use very sophisticated technology to isolate the soundwaves against all the noise in the stadium but guess what: we have it because we're the police."

"I don't think the random ramblings of a drunk will hold up in court."

"No, not on their own. But that's not the sole evidence we have for your involvement in his disappearance."

Iris had yet to offer up any evidence against the group for that crime, and he was pretty confident she didn't have any.

"The fourth dare is fairly obvious, because you're covered in bite marks and the whereabouts of a very large lion are still a mystery."

"Maybe it's found its way back to the park."

"There's no such thing as a homing lion and anyway, you know where the creature is, don't you?"

Eric shrugged.

"But I still haven't worked out what you were planning for the last dare."

Eric leant forward across the table and fixed her in his stare. "Bugging you, isn't it?"

"No," she snapped. "I'll find out; I always do. There's bound to be clues I haven't found yet, but I will. One thing is for certain, if I keep you here without charge, there's no way you can post bail and attempt to complete it by the deadline."

"But you can't keep us here much longer."

"Unless I get an extension, which shouldn't be too difficult. Your activities are on the radar of a number of agencies. Jimmy Copper from the NCA is already on his way from London to interrogate you, unless you give me the answers first. You only have until tomorrow if you want to complete the last dare."

"True, but then you'll never find out what it was."

"I will."

"And you'll also never understand who was really responsible."

She had to know. There was zero satisfaction working on a jigsaw puzzle if you accepted from the start that there was a piece missing. She always had to solve the problem, whatever it took.

"You could release us," offered Eric, "then you might find out the clues."

"I can't do that."

"Why not?"

"Because a man has been abducted and you're the prime suspect."

"What if I helped you find him, too?"

"Then I imagine that would make it more likely we'd charge you."

"Not if I provide conclusive proof that I was not responsible."

"And can you?"

"Perhaps."

"I must say I find it barely believable that four idiots like you could have pulled it off."

"How do you mean?" said Eric, taking offence, as she'd hoped he would.

"I went to the Cobley crime scene. I'm not sure the SAS could have pulled it off."

Late last Saturday night. Battersea.

Time had never been on their side. Five dares in seven days, particularly given their difficulty rating, was never going to be easy. Now, with news of Callum's betrayal, it would be that much harder. Eric's instincts that Sean was not playing fair had been borne out. His desire for a contingency plan was a good call, but it was still only a rough outline. His purposeful harassment of Carrington was certainly part of it, as was the Vice Chancellor's predictable reaction, something they'd yet to capitalise on.

Callum's confession had also confirmed Sean's real motives behind the dares, and it would no longer be enough to just complete them. Sean thought he was one step in front, but he wasn't. He was actually nine steps in front. By the seventh day, it was Eric's intention to prove, falsely, that they knew what was going on from the very start. Which meant turning the tables on the German and doing a shit load of acting.

Which meant they needed to activate Plan B.

A plan held so close to Eric's chest the others would only know their immediate parts in it. They were assigned to source specific supplies and told to meet back at the apartment no later than eleven that night. That would give them until the next morning to get everything ready. The only person without an errand to run was Eric, much to the consternation of the others. He had desk work to do. In order for his plan to succeed, he needed his external actor. Someone who could be persuaded to believe Sean was responsible for all the mayhem, not them. Someone, who Eric believed, was already watching.

When the others returned, all on time for once, the dining table was covered with massive white cardboard boxes and the smell of steaming hot pizzas filled the air. It was the fillip they all needed.

"Legend," commented Josh. "I'm so hungry I thought someone had cut my throat."

"Any ham and pineapple," asked Callum meekly.

"No! Fruit on pizza is plain wrong. Would you put meat in an apple crumble?"

"I guess it depends on the meat," replied Callum. "Kidneys, no. Bacon, probably."

"Actually, bacon does go with anything," confirmed Micky.

"Custard?" disputed Eric with a grimace.

All three nodded their agreement, killing the universal use of bacon philosophy dead in the water. Anyway, who needed metaphorical bacon when the real stuff was waiting to be devoured. They hurried over to the table to dig into the boxes.

"Do they all have olives on them?" asked Callum.

"Yep."

"I don't like olives."

"Yes, I know."

"I'll pick them off," he conceded, appreciating he wasn't in a good position to argue anything right now.

"You can, but I asked them to add some to the sauce as well," confirmed Eric.

"I'll wash it down with a beer."

"Not tonight, you won't."

"Oh come on, I know you're angry with me, but let's not go overboard."

"This has nothing to do with what you've done. I need you sober for tomorrow. You've got a big day."

"You know I'm much less effective sober."

"Yes, but on this occasion that suits us fine. It's up to you, Callum: you either have a dry evening and do as we tell you or we ring the Tax Evasion Hotline and tell them about all your dodgy financial planning."

Callum watched mournfully as they gorged on pizza and swilled down pint after pint of sparkling, cold amber nectar. Every time one went down their necks, it increased the delirious tremors coursing through his body from the dual effects of his physiological and psychological deficiency. For a man with his dependency, it was like taking Josh to a strip club gagged and blindfolded.

"What is it you want me to do tomorrow?" he asked to distract himself from the sweat flowing across his body.

"All in good time, Callum. Did everyone get what I asked for?"

"Eventually," added Micky. "It's not easy to go clothes shopping this time of night."

He emptied a bag onto the floor.

"Impossible, I'd imagine," suggested Josh. "Where did you get those from?"

"Jessica."

"I thought you were keeping your distance?"

"She texted me so I popped over…"

"Under the thumb already," scoffed Josh. "Natasha mark two!"

"It was lucky, actually, because she had exactly what we needed. Actors have lots of black clothing for rehearsals. I have three sets of plimsolls, leggings and t-shirts but only two black balaclavas," he said, pointing to the items he had dumped onto the floor.

"What's that?" asked Eric, noticing something multi-coloured peeking out from underneath all the black fabric.

"It's one of those jester's hats. It's all I could find to fit Josh's massive head!"

"I'm NOT wearing that! Bloody embarrassing."

"Said the man who walked into an airport in his rhino pants," muttered Callum.

Josh shot him an evil look.

"Good work, Micky - these should do fine. What about you, Josh?"

"Yeah, I got what you needed," he said, placing a plain white envelope on the table.

"Will it work?"

"I don't see why not. They work on animals."

"Yeah, but not normally on the inside of them."

"What's in there?" asked Callum suspiciously.

"Dessert, just for you."

"I'm not putting any drugs in my body!"

"Said the man who's spent most of his life embalming himself," Josh countered.

"It's not a drug - it's a tracker." Eric opened the envelope and poured a chunky black microchip onto his palm. "Vets use them to locate missing pets."

"But…I'm not…"

"Not yet. But you will be. Right, open up."

"Can't you track my phone instead?"

"Not if they take it from you and disable it, we can't."

"Who are 'they'!" screeched Callum.

"Logan and the other 'Horsemen'. Now pop it in."

"It's bloody huge! I can't swallow that."

"Course you can."

Callum shook his head and put both hands over his mouth.

"It doesn't have to be taken orally," noted Josh to the others. "It'll be just as effective as an enema!"

Callum moved one hand from his mouth to cover his arse and fend off attacks on both fronts.

"Do I have to remind you that you've put yourself in this situation."

He shook his head gently and held out his hand. Eric placed the microchip on it.

"Can I get something to wash this down with, at least?"

"Of course. Get him a glass of water, Micky."

"Water! My God, that's three glasses in a month,"

complained Callum. "I don't think I'll ever get used to the taste."

He stared down at the device in his hand. It was square and about the same size as a sherbet lemon. It also had razor sharp edges capable of slicing open the roof of the mouth…much like a sherbet lemon. He placed it on his tongue, filled his mouth with water and swallowed. He felt the sides scrape his gullet on its way to a boozy grave.

Josh removed his phone and opened an application to check it was working. A white dot pulsated on the map between the banks of the Thames and Battersea Power Station.

"Is it on?"

"Yep," he said, turning the display. "Accurate to within five metres."

"Well, as long as they don't bury him, we should be fine."

"Bury me!"

"I think there's only a moderate chance of that."

"Moderate!"

"One in ten, tops."

"Oh good, you had me worried for a second! What am I supposed to do, anyway?"

"You're going to threaten Logan Cobley."

"I'm dead…"

"Not immediately. I imagine they'll torture you for a while to see what you know."

"Which is why you have the tracker," explained Josh helpfully.

"What, so a pharmacist, an advertising executive and a man in a jester's hat can come rescue me?"

"Yes."

"I'm dead…"

"I promise we'll not let that happen to you," said Eric

confidently. "We need to provoke Logan enough that he gathers his team together. You said yourself they're like a brotherhood."

"But why do we need all of them?" asked Callum.

"Plan B. We're going to complete all of Sean's dares and at the same time pin the crimes on him. To do that, we need help from Logan's crew and…" Eric removed a folded photocopy from his pocket. "…this woman."

"Who's that?" asked Micky.

"More importantly," inquired Josh predictably, "is she single?"

A short brunette woman in her early thirties stared back at them from a highly staged profile photo. There was something about her piercing eyes that made them feel uncomfortable, like she was looking directly at them no matter where they sat around the table.

"Oh, she's definitely single," declared Josh, assessing the photo more closely, "and big trouble. Believe me, I can sense these things."

"This is Detective Inspector Iris Whitehall," announced Eric, "and she's going to help us catch and arrest Sean Heschmeyer."

"Why? What's he done?"

"He's going to abduct Logan Cobley and steal a lion."

"But Sean isn't going to do those things," Micky pointed out. "We are."

"Correct, which is why we need to convince Iris that he did and we didn't."

"And how are we going to do that?"

"The less you know about it at this stage, the better."

"You don't know, do you?" said Micky.

"Of course I do," replied Eric, only partially believing his own answer. "Plan B."

"But where did this chick come from?" asked Josh.

"While you were away getting supplies, I was reviewing all of the hits we've had on the WDWC Live channel. There have been a few thousand since the bomb went off in Exeter, but most people haven't bothered to watch the one of Micky and Jessica. One user, however, watched both more than a dozen times. I did some digging and identified the user as Iris Whitehall - it didn't take me long to find out who she was. She's part of the Devon and Somerset Constabulary and guess who her ultimate boss is very good friends with?"

"Sir Andrew Carrington," Micky responded.

"Bingo! There's even a picture of him with the Police and Crime Commissioner on his office wall."

"Are you saying Carrington requested that Whitehall investigate us?"

"Absolutely. My surprise visit, very much against everyone's wishes might I add, provoked him."

"And this is why we didn't want you taunting Carrington. If the police know what we've been doing, they might catch us," said Micky anxiously.

"It's essential that they do."

"Have you lost your mind!"

"No. How else are we going to convince them that Sean is responsible unless we talk them into it? It's not as if we have any evidence for it."

"That's because there isn't any, you nutter," contested Micky.

"No, but there will be. We just have to make sure DI Whitehall catches us at exactly the right time."

"Which is?"

"After we successfully steal a lion."

"Couldn't we get arrested before stealing the lion," suggested Callum.

"Afraid not."

"We don't even know how to steal one," added Josh.

"Now I do," announced Eric.

"Feel free to share it."

"All in good time. We need to complete dare three first. Callum, I asked you to get something too," he said, turning to his increasingly pale friend.

Callum placed his own envelope on the table. It was larger and more official-looking than Foxie's.

"If this falls into the wrong hands, or anyone knows we have it, we'll be enemies of the state. It won't be the police tracking us, it'll be the secret service."

"What's in it?" said Micky, pushing his chair back in case the envelope jumped up and bit him.

"These are all the details relating to Peter Francis's true identity. My MoD contact needed a lot of persuasion…one million pounds' worth in fact…"

"Jesus, Callum, that decision cost us two hundred and fifty thousand pounds each."

"Not at all," replied Eric. "It'll come out of Callum's share, won't it?"

Callum nodded reluctantly.

"What do we do with it now?" asked Josh.

"We're going to let Mr Francis know that Callum has it. Then, if he's lucky, Callum might get his million quid back."

"We're going to blackmail a bunch of lethal black op mercenaries!"

"You only live once," said Eric.

"And now we know for how long," whimpered Micky.

TWENTY-THREE
PUNISHMENT

Last Sunday. London.

"HE'S ON THE MOVE," said Josh, holding up his phone like a trophy.

The tracking dot moved at speed, and its perpendicular pattern indicated that Callum was travelling by car. Either that or he was stuck in a maze.

"Have you considered the possibility that Callum might have hired a car and decided to make a run for it?" asked Micky.

"Not for a second," replied Eric, who reacted without enthusiasm to Josh's excitement. "He'll do the right thing."

"Shouldn't we go?"

"Not yet. Let's give them a bit of time to torture him properly - after all, he did betray us for an extra ten million."

It had only been an hour since an uncooperative Callum left for his rendezvous. That was eleven o'clock and they'd only sent the email to Logan at nine: a photograph of the contents of the envelope and a ransom letter which Josh insisted had to be done properly. He'd returned from a trip to a local newsagents with a pile of magazines which he proceeded to use to cut out letters of irregular size and colour. Josh arranged them meticulously to spell out their demands and the location to make the exchange. One million pounds in return for the envelope. According to Josh, all of this effort was essential to protect their identities. In truth, it was a complete waste of time because they'd sent it from Callum's personal email account.

Logan's response was almost immediate.

Eric imagined, given the nature of Logan's day job, it wouldn't take him long to plan to extract and then torture their unprotected friend. The 'Five Horsemen' were used to working under extreme pressure and in hostile environments; Hyde Park could hardly be described as either. Eric couldn't speculate what had happened to Callum since he'd left the apartment, but he hoped they'd give him a decent kicking somewhere along the line to teach him a lesson.

"Heading east now towards Docklands," said Josh, offering a running commentary of the blinking dot.

"What if they've already killed him?" asked Micky anxiously. "Have you even considered that?"

"As long as they've still got his body, it doesn't affect the plan," replied Eric.

"Are you serious! This isn't a game, Eric. A man's life might be in danger. A friend's life, and we're sitting about drinking tea like it doesn't matter. We're supposed to be a team."

"Maybe he should have thought about that before doing deals with the enemy."

"Sean isn't the enemy, Eric. He's just a pissed-off rich dude with an entirely appropriate vendetta against us.

When all of this is over, everyone will go back to their normal lives and hopefully none of us will be dead. That's the only outcome that's important."

"None of us will be going back to our normal lives after this," predicted Eric ominously.

"I bloody well am," vowed Micky.

"It's impossible. Our lives have been disrupted beyond repair. Even if we beat Sean, there's no going back to how things were."

"What are you suggesting?" challenged Josh.

"Jobs, homes, relationships, businesses, social standing, criminal records – they're all going to change once this is over."

"You're exaggerating."

Eric remained passive in response.

"But what about friendships," added Micky. "They're the oldest things any of us own and the only things that can't be replaced. Are you going to dispense with those as well?"

"He's right," replied Josh. "Whatever our differences, the four of us have to stick together."

"Eric, give me your car keys," demanded Micky, losing patience.

"Are you going to force me?"

"If I have to."

"You'd lose."

"Maybe, but I'd lose doing the right thing," answered Micky, glaring at him dispassionately. "That's more important to me than winning."

Eric never considered losing. Principles, ethics and morals went out of the window if they stood in the way of victory. The fruits of that mindset were all around him to see in the prizes that adorned his plush pad. And yet no one did see them. The apartment had become his well-stocked cage. This week had been the only time he'd shared any of it with people he genuinely cared for. He'd lost them once before; did he want to lose them again?

"Let's go, then," he said, after reflecting on the situation for a moment.

"Can I drive?" asked Josh.

"No!"

"Oh go on, I've never driven a sportscar."

"I've never ridden an ostrich but you don't hear me crowing about it," replied Eric.

"If we get through this, Josh," promised Micky, "I'll buy you a track day."

"Aww thanks, man."

The basement of Eric's building was packed with expensive cars. No one with the means to live here would drive an old banger. Bright red Ferraris polished so carefully that the glare from their bodywork was almost blinding. Massive Bentleys that each took up more than its allotted single parking space. Gigantic Range Rovers with blacked out windows and shiny running boards that came up to their knees. There were car museums that couldn't claim to house this many rare and expensive models. Only one of its vehicles was clearly out of place. Next to Eric's Nissan GT-R was a tired Ford Granada hearse. They'd tried to contact Dubious Barry to arrange collection but he was otherwise unavailable. As long as it remained here, the authorities wouldn't detect it or make a connection with them.

They jumped into the Nissan. Josh was again forced into the back having lost the paper-scissors-stone best of three against Micky on the way down in the lift. Eric started the ignition and the blinding headlights cast its illustrious automotive neighbours in shadows like technological ghosts. The Nissan flew out of its space and up the ramp to street level. The parking lot doors eased open effortlessly as the car triggered their sensors, and within moments they burst out onto the main road.

"He's stopped moving," Josh informed them as Callum's dot pulsed on the map.

"Location?" said Eric as he dashed through London smashing every speed limit as he went.

"Factory Road, Woolwich."

"Where exactly?" asked Eric as he prepared to tap the details into the SatNav.

"Not sure. It looks like an old warehouse. Get as close as you can and we'll follow his signal."

North Woolwich was an area of the historic Docklands yet to experience an urban facelift like its nearby cousins, Stratford and the Isle of Dogs. It was home to an increasingly diverse ethnic working-class community, mostly living in poorly-maintained social housing. Much of the thriving industry which once hugged the riverbanks had been abandoned, and they waited like haunted houses for the public or private financing needed to convert them into expensive apartment blocks to attract a more affluent breed of homeowner. An act that was likely to further marginalise the current natives. It was the type of place Eric had grown up in, and with that knowledge, he knew parking a supercar on the main road wasn't a smart move if you wanted it to be in one piece when you returned.

Callum's locator chip indicated that he was on the river side of Factory Road, directly opposite London Airport. Eric turned off the slip road and headed for one of its car parks. It would have been cheaper to park it on the moon, but at least it would be safe. They bundled out of the Nissan wearing the dark clothes Micky had borrowed from Jessica but before they set off on foot, Eric flipped open the boot and removed a small wooden box with a metal handle. On the front, the year eighteen twelve was written in beautiful flowing calligraphy.

"What's that?" asked Josh.

"Protection."

"Guns!" said Micky.

"Yes. Did you really think I'm going in to face a team of highly trained mercenaries unarmed."

"You've lost your mind. Don't you think we're in enough trouble?"

"I'm not going to use them."

"What sort of guns are they?" queried Josh as he examined the worn, ancient box.

Eric placed it on the bonnet and flicked open the catch. Inside were two exquisite antique pistols.

"Attempting a highway robbery, are we?" Josh quipped sarcastically.

"They're guns. Does it matter what year they were made?"

"I think it depends on whether you're trying to look hard or you're heading for the Antiques Roadshow! Do they even work?"

"How should I know, I've never used them. They cost me a fortune so I'm not going to damage them by taking pot shots at pigeons from my balcony window."

"They're still illegal!" cried Micky.

"Ah, well…that's where you're wrong," said Eric defensively. "I have a licence for them."

"And that gives you permission to wander around Woolwich threatening trained assassins, does it?"

"It doesn't stipulate on the paperwork that I can't."

"Look, Micky, there are only two," added Josh excitedly, "so if you don't want one, that's fine."

"I certainly do not."

"That's agreed, then," confirmed Eric. "Josh and I will

have one pistol each and you can make do with a jester's hat."

Micky frowned. "Come on, let's go and collect what's left of Callum."

They followed the dot on Josh's phone out of the car park, through the airport passenger exit and out into the town. On the other side of the almost empty main road, they halted at a dilapidated factory long since abandoned.

"You didn't think this through, did you?" commented Micky as the three of them stared up at the building.

"How many floors do you reckon?" asked Josh.

"Five."

"And he could be on any one of them."

"Trackers aren't very good in three dimensions, are they? Thank God they haven't converted it into a hotel or flats – we'd be knocking on doors for hours. 'Hello, Madam, have you seen our friend!'" laughed Josh.

"Keep your hair on, boys," directed Eric calmly. "We'll just start at the bottom and work our way up."

"How many ears do you think Callum has left?" posed Micky.

"One," suggested Josh grimly. "But if he's on the top floor, it'll probably be none by the time we get there."

There was little of interest on the ground floor other than rats scurrying around between the rusty remains of light industry in search of lunch. Much of the building had been stripped of any assets, either by the last owner or local residents seeking a quick buck by selling what they found to scrap metal merchants. Most of the windows were smashed, and the floors were covered in litter discarded by desperate folk seeking shelter from the world. The surface area was vast and set out in an open plan affair with fragile metal stairs that hugged the walls on their journey to the next. There wasn't much of interest on the first floor, either, but when they reached the second, the atmosphere changed.

Eric was the only one with any experience of the army, having attended a team building course at the Royal Military Academy at Sandhurst. This had mostly involved being shouted at by a disgruntled ex-army captain and being forced to drag his body around an assault course not designed for advertising executives. Eric believed he'd done fairly well at their tests until the instructor pointed out it was designed to test teamwork rather than individuality. Eric had frequently barged colleagues off the assault course netting, purposely tripped some of them up on the hike and even dunked a few of them in the freezing water hazard as they went through it.

He'd come first, but apparently that wasn't the point.

Even so, it was more 'training' than the others had had outside of video games. Eric instructed them to spread out and only climb the stairs after the person in front gave the all clear. Josh would take the lead, pistol at the ready, Micky second and he'd bring up the rear. When Josh reached the entrance to the second floor, he gave the agreed hand signal that the coast was far from being clear. Eric and Micky eased their way up the creaky stairs to see what he'd found.

In the far corner of the room, a small group of people were huddled with their backs to them. Eric signalled for Josh to creep down the opposite side of the room and told Micky to keep guard at the entrance. Their pulses raced as they eased ever closer to the group in a pincer movement. The ancient wooden handle of the pistol shook in Josh's palm and a bead of sweat ran down his forehead. The group were sitting or lying on the floor around a small camping stove.

Eric stepped out from the shadows assertively, pistol raised. "Where's Callum?"

The group's reaction to his unexpected appearance was decidedly unnatural. Two of them glanced around as if they weren't sure where the voice came from, one was wrapped in a shabby sleeping bag and apparently out for the count while a fourth man continued to do whatever it was he was doing before their arrival. Which, as it turns out, was tripping his tits off.

"Callum's not here yet," replied a ghostly pale face whose eyes had sunken half way into his skull. "Join us."

"Junkies," whispered Josh.

Spread out on the floor next to the stove was a collection of dirty spoons, syringes, notebooks and small dots of white powder. Eric focused in on the man in the sleeping bag and his heart sunk. The man's dark skin clung to his skull and his eyes stared vacantly out into the gloom. It was impossible to know whether the man knew who he was; there, Eric certainly didn't have the same luxury. He'd seen him and he'd never unsee this. A ravaged body of a forty-something local man who'd consumed too many drugs and not enough nutrition over the last two decades. A solitary tear rolled down Eric's face.

"You okay?" nudged Josh, noticing Eric's sudden change in body language.

"Not really," he gasped.

"Haven't you seen junkies before?"

"Yes. Just not this one."

"Cool gun," croaked a second man who had long dirty hair that clung to his face and a torso which was even thinner than first man's. "Can I borrow it?"

"No."

"Callum's not here," stated Eric.

"He'll be back soon," insisted the first junkie.

"It is the kind of company he keeps," suggested Josh with a knowing shrug.

"Not today, it isn't."

"You don't see many eighteenth-century ninjas in Woolwich anymore," wheezed the second junkie, referencing their unusual dress sense. "Time travellers?"

"No."

"Hallucination?"

"Yes," agreed Eric, who had started to back away from the group. "We're not really here."

"Don't go. Stay for a shot. Plenty of needles to go around…actually one…but we all share it."

"No thanks."

"We'll tell Callum you were looking for him?" said junkie number one as the pair eased further away.

"If you like."

When Eric and Josh's slow reverse put them out of earshot, the second junkie gave one of the passive members of their group a nudge.

"Callum, couple of time travelling ninjas were looking for you."

"I'm not Callum."

"Aren't you. What's your name, then?"

"I don't remember…Cheryl?"

"Isn't that a girl's name?"

"I am a girl…aren't I?"

"Search me; I thought you were a figment of my imagination."

When Eric and Josh returned to the metal staircase, Micky was nowhere to be seen.

"Where'd he go?"

"Probably legged it, wuss."

"No, he wouldn't do that," whispered Josh, getting

more nervous about the whole situation. "Maybe he's gone to check the floor above. I'll go look."

"Well, you wanted to be in the lead."

Josh ascended the next flight of stairs, stopping every step or so to listen intently to what might be happening above him. Unlike the first few floors they'd seen, the next one had partition walls between the staircase and the room above. Josh took a step out of sight and Eric waited anxiously for the raised thumb signal they'd agreed on. None came. A minute passed and there was still no signal. Two minutes and nothing.

The factory suddenly felt like a vacuum. No sound penetrated the air. Even the draft through the broken windows which had been ever present since they'd entered no longer felt inclined to whistle around his ears. Something was happening up there, and Eric's senses decided it was probably bad. Unless he was prepared to recruit four smacked-up junkies for protection, it was down to him to get his friends out of trouble. He took a step onto the metal staircase and it clattered like falling pots and pans. He held the pistol confidently in front of him, fully prepared to use it if called upon. When he reached the last step, he paused. On the floor below him, he noticed two ends of a thin metal thread and a sensor on the doorframe. He studied it carefully. This technology wasn't available in a local hardware store. It looked like sophisticated military grade tripwire, the kind he only saw in movies.

Logan and his team were here, and they'd come prepared for the fight.

He stepped through the broken wire and onto the third floor of the factory which had originally been designed to house a series of offices, each hidden behind flimsy partitioned walls. This made it much gloomier than the ones below. He moved tentatively down the main corridor like a nervous contestant on *The Crystal Maze*, constantly poking his head through doorways to see if his friends were inside and each time expecting someone to jump out at him. At the far end of the corridor only one door was firmly refusing to give up its duty. It stood defiantly shut and bore the words 'NAGING DIRECTOR' on the glass in dishevelled black lettering. Upon closer inspection, a couple of the letters had been scraped off and never replaced – a sign perhaps that the staff felt the title continued to describe the occupant.

"Don't turn around," came a gruff voice from behind him. "Step inside."

Eric complied. It wasn't something he was accustomed to doing, but his instincts told him sternly that the result of acting normally would probably be severe pain.

Inside the room, his three companions were tied to chairs. Callum sat in the middle, his face covered in blood and his eye black and swollen. It wasn't unusual for him to be unconscious but it was rarely inflicted on him by someone else. Josh and Micky desperately tried to communicate through thick gaffer tape around their mouths. Behind the prisoners, standing in commando-style uniforms which revealed nothing more than their eye colour, were the rest of the 'Five Horsemen'.

"Eric Gideon. Now I have all the idiots," said the man immediately behind him. "What do I win for a set!"

"There's one of us missing," Eric replied cockily.

"That's right. You let Sean Heschmeyer play your stupid games, too, didn't you. I think I'll take your weapon off you before the British Museum come looking for it," he said, taking the pistol from Eric and placing it on the table next to the other. "Sit down."

They made no attempt to restrain him because they didn't need to. Even with Eric's renowned ingenuity, he wasn't fighting his way out of this one. It was impossible to 'walk the walk' with these boys, but he might be able to 'talk the talk'. Logan removed his face covering and sat down opposite. He had a weathered look these days, and out of all the people Eric remembered from University, this face was the least recognisable.

"Did you honestly think you could threaten us?"

"Not at all, in fact," admitted Eric honestly.

"So you were willing to send your friend into battle with no exit strategy?"

The other members of Logan's gang growled aggressively at the notion.

"You're assuming he's my friend," replied Eric.

"Well, is he?" demanded Logan, pointing a gun towards Callum threateningly.

"Yes," confirmed Eric, "and this is our exit strategy."

"What, pistols from the Battle of Waterloo and a plucky attitude?"

"Not quite."

"I think your friend deserves better. If you're in a brotherhood, you remain conjoined until death." Logan rolled up his sleeve to show off a rather complex tattoo with five men on horseback.

"I thought there were only four horsemen," inquired Eric. "Or have you expanded the scope of the apocalypse?"

"It's an artistic representation of our commitment to each other and what we will do if anyone stands in our way. Death, Famine, Pestilence, War and Debt."

"Debt?"

"Yes, wherever the other horsemen ride, there will always be a debt to be paid."

"So, Death wields a scythe, War has a sword and Debt carries a calculator? Scary."

"You're not in a position to mock," Logan growled, grabbing him firmly by the neck. "We're trained killers. Have you ever heard of Abu Mohammed Abubakar bin Mohammad al-Sheikawi?"

"No, but I'm guessing he struggles when it comes to printing business cards."

"Not anymore, he doesn't. He's the former leader of Boko Haram. The Nigerian army tried to kill him for over a decade, and according to their reports, he died more frequently than an iPhone battery. Slippery little bugger, though, always managed to escape. Until we came along, that was. When governments need the job done properly, they call us and we collect a tidy fee. We extracted him from his camp without leaving a crumb of evidence. No DNA, no sightings and no proof. Boko Haram still claim he's alive but we know where he is."

"Where?"

"If I told you that, I'd have to kill you."

"You're bluffing," suggested Eric bravely.

"I think you need to teach this dog a lesson," said one of the mercenaries, who was obsessively cleaning a huge blade behind the back of the three captives.

"I assure you he doesn't have the bottle for it," goaded Eric. "I've always been harder than him."

The room erupted in muffled laughter.

"I could kill you with a stare," threatened Logan unconvincingly. "Ask Taliban chieftain Mullah Muttaqi."

"How can I…if you killed him?" chuckled Eric.

"Watch your tongue! I'm trained in eskrima, bojutsu, kendo, medieval torture - and I know where every pressure point is in your body if you attempted to attack me."

"I can still have you," boasted Eric.

Micky and Josh's eyes expanded at the unbridled arrogance which was bound to hurt them just as much as it was him. While Eric remained steadfastly composed, it was clear to him that Logan was showing signs of frailty. His hands didn't know what to do with themselves as they fiddled needlessly with his clothes. His eyes wandered from their target in case they gave the game away. When it came to physicality, Logan was obviously Eric's superior on every front, notwithstanding he had four equally trained colleagues to step in as backup if he needed them.

But physical strength wasn't the whole story.

The body can be trained, honed and improved. Skills can be practised and enhanced. Tactics can be learnt and assessed. But memories, they weren't so easily altered. Taliban warlords, ISIS terrorists and enemy combatants might be easy to overcome, but you never forget the beatings from history. Eric certainly hadn't forgotten his and he was certain Logan hadn't, either.

"You and me," offered Eric casually. "Just like before. You do remember, don't you? The day you put your nose into my affairs one too many times."

"You're delusional!"

"What's he talking about, War?" mumbled one of the mercenaries.

"Oh, you're War. How grandiose of you! Sounds like someone's got an inferiority complex."

"SHUT UP!"

"Which one of you is Debt, then?" said Eric, turning around.

One of the men half-heartedly raised a hand.

"Nice to meet you. War here may not have told you about me, but I kicked his arse once."

"No you didn't. STOP TALKING."

"It was after I broke into his house and hid in his wardrobe. Sean let me in, did he tell you that?"

"I'm warning you. I'll remove your thyroid with a tin opener if you don't stop."

He didn't stop.

"I waited in that wardrobe for ages, didn't I, War? For a while I just watched and listened to see what you were doing."

"Right, that's it. One more word!"

"It was the sound of a pump that I found most surprising. I thought maybe it was a Lilo, but imagine my shock when I peeked through the key hole and saw the figure of a woman slowly growing out of the floor. She wasn't very chatty from what I could hear..."

"STOP!" Logan lashed out and caught Eric across the face with the back of his hand.

Eric casually wiped the blood from his split lip. "You may have made a name for yourself as Peter Francis, the gun for hire, but to me, Logan, you'll always be that freaky, meek, do-gooder who no one liked. Who no one respected. But I can change that if you want."

"What do you mean?" barked Logan.

"I can give you what you want."

"Which is?"

"Inclusion."

Logan took a moment as flashes of his past rushed through him. "Inclusion! I have it here."

"It's not the real thing, though, is it? I can give you that."

"In return for what?" he said sarcastically.

"Well, we need you to let us abduct you...and film it."

Where his suggestions had once been met by laughter from the horsemen, now the room fell silent. It was such a preposterous idea but he'd delivered it with such conviction it was obvious he was serious.

"You want to abduct me? Why?"

"Because Sean dared me to, and I can't allow him to win."

"Why did Sean dare you to do that?" said Logan, looking baffled.

"Initially, I thought it was because you were firmly on his side."

"I hate the little weasel," spat Logan.

"Good, then we have something in common. Perhaps he dared me to do it because he thought it was impossible."

"It is impossible," insisted Logan. "There's no way on this Earth you could abduct me. These boys would immediately rescue me even if, and it's a big if, you managed to get anywhere near me."

"But I did get near you. I'm here now."

"Yes, but we've restrained you, haven't we? It's not the other way around."

"Only because I designed it to be so. I believe there is a way on this Earth that it can be done."

"Reinforcements on their way, are they? Better be a bloody big battalion, because we've fought off more enemy combatants than they faced at the Battle of Rorke's Drift."

"No. It's only me. It's all I need."

The situation became all too much for Micky, who fainted into unconsciousness alongside Callum but achieved it with a great deal less pain.

"Tell me something, Logan," asked Eric. "Why did you always grass up *The Idiots' Club* to Carrington every time we were doing a dare?"

"Because it was dangerous."

"And extracting a VIP from enemy territory isn't? Tell me the truth."

"Because I applied to be in your club and you didn't even reply. You took him instead." Logan pointed at

Micky. "He wasn't even an outsider; he didn't deserve his place."

Micky was the only member of the club who'd applied to be a member. After Eric and Josh had invited Callum to join, they felt they needed a fourth member to increase the variety of challenges. They put up posters on the Guild message board inviting new recruits. They were inundated by a grand total of three volunteers. Micky was the first they interviewed. Logan was right, Micky wasn't the normal type of underdog they attracted, but Eric saw the pent-up anger in him for the way his father had controlled his life. *The Idiots' Club* were best placed to encourage it out of him and set him on a new path. He was in and they never bothered to follow up on the other candidates. Eric never even knew who they were.

"Then this, my friend, is your lucky day. How would you like to join the club?"

"And let you abduct me? That sounds like I'd be the victim of your dare."

"We're only going to pretend to do it. You'll be working with us all the time. These boys can join in, too," he said, nodding toward the horsemen.

Logan considered his schedule for the next week before the 'Five Horsemen' flew to Yemen on a secret RAF night flight. It mostly included doing the school run, redecorating the downstairs toilet and spending time with his in-laws. Anything was better than that.

"It's time we taught Sean a lesson," added Eric.

"No. We don't work like that," argued Debt, who had one of the gruffest voices Eric had ever heard. It was like listening to nails being sucked into a hoover. "We're not a charity, for fuck's sake."

"Debt's right," confirmed Logan. "We won't do it."

"The way I see it," said Eric, "the 'Horsemen' are basically a fraternity of bounty hunters working for the highest bidder, right?"

"Right," replied Debt.

"So if you don't want to join us, can we hire you instead?"

A few of the horsemen nodded readily.

"How much will it cost?" asked Eric.

"What, to fake my abduction?"

"Yes."

"What else is involved?" asked Debt, who actually did have a calculator on him. He removed it from his combat trousers and tapped it as Eric explained what he needed.

"You'll need to be away from home for a few days."

"Easy. Anything else?"

Eric knew the buying signals when a client was close to agreeing to a deal. The language was suggestively positive, the body language open and the motivation obvious. Eric also knew that when a customer was committed, there was never a better time to upsell.

"We also need you to help us steal a lion."

"A lion?"

"Yeah. Can you do it?"

"We can do anything for the right price."

"Which is?" Eric turned to their killer accountant.

"Half a million," said Debt with a Scrooge-like grin.

"Bargain…"

"Each," he added.

"Two point five million," stated Logan. "Payment on completion."

"And ten percent upfront, " Debt reminded him.

Eric did a quick mental calculation of how much the four of them might be able to muster for the deposit. Josh was notorious for spending his wages well before payday, so he was out. Callum had less than ten pounds in cash and owed the government millions in back taxes. Micky was middle upper class and although people were caught up in the illusion he was wealthy, he had less in liquid assets than the other two combined. Which only left him. Should be easy enough.

"Cheque?"

"Cash."

"Done," he stood up and shook Logan's hand. "Welcome to *The Idiots' Club*."

TWENTY-FOUR

THE DISAPPEARANCE OF LOGAN COBLEY

Monday morning. London.

DI WHITEHALL WATCHED the abduction in real time on the WDWC Live channel. It wasn't easy to follow what was happening, because it was being broadcast in the early hours of the morning and the perpetrators were wearing what appeared to be black lycra onesies and poorly-knitted balaclavas. There was no doubt about their identities, though. They'd specifically taken time to introduce themselves.

Gaydaffi, Turnip, Foxie and Gloomy.

Otherwise known as Eric Gideon and his currently unnamed associates.

The same people who'd successfully stolen a WWII bomb from a building site in London, evacuated a major University - damaging a significant portion of it in the process – and who'd made a fool of themselves at an international rugby match, in less than a week. The same man her boss, the commissioner, had instructed her to investigate only hours before the first of these videos was posted, transforming the seemingly routine into something altogether more intriguing.

Now they'd struck again, the abduction of Peter Francis from his heavily protected central London home.

None of these incidents appeared to have a pattern or any obvious links to each other, which was exactly why Whitehall's pulse was racing. Crimes weren't normally irregular or mysterious. They were normally motivated by simple factors like greed or anger. Not these. Without the benefit of the livestream, it would have been almost impossible to draw them together into the same investigation. But the randomness of the crimes wasn't the only confusing aspect; even more baffling was why any criminal would actively encourage her to catch them by making their own documentary series. That's not how felons behaved. They normally did everything possible to avoid being caught. They didn't set up their own TV channel, for the same reason they didn't open an online shop and sell official merchandise. The people behind these crimes were either geniuses or total lunatics, but whichever it was, Iris had to know the truth.

As soon as the livestream ended, Iris leapt into her car and drove through the night to London. Requests were made, through the normal channels, to allow her access to another force's crime scene in the expectation that sharing information might bring about a faster resolution. In truth, police forces were as competitive as any other fragmented organisation. They all had targets to hit to demonstrate their value, and that made them defensive or suspicious of outsiders. Even a detective from Somerset, a place of simpletons according to most regional colleagues, still couldn't be trusted.

Just after seven o'clock in the morning, a bleary-eyed

Iris Whitehall pulled up outside one of the wealthiest roads in Britain - the recently renovated, Grade I listed properties of Cornwall Terrace which nestled on one end of Regent's Park. To say she pulled up outside it was misleading. Given the cordon and the massive police presence on both sides of the building, she parked as close to it as possible. Only her London colleagues, with the benefit of blue flashing lights atop their cars, would still find them parked up on the curb when they returned. Her unmarked vehicle would be whisked away before she could say 'tow truck'. The nearest place, as it turned out, was more than half a mile away and it took her longer to find it than it took to drive to the capital from home.

Cornwall Terrace was more than a road, it was a building. It stretched along the southwest corner of the park with the shadow of Baker Street directly behind it. The Roman/Greco architecture oozed elegance, and it was hard for Iris not to stop to admire its magnificence. What was once a row of nineteen properties had, over the years, been amalgamated into just eight terraced mansions, and last night, the owner of Number Six had been taken against his will. Given the scale of the police operation, anyone would have thought all the residents had been abducted. The scale of the resources would have been somewhat less if someone had been kidnapped from a council estate. Not only were Cornwall Terrace's owners immorally rich, they were also extremely persuasive, which probably explained the excessive turnout.

Iris crossed the concrete walkway which extended over the basement levels and up to the doorway of Number Six where an intensely groomed man in his late twenties was barking orders at a group of disaffected uniformed officers. Iris waited patiently for him to finish his rant before attempting to grab his attention.

"Are you the Senior Investigating Officer?" she asked confidently.

"No," came the abrasive reply.

"Can you tell me where I might find them?"

"No."

"I'm DI Iris Whitehall," she offered with a friendly outstretched hand which he ignored. "From North Somerset."

"Good for you," he replied disparagingly.

"My superior officer made arrangements for me to visit the crime scene?"

Finally, the man stopped what he was doing but only to exhale a long and irritable sigh. "Fucking tourists. Credentials."

She took out her ID badge and flashed it back at him. "Somerset Investigative Branch."

"Jimmy Copper...no need to smirk," he added automatically.

"Why would I?"

"Copper...you know...as in police, filth, pig, rozzer..."

"I rarely notice humour, sir, only crimes."

"Then you're in the right place, DI Whitehall. National Crime Agency," he said, gently brushing her hand with his in a reluctant excuse for a shake. "Anti-Kidnap and Extortion Unit. Looks like everyone wants in on this one."

"How do you mean?"

"Multi agency affair. Bloody rich folk give the Prime Minister an arse ache if we don't send in Uncle Tom Cobley and all. They want to know their taxes are being well spent, not that one of these bastards actually pay any. The bloke at Number Thirteen has been avoiding extradition to Kenya for money laundering for over a decade. There are more crooks in here than down at the nick. What's your interest in it, then?"

"It crosses over into my own investigation."

"Into what part?"

"A criminal gang," she replied vaguely, not certain if any of her London colleagues had seen the video of the crime yet and not wanting to lose her competitive advantage.

"We don't have any suspects yet, so what's your criminal gang got to do with it?"

"Similar M.O., sir."

Jimmy scowled at her suspiciously. "You do understand, DI Whitehall, that any evidence relating to this crime scene must be disclosed to my team immediately."

"I'll keep that in mind, sir. Who was the victim?"

"Peter Francis, but he's also known in some corners as Logan Cobley."

"Why the alias? Renowned criminal?"

"No, quite the opposite. His identity is protected by the highest level of government, and from what they've told me, he's involved in international security and protection."

"Doesn't sound like your typical abductee, then," commented Iris instinctively.

"No, but a man like that must collect enemies in high places."

"Can we go inside?"

"Not looking like that, you can't." He gestured at her clothing as if she wasn't wearing any.

Iris was hastily rehoused in a white hooded coverall, double thick plastic gloves, face mask and shoe protectors, as well as having her own mouth swabbed in case any of her DNA was subsequently discovered at the property after her visit. Looking like a pair of deflated Michelin Men, they rustled up to the main door, and Iris immediately noticed there was no sign of forced entry.

"The front entrance is controlled by retina and fingerprint scanning," said Jimmy. "It can't be fooled or faked."

"How did they get in, then?"

"We have absolutely no idea, only to say that we know they did because there's security camera footage of four men dressed in black wandering around aimlessly in the hallway."

Iris thought back to last night's video stream. She'd witnessed all four of her suspects cross the same walkway and approach the door just as she'd done moments earlier. Then one of them, although it was impossible to say which, placed his finger on the scanner and eye up to the panel, unlocking the doors. If the technology couldn't be faked or fooled, how was that possible?

"Who first reported him missing?"

"His wife."

"Where was she at the time of the abduction?"

"In bed."

"And Mr Francis?"

"In bed next to her."

"And you've got that information from her?"

"Not solely. There are at least nine separate security measures between here in the hallway," he said, leading her into the plush and completely untarnished entrance, "and the couple's bedroom on the second floor. Burglar alarms, sensors, cameras, two Alsatians, and a six-digit combination lock on the second floor with a hundred thousand different combinations."

"And they beat all of them?"

"Yep. Every one."

"What about the dogs?" Iris had no memory of seeing any on last night's livestream.

"Both apparently slept through the break-in, but that's

not surprising because the whole operation took less than five minutes."

"You sound kind of sceptical, sir."

"Of course I am; it can't be done. It's impossible. Even James Bond would struggle to pull it off. I'd say it has to be an inside job, but it's clear that's also unlikely."

"Why would you say that?"

"They cut one of his digits off."

Iris cringed. "How do you know it's one of his?"

"It had his wedding ring on it and his wife confirmed it," replied Jimmy.

"Jesus," replied Iris, grimacing.

"What do you expect! This is London, not grockle-land," he sneered insultingly, believing falsely that her most serious cases consistent of tractor thefts and missing geese. "We're talking about a serious organised criminal gang, not some bungling opportunists. I wouldn't be surprised if it's not the work of a hostile state, Russia perhaps; they're known for their brazen attempts to disrupt Western powers or enact reprisals on those they feel warrant it."

Iris considered what she knew already about Eric Gideon and his associates, a picture that couldn't be further from her colleague's assessment. The only state they represented was a damaged mental one.

"It won't be the last piece of Mr Francis we're gonna find, either," added Jimmy, "not if the ransom note is anything to go on."

"There's a ransom note?"

Jimmy Copper motioned with his index finger and Iris obediently followed him through the hall and into the largest kitchen she'd ever seen. It was bigger than all of her family's houses combined. She struggled to simply focus on objects on the far side of the room, such was the distance. A forensics team was busy brushing surfaces for prints and combing the area for fibres. There were five people in all, and not one of them looked up to acknowledge her arrival. Bagged-up evidence was arranged in rows on a kitchen island ready to be removed for further analysis. In the middle was a single piece of paper with colourful and unevenly-sized letters stuck to it.

"Is this it?"

Jimmy nodded.

"You're kidding, right?"

He shook his head.

"And you still think this is the work of the Russians or some drug lord, do you?"

Jimmy looked crestfallen by the criticism. He wasn't used to being told he was wrong. After all, he was twenty-nine and had more degrees than a triangle.

"Are the Russians particularly known for leaving notes in the style of a poorly funded Sherlock Holmes TV adaptation?"

"Not especially. They generally spread Novichok around the place and have done with it."

"Not the Russians, then," said Iris, reading the note once more. "And I think we can rule out an organised criminal gang as I imagine, and you're the expert on this, they tend to demand money - unless this is some kind of Cockney slang I don't understand."

"I'm not following."

"Don't Londoners use animals to describe different quantities of money?"

"Oh, you mean like a pony or a monkey?"

"Yeah. How much is a monkey, exactly?"

"Five hundred quid."

"And do they have one for this?"

"No."

Iris read the note out loud, still struggling to comprehend its meaning and hoping the sound of it might help. It didn't. "We'll swap Logan for a lion."

"What does it mean?" asked Jimmy.

"I don't know."

"We've got our intelligence analysts working on it to see if it's code for something."

"I wouldn't bother. With this lot, I imagine it's self-explanatory. They actually want a lion."

"Why?" implored Jimmy desperately.

Iris shrugged.

"Okay, spill the beans. You've seen what you came to see, detective. It's time you divulged what you know about this case. The chief wouldn't have authorised your visit unless you knew something."

She was on the starting line. As soon as she opened her mouth and revealed what she knew, the gun would fire and the race to capture Eric Gideon and his companions would be on. A race she had to win. She needed to hold on to her slim advantage. Copper was with the big boys, connected to specialist teams who could muster personnel and resources she'd only get access to by filling out reams of paperwork for the next three weeks. By then, it would be too late. Gideon had left an embarrassment of rich evidence in his chaotic trail and now his crimes were serious. A man was missing, and missing a finger. A serious individual with powerful connections if his alias and multi-million-pound house were anything to go on. She had to disclose what she knew, but that didn't mean all of what she knew.

"I'm investigating a man called Eric Gideon," she offered.

"Is he known to the authorities?"

"Known, yes. Convicted, no."

"Foreign intelligence services?"

"Ad executive."

Jimmy's face screwed up into a ball.

"He's working with three accomplices, but we've not identified their real names yet."

"What makes you believe this gang is involved?"

Revealing the existence of the online video would throw away her head start, but she couldn't avoid the truth any longer as she had no other way of connecting them to the crime scene. This was her case, so she'd have to get a little creative. As long as Gideon was brought to justice, what did it matter.

"The suspects are connected to the victim," she said with confidence.

"How?"

"I understand they're involved in a long-running business dispute."

"And that's the motive?"

"I believe so."

"But it's obviously not extortion."

"I guess not. Look into Eric Gideon; I'm sure with your resources you'll discover more than I have. Thanks for your time, Jimmy."

"I'll be in touch, DI Whitehall – you're part of my investigation now," he said as she turned on her heels and marched out of the kitchen.

When she re-emerged in the fresh air of Sunday morning, she checked her phone for messages. There were several missed calls from the station and, once she was out of sight of the police cordon, she hurriedly rang them back.

"What have you got?" she demanded as soon as a voice answered on the other end.

"We have ANPR hits on that Granada you asked us to trace, ma'am."

"Good work, Patricia. Whereabouts?"

"About a dozen hits in London from York Road to Heathrow, followed by a few more on the M4 motorway heading west. The last one was just outside Reading."

"When?"

"Last one was over an hour ago. We're checking surveillance cameras, but there's been no trace of them since."

"Okay, keep looking. Get a message out for all patrols in that area to keep an eye out for them," she added, ending the call abruptly.

The walk back to her car gave her plenty of thinking time. Gideon's crimes made no sense to her. There was no obvious pattern outside of their desire to broadcast to the world what they were doing.

"Why would they film it?" she muttered to herself repeatedly.

She considered only three possible explanations. The first she dismissed almost immediately. There were a lot safer ways to get publicity, and it wasn't obvious what they wanted it for. It was also plausible they were being forced in some way to prove their crimes had been successfully completed, but that didn't explain the strange pattern of their activities. Then there was the third possible reason. She'd certainly studied it during her criminology course, but she'd never witnessed it herself. It was a more common trait in serial killers than crimes such as these, although there was certainly a precedent. Psychopaths had an unshakable belief in their abilities and a complete lack of capacity for accepting responsibility. They thought themselves too clever to be caught and often purposefully left clues to taunt their less intelligent hunters. This pattern of behaviour was certainly evident here. Was Eric Gideon testing her? Did he want to be caught?

Why else would he ask for a lion in a ransom note unless it was a clue?

Iris jumped in her car and did a quick internet search. Eric's last known location was Berkshire and he was heading west. According to Google, there was a limited number of zoos in that direction and only one with a ubiquitous link to the king of the jungle; Longleat.

Monday Lunchtime.

Josh finished attaching the fake number plates which Logan had sourced for them to the Granada hearse. Callum, still bruised from his brief torture session and more sober than at any point in recent history, stood with his back to them, cautiously sipping boiling coffee from a disposable cup. Micky fiddled with his phone as the pings of texts arrived at a rate faster than the beat of his heart. Eric leaned against the hearse's bodywork, deep in thought.

"That should do it," confirmed Josh, brushing the dust from his jeans. "Think it'll work?"

"It'll lead DI Whitehall this far; the rest will be up to her," muttered Eric, his mind elsewhere.

"And Logan?"

"On his way to the drop-off point," said Micky, looking up from his text stream.

"If Jessica is driving, how come she keeps texting you?" asked Josh inquisitively. "Bloody dangerous, that."

"It's a balance of risks. Apparently, texting is one of the things that keeps her awake. Which is more dangerous - a narcoleptic sleeping at the wheel of a supercar or a fully conscious narcoleptic sending texts from the wheel of a supercar?"

"Neither! I still can't believe you let her drive it," he groaned to Eric. "You've never let me have a go."

"That's because a narcoleptic with a fifty percent chance of falling asleep on a motorway is ninety percent safer than you driving it anywhere. I've seen your cars. Not a smooth panel to be seen."

"Objects seem to get in my way," said Josh seriously.

"That's why cars come with steering wheels," replied Eric, miming Josh's erratic driving style.

"Remind me why Jessica is even involved?"

"Because we needed someone to drive the other car," replied Eric.

"Couldn't Logan drive it?"

"Not if we want his abduction to look realistic, no. The police will be looking for him, me and probably the car, too."

"Then why Jessica? Why not one of us?"

"Because we have a dare to complete and it requires all of us."

"She will be alright, won't she?" inquired Micky anxiously.

"Probably, but it doesn't concern me," Eric responded coldly. "She volunteered - we didn't force her. Maybe you shouldn't have made such an impression on her. Anyway, her safety is your responsibility, not ours."

"Don't worry, once we get to that part of the plan, I'll look after her."

"Talking about the plan," said Josh, rolling up a cigarette for one final nicotine hit before getting back in the car. "I'm still a little confused, if I'm honest."

"Normal, then," teased Micky.

"We've been over it for the last couple of hours," groused Eric. "Which bit is confusing you, exactly?"

"I understand how we're planning to get to Longleat, how we'll take care of any security, how we'll tranquilise the lion and what we do with it when we get it into the hearse," outlined Josh as he attempted to blow smoke rings between sentences. He'd been trying to master the talent since the early nineties but was still rubbish at it.

"Right. So what's the problem?"

"I've looked at the map of the park. The lions are in a fenced enclosure right in the middle."

"Which is why we've got the bolt cutters," answered Micky before Eric snapped in irritation.

"Yes, but lions weigh – how much did you say?" He looked at Eric.

"Approximately two hundred kilos unless we're lucky enough to spot a cub."

"Won't that piss off the pride?" Micky inquired. "I hear they're extremely protective of their young."

"Very. Anyway, we're not going for a cub. It doesn't seem right somehow."

"Nothing about stealing a lion seems right," acknowledged Micky.

"So we're going for a big one, then?" clarified Josh.

"Specifically, we're aiming for a female called Sweetie Pie."

"Don't female lions all look the same?"

"To us they will, especially in the dark," confirmed Eric.

"How are we going to know which one is Sweetie Pie, then? Does she respond like a dog when you call her!"

"I doubt it. According to my research she almost always sleeps up a tree, which means she won't be inside the lion house."

"Okay, so we shoot her with a dart and hope she falls out of her tree. Then we remove her from the enclosure, while avoiding being mauled by the two dozen lions who might be out for a late-night snack."

"Yes."

"But there's still something we're missing." Josh stamped on the dog end of his cigarette and removed a piece of paper from his back pocket. He held it up against the window of the Granada. It was a basic printout of the safari park with minimal detail or scale and various scribbles they'd added themselves. "Here's our entry point, and this is where we'll leave the hearse, right?"

"Correct."

"And this is the distance between the lion den and the car, right?"

"Yep."

"How far would you say that was?"

"How should I know - it's not to scale, is it?"

"I went there recently with the kids," said Micky. "I'd say it was about half a mile."

"Half a mile!"

"Approximately."

"And there's my issue," noted Josh.

Eric looked at him blankly.

"Don't you see! Two-hundred-kilo lion, half a mile and four - sorry, three," he said, discounting Callum, "blokes who haven't exercised regularly since the last millennium."

"Why do you think we've stopped here?" replied Eric casually.

They spun around to assess a rather uninteresting retail park on the outskirts of Trowbridge, Somerset. What role did the car park of a DIY store have to do with the removal of a lion from a safari park?

"Okay, you're going to have to spell it out for me," said Josh, shaking his head.

"We have all the equipment we need except for one thing. One of those." Eric pointed at a fragile old man struggling with a flatbed trolley that contained a few boxes of tiles and a couple of tins of paint.

"I suppose it's better than dragging the damn thing along the ground," approved Josh, who regretted ever questioning the plan.

"Anything else?" said Eric.

"No."

"What about him?" whispered Micky. He waved toward Callum, who was sitting on the car park curb a few metres away rocking back and forward like he'd just been in a traffic accident. "He's in no fit state for this."

"You okay, mate," shouted Josh sympathetically.

"Fuck the lot of you," Callum croaked, his voice fractured and his body shaking with an unseen internal force.

"No need to be like that. You brought it on yourself."

"It's wrong," he mumbled. "Everything is wrong."

"Wrong?"

"The world is distorted and I can't focus properly. My brain can't remember the right…words…" he said to prove his point. " My body feels numb and unresponsive."

"Has he been drinking?" asked Josh quietly.

"Not since Saturday."

"Maybe he can't function without it. What if he buggers off to the pub when we're in the middle of the next dare?" said Micky.

"We can still track him," smiled Josh, holding up his phone.

"Is it still in there? I thought it would have passed through his system by now."

"God no! Passing something that big would be like childbirth. We'll definitely hear him when it happens."

"You two go get a trolley and I'll have a word with him," said Eric assertively.

They nodded and Eric sidled over to Callum, taking a seat next to him on the cold stone floor.

"How you feeling?"

"Deathly." Callum held his head in his hands. "My face throbs…as much as my brain. I'm sore everywhere. It's like my…skeleton has gone to war with my flesh. I'm not sure…if I can do this?"

"Of course you can, mate."

"I'm not talking about the dare," he replied solemnly. "I'm not sure I can go on in general. Life's too hard."

In normal circumstances, this would be the kind of attitude that Eric met with disdain and anger, but this wasn't the time or the place for it.

"We've all got problems, Callum. This week has proved it more than I realised."

"You're doing alright," he countered.

"Am I? The facts don't bear it out. Perhaps I'm just better at hiding it."

"I am sorry about what I did," said Callum, removing a hand to reveal his bruised eye socket and battered flesh.

"I know. Do you think any of us would have reacted any differently? When we're forced into a corner, we do what we have to do to survive, right? The four of us have always found a way to overcome adversity. But we're learning tough lessons this week. We've all been trying to outrun our problems and you've run out of puff. The only question is: what are you going to do about it?"

"How do you mean?"

"Face up or give up."

Callum's body looked in favour of the latter.

"Did you ever meet my brother, Winston?" asked Eric, seemingly changing the subject.

"Is that the plasterer or the one who's serving ten years in Wormwood Scrubs Prison for manslaughter?"

"Neither," replied Eric. "I'm not sure any of you ever met Winston properly. He was the second youngest in my family, only a bit more than a year between us. I always felt closest to him and he was certainly less mean to me than the other two. But he wasn't born with resilience, and it pains me to think of what he might have achieved if he'd understood his potential. Winston was so smart, Callum, much more than me, but he was naïve."

"Naïve like Josh?"

"Not quite. I'd say Josh was gullible rather than naïve."

"I heard that," called a panting, distant voice.

"You see, when you grow up in a place like we did," continued Eric, "it's almost impossible not to fall in with the wrong sort of people. In those days, if you weren't in a gang, you didn't have much hope of surviving."

"Were you ever in a gang?"

"Yes," replied Eric. "They were called *The Idiots' Club*."

Callum forced a smile but winced from the pain it caused him.

"We might not have been popular, but compared to the one Winston was in, we were bloody saints."

"Did he get into trouble?"

"Oh yeah. Big trouble."

"And do you still see him?" asked Callum.

"I hadn't for many years, but bizarrely, I saw him yesterday."

"Yesterday? I thought you were busy getting me beaten up and pretending to abduct someone."

"It wasn't a planned reunion by any means. Took me a little by surprise, if I'm honest."

"Where was it?"

"When we were searching the old sugar factory for you, Josh and I stumbled upon a group of heroin addicts shooting up on the floor below. There was this waif-like character sprawled out in a dirty sleeping bag. His eyes were open but I'm not sure he knew where he was. Even with the grime on his withered face, I knew who it was. It was Winston. Do you know what I thought when I saw him?"

"Don't do drugs," suggested Callum weakly.

"I thought about how his predicament was partly my fault."

"Your fault? What did you do?"

"Nothing."

"You shouldn't blame yourself, then."

"But that's precisely why I felt guilty. I should have done something. I've always believed in people's right to live any way they want to, but what if they aren't equipped to do that? When does support become control? Should we intervene in someone's life when they don't want us to? Should we sit back and watch them destroy themselves?"

"No, I think we should step in and help. That's what a real friend does, even if it's difficult, " sobbed Callum, correctly interpreting Eric's analogy.

"But none of us have," added Eric. "None of us told Micky that his wife was controlling and mean. None of us told Josh it was time to settle down and find love. None of us confronted you about your drinking, which might be the main reason your businesses have failed down the years."

"None of us told you it was okay to say no."

Eric instinctively wanted to deny he had a problem, such is the way beliefs infect our personalities, but what sort of example would that be. "True."

"You are my friend, Eric," he responded, reaching out

his shaky hand and firmly gripping his friend's. "I'm ready to accept your help."

Eric reached inside his leather jacket and removed a small, shiny, ornate hip flask. He unscrewed the cap and gave it sniff. The aroma of whisky wafted through the air and Callum's body started to convulse.

"This is the really good stuff," remarked Eric as he passed it to Callum. "Don't tell Micky."

"I thought this chat was about us facing up to our demons, not giving them an energy boost," said Callum, torn between his desire to drink and his motivation to refuse.

"It is. You need to find a way to get off the booze, but that process won't happen overnight. It's going to be a long, painful road and the three of us are going to be there for you." He pointed to the back of the hearse, where their companions were struggling to shut the boot door on a flatbed trolley. "But for now, we need your 'A-game' and if that means a few shots of spirits, then so be it."

"Thanks, Eric." Callum took a sizeable gulp of whisky. "I'm going to get help."

"Excellent. What say we go steal a lion first?"

TWENTY-FIVE

THE LION KING

TODAY. FROME POLICE STATION.

IRIS HAD ENDED the interview abruptly, just as it was getting interesting. Eric knew it was a tactic. She was playing with him and he loved it. While she'd no doubt returned to her home for a restful night's sleep, he'd not got a wink. It was all too exciting. Today was Wednesday, the seventh day. There was only one dare left and it had to be completed before today gave way to tomorrow. There was much to do but first he had to get out of Frome - more specifically, Frome Police Station. The interview reconvened in the same poky little room they were in yesterday. It was early and the sun had barely had a chance to crawl into view, not that anyone would see it with today's grey skies.

DI Iris Whitehall looked refreshed and in a bullish mood. She had plenty of time to dwell on her advantage and plan her next move. Eric knew she was going to pick up where she left off, the abduction of Logan Cobley. Iris opened her folder and removed a number of photographs, all blown up to A4 size to more easily analyse the details. She pushed one of them across the table for him to consider.

"Can you tell me what this is?" she asked.

"Obviously."

"And?"

"It's a massive finger."

"It's actually a regular-sized finger that has been blown up in scale. What's the most unusual thing about it?"

"It's not attached to a hand," replied Eric plainly.

"Very good," she replied sarcastically. "And can you tell me to whom it belongs?"

"A nine-fingered man?"

"Yes, and what's his name?"

"I have many skills, detective, including reading body language, but I don't know anyone in the world who can identify someone by looking at a single finger unless it happens to have a tattoo on it."

"It belongs to Logan Cobley. It was discovered at the scene of his abduction and according to your livestream, you were there. Is that what you call 'indisputable proof' that you weren't responsible?"

"No, I'd say it was indisputable proof that Logan Cobley only has nine digits, but you have no evidence that I removed the tenth."

"I have the video!"

"And what does that show you, exactly?" said Eric, growing in confidence.

"It shows the four of you loitering outside Logan's home in Cornwall Terrace before you miraculously over-came his security system and broke in."

"And you'll notice all four people in that video are wearing balaclavas, apart from the moment immediately before they enter the building and the very last part after they've bundled Logan, bound and gagged, into the back of a car."

"What's your point?"

"Have you found any of our fingerprints or DNA inside the house?"

"No."

"Is there any security footage from inside the house that identifies any of us being there?"

"No," she replied subserviently.

"Is there any proof from the video, or evidence collected at the crime scene, that any of us cut Logan's finger off?"

"No, but that doesn't prove it wasn't you."

"And neither does it prove it was."

"Then how do you explain your claim at the end of the video that you'd…" Iris reached for her notes, "…'Caught the bastard, Sean'."

"Caught isn't the same as abducted and bastard doesn't necessarily mean Logan."

"But you're not denying that someone dared you to abduct him."

"No, I'm not denying that."

"Then I have probable cause, and the fact remains that Logan is missing."

"Agreed."

"But you're saying it wasn't you."

"Not directly, no."

"But you were involved?" said Iris, her head starting to spin from the cryptic nature of Eric's answers.

"Define 'involved'?"

"You know what happened!" she shouted.

"Yes."

"Then you also know where Logan is?"

"Absolutely."

"Then tell me!" she shouted, losing her cool.

"I could, but I'd need something in return."

"Why?"

"Because if you don't give me what I want, two things will come to pass."

"And what are they?"

"Firstly, you'll never find out who was really responsible for everything you've been investigating this week. The only charge that will hold up against us in court will be the removal of a World War II bomb, the only crime for which you have substantial evidence. Given that this is a first offence for all of us, the worst we can hope for is a suspended sentence and some community service. Secondly, and much more importantly for you I think, you'll never know how the story ends. You'll never solve the puzzle."

"I don't care about that."

Eric fixed her with his stare, "Yes, you do."

"What is it you want from me, Eric?"

"Let us go."

"Ha! I don't have the authority even if I wanted to. This is a multi-agency investigation now. We've got people all over the country searching for Logan. My own investigation was sanctioned by the Police and Crime Commissioner. Imagine the shit storm I'll face if I release our main suspects when there's so much evidence against you."

"In life, sometimes you have to break the rules to get what you want."

"You mean like you? How's that going?" she asked sarcastically.

"Very well."

"Your circumstances suggest otherwise."

"You and I are more alike than you think." Eric stood up suddenly, somewhat to Iris's surprise. "We're both incapable of giving up and we share an insatiable obsession for winning. The only difference between us is our approach."

"I believe in rules."

"Yes, given your background, I find that fascinating."

"What do you know of my background?" she replied bitterly.

"I know about the discrimination," he said, leaning over the table towards her.

"Eric, please sit down. You're becoming agitated, and I'd hate to have to physically restrain you."

"I'm just stretching, " Eric replied, his arms moving clockwise around his body in an oddly robotic manner.

"Sit down!"

Her anger forced him to comply.

"You don't like men much, do you?" stated Eric.

Iris tried not to react, but her body language told the truth.

"If I had to guess, I'd say you've been fighting chauvinism since the first moment you joined the force. Childish pranks, testosterone-fuelled insults, maybe even worse than that. Whether the discrimination stretches back to your childhood is hard to say, but I wouldn't be surprised if you didn't have older brothers whom your parents always preferred."

"Stop."

"What I do know, from observing you for hours, is that you have a frightening determination to prove that a woman can outdo a man. And because you have an undoubted disadvantage, because the system is designed to impede you, I'm intrigued by your loyalty to it. You follow their rules and they will always limit you. The system was designed to favour men, Iris, just like your parents. My horizons are boundless because I don't follow any. Sometimes stepping over the line is the only way to come out on top."

"No more games," she huffed, Eric's words adversely affecting her mood. "I took an oath and I'm not willing to break it."

"But what if I gave you mine?"

"Your oath?"

"My promise."

"Go on."

"I'll tell you where Logan is, alive and well, and you can take the glory. Think about all those colleagues of yours fighting for the prize and talking down your chances. You can win, but only if you agree to release the three of us temporarily. If you do, I promise I'll return to a police station of your choosing by midnight, unless you've gathered enough evidence to prove our innocence."

"There's no promise you could give me that I would trust."

Eric leaned back in his chair, rather deflated that she'd spurned the opportunity.

"There is something I can trust, though," she continued.

"What?"

"Eric Gideon, I dare you to turn yourself in to the police by midnight."

Eric grinned, "You've been paying attention."

"I always do."

"The answer is yes, because it always is," said Eric, extending his arm and holding his hand open expressively. "Shake on it?"

She gripped his hand and metaphorically passed to the dark side. The race was going to continue and this time they'd be chasing her as well.

"That wasn't hard, was it."

"Time will tell."

"Time will be your guide."

"Where is Logan?"

"Netherswell Manor in the Cotswolds, the same place you'll find a rather groggy lion."

"You're giving me two for one?"

"Not really, but if you find one you'll probably find the other."

Iris grabbed her phone and made a call requesting all available units to mobilise around the property but to wait for her arrival. She gathered up the various documents from the table and stuffed them hurriedly into her folder.

"It's about an hour and a half from here, so it won't be long until you know the truth."

"What's the last dare?" she demanded.

"Now, that's not what we agreed, is it? The fifth dare is your test, DI Whitehall, to see if you're worthy."

"At least give me a clue?"

"I've given you plenty already."

Iris jumped up out of her seat and swung open the door of the interview room.

"Am I free to go?"

"Once I've signed the paperwork. It'll take about an hour."

"Excellent. Until next time, Iris Whitehall."

"Until midnight, Eric Gideon."

MONDAY. *Longleat Safari Park.*

ERIC and the boys spent most of Monday keeping a low profile and waiting for night to fall. They'd arrived in the area at a time when normal people were heading out to work and yet they'd only just finished their last assignment. They loitered in country lane laybys where the hearse might be inconspicuous - a task made almost impossible thanks to the B&Q trolley hanging out of the back and two middle-aged men in a place which ordinarily housed a coffin.

They passed the time recounting stories of their Uni days, listening to the radio, internet surfing on their phones - when the signal allowed it - and topping up on sleep. Only Eric stayed awake. He had an uncanny ability to stay alert on a minimal amount of nap time - the antithesis of Jessica in that regard.

Every couple of hours, they'd drive somewhere new to avoid the suspicion of ramblers or local farmers. It was never too far from the perimeter of the safari park, which occupied an area of one thousand acres in the heart of Wiltshire. Occasionally Josh, who found silence more challenging than most, would chip in with some benign and forgettable fact he'd found on the internet about the place they were illegally planning to enter later that day.

"Apparently, the parklands around the manor house were landscaped by Capability Brown."

"Fascinating," wheezed Micky through firmly closed eyes.

"Who's he when he's at home?" asked Callum who, thanks to regular medicinal shots of whisky, had returned to being a semi-functioning member of society.

"A gardener, I suppose. I wonder why you don't get names like that anymore? I mean, if you call your child Capability it sets a pretty high level of expectation on the kid."

"Yeah, but they weren't going to call him Inability Brown, were they?" said Eric.

"It's bloody cruel to call him either," added Callum.

"Who's to say it's even a bloke?" continued Eric.

"I think most gardeners were dudes in the eighteenth century," insisted Josh, not known for being a solid source of truth about anything outside the previous twenty-four hours let alone ancient history.

"On his Wikipedia page he does look like a man," said Micky, scrolling through his phone, "and also a little bit like Droopy the cartoon dog."

Eric peered over Micky's shoulder and nodded.

"According to this," Micky continued, "Capability was only a nickname."

"There you go," confirmed Callum. "I don't believe any parent purposely gives a child a cruel name."

"What was his real one, then?"

"Lancelot."

"They obviously decided they didn't like him from the get-go," suggested Eric.

"If you boys ever have children…" said Josh.

"I already have three," interrupted Micky, a little offended.

Josh marched on obliviously. "What strange names would you go for?"

"Always," answered Callum before anyone else. "Always Jollie."

"Not a good name for the Spitz family," chuckled Josh. "I think I'd go with Flexibility Foxole."

"That's why we always put you in the back seat," said Eric. "I think I'd go with Unpredictable Gideon."

"Perfect description."

"What about you, Micky?" said Josh.

"Quentin, Eloise and Buster."

"Buster!" Josh burst out laughing. "That's hilarious."

"They are my children's names."

"Oh."

This mode of banter continued throughout the afternoon and deep into the evening until their conversation took an unexpected detour into more poignant territory.

"I was thinking," said Callum, "if all goes well tonight, we'll only have one more dare to go, and that's the easiest one."

"Sometimes it's the easiest ones that catch you out," warned Eric.

"That's true of women," Josh mistakenly said out loud. "I think it might have broken a record, too."

"Record?"

"This is the longest period of time I haven't had sex since I lost my virginity at thirteen."

"How do you feel?" asked Eric.

"Heavy."

"You were thirteen!" exclaimed Micky. "Two of my children are older than that."

"We're not seriously taking Josh as an international benchmark, are we?" argued Eric.

"No," confirmed Callum.

"My kids are definitely not doing it," insisted Micky forcefully. "They're still interested in Lego and computer games."

"Sure," mocked Josh. "That's what I told my foster parents, too."

"That's almost thirty years of chasing women," calculated Callum.

"Wow, that is a long time."

"You're never going to find what you're looking for playing the field, you know?" said Eric sternly.

"If you're talking about sex, then I think you should check my record!"

"I'm not," replied Eric seriously. "I'm talking about love."

"Love! When the fuck have the four of us ever talked about love?" Josh almost gagged as the word came out of his mouth.

"We haven't, but perhaps we should have. We were all dealt a bad hand and we've been shouting 'twist' to the dealer ever since. We're all searching for better cards, but maybe we have to accept the ones we've been dealt."

"Personally, I love a good twist," said Josh with a wink.

"Be serious for once. You can't get out of every situation with charm and comedy," snapped Eric.

"Who yanked your chain?"

"I did. This week has been a wake-up call for me. I've not acted as I should have with you boys. Guardians mistreated you badly down the years, Josh. It's not your fault. They didn't show you love but you do matter…and I just wanted to say," Eric hesitated, "that I love you."

Josh's face curdled and for the first time in years he couldn't think of a funny response. In fact, there was only one word available to him.

"Gay!"

"And there's the problem in a nutshell. Emotional availability."

"Please stop acting weird," begged Josh, a little frightened by the conversation.

"You think love and sex are the same thing, Josh. They're not. Until you accept that, you're never going to be truly happy. I love you in a purely platonic sense, like a brother. I love all of you, and I wanted you to know," expressed Eric honestly.

Josh's bottom lip started to tremble. The more he focused on keeping it still, the more it vibrated. A lump forced a path up his throat from a knot hidden from the world deep in the pit of his stomach. Finally he released it and broke down in tears. Within five minutes, the whole group were wailing like babies, hugging and professing their undying affections for each other. It was usually only something they witnessed from Callum after eleven pints.

Once their tears ran dry and their composures returned, an awkward period of masculinity mobbed the car as if their normal personalities had regained control and were trying to backtrack any embarrassment their alter egos had caused them. There was a lot of shoulder punching, gibbering references to recent football matches and deeper voices than normal.

"I'm going to miss this," said Micky.

The contract they'd signed with Natasha meant they weren't only approaching the end of their dares, they were approaching the end of *The Idiots' Club*.

"You have a choice," professed Eric. "All contracts can be broken."

"If I've learned anything from my father, then it's to follow through with your obligations."

"Difficult if you've agreed to do different things with different people, though," offered Eric.

Micky nodded.

"This might be the last time we're together, but what a way to go out! One last hurrah," explained Josh. "Callum will get the money he needs and we've all had a blast."

"There certainly was a blast."

"There won't be a lot of money left," moaned Callum. "Out of the ten million we get from Sean, we owe my MoD contact one, the horsemen two and half, Jessica something substantial and over a hundred grand to Dubious Barry."

"Why does he get any?"

"For the hearse."

"This piece of shit isn't worth a tenth of that."

"Now you know why they call him Dubious."

"It still leaves more than a million each," said Josh.

"We'll be getting more than that, trust me," said Eric, whose reply was briefly interrupted by the ping of a text message. "They're in position."

"How long did they say they needed to deal with the security?" asked Micky.

"About an hour. Has Jessica sent you an update?"

"Not since she confirmed they'd arrived a couple of hours ago. I'm guessing the concentration was all too much for her."

"She's earnt a nap, and don't worry, you'll join up with her before morning. Time we got to the rendezvous point."

Eric turned the ignition key and sparked the noisy, reticent engine into action. Under the cover of darkness, the perfectly camouflaged hearse weaved its way down the narrow country lanes flanked by vast hedgerows that clung to muddy banks. Micky offered directions from a printed map, an object none of them had used for many years. Thankfully, there were no cars in their path, as there were only a limited number of spots to smoothly and speedily pass oncoming traffic. Through the gaps in the hedgerows peeked the occasional quaint cottage, advertising itself with billowing smoky chimneys and moody lighting. It was surreal to think there were monkeys, giraffes and wolves nearby when all they saw through the car windows were sheep and horses.

The road narrowed further and the hearse slowed as they approached a farm gate. The weak headlights illuminated a sign.

'WARNING. This gate is locked at night.'

Fortunately, that was the extent of the security. No cameras. No security guard post. No spikes in the road.

Just a rather rusty padlock and a sign with red letters. Eric eased to a stop as quietly as possible to avoid drawing any attention from the owners of two nearby houses. Micky jumped out to cut the chain, pulling the gate back into position once the car passed through. The bumpy lane rose steeply and a second, more convivial, sign greeted them.

'WELCOME TO LONGLEAT.'

From here, not even a sat nav would help them. They were on the inside of Longleat's northern perimeter, and the only way to navigate it was to follow the park's signs like a normal visitor. At the top of the hill the main track curved to the right, but an even rougher trail - protected by a flimsy gate proclaiming 'STAFF ONLY' - went straight on.

"I can't believe there isn't more security?" whispered Micky.

"Wild animals are similar to old bombs," murmured Eric. "There's probably more protection for Serengeti lions than for these ones."

Micky hopped out again to find, as expected, that the padlock had already been removed. It was half a mile further down the track when they finally acknowledged where they were. Animal noises, designed for foreign continents, rumbled at them through the darkness. These grew in prominence as the track came to an end in a courtyard of barns and disorganised pens. The largest building looked ramshackle, like it was built in a half-hearted rush. Its corrugated roof was only marginally more effective than it having no roof at all, and the chipped red bricks clung to each other out of fear rather than design. At the rear of the barns, two off-road vehicles in zebra camouflage were parked shabbily.

"Is this it?" said Josh.

"Yes," answered Eric.

"Where are the 'Horsemen'?"

"If they've done what we've paid them to, they'll be long gone by now."

It didn't take them long to discover that the horsemen had already been here. A man in a park uniform lay slumped over the steering wheel of one of the Jeeps. Two more keepers were asleep in the hay of an open-air shed, legs bound with plastic straps for good measure. There were a minimal number of cameras attached to walls or telegraph poles and all of them looked deactivated. Although human activity had been muffled, it was anything but quiet inside the compound.

A high-pitched bleat made Callum jump out of his skin.

"What was that?"

A series of groans, moans, roars and an elongated bellowing noise echoed around them.

"I don't like it," added Callum. "It's freaking me out."

"Camels," said Micky. Only the light of the moon and the very occasional low wattage neon lamp helped their eyes acclimatise.

"Everyone unload," commanded Eric. "We don't have much time."

Josh grabbed a small rucksack from the passenger footwell, Eric picked up a bag of tools and the other two grappled to free the B&Q trolley from its unorthodox berth.

"I think you're forgetting something?" said Eric to Josh.
"What?"
"The hat."
"What hat?"
"The one Jessica kindly lent you."
"I'm not wearing that."
"I dare you!" said Eric with a wink.

"I hate you, " Josh replied, before searching the back of the hearse to retrieve the multicoloured jester's hat. He pulled it down over his crown. "For how long?"

"Until we've dispatched the lion."

"Fine, but I'm not pushing the trolley. I bloody hate those things. They've got minds of their own."

Most supermarket trolleys desire to go in the opposite direction to which they're being pushed and have an almost supernatural talent for moving of their own free will, but in every shop's fleet there will always be one trolley with extra special powers. Every supermarket on the planet has a trolley whose wheels were purposefully attached to the frame back to front. These little metal freaks will frequently seize up and stop without prior warning, or decide to swivel at right angles to the current direction of travel. To make matters worse, all four wheels will behave with zero regard for what the others are doing. It makes shopping more difficult than scaling Everest in a suit of armour.

Out of all the available candidates Micky and Josh might have chosen from the Trowbridge branch of B&Q, they'd picked this one. One of the freaks, and it was keeping its talents secret for now.

"Which way to the lions?" asked Eric.

"Hold on, let me look."

Josh pulled out an official Longleat map. The park handed these out to every visitor as they passed through one of the three ticket booths dotted on the east, west and south sides of the park. As they weren't planning to go through official entrances, they'd printed theirs out from the internet in black and white. It was about as much use as the trolley.

"That's Monkey World," said Josh, struggling to unfold it, read and point at the gloom simultaneously. "On the other side, next to the loos and the smoking hut, is vulture valley, which must mean the area to our right is the big game park. That must be correct because there's a picture of a camel. If we walk straight forward until we reach those trees, then we should find the lions."

The safari park had miles of good-quality tarmac roads, except none of them went in a straight line. They weaved across the park like a drunk taking a long, meandering walk home from the pub. They were purposely designed to trick visitors into believing that the park was bigger, and better stocked with interesting animals, than in reality. Micky explained that the last time he'd been here, all they'd seen were a few monkeys and a rather moody-looking warthog. As they didn't have time to follow the track, and none of the roads lay straight in front of them, they only had one choice. Cross country.

Micky and Callum struggled to push the trolley through the grass, occasionally losing control of it altogether as it hit a lump of turf or concealed stone. After several aborted attempts to tame it, they agreed it would be quicker to carry it between them. A luxury they'd not have on the return leg if all went well with Sweetie Pie.

The first indication they had of reaching the lion pen was when Josh walked into a wire fence. He stumbled backwards and landed in a heap, jester's hat covering his face, grumbling experimental expletives.

"How are we meant to work without any light?" he groaned, as he dragged himself back to his feet and fumbled around his clothes to find his tobacco tin.

"What are you doing?" said Eric.

"Rolling up."

"There are designated smoking areas," established Micky, referring to the park map, "and this isn't one."

"But it's miles away!"

"Smoking isn't allowed."

"Hold on, we're attempting to steal a lion – that's not allowed, either," huffed Josh, putting the tin back in his pocket.

"Which one is Sweetie Pie?" asked Callum, staring through the wire fence. "All I can see are trees."

The fence encircled a copse of oak and sycamore trees and ran as far as they could see in both directions, although current visibility was less than twenty metres. Amongst the distant trees were concrete walls with lion-sized entrances which opened up into a sparsely turfed field. It was both a blessing and a curse that as hard as they stared through the wire, none of them saw or heard any lions.

"Are you sure this is it?" asked Eric.

"I believe so," said Micky. "Although last time I was here I didn't see any lions, either. Perhaps it's all a big lie."

"We should ask for our money back," joked Josh.

"Look," announced Callum excitedly. "There!"

It was a peculiar truth that Callum had the keenest eyesight out of all of them, and it was remarkable for several reasons. Firstly, while most people suffered a reduction in vision when they drank heavily, Callum's eyesight functioned almost exactly like a sober person's even when he was hammered. Which explained why he was able to carry on drinking long after others had to stop. This superpower didn't extend to his limbs, which flailed around like a synchronised swimmer suffering vertigo. Secondly, it meant he was the only one who saw the lion approach, a revelation the others completely overlooked right up until the moment it roared.

A broad, muscular and world-weary lion with a hefty heavy metal haircut broke through the gloom and padded casually towards the fence.

"Shit, look at the size of him!" whispered Micky.

"Why are you whispering?"

"Because he might hear us."

"I think he already has," replied Callum. "He's licking his lips."

"Maybe we should take this one," suggested Josh, as if he was picking a goldfish at a pet store.

"No," countered Eric. "We'd not get even half of him on the trolley."

The lion paced up and down the fence, occasionally stopping to eyeball one of them. The message was obvious, 'This is my pride, sod off.'

"Shoo." Callum motioned with his hands.

"It's not a seagull."

"What are we going to do? We can't get in there if he's prowling around."

"How much of that tranquiliser do we have, Josh?" asked Eric.

He rummaged around his backpack and found two vials of liquid. "I'd say enough for four shots."

"Okay, get a dose ready."

"How do we know what strength to use?" quizzed Micky.

"According to the guy I picked it up from, it really depends on the lion," answered Josh. "It's similar to alcohol tolerance in humans."

"So if the lion was Callum?"

"We probably wouldn't have enough."

"And if it was Sean?"

"Probably a sniff of the vial would do it! Every lion will react differently. It depends on weight, where the dart lands and the emotional state of the animal."

"How can you tell if a lion is depressed?" inquired Callum.

"Maybe they have lion psychiatrists?"

"I think it's generally more about the stress the animal is under," replied Josh.

Callum looked through the bars. "He looks a lot less stressed than we do."

The lion roared and their pressure increased.

"I'm going for a double shot; someone give me a little light from their phone."

Eric obliged and Josh went to work mixing two separate clear liquids into a small measuring cylinder before pouring the result into the clear shaft of a six-inch-long dart. He removed a dart gun from the bag and inserted the dart.

"Who's the best shot?" said Eric.

"That'll be me," stated Josh confidently.

"Bollocks it is. Don't you remember that time we went paintballing?"

"Yes. I destroyed you all."

"Crap! You looked like you'd been on paint run you were covered in so many colours."

"Rubbish."

"How often do you shoot?"

"Laser quest every now and again."

"I shoot most weeks with the Herefordshire Clay Pigeon Society," boasted Micky.

"Do I look like I care?"

"You look like a tit," said Micky, referring to the hat.

"It's my gun and I'm taking the shot."

"Don't be stupid - you couldn't hit a barn from the inside!"

Micky lumbered over to Josh to wrestle it from him. "Hand it over."

"No!"

"Look, this is not helping," barked Eric.

The lion watched, utterly bewildered. If they ever opened human safari parks for animals, this is probably what it would be like.

A brief struggle broke out as Josh and Micky wrestled for control of the dart gun. A popping sound pierced the air and the dart burst out of its chamber. The lion followed its trajectory as it landed with a thud in Callum's butt. A roar, to rival the lion's own, galloped across the open valleys of the park and a few seconds later a body collapsed on the ground.

"Oh, brilliant," sighed Eric.

TWENTY-SIX

TANTRUMS AND TRANQUILISERS

IN THE PANTHEON OF HARDCORE DRINKERS WHO frequented Exeter University in the mid-nineties, there were many pretenders to the crown but only ever one king. Callum Jollie's alcohol tolerance was the stuff of legend. Stories turned into rumour, and rumours mutated into myths which persisted long after his graduation day. One often-told fairy story recounts his completion of the 'top shelf' of spirits in the Ram bar, a feat long thought suicidal. There's even a version of the yarn that suggests he completed it at lunchtime and went back later that evening to do it all again.

Like all good tall tales, the gap between truth and exaggeration expands with the erosion of time. There's Callum's world record for consuming pints of 'snake bite and black' in one sitting which multiplied from twelve then to fifteen and currently stood at thirty-four. The source for much of this misinformation came from the man himself. Indisputably though, whether truth or fiction, when it came to drinking challenges not even Eric could claim to be Callum's master.

Most people have an aversion to one type of spirit because of a bad experience which results in never touching the stuff again. The very thought of its consumption will send them into a traumatic spin. It might be a reaction to whisky after sneaking into your parents' drinks cabinet when you were fourteen and spending the rest of the evening with your head down a toilet. Or you might have developed an allergy to gin after attempting to finish an entire bottle of Bombay Sapphire in a single visit. But none were true of Callum. To add to his infamy he'd conquered every craft beer, dodgy Hungarian red wine and homemade basement brew before eagerly going back for seconds.

Down the years, nothing had stopped him.

Now they knew what would.

A large measure of medetomidine with a zolazepam-tiletamine mixer.

"Perfect," wheezed Eric, rushing over to check Callum was still breathing.

"Is he okay?" asked Micky.

"No! He's got a lion-sized dose of tranquiliser in his arse."

"But he's alive?" reiterated Josh reservedly.

"Yes, but he's no bloody use to us."

"Sorry," offered Micky sanguinely.

"So you bloody should be. This isn't a game, you know."

"Hold on, I thought that's exactly w…"

"Not now," recommended Micky quietly.

"Get another shot made up," demanded Eric, "and this time shoot the bloody lion. I'm going to search for Sweetie Pie."

Eric stropped off down the side of the fence to look for a female lion asleep amongst the trees. It didn't take him long to find her, and to his immense relief she wasn't too far from the perimeter's edge. When he returned ten minutes later, he discovered Josh and Micky watching the mighty male lion on the other side of the wire like a pair of confused zoologists.

"Why haven't you done it?" snapped Eric.

"We have," said Micky, pointing.

The mighty beast was defiantly conscious even though a large empty dart was sticking out of its chest.

"He's a bloody warrior," said Josh. "Look at him, he's mocking us."

"Did you use the same dose strength?"

"Yeah, he's just riding it out. God, I want to see Callum take this boy on in a drinking competition."

"Maybe we have to wait until it works."

Ten minutes elapsed and the only activity from the warrior lion was a regimen of continual consciousness, an occasional deafening roar, and subjecting them to the world's most intimidating staring competition. After twenty minutes, he finally succumbed to the drugs building up in his bloodstream, lay on the grass and passed out.

"Right, let's go."

"He's faking it," proclaimed Josh with certainty.

"Faking it?"

"Yeah, look at him. It's an act. He'll wait until we've cut through the wire and then he'll spring up and chew our legs off! I saw them do it in one of those Attenborough programmes."

"As unlikely as I think that is," answered Eric, "maybe you should stay here and keep an eye on him while Micky and I go get the other one. After all, we don't know how long the sedative will last."

"Fine by me, but just so you know, if he wakes up I'll shout and then run. Got it?"

"I think they prefer a moving target anyway," replied Eric. "Get another dose ready."

Josh mixed together the liquids for a third time and poured the contents into a new dart before passing it to Eric. "After this there's only enough tranquiliser left for one more dart, so don't miss."

Eric nodded, "Micky, grab the tool bag."

They waded through the tall grass to the area where Eric had spotted Sweetie Pie sleeping twelve feet off the ground on the bough of a sprawling sycamore tree. Eric rested the dart gun in one of the holes of the wire fence and steadied himself for the shot. Once he was confident he had the lion in his sights, he gently squeezed the trigger and the dart flew out of the barrel with a muffled pop.

"Did you hit her?" asked Micky, squinting to see through the gloom.

"I think so."

Thud!

"What was that?" Micky whispered in a nervy voice.

"That was a medium-sized lion falling out of a tree."

They waited a moment to see if the commotion had roused the rest of the pride into action. When it was clear there was no other movement within the enclosure, they went to work.

"Get cutting," demanded Eric as he rummaged around in the tool bag and removed two sets of bolt cutters.

It took longer than expected to snip through the tough wire and make a hole large enough for them, and eventually the body of a lion, to squeeze through. They scurried inside and located the unconscious animal a few metres from the base of the tree. Sweetie Pie's tongue was hanging limply from one side of her sharp jaws, and they were relieved to see the gentle rise and fall of her chest.

"Right, you grab her back legs and I'll grab the front," instructed Eric. "Let's be as quick as we can."

They picked her up by the limbs and gently dragged her body across the dirt and grass, constantly checking for signs of the pride's hairy cavalry. Although somewhat smaller than the lion they'd recently sedated, Sweetie Pie was still a handful to move, not helped by the poor physical state of her escorts. After they were safely through to the visitors' side of the fence, Eric passed Micky a very different type of gun.

"What's this?"

"Cable tie gun. We don't want to leave a hole or the park might not have any animals in it by morning. It'll be like a lion buffet. Get to work."

"Makes sense."

"Josh, bring the trolley," Eric called through the darkness.

Trundling wheels ruined the silence with a loud clatter as the vehicle spontaneously changed directions and collided with the fence.

"Could you be any nosier?" commented Eric ironically as Josh finally managed to navigate his way to them.

"Honestly. No."

"How's Callum?" asked Micky.

"Still out cold."

"Bugger," uttered Eric. "Looks like we have two bodies to carry. Josh, help me get this one onboard."

They grappled with the beast and eventually managed to secure most of her muscular frame onto the base. The wood creaked under the weight, and her legs and tail cascaded unavoidably over the side. It would make their progress slower because they'd have to be careful not to run them over.

"All done." Micky returned the tools to the bag after

giving the fence a rigorous shake to check his handiwork was up to scratch.

"Great, let's get out of here. You'll need to give Callum a fireman's lift."

"Why me?" moaned Micky.

"Because it'll take two of us to push the trolley."

"What about all the stuff? We can't leave it here."

"Of course not. Put it in the backpack and I'll carry it."

"Um, do any of you remember the way back?" said Josh, squinting into the distance.

Over the hour or more that they'd spent arguing, shooting each other with tranquilisers and removing a lion, the moon - their only source of light - had been mobbed by thick, menacing clouds desperate to drop their watery payload at any moment. As a result, they'd lost all reference points by which to navigate. The main one, the outline of the keeper's sheds where they'd parked, had seemingly disappeared. The only things they did see were an expanse of unfamiliar fields and the ominous shadowy outlines of nocturnal creatures going about their business.

"Which way?" Josh asked.

"Follow the trolley tracks," suggested Eric.

"There aren't any. We carried it here, remember?"

"I'm pretty sure it's straight in front of us," groaned Micky, struggling for breath under the excess weight of Callum's body across his shoulder blades.

"What makes you so sure?"

"I've been here before."

"You were in a car!"

"I can see a road to our left," announced Eric. "Let's take that; at least the trolley will be easier to manage."

"But if we follow the tracks, we'll end up going around

in circles. What if she wakes up?" said Josh, pointing at the doped-up lion.

"We'll turn off when we see the sheds."

"Fine," huffed Micky. "The sooner I can get this lump off my back, the better."

Progress was painfully slow. The trolley was even less responsive with the weight of a lion pushing down on its castors than it was empty. It frequently decided to shoot off the road at right angles of its own free will. When they did manage to keep it on the tarmac, the uneven surface made it bounce up and down, occasionally displacing the lion's head off the back, requiring them to resecure her in case anything got caught underneath the wheels. Micky moaned constantly, chuntering all manner of future threats against Callum's life, even though he'd been partly responsible for his friend's predicament.

Every time they passed a junction in the road, they argued amongst themselves about whether taking it would move them closer or further away from the exit. Mostly they decided against it, hoping that the comforting sight of the corrugated barn would soon appear through the gloom. As they passed through changes in topography, inquisitive nocturnal residents gathered around to watch the unexpected entertainment. It was almost as if the purpose of the park had been turned on its head. It was no longer the humans excitedly watching to see what the animals might do; now packs of hyenas cackled at the sight of a man in a jester's hat struggling to push a lion on a makeshift stretcher as another stumbled under the weight of his piggyback rider.

After an hour of bitter tantrums and bruised shins, Eric made an executive decision to turn off the track. It was partially a wise call. On the positive side, it took them in the right direction and happened to be a shortcut to the exit. On the downside, and unknown to them at the time, getting to it was via the monkey drive-through.

Anyone who's visited Longleat, or any safari park for that matter, will know that monkeys are kleptomaniacs with an insatiable desire to remove any objects that aren't welded down securely to your car. It doesn't matter to them what type of vehicle it is, or what accessories are hanging off the sides, because they're the monkey equivalent of teenage yobs with half a bottle of vodka and suspect morals. Radio aerials, wing mirrors, parking sensors, roof racks and spoilers are easy pickings for light-fingered monkeys. These automotive appendages were absent from the idiots' ride but that didn't mean there wasn't anything which took their fancy.

One of them was wearing a rather fetching multi-coloured hat.

Fortunately for Josh, most monkeys slept at night.

All of them except the night monkeys, obviously.

"I can see the barn!" Josh exclaimed.

"Thank god," puffed Micky.

A small orange monkey with huge round eyes appeared out of nowhere and clambered on top of Sweetie Pie. It prodded the lion's fur as if assessing the quality of the goods before rummaging through her follicles in search of a tiny late-night insect snack.

"Oi, fuck off," said Josh. "That's our lion."

A dozen of the scavenging little buggers suddenly appeared on all sides of them.

"Shit, we're surrounded."

"They're only monkeys," Eric stated calmly.

"I've seen these little hooligans," argued Micky. "They can rip a car apart quicker than a scrap metal merchant."

"Don't be melodramatic. They're tiny and we're not in a car."

One of the monkeys boldly jumped up on the handle-bars of the trolley, mesmerised by the jangling bells on the ends of Josh's hat. It took a swipe and Josh ducked instinctively.

"He's trying to steal my hat, cheeky sod."

"Throw it away - maybe that'll distract them."

"No."

"You hate that hat."

"But it's a dare! I'm not giving up just because some goofy-eyed gibbon takes a fancy to it."

The monkey tried again and Josh slapped him away with a lucky parry. This appeared to anger the primate. It screamed, hooted and jumped up and down in fury like a spoilt toddler who'd been told to get off the trampoline. Its chant drew in more of its friends and soon there were a few dozen monkeys hopping excitedly around Josh, each attempting a different strategy to steal the hat. There were stealth attacks from the rear, full frontal assaults and one even defecated on his leg to distract him from a brazen attempt on both sides. Josh swung his fists in disorientated panic, accidentally clobbering one full in the face with a right hook. The monkey flew through the air and landed in a dazed heap on the ground.

"You can't knock out a monkey!" alleged Micky judge-mentally.

"Why not?"

"They might be endangered."

"But there's thirty of them and only one of me. I should be protected not them."

"But it's not a fair contest. They're only small."

"Not when they gang up on me they're not!"

"Oh shit," said Eric, watching as the family of nocturnal monkeys regrouped in response to the knock-out blow. "Now they look really pissed off."

The noise of monkey revenge grew deafening as more and more of the little critters bounded out of the dark and swarmed around them.

"Run!"

The trolley wobbled and bounced as they pushed it in hasty retreat, Josh's hat jangling like a monkey beacon throughout. Micky found a new level of pace as the night monkey swarm skipped and jumped through the grassy meadow hot on their trail, squeaking and flinging faeces over their heads. To their relief, the barn emerged out of the horizon and all they had to do was get inside the hearse before their simian pursuers.

But the monkeys beat them to it.

They scrabbled over the black bodywork of the Granada, ripping at anything not securely attached, which with this particular motor was almost everything. Eric opened the boot door and the men carelessly bundled the still-unconscious Sweetie Pie into the back. They squeezed Callum down the side next to her, discarding the trolley before all three of them clambered into the front seats and slammed the doors.

The monkeys congregated on the windscreen as if intent on blocking their escape. Most of them were wielding the spoils of their vandalism like a bunch of tiny volunteer soldiers. One held the Granada's aerial and brandished it like a sword. Another held up the Ford badge as if presenting its identification. One was wearing the casing of a wing mirror as a helmet. A host of tiny claws scraped at the roof as others tore at the side panels or tried in vain to chew through the glass windows.

"Floor it!" shouted Josh.

The engine backfired and most of the monkeys scattered in panic. The hearse chugged up the track uncontrollably as Josh and Micky clung to each other in the single passenger seat. One solitary monkey remained on the windscreen by grabbing hold of the wipers. His shocked little monkey features flapped around like a dog with his head out of the window.

"Get him off!" shouted Josh.

"How?" screamed Eric, whose foot was flat to the floor.

"Use the wipers!"

"No, it's cruel."

"Do it!"

Eric relented, and like a furry pendulum, the night monkey swept the glass from side to side, his eyes peering through the windscreen in confusion. Eric stamped on the brakes. The sudden change of direction, combined with deceleration, broke the monkey's will. He flew off to the left like the contents of a medieval trebuchet and a shrill, surprised shriek faded into the distance.

"Is he alright?"

"He looks a bit woozy, but he'll survive."

Eric accelerated again and they careered down the service lane before rejoining the road they'd taken up the hill. Once they were through the closed gate near the cottages and back in the country lanes away from the park, everyone exhaled a long and adrenalized sigh.

"Jesus, that was intense," exclaimed Micky. "My back is in tatters."

"Stealing a lion must be the stupidest thing we've ever attempted," wheezed Josh.

"Succeeded," added Micky, waving a hand towards the boot.

"We're not stealing it," countered Eric.

"Then I'm confused as to what that was all about."

"We're only relocating it without permission," explained Eric. "We'll get it back in no time."

"Bloody salesmen," huffed Micky.

"I thought we were meant to be livestreaming the dares," said Josh.

"We are, but which of us had any hands free to do that? It was supposed to be Callum's job."

There was a pathetic whimper from the back as Callum regained some of his senses.

"Looks like he's back with us. Quick, take my phone and start recording," said Eric, pointing to the glove box.

Josh removed the expensive, top-of-the-line smartphone and accessed the WDWC Live channel. "We're rolling."

"Blimey…what…did…I…drink?" mumbled Callum, rubbing his eyes.

"Medetomidine," answered Josh.

"How many shots?"

"Just the one."

Callum finally turned over and his eyes focused on the huge, rancid jaws of a lion staring back at him. He screamed like a six-year-old girl and pushed himself as far from the creature as possible – which was no more than six inches. "Let me out!"

"Stop panicking; she's tranquilised."

Sweetie Pie's tongue twitched.

"LET ME OUT!"

The lion's jaws quivered, her eyes opened, and a pupil dilated spotted her first meal of the day.

"NOW!"

Eric forced the hearse into a unexpected emergency stop which caused it to skid off the road and nosedive into the hedgerow. A plume of smoke discharged from under the crumpled bonnet and the engine offered a terminal groan. Callum tried hysterically to open the boot, something that was only possible from outside, a ridiculous safety feature given how the usual occupant was in a large wooden box and hopefully very much deceased. The lion twisted and turned to escape her cage. Her tail whipped about like a rattlesnake as she tried to claw her way into the front seat. The car was filled with deafening, angry roars as Sweetie Pie voiced her disapproval at being rehoused. Micky tumbled out of the side door and rushed around to the back. The decision to open it was somewhat of a double-edged sword. Callum would be free but so would the lion.

"Josh, get another dart ready!" shouted Eric.

As the boot door flew open with a creak and a bang, Callum and Micky immediately scampered back to the passenger seat and squeezed themselves on top of Josh. Totally disorientated, Sweetie Pie lumbered out of the hearse and went on the attack. The sound of a wheel bursting pierced the air, and the car sank down a few inches from the puncture.

"Give me the dart gun," ordered Eric.

"I would if these idiots would give me a bit of space," screamed a muffled Josh from somewhere under the one-seater pile-on.

"Quick, before she decides to explore Somerset!"

Josh's arm, holding a fully loaded dart gun, appeared from under the bodies.

"Keep the video rolling," said Eric, leaping heroically out of the driver's seat. "And someone find the manual - we're going to need the spare tyre."

TWENTY-SEVEN

ON THE SEVENTH DAY

TODAY. FROME.

ACCORDING TO THE BIBLE, after creating the Earth, on the seventh day God rested. There's very little detail as to what this involved. God had covered a lot of ground in the previous six days - what with all the creation of lights, oceans, land, heavens, creatures that creepeth, beasts and man - but there's no mention of any golf courses. No doubt this was an oversight. In the absence of hitting a pimply white ball across a field into a very small hole, God insisted that everyone should go to church. It's a trend that has been slowly reversing ever since.

It was Wednesday morning, the seventh day since *The Idiots' Club* began their dares, and there definitely wasn't time for golf, church or rest.

They might have enough time for a quick pray, though.

Eric perched on a damp, rotten picnic table outside the Royal Oak pub a few hundred metres from the police station. There was a sustained drizzle in the air. Not enough to get you soaked but certainly enough to cause mild irritation. Eric's tattered clothes made it feel worse than it was. Only one foot had a shoe and most of his left leg was open to the elements. Despite this, his smile remained resolutely tattooed to his face.

Eric watched as Callum and Josh sauntered towards him up the street. He knew it was them even a hundred metres away. Not many people wore hats at this time of the morning and certainly not this type.

"Is it open?" asked Callum, pointing at the pub as soon as he was in range.

"If it was, do you think I'd be out here in the rain?"

"I thought it might have been because of a dress code violation."

"This is downtown Frome, Callum, not Royal Ascot. I think they'd serve you if you were wearing a mankini."

"It's a little early, Callum," Josh observed, checking his watch. "It's only nine."

"Damn it," he replied, shaking from an extended period of sobriety. "Do you have the flask?"

Eric reached inside his damaged jacket and passed the almost empty hipflask over. Callum drained it dry.

"I was sure we were done for," suggested Josh breezily. "How did you pull that off?"

"Maybe it was something Callum said," Eric replied sarcastically.

"Me? I think my interview lasted less than five minutes."

"Mine wasn't much longer," confirmed Josh. "Seems like she knew who to work on the longest."

"You're forgetting that DI Whitehall has been following us for days, having watched all our videos. She obviously knew a drunkard and a man in a stupid hat were false starts!"

"Seriously, though, how'd you do it?"

"She offered me a dare."

"A dare! Why?"

"Because she's desperate to know what this week has all been about."

"I've been wondering the same thing," chuckled Josh.

"She's desperate to know what the last dare is," added Eric.

"And what was her dare?" asked Callum inquisitively.

"We get the day off as long as we hand ourselves in by midnight."

There was an audible groan from the other two at the realisation their freedom was only temporary.

"Chill out," Eric demanded. "It was the only way we were going to get the last dare done and clear our names."

"We can't clear our names…it was us," said Josh.

"It all depends what happens next."

"What I'd like to know is where Micky and the lion are?"

Eric's phone beeped. It had been going crazy ever since he'd taken it back from the desk sergeant and turned it on. He held it to his ear to listen to the latest in a series of voicemail messages.

"Everything alright?" tested Callum after the call seemed to go on for an age. "Is it Micky?"

"No. Everything is fine - never better, actually. I've been fired."

Callum looked at him quizzically. It was an odd response to the news, given how much Eric loved his job.

"It was a message from Alan," he told them.

It certainly wasn't the only one he'd received over the last few days from Peperit Creative or someone associated with them. The oldest recordings were from Monica Silvers, his HR Director. The first couple were recorded over a week ago and she'd been casual and breezy. But with every passing update, her delivery developed a more terse and bitter undertone. Even before he picked up the final voice message - Alan West's short and succinct announcement of his sacking – he'd guessed what was coming. Several colleagues had left messages to offer their commiserations and to falsely pronounce their intentions to jump ship with him if he asked them. Their fake loyalty became obvious when most of them ended their calls by asking if they could have his office. Even a few of his clients had called to profess their dismay at his removal, even though it was clear Peperit had struck early to tie up the announcement with new contracts and better terms for any clients they thought might be flight risks.

'Follow me where, exactly?' thought Eric. There was only one immediate destination on his mind.

"Sacked," said Josh merrily. "Me too!"

"Why did they fire you?"

"Probably because I haven't been to work since last week."

"You're a salesman! You can get away with being out of contact for a week, surely?"

"In normal circumstances yes, but it's not so easy to explain what happened to all the missing medetomidine! To be honest, I think I've outgrown the role anyway. About time I thought about a career with a future."

"Your mid-forties is a good time for career planning," Eric laughed.

"That's all three of us out of work, then," said Callum matter-of-factly.

"Yes," replied Eric. "Which is why I think we should go into business together."

"Doing what?"

"Advertising."

"I don't know anything about it," grumbled Josh. "I'm a failed vet."

"You're a salesperson, mate. Between us, we can sell anything to anyone. I can teach you what you need to know about advertising and as a team I think we've proven our ability to solve any problem they throw at us."

"Will we have to brainstorm?"

"Not if you don't want to. You can try a more spontaneous approach."

"I love it!" announced Callum. "I can be Financial Director."

"No!"

"Why not?"

"I think it's pretty obvious, but in case you haven't been paying attention - tax evasion, financial malpractice and a high probability you'll be barred from any directorship."

"What can I do, then?"

"Intern."

"Intern!"

"I'm only joking. How about Human Resources?"

"I'm not qualified."

"Not traditionally, no, but I'd say you have enough life experience to make the job your own."

"This is great," said Josh. "It's a brilliant idea. We get to work together and run a business differently. What should we call it?"

"We'll brainstorm it."

Josh scowled.

"Maybe we'll call it Sweetie Pie?"

"No!" said Callum, who'd had more than enough of that name to last him a lifetime.

"Talking of which, have you heard from Micky?"

"He's on his way down south, which is exactly where we need to go."

"I still don't understand the plan," confessed Josh. "Why did we need to involve this Whitehall character at all?"

"Because she's one tough competitor and that makes the game more fun."

"I'm up to here with fun," said Callum, rolling his eyes.

"We've got a small window to tie up all the loose ends, and if we don't, they're going to throw the book at us."

"A window to do what?"

"To prove that Sean was responsible for everything that's happened."

"But…he wasn't."

"We know that, but I'm afraid that's not how it's going to look to Whitehall," grinned Eric.

THE CHARTER PLANE touched down at Cotswold Airport near Cirencester shortly before ten o'clock. The manifest confirmed only two passengers – Clarence Douville and Sean Heschmeyer – returning from a short business trip to sign contracts for one of *Heschmeyer Industries'* newest projects. Being the CEO of a publicly-listed business had many perks. Travelling by private plane, avoiding the riffraff, was only one of them. It also had downsides. His diary was under immense pressure. The company that bore his family name was nothing without Sean; every stakeholder, divisional director, local politician and trade unionist leader demanded his presence for any big decisions.

Their trip to Madrid had been fleeting. Just enough time to press the flesh, schmooze the locals, praise officials, guzzle some tapas, and sign a contract, once Clarence had had enough time to read it. After pen was put to paper,

Madrid would be committed to its newest megastructure, local construction would have secure employment for the next few years and *Heschmeyer Industries* would suck a billion Euros out of the national economy. It had happened in such a rush he couldn't even remember what it was for. He wanted to say a runway but it might as easily have been a seven-hundred-foot tower made from reinforced custard. What did he care? As long as his company got paid, the Spanish could have whatever they wanted. On this occasion, the only thing that concerned him was getting home in time.

Even a billion-pound contract wasn't worth as much as today's events.

The Idiots' Club had, even by their esteemed standards, exceeded his expectations. He'd not been surprised they'd achieved the first two of his dares, and as it happened, failure would have been a lot less damaging to the group than success. Sean had rightly calculated the consequences to be greater than the crime. As expected, Carrington had used his powerful connections to release the dogs against Eric in a personal vendetta which went back decades. Clarence had delivered the bad news to Mrs Parsons of her husband's misdemeanours of the second dare before they left for Spain. Events which, he predicted, would leave an indelible mark on the club.

More of a surprise was their success with the third and fourth dares. Sean had watched the footage of both from his swanky Madrid hotel, having been woken by an employee whose only job that week was to monitor the WDWC Live channel for any updates. Which meant he'd only experienced one uninterrupted night's sleep between check-in and check-out. Monday night, they woke him at two in the morning and he watched in disbelief as his four former associates pulled off the impossible – the abduction of Logan Cobley. There was nothing obvious in what he'd seen to doubt the authenticity of their actions and it was confirmed by the constant mystery surrounding Logan's whereabouts, which was still being broadcast on the national networks.

Around midnight the next day, he was woken again. This video stream was shorter and did not reveal everything they'd done, but it indisputably proved two things. They'd definitely stolen a lion and it hadn't gone smoothly. All four of them were showing signs of physical or emotional distress as they desperately tried to lift a partially-doped lion into the back of a hearse while one of the them changed a chewed tyre. Even if the explanation for these miracles was still outstanding, it meant they only had one dare left to complete.

Not that he felt the slightest concern about losing.

While the private jet taxied to the nearest hangar, his attention turned to poor old Callum. Sean almost felt sympathetic about what he'd have to do before the end. Having helped them complete all the difficult challenges, his job now was simple. He had to go missing to stop their progress and receive his extra reward. Sean never honestly thought he'd need it, but observing Eric over the years had been useful. Always have a fallback. However it was delivered, Sean would be there to claim victory, and now that he was safely back from Spain nothing would stop him.

Sean's phone bleeped to indicate life had been restored to the wireless world. A flurry of delayed messages flooded through the virtual sluice gates which had swelled to bursting point in the preceding few hours. He had people to deal with most of them, but some were private and his alone. He opened his message service and found something from Eric. Videos posted only an hour ago.

"Hello, Sean Coronary."

Sean raised his eyes at the childishness of the greeting and motioned to Clarence to shuffle over and watch the videos with him.

"Lovely morning," mocked Eric. He was sitting on a pub bench shrouded by grey drizzly skies and wearing clothes that must have been donated to him by a man who'd recently been involved in a nasty combine harvester accident. "While I wait for the others, I thought I'd leave you a quick message. It's Wednesday. It's the seventh day, and as you'll already know, we've completed four of your dares. They were a little bit amateurish, to be honest."

Sean grunted sarcastically.

"The police have decided to let us go without charge because as much as they've tried, they still can't locate Logan Cobley or Sweetie Pie - she's a lion, by the way. Fortunately though, I happen to know where the authorities might like to look. I'll give you a clue."

The video ended, but there was another message in the chain next to it. This one was recorded in a very different location and one Sean knew all too well.

"That's Netherswell Manor!" gasped Clarence, who was not known for showing any emotion outside of intransigence.

"Yes," replied Sean coolly.

"Where's security?"

"Engaged."

The video operator strolled alongside the property, their feet crunching through the expensive Cotswold stone shingle that lay between the manor house and the beautifully landscaped gardens. The camera turned to film through the window of Sean's glass panelled garden room. Inside, bound to a chair with cord, was Logan, sporting a number of very realistic-looking wounds, most of which were excreting blood onto Sean's terracotta floor tiles.

"But they can't do that!" exclaimed Clarence.

"Why not?"

"It's not in the contract."

"Then I blame you for not foreseeing it," replied Sean aggressively.

It wasn't really what Clarence meant by his comment, although the more he thought about it, the more he realised not having this strange eventuality in the contract might come back to bite him. It was an easy thing to overlook, but you can bet every contract he drafted from now on would have a kidnap clause added to the terms in the usual indecipherable legal hieroglyphics.

The camera moved around the building; however, they didn't need visual confirmation of what it was about to show them. They heard it.

A roar.

Then a rattle.

Finally a popping noise.

Down at the back of the house, next to the swimming pool, was the tennis court. Inside the court's ten-foot-high-fence was a lion, very much full of life and obviously irritated. It alternated between trying to ram the fence and attempting to remove the tennis ball stuck on its teeth using the umpire's chair.

"They're trying to pin it on you," gasped Clarence.

"Evidently."

"Were you expecting it?"

"With Eric you have to expect almost anything," he said calmly. " But we still have Callum."

A third video, which had been sent a minute later, completed the set.

"As you can see," narrated Eric with a grin, "this puts you in a little bit of hot water. At the very least, it's probably going to cause you and your company a great deal of embarrassment, even if your high paid lawyer – hello Clarence – can build a solid defence. Of course, I can save you the time and bother."

Sean looked out of the window to see his chauffeur-driven racing green Bentley pull up alongside the jet. He rose from his seat and held his arms out for Clarence to help him into his jacket – all the time watching the video propped up on the table.

"The police, and no doubt the nation's press, are on their way to Netherswell Manor. You have a choice, Sean. Meet them there and explain how a high-profile abductee has ended up inside your locked home and how a famous member of the Longleat pride ended up on your tennis court, or meet me face to face for one final challenge. If you choose the latter, I guarantee all of this disappointment will be washed away. What do you say?"

The video ended.

"You're not going to let him get away with this, are you? It's blackmail."

"Of course not."

"Call the police, then."

"No," insisted Sean. "I wanted to see Eric's face when he failed anyway, so this doesn't change anything."

"But he's playing you for an idiot," stated Clarence, a little more disrespectfully than he'd intended.

"Maybe I am one."

Sean moved along the aisle and out into the cold air.

"Where are you going?"

"To confront him."

"He didn't even tell you where he'd be."

"He didn't need to."

≈

DI IRIS WHITEHALL drove for an hour but covered significantly more distance than the cars travelling in the adjacent lanes. It helped if you had a blue flashing light and an
advanced driving qualification. According to her SatNav
she was less than thirty minutes from her destination,
Netherswell Manor, where Eric indicated she'd find the
evidence to add clarity to her unusual investigation. What's
more, she had the insurance policy that if he was lying
about it, she'd have the opportunity to prosecute him when
he returned to the police station as promised at midnight.

Iris didn't trust Eric, but she had trust in this.

What she'd learnt about him in the last twenty-four
hours proved that a dare was a dare and nothing would
stop him from seeing it through, whatever the ramifica-
tions. There were some lingering doubts about her course
of action, however. Just because Eric had agreed to hand
himself in didn't mean her current line of inquiry wasn't a
decoy. It was clear from local reports radioed in from
police units stationed around Netherswell that some of the
information Eric had given her was true. For one, a local
officer had witnessed a lion eating a whole tennis net.
Nevertheless, it didn't mean his intentions were
honourable, and that made her anxious.

She couldn't shift the fifth dare from her mind. The
need to know the truth burnt through her like a discarded
cigarette butt on a cheap sofa. Even more irritatingly, Eric
had implied that she already had the clues she needed to
work it out. Which meant if she didn't, he'd win their intellectual chess game.

'What clues?' she kept repeating to herself.

What had she missed? She replayed the interview in
her head but her concentration was jumbled. Certain
words and phrases were forcing themselves to the top of
her brain like buoyancy aids. She went over them time and

time again. Then, without checking her rearview mirrors, she stamped on the brakes and skidded to a stop in a layby.

Time.

Everything came back to it.

She reached onto the back seat and grabbed her notepad. She always made copious notes to retain crucial information and build a pattern. She stared at her scribbles from Eric's interview for any references to time. They were everywhere, and she'd circled each one as if she unconsciously already knew their significance. She read them out loud.

"Look at my hands."

"The three of us have less power than the battery in that clock."

"It doesn't matter how many…miles…people travel."

In total, the words 'clock', 'time' and 'hands' were referenced more than a dozen times. Not just the words, either. She recalled the odd mannerisms and vocal tone he used along with them. He'd been programming her since the moment she walked in the interview room.

"Cheeky bastard," she sighed. "Neuro Linguistic Programming."

She closed her eyes. A picture began to form. A Victorian clock tower in the middle of a roundabout. A weathered white clock face with two black hands chasing each other to be first to reach the Roman numerals. Not any clock tower. An infamous one.

The Miles Clock Tower.

"That's it!" she screamed in delight.

She immediately and quite illegally swung her car into a U-turn and flew across the dual carriageway to the bemusement and horror of drivers travelling in both directions.

TWENTY-EIGHT
OLD SCORES

THEIR ONLY REALISTIC ROUTE OUT OF FROME WAS A TWO-hour train journey. They traipsed the mile or so into town from the police station, only stopping once for Eric to nip into the shops and buy a new set of clothes. This wasn't simply to protect his body from the persistent rainfall - it was also about keeping up appearance. If he was going into battle, he had to be wearing suitable armour. Whether any military personnel currently fighting in places like Syria considered smart jeans, Nike trainers and a polo neck jumper armour was debatable.

It was the morale boost Eric needed, even if full resurgence wouldn't be achieved until he'd had a hot shower and a good night's sleep. In the last four days, Eric had only snatched a handful of hours rest, and as his butt hit the cheap fabric of the train seat, even he found himself nodding off. It didn't last long. A platform change in West-bury reduced his forty winks to about half a dozen. Clutching polystyrene mugs of boiling hot coffee procured from a small kiosk, they rushed across platforms to make their forward connection. As each of them settled down for the last leg of their journey, they silently contemplated the end of their own.

Eric considered what might happen tonight when they reached their destination. Would Sean take the bait? And if he did, how would Eric ensure *The Idiots' Club* came out on top? They'd need a little help from Iris - that was for sure. But what if she hadn't worked out his clues? His mind drifted further out and to thoughts of the future. The opportunity to work with his closest friends on a new project with mutual ideals. He glanced over at Callum and a lingering doubt crept over him that he might yet still go through with his side deal with Sean.

Meanwhile, some of Callum's attention was focused on the fate of the last member of their team. Was Micky safe? Would he manage to meet them at the time and place they'd agreed upon? What if he didn't? The rest of Callum's thoughts settled on what Eric had said to him a couple of days ago. How he'd found exactly the right words of encouragement after everything Callum had done to sabotage them.

Josh didn't do any thinking at all.

Such an activity was entirely wasted on him, and there were dozens of Tinder matches he'd missed to catch up on.

Around lunchtime, the train jolted to a stop at Exeter Saint David's Station and they bundled out onto platform one. Outside the front entrance, they stopped briefly as an unforeseen wave of nostalgia pressed down on them.

"Seems strange we were only here six days ago," said Callum.

"Feels like months," added Josh.

"A lot has happened in a week," stated Eric.

"You're telling me. If I'm honest, I didn't think we'd make it this far," expressed Josh.

"At times, neither did I," replied Eric.

The others were rendered speechless. This wasn't the Eric they knew. He'd never admit to having doubts, certainly not to them at least.

"You alright, mate?"

"Of course. You've learnt lessons this week and now I know what mine is."

"What?"

"You'll see later," teased Eric. "Shall we go?"

"Why not. Let's find out if Micky managed to beat us here."

It might have been more than twenty years since they'd lived permanently in the city, but they'd lost none of their local knowledge. Inevitably, some of the layout had changed. Some of their favourite pubs were no longer operational, having been demolished or converted into housing. Even though there were a good number of new building developments and the University campus had spread like an uncontrollable plague of algae, they still remembered all the best shortcuts. The hidden passage-ways, narrow lanes and unsigned footpaths which wound and weaved their way from the station, across the main roads and up the hill to campus.

It was early in the afternoon, and a swarm of students scurried between faculty buildings to dodge the rain on their voyage to another lecture theatre. Normally, the green spaces which separated the exquisite architecture of the impressive University would be crammed with under-graduates engaged in intellectual debates, enjoying lunch or simply taking a chance to rest and relax. Today, the inclement late-March climate had forced them inside, which was a lot more crowded than it had been last week when the huge Forum had significantly fewer cracks in it.

Eric led them into Devonshire House through the

back entrance which was on the far side of the Forum. Avoiding attention was the name of the game today, and there was one quiet place where they were likely to be ignored.

The Ram.

As they wandered the narrow halls of the Guild offices and passed the snazzy food courts, a door caught Eric's eye.

"You guys carry on," he said. "I need to make a quick detour."

"Where to?"

"In here," he said, gesturing towards the Xpression FM studios, the University's dedicated radio station.

"Why?" asked Josh, scratching his head.

"I need to give them a message. I'll explain later."

When Josh and Callum rounded the corner, the familiar signage of The Ram welcomed them nostalgically. The student pub was in a quiet corner next to the toilets and the entrance was exactly as they remembered it. Not so the interior. The Ram's once simple design of wooden beams and plain stone floor tiles had been replaced with a gaudy orange colour scheme, uncomfortable-looking leather upholstered chairs and unfathomably uninspiring cheap artwork. It immediately reminded them of the business centre at the Edinburgh hotel where their journey began.

"What have they done to her?" groaned Callum, who'd spent much of his three-year degree on the premises.

"I know," replied Josh solemnly.

"They've sucked the soul out of it. No wonder no one comes here anymore."

It was almost true today. There were only three patrons inside before they walked in. A geeky student sipped a glass of mineral water while transfixed by the false light of a miniature laptop, and two mature students canoodled on a leather sofa at the far end of the bar.

"They've made it!" Callum called out merrily, stomping through the bar to congratulate them.

Micky and Jessica were oblivious to others until Callum noisily dragged a chair out from under their table.

"Hey, boys," chirped Micky excitedly. "I didn't think you were going to make it. Where's Eric?"

"Oh, he's on his way. You two look...comfy," commented Callum, raising an eyebrow.

"Well, we are getting married," replied Jessica, doe-eyed.

"Jessica, you remember Callum...and Josh, of course," he said as Josh lingered in the background, not sure what to do with himself.

"How could I forget," she remarked chirpily.

Josh found it difficult to hide his discomfort. "Jessica," he mumbled.

"You're actually a lot cuter than I remember," she said with a sarcastic wink.

"I'm not interested," he grumbled under his breath. "This ship has sailed and you weren't on it."

"You don't have to be like that. There's no shame in being gay," she joked.

"GAY!"

"She's just fucking with you," laughed Micky. "Get a drink, boys, and join us."

Callum was adopting a nostalgic pose against the bar when Eric bounded in, his face brimming with delight. He quickly reintroduced himself to Jessica before going straight into Micky's debrief.

"Where's the Nissan?"

"Safely parked in town."

"Is she in one piece?"

"Not a scratch on her."

"And the hearse?"

"The 'Horsemen' have disposed of it."

"Shame, I was getting quite attached to it."

"Dubious Barry won't be happy," added Josh.

"I think he's got other things on his mind right now," proclaimed Eric. "Did you get any trouble?"

"Not once," replied Micky. "The whole trip was plain sailing. Logan and Sweetie Pie are safely tucked up in Netherswell Manor and the other 'Horsemen' are keeping guard."

"And what about Iris? Did you see her before you left?"

"No, was I meant to?"

"Not necessarily."

Callum placed a cold pint of lager on a coaster in front of Eric before settling himself down on a low bar stool with his own.

"God, I think we've earnt this," said Eric, eagerly quaffing a third of a pint in one mouthful.

"Is that a half?" gasped Josh, pointing at Callum like he'd seen a ghost.

"Yeah," replied Callum. "I'm taking it easy. Last time we tried to climb the clock tower, I spent most of it passed out on the tarmac."

"Probably wise."

"What are we supposed to do now?" inquired Micky.

"We wait and relax," announced Eric. "It'll be light for hours, and we have to do the last dare at night. In the meantime, we wait to see who shows up for it."

They were expecting, and hoping, a number of people might show up to help them complete their last dare, but none of them sitting around their table in the Ram were prepared for who walked in ten minutes later. They heard her long before they saw her.

"MICKY PARSONS!"

The blood drained from his face.

"Where is that good-for-nothing cheating bastard?"

"Quick…hide me!"

Natasha marched across the pub with the air of someone who owned it. She had no time for nostalgia today. The past was gone and the future was about to get messy. She stomped up to their table, her finger outstretched towards her husband, her face claret with the overload of a thousand bursting capillaries. Micky pathetically pretended to hide under the lip of the table.

"Come out, you miserable excuse for a human being!" she screamed. "How dare you!"

"How did she work out we were doing dares?" whispered Josh, confused by her choice of words.

"I don't think she's talking about this week," replied Callum under his hand.

"Darling…" gushed Micky, pretending to have dropped something valuable on the floor but returning holding nothing but an old Wotsit crisp.

"Don't 'darling' me, you moronic little shitbag. Who's this slut!"

A flood of guilt washed over him. Despicably, he'd placed Jessica in the eye of the storm all because of a stupid dare. There was always a risk she'd get hurt, but he never expected this scenario. He glanced shamefully to his left to offer his sincerest apologies and anticipating her reaction to be one of embarrassment and anger, but it was neither. Not unexpectedly, her eyes were firmly closed and a gentle, cute version of her snore wheezed through slightly cracked lips.

"She's with me," expressed Josh confidently and quick-wittedly.

"Yeah…she's…Josh's girlfriend," confirmed Micky

with an over-elaborate nod which was liable to separate his head from his neck.

It had taken him twenty years and dozens of attempts, but finally Jessica was going to spend a brief and unconscious period of time as Josh's missus. It was the only way it was ever going to happen and only one person argued against it.

"Bollocks she is, you deceitful toerag. I've seen the video."

"Oh…right…but…I can explain…"

"I don't think he can," whispered Callum.

"Ten quid?" replied Josh.

"You're on."

"It's not what it looks like…" said Micky, scrambling to defend the indefensible.

"You've totally humiliated me," screamed Natasha, grabbing hold of the nearest pint and motioning to throw it.

"Noooo!" begged Callum, like she was about to sacrifice one of his children.

The glass shattered against the wall, sending a splosh of lager over everyone sat on that side of the table. A tear rolled down Callum's face.

"I'll never be able to show my face in the village again after this. I'll be a laughingstock. You've ruined my life. After everything I've done for you over the years, this is how you treat me," she howled, slapping him across the face with a swing that had been building in power for days.

His skin stung from the impact, but the slap was precisely what he needed. The spell that she'd cast over him suddenly lifted and he saw her the way others did. What was he doing with her? She was mean and at that moment he couldn't identify a single reason why they were a couple. Yes, he'd done some unacceptable things, but why did it have to stop there? The last three days were some of the most exhilarating he'd experienced in years and it wasn't simply because of what they were doing, it was because she wasn't there to ruin it.

"Natasha, can I remind you, we have a contract." Eric interjected. "You agreed to allow us ten days and we have one more left."

"Screw your contract! Micky and I signed a more important one fifteen years ago. That's the only one that matters."

"Violations come with consequences," he said sternly.

"Eric, you can shove your contract up your arse."

"No," said Micky, bursting to his feet. "Not his contract. Ours. I'm done, Natasha."

"What do you mean you're 'done'?"

"Done. Finished. I want a divorce."

"What?!"

"A divorce," repeated Callum.

She picked up the nearest glass, which just happened to be Callum's half pint, but before it joined its bigger cousin in a watery grave on The Ram's carpet, Callum intervened, "Put it back."

"No one tells me what to do!" she replied, screaming like a grieving banshee.

"I just did," growled Callum, noticing that at least half of his drink was no longer in its glass. "People like you are all the same. You think you can take what you want. Well, you can't. This is my drink!"

She ignored him, dropping it on the floor and turning her attention back to her husband. "No one rejects me and gets away with it. You're done, Micky Parsons, when I say you're done."

"Okay…" he mumbled subserviently, shaking like a leaf.

"Come on, we're leaving," she ordered. "I'll deal with you at home."

Micky picked up his coat and complied like a well drilled robot. The others jumped in to offer him moral support.

"He said he was done," repeated Eric.

"He doesn't love you anymore," added Josh.

"You owe me half a pint!" demanded Callum, whose normal sunny disposition had sunk behind clouds of mad fury.

"You don't have to do what she tells you anymore," Eric repeated to Micky. "The only person who controls you is you. You have to decide what's best and, whatever the consequences, whether you go through with a divorce or stay married to Princess Harpy here, we'll support you."

Micky looked at Natasha, then at the Idiots and finally to the sleeping Jessica. He'd made the wrong decisions before. He wasn't making them today.

"I don't love you anymore," he told Natasha confidently. "It's over."

A switch in her brain flicked from irascible to 'no one gets out alive'. She picked up the nearest bar stool and threw it down on the table to the soundtrack of more smashed glasses. A second chair flew through the air, crashing against the fire exit and setting off the alarms. Callum finally lost it, throwing his body towards her before any more drinks were spilt. She ducked his advance, punching him accurately in the goolies. Callum hit the floor with a high-pitched shriek. The others tried to join in but anyone within range received a vicious slap. Even with the extra numbers, the boys struggled to restrict the damage being inflicted on their beloved Ram by the one-woman riot. Much to their relief, the alarms attracted the attention of security. Two uniformed brutes, probably student rugby players, stormed in to analyse the situation. Neither of them expected this.

"Get your hands off me!" Natasha shouted as they stopped her causing any more damage.

"Is this woman bothering you?" one of the guards asked them.

"Absolutely," attested Micky.

"Madam, I'm going to ask you to leave," said the barman sternly, dealing with an incident less common than aliens rocking up for a pint of bitter.

"This was always a dump anyway."

"That's it," snapped Callum. "If you don't throw her out, then I will."

"You'll pay for this, Micky!" She aggressively shook her fist at him. "I'm going to bleed you dry. You'll never see the children again, and I'm going to take your family's house. When I'm finished with you, there'll be nothing left. No money, no business, no classic cars, no home, nothing!"

"You can't take everything."

"Don't bet on it."

"I'll always have this lot," he said, pointing to the others. "You can't take them from me."

"We'll see, won't we. You have no idea what misery I'm capable of," she spat.

"Yes, I do. We were married."

"And I only did that to get back at him." She nodded at Josh, as the two security guards each held an arm to stop her flinging any more furniture around.

"Oh, was that what you were doing," said Josh in a surprised tone. "I never noticed. Bit of a waste of time, wouldn't you say?"

"I'm going to ruin all of you!"

"I'm afraid Sean beat you to it," added Eric.

"Hold on. I recognise you lot," commented one of the

security guards. "I saw you in the Forum last week when the bomb went off. One of you was dressed as a fireman."

They shook their heads in denial and waved him away like he was talking rubbish. He soon dropped the accusation when Natasha stamped on his foot and he instinctively released his grip in shock and discomfort. She dashed for the door, the security men following in hot pursuit. Even when she was out of sight, they could still hear her angry threats echoing down the corridors. When those were finally silenced by distance, Josh, Eric and Callum broke into a spontaneous round of applause and slapped Micky on the back in congratulations.

"You're two divorces closer to me now," said Josh with a wink. It was highly likely the number would rise before the year was out.

"This calls for Champagne!" yelled Micky.

"Do they have any in The Ram?" asked Eric as he headed for the bar.

"Yep," replied Callum. "It was a favourite of the Sloane Rangers. It's not very good quality, but they don't care as long as the label's right."

The noise of clapping roused Jessica from sleep. She stretched out her arms to loosen her muscles and let out a long satisfying yawn.

"Good morning!" said Eric ironically. "You missed all the excitement."

"Not really," she whispered with a smile. "I was only pretending. Being a narcoleptic can have its upsides and I'm a bloody good actress!"

Eric chuckled. "You're sneaky."

"I had to be. It was my insurance policy. I've been waiting for Micky for years, but I had to see what he'd do if he was forced to make a choice. He didn't disappoint me."

"So did you know he was already married?"

"Of course. I've been stalking him for ages."

"Right," said Josh, a little concerned by the revelation. "That's a little bit sinister."

"No worse than what you lot have been up to."

They nodded because it was impossible to argue with her.

Micky returned with a bottle sticking out the top of a rarely used wine cooler. The label on the side was written in an Eastern European language which none of them understood. It was called 'Champaine' and the contents were a pale yellow colour with the distinctive smell of marzipan. Such disparities from the genuine article wouldn't have bothered them as students, so why would it bother them now. Micky handed out the brimming glasses of bubbly and raised his own to make a toast.

"To Jessica. I'm sorry for making you wait."

They took healthy gulps but all regretted it when they spluttered at its uniquely surprising taste. Micky leant down and gave Jessica a long, passionate kiss.

Josh ruined the moment by asking, "Does this mean Natasha's a free agent again?"

"I guess so…hold on…No!"

"I would also like to offer a toast," pronounced Eric. "To *The Idiots' Club*! To ten million quid, a highly enjoyable week and new beginnings."

"You have a nerve, Gideon."

Dressed in his customary beige tweed suit, Sir Andrew Carrington was flanked by the two security guards who'd recently removed a troublemaker.

"Vice Chancellor," said Eric gleefully. "Join us, won't you?"

"I'd rather suckle from Satan's teat than share a drink

with you. This is strictly a student bar and you are not welcome."

"But I have my student card on me." Eric drew a tatty yellow laminated card from inside his wallet. "You never managed to take it away from me."

"And do you still regard yourself as a student?"

"Of course."

"Excellent."

Carrington produced a handbook, which had been concealed behind his back, opened it to a pre-marked page and recited its contents. "In general, disciplinary offences are likely to fall into one of the following categories and can be deemed as either minor or major. Number one, actions that create actual or potential distress or harm to others irrespective of whether or not distress or harm was intended."

"Who have we distressed, exactly?"

"One hundred and three students suffered burst eardrums," he replied seriously. "Number two, actions which cause actual or potential damage to the property of others."

"I'd argue that was mostly the bomb."

"Which you were responsible for setting off."

"Prove it."

"Number three, actions which disrupt the normal operations and safe use of the University including, where applicable, reputational damage to the University."

"But I don't think…"

"Number four," he continued, ignoring Eric's attempts to defend himself, "actions which impede or interfere with the pursuance of work or study of University members, or impact on normal operations."

"Is that all?" asked Eric.

"This is the first time in my thirty years someone has

breached all four clauses in the same act, and that includes you lot back in the nineties."

"We're getting better at it, then," giggled Josh. "That's education at work."

Whilst Carrington read out his charge list, Eric sent a surreptitious text message from under the table.

"Where's your evidence?" demanded Callum.

"In the capable hands of DI Whitehall, who has been investigating you on my request."

"Yes, we know."

"You know!" said Carrington, looking stunned.

"Yes. She's already arrested and released us without charge."

"That's ridiculous."

"We thought so, too, but here we are. If the police don't have the evidence to charge us, what makes you think you can?"

"Because I know the truth about you four. I know what you've done and you're not going to get away with it. I hereby expel you from our magnificent institution."

"What does that mean, specifically?" asked Josh.

"You'll no longer receive the monthly alumni magazine!" replied Micky in fake shock.

"There's a magazine…?"

The University will officially disown you, and your degrees will be scrubbed from our records," smirked Carrington maliciously.

"You don't really get it, do you, Andy?" offered Eric.

"Andy!"

"Our qualifications haven't helped us once. Josh here has a third class degree in veterinary science and yet he spends his life selling worming tablets for flamingos…"

"Actually, we don't sell those - I checked."

"Callum has a two-two in business studies and yet he's

sunk more corporate enterprises than the credit crunch. Meanwhile, Turnip here has a decent degree in biology and runs a chain of pharmacies, but I know for a fact he bloody hates it."

"He's right," confirmed Micky.

"As for me, academic performance has never made a jot of difference."

"Probably because you got an unclassified in economics," Josh reminded him sarcastically.

"It's irrelevant."

"Then it won't matter to you if I expel you, will it," stated Carrington bitterly.

"Of course it matters. University isn't just about getting good grades, it's about adapting to new challenges and building new friendships. It's about being part of something bigger. It's about expressing opinions and views. It's about discovering truth. *Lucem Sequimur*. It's about following the light. But you take that motto literally, don't you? It even relates to the colour of someone's skin. You've repressed anyone whose views and backgrounds differ from your own white privilege. You've been doing it ever since you were first appointed because you vehemently believe you're better than everyone else."

Xpression FM, which had been playing unrecognisable modern hits in the background, stopped playing music and announced an exclusive news report.

"Can you turn it up, please, barman," Eric called out. "Andy, you should listen to this."

"Listen to what?"

"The truth."

"What are you talking about, you stupid little man?"

"I'm talking about the last time I paid you a visit. I took the liberty of recording some of your comments about me.

Your views were more powerful and disgusting than even I imagined."

Carrington's words weren't just being heard in The Ram. They were being heard in canteens, study rooms, student accommodation, public transport, sitting rooms and local businesses. Anyone in range of 87.7 MHz or with access to the internet. It was by no means the most popular station in the city, but it had enough listeners to cause him catastrophic reputational damage.

"…I don't care how successful you are, Mr Gideon, because in my eyes a black man can never compete with someone like me…"

Carrington's head sank onto his chest.

"Now I imagine an opinion like that would probably have got you fired back in the nineties, but in the age we live in I expect people will demand a full public inquiry."

"You bastard," wheezed Carrington.

"Those whom the gods wish to destroy, they first make mad," repeated Eric. "Well, you did make us mad."

"Get out of my University."

"I don't think it's going to be yours for very much longer," expressed Eric. "Drink up, everyone! We're no longer welcome here."

"You never were."

TWENTY-NINE

THE LAST DARE

THEY'D WALKED THIS ROUTE A THOUSAND TIMES BEFORE. Every weekday when they'd been bothered to attend lectures. Every Friday when they'd stumbled back from a dare night in The Ram. On Mondays after playing five-a-side football, extremely badly, in the University league. Every Saturday night after an insanely claustrophobic boogie in the Lemongrove nightclub. Twice a day for over three years, the walk from Streatham Campus to their respective homes was etched indelibly into their DNA.

Over the main road and past Lafrowda Halls, then down Hoopern Lane - forever littered with more dog excrement than there are dogs - down Pennsylvania Avenue, in the shadows of the massive rear wall of the prison, then a sharp turn onto Howell Road and a short walk through the park to Woodbine Terrace. Eight Georgian townhouses squeezed together in a narrow dead-end lane inaccessible by anything larger than an old Mini. For two years, Josh and Eric lived in number seven. From Josh's second-floor bedroom window at the rear of the house, the outline of the town centre and its stunning Cathedral nestled on the horizon at the far end of Queen's Street, and below the window ledge, poking its head over the roof apexes of the adjacent street, was the pinnacle of the Miles Clock Tower.

They rounded the corner, and the clock tower was exactly as they remembered it. A little dirtier perhaps from the constant and increased traffic that circled the round-about below it, but the hands on its clockface marched towards a destination always out of reach. Twenty years ago, they'd failed to remove one of those hands. Today, one of them would have to finish the job.

"It's quieter than I thought it might be," said Josh, as they stood outside the curry house watching the end of rush hour traffic fight its way home.

"Isn't that a good thing?" replied Micky.

"I wasn't talking about the cars. I thought he might be here."

"He will be," claimed Eric confidently. "And so will she."

"But what if he doesn't come? What if the plan hasn't worked?"

Eric scowled at him. His plans always worked.

"When should we do it?" asked Callum. "By my reck-oning, the seven days ends at midnight."

"After dark."

"That's a few hours away yet," explained Josh.

"How will we decide?" asked Micky. "Draw straws? Paper, Scissors, Stone?"

"Decide on what?" posed Eric quizzically.

"Who's going up."

"That won't be necessary."

"You're going up, then, are you?"

"Let's wait and see," stated Eric. "I don't know about you, but I'm a little peckish."

"Starving," replied Jessica.

"Curry?"

"As long as it's not Greek food, I'm in," she replied, giving Micky's hand a little squeeze.

"Never again."

"Curry it is, then."

The Ghandi Indian restaurant was directly opposite the clock tower on the edge of the roundabout. It was empty, so they chose a table by the window and ordered bowls of chicken vindaloo, lamb biryani, pilau rice and enough poppadoms to wipe out a battalion of celiac sufferers. Throughout their meal, Eric kept an eye fixed on the scene outside the window, waiting expectantly to see what would happen. The sunlight, already subdued by heavy grey clouds, casually ebbed away and the street lamps flicked on like a chain reaction. There was nothing out of the ordinary - night-time dog walkers, the occasional posse of students and the waning traffic.

Inside the curry house, the mood was buoyant. The food was excellent, the lager flowed and everyone had something to celebrate. They were close to completing the world's most bizarre set of challenges, and to their surprise, none of them had died in the process. Along the way, they'd been forced to self-assess their lives and reflect on the past. Bonds of friendship had been reforged and the future for most of them looked brighter than it had done two weeks ago. They had a long road to overcoming their differing challenges but also a collective positivity about the journey. Only Eric's attitude was out of kilter.

He was distracted by the world on the other side of the glass. Plan B had always been a long shot. It involved extraordinary skill and subtlety in manipulating a complex set of characters. Not an easy thing to master when they had their own agendas. Gathering them together in the same place and at the same time was the equivalent of encouraging planets to align. The plan had delivered victories already, but there had been side effects. Carrington had got what was coming to him and Natasha was an unintentional bonus. The big fish, though, had yet to be caught. The only person who'd made a genuine fight of it. The one person who might prove to be Eric's equal.

"It doesn't look like Sean's coming," said Callum passively, noticing Eric's obsession with staring through the window.

"Sore loser," offered Josh.

Their waiter placed a silver tray with five foil-wrapped mint chocolates and a leather presenter case with their bill hidden inside on the table.

"Normal rules?" said Micky.

"Oh come on, I can't afford to pay for it," whined Callum. "I've only got nine pound twelve pence in my account."

"But tomorrow you'll have at least a million, " Eric reminded him.

"And you'll still be tighter than a sixteenth-century corset," laughed Josh. "I'm in."

"Everyone write down an estimate," explained Micky. "Furthest away from the actual bill pays."

Callum nodded reluctantly. He'd never been lucky at this game, but at least he had a one in five chance of getting it wrong.

"I'll cover Jessica's," announced Micky chivalrously.

He had a one in four chance.

"That's a bit sexist, isn't...oh right...she's nodded off again," said Josh. "I hope for your sake she doesn't fall asleep when you consommé the relationship."

"Consommé! You want me to boil her in a broth?"

"What?" replied Josh with furrowed brow.

"I think the word you were searching for was 'consummate'!" replied Eric.

"Shit, I've been saying it wrong for years."

"Well, girls do like funny guys. Maybe that's been your secret weapon all along!"

Most of them scribbled a number down without too much thought. Callum took a little longer. He asked the waiter for several bits of paper and a calculator to precisely work out what he hoped was the right amount. Finally he submitted his answer and Eric opened the leather presenter.

"One hundred and fifty-six pound thirty-seven pence."

"Is that with or without tips?" asked Callum.

"It's a good point," said Eric. "How much would you normally pay?"

"Ten percent," replied Callum.

"Fine. So that would still make you almost a thousand pounds out…and still in last place."

"Damn it."

"Eleven hundred and twelve pound. What were you thinking?"

"I put the decimal point in the wrong place."

"Starting to understand why your businesses have all failed," observed Micky.

"Right," moaned Callum. "I'll get it."

They waved the waiter over and Callum secretively removed a credit card from his wallet and hid it inside the leather presenter case. Card and machine were joined in union and after the amount was added, the waiter passed the card reader to Callum to enter his PIN.

"Thank you very much, Mr Gideon," said the waiter as the machine rattled with fury.

"That's strange," Callum replied in a fluster. "Hmm…I wonder how that got into my wallet?"

"I imagine it was after you pinched it from the letter rack in my apartment!" smiled Eric. "Don't worry, I'll deduct it from your winnings."

"Thanks," he replied sheepishly.

"Come on, let's get this done. It's dark enough out there now."

"What about Jessica?"

"Sanjiv!" Eric hollered across the restaurant. "Can we leave our friend here?"

"No problem, Mr Eric."

"He knows you?" quizzed Micky.

"Of course. He's run this place since before we lived here, and we ate here most weekends. Sanjiv never forgets a face."

"When it comes to you, no one in Exeter does."

Micky made Jessica comfortable on the velour-covered bench seat and they headed outside. The temperature had dropped considerably over the last few hours and their curry flavoured breath billowed into the air like a pack of dragons. They strolled across the roundabout and up to the base of the tower.

"I don't remember there being a camera on it," said Micky.

"I imagine it's a direct response to the last time we were here."

"Does it change anything?"

"Yes," replied Eric. "It means we don't have to film the dare ourselves."

"Is that the same as livestreaming it? You know Sean is a pedant."

The small door at the base of the tower creaked open and a man stepped out, ducking to avoid the low lintel. "I thought I'd watch this one live."

They coyly acknowledged each other.

"Sean."

"Eric."

"I was starting to think you weren't coming."

"Well, you didn't leave me much choice. There appears to be a lion on my tennis court and a missing person in my garden room."

"Interesting. I heard on the news that the police were looking for a lion and a missing person," said Eric dryly.

"I'd say they've found them both, given the cordon they've placed around my house, but I'm certain you and the boys will be able to explain how they got there."

"Perhaps," Eric responded. "It all depends what you're prepared to do to secure our honest confession."

Sean took a few paces from the door and shook the others weakly by the hand. He glanced up at the thirty-foot structure and a shiver ran down his back. The scene froze and an echo from time screamed through his memories. He grabbed his leg and winced at a pain first sustained here but constantly revisited in the manner of his walk - the limp that never left him even if the memories did from time to time. His eyes slowly scanned the tower, picking out each personal landmark where his body had struck the stone on his journey to the road a few metres below where he'd lost consciousness.

"It's the first time I've been here since the accident," muttered Sean. "That night is flooding back to me."

"I can't remember a thing," commented Callum.

"No surprise there," added Josh.

"None of you will ever know what it was like," continued Sean in a depressed tone of voice. "I've not experienced a pain like it since. It was excruciating."

"Wounds heal," stated Eric unemotionally.

"But not these wounds. I wasn't talking about the phys-ical pain. There's no bandage or drug for my injuries. You can't see or feel them. Have you ever been betrayed, Eric?"

"Yes," he replied, finding it impossible not to look at Callum, whose eyes were focused on the road.

"How did it feel?"

"Like someone had repeatedly punched me in the soul," answered Eric.

"You always were good with words. I can't think of a better description. I finally learnt the truth that night twenty years ago. The people I'd called friends were nothing of the sort. They didn't care about me, only themselves. They didn't respect me or consider me one of them. Over time, the physical pain subsided and was replaced by something else. A burning desire for vengeance against those responsible. Your actions lit a fuse and set fire to my ambitions. But I knew my success would never impress you four. I'd have to fight for your respect."

"So you decided to test us."

"I knew you'd only play if there was a suitable game."

"And for once," said Eric, "I congratulate you for your creativity. The dares you devised were commensurate with *The Idiots' Club's* high standards… but…I don't believe your motive for a second."

"Eric, I've thought about nothing but beating you for two decades," he repeated.

"This isn't vengeance, Sean. It's jealousy."

"Rubbish," he argued coyly.

"You designed these dares specifically to destroy our friendship. You believed involving Jessica would drive Micky and Josh apart, and it almost did. You thought we'd never forgive Callum for accepting your counter deal, but we did forgive him. You hoped I'd be tempted to take on Carrington again, to the consternation and disapproval of the others, but that also worked out in our favour."

"And asking a bunch of friends to steal a lion is bound to create tension!" added Josh angrily.

"But none of it worked, Sean."

"I'm still pissed off you shot me in the arse with a tranquiliser," replied Callum, pathetically raising his hand in the air.

"We did say sorry," offered Josh.

"When?"

"Actually, you were doped up at the time," admitted Micky. "Sorry."

"See," said Eric addressing Sean. "Your attempts to split us apart have only brought us closer together."

"So I see," countered Sean. "If only you'd treated me the same way."

"You're right," acknowledged Eric. "Most of us treated you appallingly badly, Sean, and it's only now I can see it. I didn't hate you. I hated what you represented. I couldn't separate one from the other, and for that I apologise."

The group was shocked by his confession and for a while no one spoke.

"We have wronged you, Sean, but that doesn't give you the right to interfere with our lives. You have attempted to inflict untold damage to our reputations, relationships, careers, future prospects - and that cannot be allowed to stand. If you attack us, we will retaliate. We will always do it together and we will always win."

"But you've not won yet," replied Sean, nonchalantly pointing up at the clock tower. "Still one dare to go. So, which one of you is going up?"

The four of them stood in a semicircle, resolute and unified, their arms crossed defiantly, all unwilling to answer his question.

"Micky?" asked Sean.

He shook his head.

"Callum?"

"No, I have a strict self-imposed three-pint limit for climbing awkwardly-shaped monuments, and I've already had four."

Eric gave him a congratulatory pat on the back for being at least six pints off his normal mark by this time of the evening.

"Josh? What about you?"

"Not today, my old son."

Sean turned to Eric. "I can always rely on you to say yes, though, can't I?"

"No."

"What do you mean 'no'?"

"I'm not doing it."

"But you always say yes. You're famous for it."

"Not this time."

"I don't believe you."

"You should," Eric replied assertively.

"But if you don't climb, you'll fail. I'll win."

"That depends on your definition of victory, doesn't it. If none of us climb and we fail your challenge then, according to the terms of Callum's side offer, you owe him twenty million pounds, which he's agreed to split with us. However, if one of us removes one of the clock's hands we can rightfully claim to have beaten your dares but we'll only receive ten million. Either way, we win. Even if your posh lawyer finds a loophole in the contract and we get nothing back, the last week will still have been worth it."

"Perhaps you're forgetting what I can do to all of you," threatened Sean.

"And what would that be?" stated Eric rhetorically. "I've already lost my job, Micky has already split up with Natasha, Callum has accepted his lot and will face any punishment that comes his way. As for Josh, well quite frankly, I don't think he's ever really given a fuck."

"Spot on!" Josh confirmed merrily.

"I can do much more damage than that," whined Sean, petulantly stamping his feet like a spoilt child. "There is a debt to be repaid and I demand that one of *The Idiots' Club* climbs to the top of this tower and brings down a clock hand."

"Don't worry, one of them will."

"Who?"

"You."

"Me! Why would I put myself through that all over again?"

"Because you're not the only one who has damaging information. If you don't climb, we'll continue to frame you for the abduction of Logan Cobley and the theft of a lion."

"There's no evidence."

"On the contrary. There's a tonne of evidence left at both crime scenes with your mark on them."

"Such as?"

"Fingerprints and DNA."

"Taken from where?"

"The contract you signed was covered in them. Then there are the eyewitness accounts by Logan's wife and a dozen neighbours who will all positively identify you as the culprit."

"But I didn't do it!"

"Correct, but we've made it look a lot like you did. Sorry about that."

"I'm not climbing!"

"I expect Clarence will probably get you off, but think about the damage to your brand. Think about how it'll affect your company's share price and how those high profile friends might react. There's no smoke without fire, right? We can stop that happening…if you climb."

"You can't blackmail me."

"Fair enough," said Eric, raising a thumb in the air in agreement. "There's also another reason why you should do it."

"Another reason?"

"Last time you failed. The trauma has haunted you for two decades and you thought, wrongly, that holding us to account for our personal failures would give you closure. It worked to a degree. We have all changed as a result. But it won't end here for you. Closure will always be out of reach. You want our respect, but even if you beat us, we won't give it to you. If you face your fears and climb, though, it'll certainly be yours."

The others nodded in affirmation as they witnessed Sean's demeanour noticeably soften and shrink. The millionaire CEO of *Heschmeyer Industries* had been replaced by a geeky teenage ghost - vulnerable and meek, but no longer persecuted.

"I can't do it," Sean uttered nervously.

"Of course you can," said Micky.

"You're an idiot," added Callum.

"That's a compliment," said Eric.

"And this time we'll be behind you one hundred percent," added Josh.

Sean looked down at his pointy black brogues. They looked identical to the ones he'd been wearing the last time. He slipped them off and felt the sopping wet concrete through his socks. He wondered why he hadn't done that before. The only challenge akin to climbing anything wearing winkle picker shoes was trying to win a hundred metre race wearing welly boots. He turned to face the tower. How far did he get last time? He certainly got above the horses' heads on the corners of the buttress because he remembered hitting one of them on the way down. Did he get as far as the overhang just below the clockface? Yes, he believed so. The more he visualised it, the more he realised how close he'd come to reaching his objective. Only another metre or so and his life might have been so much different. Not necessarily better but different. Certainly one without a limp.

Sean took a pace forward and reached up the side of the nearest buttress to find a secure handhold.

"I think he's going to do it," Josh mouthed to the others.

Sean pulled hard at the red brick and swung his left foot up to a ledge a few feet from the ground.

"He bloody is," hollered Callum.

The only one who didn't look surprised was Eric.

In the distance behind them, the shrieking sound of a car obliterating Queen Street's speed limit forced them to turn around. A blue flashing light whirled mesmerically on the roof of an unmarked car before it was soon joined by a dozen uniformed automotive siblings. They approached from every side street that fed every junction of the clock tower's roundabout. The first car skidded to a halt right next to the door of the tower like a stuntman pulling off a tricky action sequence. As the cavalry cars followed hot on its heels, blocking the adjoining roads, the figure of Iris Whitehall dispassionately stepped from the driver's seat.

"Everyone stay exactly where they are."

Eric smiled. The last piece of the Plan B jigsaw was falling into place.

THIRTY

THE HANDS OF TIME

"DETECTIVE, GLAD YOU COULD MAKE IT," SAID ERIC, AS Iris joined them on the tiny island roundabout. "I see you worked it out?"

"Mostly," she replied, adopting a stern and unfriendly manner. "But you're going to fill in the gaps before my boss arrives."

"I imagine explaining all this to him will be a challenge. I look forward to watching you work."

"I could just bundle you into the back of the car and present you as Exhibit A."

"That wouldn't be very sporting, would it. I'm sure we can clear everything up, but at the moment," said Eric, gesturing at the tower, "I'm a little preoccupied."

"The last dare," said Iris, gazing upwards as Sean moved out of reach of even the tallest of the constables she brought with her. "Why is he climbing it?"

"Closure," offered Micky.

"You must be Turnip," she exclaimed, as she spotted a face she didn't recognise.

"Nice to meet you," he replied politely.

"I'm definitely going to have some questions for you."

"I'm at your disposal, detective."

The police had already sealed off the area with tape, and a large crowd of onlookers were enticed out of the local pubs and nearby living rooms by the power of the blue flashing lights. Iris retrieved a loud hailer from her car's back seat and delivered a crackling message into the sky.

"Sean Heschmeyer, I'm arresting you for the abduction of Logan Cobley. Please come quietly...and...down."

Fuelled by a dizzying cocktail of adrenaline and unresolved trauma, the German had already made startling progress up the side of the brickwork, but as he hit the tricky halfway mark he faltered, unable to find comfortable handholds to lift him past the overhang and up to the final section. As he attempted a complex manoeuvre, he ran out of talent. His right foot slipped and he was forced to grab hold of the narrow windows carved up the centre of the stone blocks by his fingertips.

"Arghhh!"

"I'm not sure he's coming quietly," said Eric.

"No, but by the looks of it he might come quickly," replied Iris.

"Did you find the evidence against him that you were looking for?"

"Yes. Logan's witness statement. He's identified Sean as his abductor."

"How interesting," exclaimed Eric breezily. "Do you believe him?"

"More than I believe you."

"And what's happened to the lion?"

"It managed to chew a hole through the tennis court's fence and is currently on the run in Cheltenham somewhere."

"Oh," replied Eric gravely.

"We have specialist teams searching for her."

"I've heard of the Flying Squad but not the Lion Squad," Josh chuckled.

"Will you add that to Sean's charge sheet, too?" asked Eric.

"Sadly, she didn't give us a statement," replied Iris sarcastically, more interested in something on her phone than Eric's mind games.

"But she was on his property."

"Don't take me for a fool, Eric. There's enough evidence to question Sean, but I have more than enough to charge you for all of these crimes and probably more."

Eric checked his watch. "You'll get your conviction, Iris, but I still have two hours left. Which police station would you like me to attend?"

"None. I'll be taking you back into custody personally."

"Of course."

A whimpering cry drifted down to street level. "Heeell-llppppp!"

"Come on, Sean, you can do it," cheered Micky, Callum and Josh in support.

Eric knew full well that he couldn't do it. It wasn't really a question of strength or flexibility. It was purely a question of belief. Sean never truly believed he had what it took to complete any of their dares. Not then and not now. What he needed was guidance and support. What he needed was teamwork.

"Where do you think you're going?" demanded Iris as Eric walked away from her.

"I've seen this movie before," answered Eric. "I'm doing what I should have done the first time around. It takes a coward to dare someone to do something ridiculous and a brave one to do it himself."

"Stay exactly where you are or I'll be forced to get my handcuffs."

"Woohoo," interjected Josh. "I'm ready!"

Eric flung himself at the tower before the rank and file officers had any chance to restrain him. In a few moments, he'd pulled himself up onto the buttresses and was plotting a strategy for the difficult middle section. There were no obvious protrusions to grab hold of other than the vertical windows in the white concrete blocks and the occasional spot which had been eroded away by a hundred years of British rainfall. Sean had made it to the second of these windows and was holding on for dear life. It wouldn't be long before he lost his grip and he repeated his painful fall.

"Hang in there."

Eric called up confidently but wheezed with personal exertion.

It was difficult to explain how he managed it. Not even he knew for sure. Eric had no official climbing experience and had no formal techniques to fall back on. The moves he made were not based on skill or logic, merely an insatiable desire to overcome the obstacles without dying. In many ways, the climb was a metaphor for how he approached everything in life - with guts, determination and not a huge amount of genuine ability. In his brain he'd reached Sean's position as stylishly as a tightrope walker. In the eyes of the onlooking crowd, it looked very much like a middle-aged man was trying to run uphill, hump a tower and chew concrete simultaneously.

"Stopped for a rest?" puffed Eric, as he pulled himself level with Sean.

"Pe…tri…fied," jabbered Sean in terror. "It's…going to…happen…again."

"Not this time. Hold my hand."

Eric managed to reach up and grab the overhang with

one huge hand while holding onto Sean's with the other. For a while the pair dangled uncomfortably in mid-air, unable to progress any higher due to a lack of energy and ideas.

Meanwhile, some distance below them Micky and Callum engaged in interesting wagers about what might occur next.

"Ten quid says Eric beats Sean to the top?" offered Callum.

"Obviously, I'm not betting on that. What about - twenty pounds says Sean wets himself."

"Done. You in? Josh?"

Whilst everyone else was distracted by events up high, Josh had seized the opportunity to pursue his own conquest. It had been at least a week since he'd chatted anyone up and the only available subject happened to be the same person responsible for his recent arrest. It didn't bother him; he'd never been very picky.

"I love your blouse," said Josh, sauntering casually over to DI Whitehall. "It's a great colour on you."

"It's white," said Iris gruffly.

"Accentuates your curves."

"It's only a work shirt."

"Then maybe after work I'll take you out for dinner," he announced assumptively.

"I don't think so."

"Anywhere you like, I'll pay."

"No."

"Money's no object."

Iris finally pulled her gaze from the tower. "Are you deaf or stupid?"

"What?" he replied in surprise.

"Both, then."

"Don't be like that. You won't get a better offer all night."

Iris's face soured further. "A date with a tramp with no shoes on would be a better offer than a date with you. I've seen more eligible bachelors in my morgue after road traffic collisions."

"Ha-ha! I love a girl with a sense of humour."

"Mr Foxole, what gives you the right to pester women like this? Hmmm. No is no. Why would I be interested in a washed-up gargoyle like you?"

"Um…sex?" he replied tentatively.

"Ugh! I think I've regurgitated a little sick in my mouth. You're a caveman, Mr Foxole. You have zero respect for the opposite sex and little awareness of what century you live in. You don't even remember the names of the women you married."

"Of course I do," he complained defensively.

"What was your third wife called?"

Josh strained his synapses and a few of them snapped. "Vanessa! She was from Toronto and worked at Great Ormond Street Children's Hospital as an oncologist."

"Nope. She's called Samantha and she's from Tulsa. We contacted all of your ex-wives to get information about you."

"I wouldn't trust what they say. Totally bitter and biased against me."

"Do you know what the funniest thing about talking to Sam was?" asked Iris rhetorically. "She's not even an oncologist. She runs a colonic irrigation clinic. She injects water up people's arses to remove impurities."

"So that's what that was! I thought she was just being kinky."

"It didn't work," remarked Iris. "There's still a lot more

shit inside you that needs removing. Now fuck off and let me do my job."

Josh returned to the others, pretending everything had gone well. Sadly for him, they'd overheard the whole exchange and were desperately trying to contain their laughter.

"How did it go?" enquired Micky sarcastically.

"I don't get it. That's the second time it's happened."

"It's starting to look like a pattern," giggled Callum.

"I think I've lost my mojo."

"Perhaps it's time to let it go, Foxie. Stop chasing and enjoy holding on to what you have," recommended Micky.

Josh thought about this for a moment. The others had made giant strides over the last week to iron out some of their imperfections, but what lessons had he taken from it?

None.

"Sod that for a laugh! I'm a bloody sex machine."

"Whatever you say, mate," laughed Callum.

Micky gazed up to see if the climbers had made any progress. "Oh, look. They're almost there."

"They'd better hurry up," replied Callum, pointing down Queen's Street, "before the police get that thing in position."

"Oh, shit! Get a move on!" Josh shouted up the tower when he saw what was coming.

Eric had managed to pull himself up to the clockface level and was leaning over the edge, where a visibly distressed middle-aged millionaire was clawing at his shirtsleeves.

"Sean, open your eyes!"

"I…can't."

"Look, you've almost made it, but you have to believe."

"I…don't believe."

"Yes, you do," said Eric sternly. "Look at me."

Sean opened one eye and witnessed something he'd not seen before. Eric's face was warm and welcoming, quite a contrast to the cold and hostile one he remembered from history.

"You've already proven yourself to me," offered Eric sympathetically. "Your dares were incredible, even if they were motivated by hate, but it takes real balls to revisit past failures. You have my respect, Sean, and I believe in you. Now you have to believe in you."

Eric had always known that words were powerful. They were all he really had. Sometimes he used them to manipulate or deceive. Sometimes to confuse or misinform. Sometimes to offend or demoralise. At any given moment, they were weapons of war or peace; comfort or humiliation; help or hindrance. They could be anything he wanted them to be, and right now they had to be a steroid. The words soaked through Sean's pores and pumped up his muscles. A power surged through him, wiping away the physical and mental barriers that had kept him frozen to the spot.

"That's it, Sean! You're doing it."

Sean pulled himself up over the edge, exhausted but ecstatic. Without even thinking about it, he hugged Eric exuberantly and chuckled like a three-year-old child.

"YES!"

"Longest climb in history."

"Yes…but worth it."

"Do you understand now?" asked Eric.

"Yes."

"We do difficult things because no one believes we can. Welcome back to *The Idiots' Club*," he said, holding his hand out warmly.

Sean shook it eagerly.

"I think the dare requires us to take a clock hand," stated Eric.

"We'll take one each."

While they fingered the hands of the clock to find a way to remove them, a figure rose slowly through the air behind them. As her voice burst out of the megaphone, they jumped in shock and grabbed hold of the hands for fear of falling.

"PUT THEM BACK!"

Iris stood on the platform of a cherry picker, which had recently been manoeuvred into position by the side of the tower. The Idiots on the ground had certainly seen it, but up here Sean and Eric had been somewhat distracted. It was simply another example of how far Iris would go to win.

"BOTH OF YOU STEP INSIDE," she shouted with the tone of a mother scolding her children for a garden misdemeanour.

Eric knew the game was up, but as he went to step into the metal compartment of the cherry picker, the hour hand snapped off in his fingers and he lost his footing. He tensed up in anticipation of the inevitable fall into pain, broken limbs, reconstructive surgery and sucking meals through tubes for the next six months. He closed his eyes and life flashed before them. Every mad dare and close shave to which he'd subjected himself. Every near miss and glorious victory. Every adversary and innocent bystander. A second of time seemed to take an hour but he was still floating in blissful nostalgia. Something had stopped his fall. He felt his neck tighten and his shirt collar squeeze the air from his throat.

"I wouldn't wish it on anyone," wheezed Sean, who had grabbed hold of his shirt.

DI Whitehall opened the door of the cherry picker and the two of them bundled inside.

"Sean Heschmeyer. Eric Gideon. I'm arresting you for trespass and theft. You do not have to say anything, but it may harm your defence if you do not mention when questioned something which you later rely on in court. Anything you do say may be given in evidence," she announced, securing handcuffs on both of them.

"Bloody brilliant," said Sean joyfully.

It was the oddest arrest in history. No high-speed car chase. No fugitive being pursued on foot through a bustling crowd. No surprise sting operation. Just the odd warning bleeps of a slow moving construction vehicle taking an age to reach the ground. When they finally did arrive, a bemused crowd looked on as Micky, Josh and Callum gave them an ironic slow handclap. It wasn't long before their actions became impossible as Iris signalled to colleagues to read them their rights and place them in cuffs as well.

"Not that one," instructed Iris to the uniformed officers as they went to lead Eric away. "He stays here."

They left him alone at the base of the tower while the others were led away to the police vans. Iris sat on the curb next to him rolling her sleeves up and lighting a cigarette in victory.

"How does it feel?" she said.

"How does what feel?"

"Beating him."

"Who, Sean?"

"Yeah."

"It wasn't really about that. It was about something more important," replied Eric happily. "Sean was a decent adversary, but it's only a proper competition if you face a worthy opponent. In the end, I wasn't competing against him at all, I was competing against you. And you won. Congratulations."

"I was just doing my job," she replied casually.

"No, you weren't. Along the way, you broke the rules because, like me, you need the game. You need to understand the puzzle and solve the clues. You worked it all out and, ultimately, you beat me. You have my respect."

"That must be a difficult thing to say."

"Not really. I'm getting used to it. If anything, it's a relief. I don't have to pretend that the world is against me anymore."

It had been one of the most extraordinary cases Whitehall had ever worked. The motive was unusual, to say the least, and the suspects intellectually challenging. Well, not Foxole, but certainly the others. Irrespective of how much it had boosted her sense of job satisfaction, crimes had been committed and someone had to be punished.

"You ran a good race, Eric, but I'm afraid it's time to pay for it."

"Fair enough." Eric got to his feet, ready for the solitary walk to the police van. As he set off, Iris's phone rang.

"Yes, sir," she answered, acknowledging the contact card flashing up on her screen.

"Whitehall. Have you arrested the suspects yet?"

"Yes, sir. I'll be charging them as soon as we get back to the station."

"Good. I'm sending you an email with some new developments," he replied gruffly.

"Developments, sir?"

"Yes. Longleat have been on the phone. Their missing lion is safely back in its enclosure."

"That's great news. Where was she?"

"In her enclosure."

Iris twitched suspiciously as she caught Eric supressing a smile. "But…she was on the run around the Cotswolds!"

"And now she's running around in a purpose-built pen with the rest of the pride."

"But, how did she get there?"

"Beats me, but the park officials only care that she's back. They'll be running a full security review, of course, to identify gaps in their systems."

"I suppose it is good news, sir. Can I still charge Gideon for her theft?"

"No. Not unless we can gather more evidence. All we have is some dodgy video of a lion next to a hearse and a man in a jester's hat having a fag."

"What if I find the hat?" replied Iris desperately.

"No."

"But, sir, I know it's them."

"I can't go on hunches, detective. There's also news about Logan Cobley. He's withdrawn his statement identifying Sean Heschmeyer as his abductor."

"WHAT!"

"He's claiming that he's an old friend of the Heschmeyer family and was staying the weekend but forgot to tell his wife."

"But, sir…he was tied up in the garden room!"

"I know, but weirdly, he says it was a dare. Imagine that, grown adults doing dares!"

"Yeah, imagine that…"

"Apparently, Sean tied him up and dared him to escape."

"Sir, with the greatest respect…that's bollocks."

"Whitehall, remember who you're talking to."

"But, we have video of Logan being abducted from his house in London!"

"Apparently that was an operational exercise, part of

his job. Did you know he works for a top-secret government agency? Very interesting stuff."

"Then who chopped his bloody finger off!"

"Probably an accident."

"Accident!"

"Anyway, it's not your case. There's a colleague in London called Jimmy Copper who's leading it, and he'll be in touch soon for a debrief."

"Are you saying I can't charge Eric Gideon with either of these crimes?"

"Not immediately. I want you to review the case file and then talk with the Crown Prosecution Service, see what chance there is of securing a conviction."

"Fine," she growled.

"Sir Andrew Carrington has also dropped any claims that Gideon harassed him."

"Jesus, is there anything I can charge them for?"

"Not unless they've done anything else I'm not aware of."

"They stole the hands from a clock – I saw it myself."

"Great. Get him on that. I'll expect a full report on my desk in the morning."

The line went dead.

"Trouble?" said Eric.

"There will be. I'm starting to understand why you've been arrested so often but never charged."

"You just need a good Plan B."

Eric wandered off to join the others without asking her permission.

"Wait," said Iris, hurrying after him. "There's one part of this I can't figure out. Obviously, you've had some support in the background, but the security system on Logan's house can't be fooled or forged. That leads me to believe he was with you when you broke into his house. That's why his dogs didn't react, right?"

"Now if I confirmed that theory, I'd implicate myself, wouldn't I?"

"But why on earth did he cut his own finger off!" she said, following her own one-track mind.

"He didn't," Eric whispered. "Logan lost it in an explosion while working in Afghanistan but he keeps it in his freezer as a prank to play on his kids. Defrost it, cover it in a bit of his fresh blood and it looks really convincing!"

Iris wanted to be angry but all she mustered was an exhausted chuckle. "If only all criminals were as interesting as you, Eric Gideon. I doubt I'll have a week quite like this one again."

"You never know," he replied with a wink.

In the back of the police van the five members of *The Idiots' Club*, reunited for the first time in two decades, shared their experiences and stories of the last week to help Sean understand how they'd pulled it all off.

"Looks like you owe us some money," said Callum.

"Ten million, to be precise," added Josh.

"Twenty," countered Sean. "You've earnt it - although strictly speaking I completed the last dare so according to the contract, you failed."

"We did it together," Eric reminded him.

"Either way, I don't need the money."

The police van pulled away, shaking them up and down like a broken blender.

"What's everyone going to spend it on?" asked Sean.

"We have a few debts to settle," replied Eric.

"Most of mine is to cover back taxes," stated Callum.

"I might go for some plastic surgery," suggested Josh, who was still processing his second ever rejection.

"I think I'll buy a little cottage in the country with Jessica…shit, Jessica! We left her in the curry house."

"Don't worry, Sanjiv will look after her."

"She'll probably still be asleep when you get back," joked Josh.

"It appears everything has worked out for the best, and I'm glad we've found a fitting way to bring the curtain down on *The Idiots' Club*," said Callum. "All of us together, some lessons learnt and old wounds healed."

"Who says this has to be the end?" stated Eric defiantly, winking at Sean.

"Oh no, I'm one hundred percent done," insisted Micky forcefully.

"Eric," said Sean mischievously.

"Yes, Sean."

"I dare you to escape from this police van."

"Don't you bloody dare," said the other three in harmony.

A grin crawled across Eric's face.

THE END

Sign up to the newsletter
www.tonymoyle.com/contact/

It makes all the difference to an author's career if you leave a review in the store where you purchased this ebook to help other readers find it. I would be most grateful if you did.

Printed in Great Britain
by Amazon